The Seventh Crow

Dreaming Robot Press
quality middle grade and young adult science fiction and fantasy
• Las Vegas, New Mexico •

Dreaming Robot Press
Published by Dreaming Robot Press
Las Vegas, New Mexico

1 3 5 7 9 10 8 6 4 2

First published in the United States by Dreaming Robot Press. 2016

Copyright © 2015 by Sherry D. Ramsey. All rights reserved.

Publisher's Cataloging-in-Publication data

Names: Ramsey, Sherry D.

Title: The Seventh Crow / Sherry D. Ramsey.

Description: Las Vegas, New Mexico: Dreaming Robot Press, 2016.

Identifiers: ISBN 978-1-940924-08-3 (pbk.) | ISBN 978-1-940924-09-0 (ebook)

Summary: The day a talking crow meets her on the way home from school, fourteen-year-old Rosinda is plunged into a forgotten world filled with startling revelations: magic ability flows in her veins, she's most comfortable with a sword in her hand, and the responsibility for finding a missing prince rests solely with her.

Subjects: LCSH Magic--Juvenile fiction. | Amnesia--Juvenile fiction. | Fantasy fiction. | Adventure fiction. | BISAC JUVENILE FICTION / Fantasy & Magic.

Classification: LCC PZ7.R1483 Se 2016 DDC [Fic]--dc23.

For my long-ago English teacher, Patrick Reilly,
with gratitude.
"A teacher affects eternity; he can never tell where
his influence stops." - Henry Adams

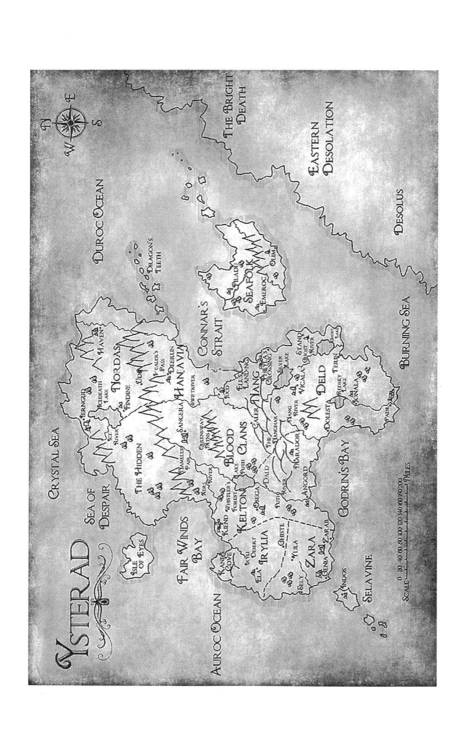

CHAPTER ONE

Rosinda trudged home with her head down, her backpack weighted with the homework Mr. Andrews had assigned for the night. Skeletal leaves crunched under her feet along the side of the road.

A low croak made her look up, and she saw the crows. They stood scattered in a loose line in the grassy swath beside the road, their glossy black feathers reflecting the late-afternoon sun, each just a wingspan away from the next. Every one had its bright black eyes fixed on her. Rosinda stopped.

The words of Aunt Odder's crow-counting rhyme popped into her head. This was one of the many things she had struggled to relearn over the past year. She counted the crows under her breath, chanting the rhyme.

"One crow, sorrow; two crows, joy; three crows, a letter; four crows, a boy," Rosinda said, her eyes resting briefly on each crow as she counted down the line. "Five crows, silver; six crows, gold—" She trailed off, looking around for a seventh crow. The rhyme always seemed to run out after six. Maybe crows didn't like big groups.

Just like me. She turned back to the road.

From a tree just ahead, a black shape dropped like a falling branch. A seventh crow. This one, bigger than the others, swooped on silent feathers to the ground just in front of Rosinda.

"Seven crows, a secret that has never been told," it said in a gravelly voice.

Rosinda froze, the weight of her backpack forgotten. Had

that just happened?

Someone's playing a trick. It wouldn't be the first time. She forced her eyes from the crow, looking to both sides and glancing over her shoulder. Someone could have followed her from school, one of the boys, with one of those gadgets you could talk into and play your voice back in all sorts of weird ways. They must have heard her saying the crow rhyme. A chance to tease her. Yes, they must be hiding in the long grass, or behind a tree—

"There's no one else here, if that's what you're thinking," said the crow, hopping closer. "Just you and me. And them," it said, cocking its head toward the other six crows, "but they don't really count, since they won't be joining the conversation." The crow made a sound almost like a chuckle.

Then it's the accident. Rosinda's throat tightened. The head injury had taken away practically all her memories except for the past year, and now she was losing her mind.

The crow seemed to read her expression. It shook its head, black feathers ruffling. "There's nothing wrong with you. This is real, and it's important."

Rosinda swallowed. "What do you want?" she asked. Her voice was a raspy croak, almost like the crow's. The world seemed very tiny, shrunk down to this autumn-splashed stretch of road, herself, and the seventh crow. She hoped she wouldn't faint.

"I have some things to tell you, Rosinda," the crow said.

Rosinda's hands flew up to cover her mouth. The crow knew her name?

"Please try not to be alarmed," the crow said kindly. It cocked its head to the side, studying her. "Do you want to keep walking or sit in the grass over there?"

Rosinda's legs felt wobbly. "I'll sit," she whispered. Almost as if they knew what she'd said, the other six crows hopped off a little distance. Rosinda walked to a nearby tree, sliding her backpack off and hugging it to her chest. She sat on the carpet of multicolored leaves with her back against the rough bark. The crow followed and stood just beyond her feet, regarding her with bright eyes.

"I'm afraid this is not the best news," the crow said. "Your Aunt Oddeline has been kidnapped."

"What?" Rosinda's heart thudded in her chest. Her Aunt Odder was the only family she had here, with her parents in a hospital in Switzerland for the past year. The year since the accident. "How do you know this?"

"I know because of who I am and where I come from," the crow said. "I think she's safe for now, but you're going to have to trust me. My name is Traveller."

"Who would kidnap Aunt Odder?" Rosinda asked, jumping to her feet. The backpack rolled unheeded in the leaves. "I have to call the police!"

The crow lifted a wing. "That won't do any good. The guards of this land—your police—will have no way to find her."

Rosinda's breath caught in her throat as if she'd been running. "Who kidnapped her?"

The crow shook its head again. "I don't know. I have suspicions, but—no."

"Can you help me find her? There must be something I can do!"

"I don't suppose you know where Prince Sovann is?"

Rosinda shook her head impatiently. "I don't even know who that is."

The crow made a sound like a sigh. "Then you'll have to come with me, Rosinda. You'll have to come home to Ysterad."

For a brief moment something shimmered at the back of Rosinda's brain, the stir of a thought, or a memory, triggered by the name. She struggled to catch it, bring it to the front of her mind, but it was gone as quickly as it had come, leaving her feeling tired and slightly sick. The autumn air pricked her skin, suddenly cold. The hard, hot feeling in her stomach was anger.

"I have to go home," she said.

"Yes," the crow agreed, "we'll need to gather some things."

"No, I mean I'm going home. Alone. Home to my house. Mine and Aunt Odder's. I don't believe any of this. I'm dreaming, or hallucinating, or maybe I have a brain tumor. Maybe this is something else left over from the accident. I don't know and I don't care." Rosinda's breath came hard and fast. She grabbed her backpack and slung it over her shoulder. "Don't follow me," she said, and hurried back to the road. Rosinda felt the crow's gaze on her back but she wouldn't look at him.

She strode along the graveled shoulder, her thoughts in a jumble. There was no sound behind her, no soft flapping of wings overhead. Maybe the crow had taken her seriously and stayed behind. Rosinda had a flash of misgiving. *What if she got home and Aunt Odder wasn't there?*

She pushed the thought aside and kept walking, the riot of red, gold, and orange leaves now garish and too bright. No cars passed. She and Aunt Odder lived in a small house on an out-of-the-way road, and it took her half an hour to walk home from school. Rosinda didn't mind. She was a loner by nature. She hadn't made many friends in the year since she and Aunt Odder had come to Cape Breton. Maybe other kids were wary around her because of her memory loss, the way sometimes she couldn't think of the right word for something, but she didn't think that was all of it. She just didn't fit in.

Rosinda rounded the last corner, and the house came into view, a narrow, two-story cottage at the top of a curving gravel driveway. It looked completely normal, and Rosinda let out a breath she'd barely realized she was holding. *Everything must be fine.* A wisp of grey smoke curled out of the chimney, Aunt Odder's beat-up little hatchback sat in the driveway. The kitchen window framed the silhouette of Filara, Aunt Odder's cat. Rosinda hurried up the driveway.

"Aunt Odder!" she called when she opened the kitchen door. The radio played softly on the counter. Filara jumped down from the windowsill and bounded across the kitchen floor to Rosinda on silent feet, curling around her legs. Rosinda reached down and stroked the animal's silky head absently as she listened for Aunt Odder's welcoming voice.

It didn't come. The house was silent, as if it also held its breath.

Rosinda slung her backpack onto the kitchen table. "Aunt Odder! Where are you?" she called again. The kettle was still plugged in, the teapot standing beside it with the top open, waiting for hot water. She glanced inside. Two teabags lay on the bottom. Rosinda touched the side of the kettle and felt a bare hint of warmth. It must have boiled a while ago and then shut off.

It wasn't like Aunt Odder to boil water and not make tea.

Rosinda went to the tiny sitting room, her throat and chest tight. The computer hummed quietly on the corner desk near the window. The television was off. Rosinda ran up the stairs two at a time. It took only a glance to see that the two bedrooms and the bathroom were empty.

The house was empty. Aunt Odder wasn't here.

Hot tears blurred Rosinda's vision, but she blinked them back. Before she could decide what to do next, a terrible racket erupted downstairs. Rosinda glanced around, grabbed a heavy, wooden-handled umbrella from beside Aunt Odder's door, and raced back down the stairs. *Could this day get any worse?*

She plunged through the kitchen door and skidded to a stop. Filara stood in the middle of the table, her patchwork of calico fur standing straight out. She hissed and spat in obvious fury.

The crow perched on the corner of the counter near the radio, wings spread wide as it screeched at the cat.

Whether it was the sudden reappearance of the crow, or the

noise of the creatures, or her growing concern for Aunt Odder, Rosinda felt her worry turn to anger.

"Stop it!" Rosinda shouted, striding into the kitchen. She banged the umbrella down on the table and scooped Filara up. The cat struggled for a moment, then went quiet in her arms.

The crow immediately folded its wings, ruffling its ebony feathers for a moment until they fell elegantly into place. It made a sound that reminded Rosinda of a man clearing his throat. "Ahem. I apologize, Rosinda," it said in a quiet voice. "The cat startled me when—"

"When you broke into my house?" Rosinda snapped. She didn't want to imagine how the crow had done that.

"Well, yes," the crow admitted. "But you've seen by now I was correct. Your aunt is not here."

"That doesn't mean she's been kidnapped," Rosinda started, but her voice trailed away. What did it mean, after all? Aunt Odder was always here when Rosinda came home from school. If she'd been out in the garden, Rosinda would have seen her. And she hadn't finished making her tea.

Rosinda had to accept that the talking crow was not a hallucination. She felt her anger and her energy drain away. Keeping the cat on her lap, she lowered herself into Aunt Odder's creaky wooden rocker.

"What did you say your name was?" Rosinda asked quietly. Her hands trembled slightly as she stroked Filara's fur for reassurance.

"Traveller," the crow answered. "Do you think we can talk now?"

Rosinda nodded. "I think," she said slowly, "you'd better tell me everything."

CHAPTER TWO

"I expect your Aunt Odder has told you why you're here," the crow said.

Rosinda nodded. "It's a nice, quiet place for me while I'm recovering from the accident. And my family has owned this place for years—" She trailed off, realizing the crow was staring at her with a strange intensity. *He has a name*, she reminded herself. "What's wrong?"

Traveller flicked his feathers. "I meant the *real* reasons," he said. "You're old enough to know—how old are you?"

"Fourteen," Rosinda said defensively. "Almost fifteen. What do you mean, 'the real reasons?'"

Traveller paced along the edge of the counter, shaking his head. "Unexpected," he muttered. "This makes it much more difficult."

It was strange, Rosinda mused, how quickly one could get used to the idea of a talking crow.

He turned back to her. "Does your aunt have any large crystals in the house?"

Rosinda frowned. What a weird question. "Not really," she said. "Well, she gave me a sun catcher for my birthday. It's sort of like a big crystal."

"May I see it?"

"I guess so, but I don't see what—"

"Please?"

"Okay, okay. It's in my room." Rosinda took Filara with her and ran upstairs. It was annoying the way Traveller kept asking questions and saying puzzling things, and never answered any of her own questions. But how do you rush a crow? He'd said he wanted to tell her things, so presumably he'd get around to it. She just wished he'd hurry up.

The sun catcher hung from a gossamer thread in her window, an emerald-green crystal almost as big as the palm of her hand with a filigree of silver at one end. The late-afternoon sun caught it and spun rainbows around her room. Rosinda carefully took it down and returned to the kitchen.

When she opened her hand and showed it to Traveller, he excitedly bobbed his head. "Yes, it must be. Well, that's one problem solved, anyway. Your aunt is a wise woman, Rosinda."

Rosinda thought of Aunt Odder, with her long, crazy blonde hair flying in all directions and her crooked smile, her endless puttering in the herb garden and the strange-tasting things she brewed up out of the herbs sometimes. She had never thought of Aunt Odder as particularly wise, but she did love her. Her aunt took very good care of her. Rosinda's throat tightened up again.

"Where is she? Please tell me," she begged the crow.

"It's just difficult to know where to begin," Traveller said.

Rosinda moved toward the counter to set the sun catcher down. She hadn't been this close to the crow before. Tiny rainbows iridesced on his feathers where the sun touched them. She felt the urge to stroke them, but she still held Filara, and the cat hissed at the crow again.

Traveller scrabbled backwards on the counter out of reach of the cat's claws. "I don't trust those creatures."

Rosinda tightened her hold on the cat and went back to her chair. "What was the name you mentioned—the place? Ister-something?"

The crow nodded. "Ysterad," he said. "You don't remember it?"

Rosinda shook her head. "No. I don't, although I feel… strange, when you say it, like I should know it. But I don't remember anything before about a year ago. Before the accident," she added.

Traveller fixed her with a beady black eye. "Rosinda, there was no accident."

She stared at him. "What? Of course there was. It was a car accident. My parents and I were all hurt. I wasn't too bad physically, but I lost my memory, and my parents have been in rehabilitation in a hospital in Switzerland since then—" She stopped. The crow was shaking his head.

"I'm sorry. That's not true. You and your parents were attacked in Ysterad. Someone targeted your family as a way to get to...something important. Your Aunt Odder rescued you and used her talents to bring you here out of harm's way."

Rosinda started to shake her head but stopped. It didn't make sense, but neither did her missing aunt. Or a talking crow. If she was willing to accept Traveller, perhaps she had to be willing to accept what he had to say.

"Are my parents okay?" she asked in a whisper.

"I think so," the crow said. "They haven't been heard from in a while, but I don't think anything terrible has happened to them."

"Okay." Rosinda fetched a deep breath. "So where is Ysterad?" she asked. "It sounds like somewhere in Europe."

Traveller made a raspy, coughing sound that Rosinda realized after a moment was laughter. "No," he said, "It's not in Europe. It's further away than you can imagine, and closer than you'd think."

Rosinda frowned. "I don't like riddles."

"Neither do I," he said. "But sometimes nothing else will do. Do you have a heavy cord or chain that you could wear around your neck?"

"I guess so," Rosinda said. It was hard to keep up with this conversation. "Do you want me to get it?"

The crow opened his beak and then froze, his head cocked to one side. He didn't answer her.

"Traveller?" she said.

He stretched his wings wide. "We have to get out of here quickly," he rasped. "I thought they'd be satisfied with your aunt, but they're coming."

Rosinda stared at him, bewildered.

"Girl, I need you to move, now!" the crow ordered. "Get that cord, and put the crystal on it, and hang it around your neck. Grab anything you need out of your room. Go! *Go!*"

Rosinda dumped the cat off her lap and flew up the stairs to her room. The cord hung in her closet. She grabbed it and a warm sweater, the book she was reading, and the change purse with her bit of money. *Grab what I need? How can I know what I'll need when I don't know where I'm going or what's happening?*

Back in the kitchen Rosinda snatched the crystal from the table and strung it onto the cord with trembling fingers. She looped the cord over her neck, and the shimmery feeling tickled her mind again, like a memory just beyond her reach.

Her schoolbooks lay strewn in a heap on the table, and the open backpack now held bread, cheese, some apples and pears from the fridge, and bottled water. Traveller perched beside it. How had he managed to do all that? She dug her journal and pencil out of the pile.

"Throw those inside," he ordered, looking at the sweater and things she'd brought with her. "Now listen to me, Rosinda."

She looked at him, caught by the seriousness in his voice.

"Does your Aunt Oddeline have a book or a collection of papers— something she uses a lot? Maybe she keeps it in a special place? Think hard."

"I don't have to think hard. It's right here." She reached up to the cupboard above the stove and pulled down Aunt Odder's "everything book."

"Is that the only one?" the crow asked sharply.

"I think so," Rosinda said. "She calls it her 'everything book.' She uses it all the time, for recipes, and looking up gardening stuff, and writing in—" She turned the book over in her hands, the rough brown leather of the binding worn soft from use, the book itself bristling with odd loose papers collected inside. The cover and spine were blank, although she knew Aunt Odder's name, "Oddeline Dealanda" was written inside on the flyleaf in a spiky hand.

Holding the book, Rosinda felt a hollowness in her stomach. Everything Traveller had told her must be true. Aunt Odder wouldn't have gone anywhere without her book. She even carried it in her enormous purse when they went grocery shopping.

Rosinda stuffed it into the backpack with the other things and turned to the crow. "Okay," she said breathlessly. "What now?"

"We'd better put some distance between ourselves and here," Traveller said. "I can't believe I'm saying this, but could you bring the cat? She might be helpful."

"I don't know if she'll follow me or not," Rosinda said doubtfully. "She's really Aunt Odder's cat. But I'll try." She took the bag of kitty treats from the cupboard and was gratified to see Filara perk up her ears.

Rosinda took one last look around the kitchen. She unplugged the kettle, and without thinking about why took the small teapot and slipped it in with her other things, teabags and all. She hurriedly dumped the other teabags from the canister in as well. The crow had already hopped to the door.

"We really must go," he said urgently.

Rosinda nodded and they went out into the cool fall air, the cat trailing them. Rosinda took a moment to lock the door behind them.

"Where are we going?"

"This way for now," said the crow. Traveller launched himself into the air with a few heavy flaps of his wings. He flew toward the woods at the back of the property. Rosinda took one deep breath and set off running behind him.

CHAPTER THREE

The four watchers had made themselves comfortable in the blasted lands of the Eastern Desolation. The landscape here was stark and barren, the legacy of a long-ago magical battle in Ysterad. It was perfect for a gathering of homeless gods.

Sekhmet, once known to her Egyptian worshippers on Earth as the Lady of Slaughter, had conjured herself a palace of sunlight, warm as the yellow sands of her ancient Memphis home. Morrigan had created her own highland forest, with a throne of standing stones near a clear-voiced stream. Gradivus lounged in a pillared Roman temple, with floors of polished marble and walls lined with weapons and armour. And Tyr, the one-handed god, had fashioned his throne on a chilly, windswept mountaintop.

It was all illusion, of course, but it helped each god feel at home in this foreign land they now inhabited and would eventually battle over.

Their alliance was an uneasy one, and they kept mostly to themselves. When they met for a conference, each brought their illusory surroundings with them. Even gods in less-than-perfect circumstances felt the need to display their powers. The melding of the four environments created an eerie, unearthly scene as heat and cold, desert and forest met and merged.

As usual, Sekhmet spoke first. "Have we made any progress?" she shrieked, as the four gods and their illusions shimmered into one shared space. The ancient Egyptians had worshipped Sekhmet as a war goddess. She wore the head of a lion atop her lithe woman's body, and her dress was the color of fresh blood. Two inscrutable cats entwined themselves around her feet.

Tyr shrugged under his ragged fur tunic. "The people of Ysterad grow more disquiet every day," the one-handed god said in a voice with the depth of mountains in it. "It shouldn't be long, now."

"Any news of the Prince?" Morrigan asked from her forest glade. Today she wore the aspect of a beautiful, auburn-haired young woman, although if one looked hard enough at her, the form of a hooded crow seemed to exist in the same space. For the ancient Celtic peoples of Earth, she had represented war, strife, and the birth of many children. She avoided looking at Sekhmet as much as possible. The burning aura of light surrounding the Egyptian goddess hurt her eyes.

"No," said Gradivus. To the Romans he had been Mars, the bringer of war, and the Greeks had called him Ares, but now he preferred the name Gradivus. He absently polished a spot on his gleaming bronze armour. "I find it hard to believe some hedge-witch could manage to hide him, even from us, for so long."

"She is not a hedge-witch, she is a Kelta," Morrigan snapped.

"If I had my full powers," growled Sekhmet, "she would have felt the wrath of the sun before now. Her entrails would fry as her blood seeped into the sand." She preened the fur on her neck with one hand, as graceful as a cat. "But I do have news of the hedge-witch," she continued, ignoring Morrigan. "She is back in Ysterad."

"What? How?" asked Tyr. The Norse god of war and justice was usually calm, but if anyone could break that calm exterior, it was Sekhmet.

Sekhmet stretched lazily in her seat. "I found someone who was willing to go and fetch her for me."

Morrigan stood. "I thought we had agreed to work together until the wars had actually begun," she said accusingly. "If we make any mistakes, all will be ruined."

The Egyptian goddess regarded the Celtic one with a condescending smile. "You three are far too willing to sit around and wait for the people to decide to go to war," she said. "I prefer direct action. One of those wanderers from the Irylian Desert was all too eager to listen to my whispers as he slept."

"He crossed the Worlds' Edge?" Gradivus asked with interest. "How did you manage that?"

Morrigan thought the Roman god's question was more than simple curiosity. They were all wary of the Egyptian's impetuousness and fast-growing power, but Gradivus made little attempt to hide his suspicions.

Sekhmet shrugged. "I thought there was probably a travelling-stone lost or hidden somewhere in that desert, so I spent time searching for it," she said. "The power of the sun can light up the darkest corners. When I found it, I revealed it to my follower in a dream. The rest was easy."

"And where is the travelling-stone now?" asked Tyr. "An item of such great power should not remain in your follower's hands."

The Egyptian goddess laughed. It was not a pretty sound, a dry rasp like disturbed mummy wrappings. She picked up one of her cats and stroked its fur. "It is not. It is in *his* followers' hands. I've sent them back for the girl. I doubt she will be of any use to us, but her presence might help convince the hedge-witch to cooperate."

"Bad enough you entrusted it to a human you barely know," Tyr scolded, "But now you have let him pass it on to others? Foolhardy!"

"They will return it to their master as soon as they are reunited. My follower instills both loyalty and fear in his men." At Tyr's look she continued, "Oh, if you insist, I shall place a geas on him against using it any further," she said. "Would that satisfy you?"

"All objects of power should be brought here to us," Tyr said stubbornly. "We should divide them among our followers before the final battle. That would be fair."

"Don't start bickering about a stone," Gradivus interrupted. "Where is the hedge-witch?"

"Kelta," Morrigan corrected again, shooting a cold stare at him.

"My follower is taking her to his camp," Sekhmet said.

"He should bring her here," Morrigan said. "There are others who would want to question her if they discovered she were back in Ysterad."

"He will bring her here soon," Sekhmet said angrily. Her temper was always simmering, barely under control. "He argued he had to return home first and prepare a caravan before making the journey here."

Tyr laughed nastily. "Your follower argues with you and tells *you* what he will do, and yet you say you're in control of the stone? It doesn't sound like he cares much for your orders."

The lion-headed goddess leapt from her sun-baked throne and paced dangerously toward the Norse god but stopped at the edge of her own illusory space.

She's no more powerful than the rest of us, Morrigan thought. *She only wants us to think she is.*

"He will do my bidding," Sekhmet snarled. "It is more than any of you have been able to accomplish."

"The Kelta is too important to be risked," Morrigan said firmly. "She is the only one with knowledge of the Prince. We should each send a follower to assist in conducting her here."

"I agree," said Gradivus. "You will tell us, Lady of Slaughter, where they are to be found."

Sekhmet's green eyes blazed. "If you insist," she said. She turned and paced back to her throne. "I will inform you all once I have spoken with my servant," she said, and her sunlit throne room vanished.

There seemed to be little else to say, so Gradivus and Tyr, with a nod to Morrigan, also faded from view, leaving the Celtic goddess alone. She sighed and sat down on the grass with her back against the smooth grey side of one of the standing stones. She was not pleased with this alliance, but it seemed the only way. There was no place—and no power—for gods without followers, and no followers for war gods without war.

She narrowed her eyes, looking into the clear waters of the stream. With a thought she called into view an image of the land known as Ysterad, and it shimmered on the surface of the water. Morrigan smiled. There would be war by the time the four had put their plan to work, war enough and followers enough for all of them. But only one would ultimately emerge victorious, and Morrigan was concocting a plan to make certain she would be that one. She expected the other three were doing the same.

CHAPTER FOUR

They weren't far into the woods before Rosinda was breathless. The backpack, heavy with supplies, caught on branches and bumped against trees, slowing her down. Traveller flew slowly so she could keep up, but he was still too far ahead for her to call to him to stop and wait. Filara trailed easily behind, pouncing on things in the underbrush and then bounding back to the path.

Rosinda stopped and turned to look back. The path was empty, so she slipped the backpack off her shoulder and sagged against a nearby tree, letting her back slide down the rough bark until she sat on the ground. A moment later she heard the soft flap of Traveller's wings overhead. He swooped down to land close to her.

"Are you all right?" he asked. "Why have you stopped?"

"Because I'm exhausted, and I don't see anyone behind us, anyway. Are you sure someone's following?"

Traveller cocked his head to the side and closed his eyes. Rosinda wondered how he could see anything that way.

He opened them and looked at her. "There is definitely someone—several someones, as a matter of fact—from Ysterad in the vicinity. I can't tell how close they are, but I suppose we can take a brief rest."

"How do you know that?"

"I can sense those from Ysterad," the crow said, with a ruffling of wings that looked like a shrug. "That is how I found you."

"But I'm not from—" Rosinda stopped suddenly. She

couldn't be sure where she was from anymore. She'd believed what Aunt Odder had told her, but more and more it seemed to have been a lie.

"Who's after us?" she asked.

Traveller shook his head. "I'm not certain," he said. "But I fear it is the same ones who kidnapped your aunt."

"It could be someone coming to help me," Rosinda suggested.

"*I* was sent here to help you. Anyone else from Ysterad is not here for that purpose," he said with certainty.

Rosinda stood. She was ready to keep moving, but Traveller's words raised another question.

"Who sent you?"

"Someone who thinks you're important," was the crow's only answer, and he flew off ahead again.

She took a few hesitant steps after him, frustrated by his answer.

"Rosinda!"

For an instant she felt as though she couldn't catch her breath. Had her pursuers caught up faster than Traveller had expected? She spun around, but there was only a boy her own age running to catch up to her, a pack jouncing on his back.

Jerrell? What can he want?

Jerrell was in her grade at school, although not in her class. He was thinner and shorter than she was, and he had a mass of spiky dark hair and eyebrows that almost met in the center of his face. He lived on this same road, just a short way past her house, but they never walked together. She usually saw him pass the house a little while after she got home. He always walked alone, too.

He slowed and trotted the last few feet to where she stood.

"What's wrong?" Jerrell asked. "I saw you run out of your house like something was after you."

"I—I can't talk right now, Jerrell," she stammered. "I have to go."

He narrowed his eyes, studying her. "You're in trouble, aren't you? Where's your aunt?"

"She's gone out. I'm just going for a walk. Alone," she added, hoping he'd get the hint.

He shrugged. "I don't care if you don't want to tell me, but don't lie to me. I'm not stupid."

Rosinda swallowed. She'd barely ever even talked to Jerrell before. *Why did he even care?* A flutter in the trees overhead told her Traveller had flown back to see what was happening. She hoped he wouldn't suddenly start talking in front of Jerrell. The crow settled on a branch and watched her with bright, interested eyes.

"Okay, look," she said. "You're right. I might be in trouble. I'm not sure where Aunt Odder is, and I'm...I'm going to find her. You should just go home, though. You don't want to get involved in this."

He didn't blink. "Are you all alone?"

She nodded, then thought of Traveller. "Well, not quite," she said. "I think I have help."

Jerrell pointedly looked all around them. "You look pretty alone to me," he said. "I think I'd better come with you."

"I don't know what you might be getting into," Rosinda told him, "and it isn't really your problem."

Jerrell hefted his backpack a little higher on his shoulder. "I'm okay with that. And I'm pretty handy to have around," he added, flashing a grin. Then his face became serious. "Look, if you really don't want me to stick around, I won't. But I mean it when I say I'm willing to help. And I'll stop asking you questions, if it makes you happy. I just...if you're in trouble, maybe you could use a friend."

Rosinda took a deep breath. Maybe Jerrell had a point. Just

because she was used to being alone...maybe it didn't mean it always had to be that way. Explaining Traveller—she had no idea how she'd do that. But maybe she'd just deal with it when the time came.

She half-smiled. "You might have a point."

He grinned back. "Great. Now are we just going to stand here, or get to...wherever it is you're going?"

Rosinda looked up at the crow again, but it launched off the branch and flew off down the forest pathway. "I guess we're going," she said. She looked at Jerrell with a strange mix of exasperation and relief. What was he thinking? She felt like she had to say something else. "Um...thanks, you know?"

He shrugged. "Didn't do anything yet." Then he grinned. "But I'll remember you said it, for when I do."

•••

They walked in silence through the woods for perhaps fifteen minutes. Finally Jerrell asked, "How do you know where you're going?"

Rosinda glanced back at him. From somewhere he had pulled a compass and stared at it as he walked. "I thought you weren't going to ask me any more questions."

"So I lied."

"I just...know the way," she said.

Jerrell looked up at her skeptically. "You're going in a straight line, and there's no real path here. That's pretty much impossible without a compass or a GPS."

Rosinda didn't answer. How could she tell him she was following a talking crow?

They broke through the edge of the woods into a small clearing. Traveller perched on a wizened tree stump just ahead of them.

"Wow," Jerrell said. "Look at the size of that crow!"

Rosinda stopped. She couldn't just walk up to Traveller and start talking to him, with Jerrell standing right there.

Traveller solved the problem for her. He quirked his head, motioning them closer. Rosinda took a couple of cautious steps forward, wondering what the crow was planning.

Jerrell dug in his backpack. "Shh! You'll scare him!" he hissed.

"Just follow me," Rosinda said desperately.

"I want to get a picture." Jerrell had pulled a tiny digital camera from his pack and held it up to his eye.

Traveller spread his wings wide, and Jerrell gasped. "Cool!"

He's posing, thought Rosinda, a smile twitching at her lips.

Jerrell snapped the picture and walked forward slowly with Rosinda. "I wonder how close he'll let us get," he murmured.

"As close as you like, young man," the crow said, settling his wings back at his sides. "But we really don't have time for any more pictures."

Jerrell's camera slipped from his fingers, but he scooped down and caught it before it hit the grassy ground.

"Wh-What?" he stammered.

Rosinda was pleased to see something ruffle his calm exterior.

"I heard you offer to help Rosinda," Traveller said. "That was very good of you. I'm impressed."

Jerrell turned to Rosinda. "Is that crow talking to me?" he demanded.

She nodded. "He talks to me, too. He's the help I mentioned."

Slowly and deliberately, Jerrell put the camera back into his pack. Then he faced Traveller again. "My offer still stands," he said firmly. "Seems to me she must be in even more trouble than I thought."

"Okay, shouldn't we keep moving?" Rosinda asked.

Traveller glanced around the clearing. "We're all right here for a bit," he said. "Fairy ring."

Jerrell followed the crow's gaze. "Fairy ring?"

"It's a dead magic area," Traveller explained. "See how the grass is darker in a ring where we're standing?"

"I thought fairy rings were caused by a fungus," Jerrell said, frowning.

"Well, I'm sure that's how it seems to people who don't know any better," Traveller said kindly. "But where do you think the fungus comes from? Fairies spread it in spots they want to protect from magical spying."

"So whoever's following us can't see us here?" Rosinda asked hopefully. She hadn't believed in fairies before today, but the appearance of a talking crow made her question everything.

Traveller ruffled his feathers. "They'll sense us if they get close enough," he said. "But not from a long distance away. That gives us time to try something."

"Try what?"

Traveller was silent for a moment. Then he said, "Rosinda, did your aunt ever teach you any talents?"

Rosinda frowned. "I don't think so. I thought you had to be born with talents."

"No, I mean, say, something out of her 'everything book'?" he pressed.

"You mean like a recipe?"

He shook his head and sighed. "No, I mean magic. A spell, a charm, a hex."

She stared at him. Now he was telling her that Aunt Odder did magic? It was too much. Rosinda burst out laughing.

The crow looked affronted. He waited until Rosinda caught her breath. "I suppose I have my answer," he said.

"You know," Jerrell mused, "Your aunt *is* kind of strange, Rosinda. She could be a witch or something."

Rosinda glared at him.

He put his hands up. "Sorry, sorry, it was just a thought. And I don't mean a *bad* kind of witch."

But he was right, Rosinda realized. Aunt Odder wasn't like anyone else. She knew all kinds of stuff about plants and herbs and the earth—more than just normal gardening facts. Aunt Odder guarded that book as if it was the most precious thing in the world—next to Rosinda herself. Aunt Odder was fun and loving, but Rosinda sometimes felt a fierce protectiveness in her, too.

"*Is* my Aunt Odder a witch?" she asked Traveller.

"Yes and no," the crow said. "Your aunt is a Kelta, one who knows the lore of the earth and practices healing magic. Kelta have a close affinity with everything natural—plants, birds, animals, weather—and their powers extend into all those realms."

Rosinda swallowed. "And you thought she might have taught me some of that?"

"I thought it was worth asking," the crow said. "Your mother—" He broke off.

"What about my mother?"

Traveller made a sound like a human sigh. "Your mother's a Kelta, too, and your father's an Enchanter. There must be some magical talent running through your veins."

"Not that I'm aware of," Rosinda said dryly. *If I could do magic, I think I'd have more friends.*

"Would you be willing to try some?" the crow asked.

"What?"

"Just something simple," he added. "I've been thinking about the cat."

"Filara?" Rosinda glanced around and caught sight of the animal sniffing at one of the brown-speckled mushrooms encircling the clearing. "What about her?"

"There should be a charm or spell in your aunt's book for communicating with animals. The cat might be able to give us some clues about who took your aunt."

Rosinda looked doubtful. "You want me to make the cat talk?"

"Oh, no, that would be a very complex spell. I'm thinking of a simpler charm, to let you read her mind, see her thoughts.

Just for a few minutes. To see what she might have observed."

Rosinda turned to Jerrell. "Having second thoughts about coming along?" she asked him. "Or does this all seem quite normal to you?"

He grinned. "Actually, this is the best time I've had in a long time," he said. "I think you should go for it."

She shook her head. "I'm not the only one who's crazy around here, I guess. Okay, I'll try it. If there's such a thing in here," she said, pawing through the backpack for the book. It seemed heavier than it had when she'd taken it down from the cupboard, and it smelled like Aunt Odder—herbs and garden loam and fresh grass. Rosinda blinked back tears and opened the cover.

She'd never paid much attention to it before, although the book was usually open on the kitchen table or counter. Now she laid it carefully on the stump in the middle of the clearing so none of the loose papers stuffed in every which way would fall out. "What am I looking for?" she asked Traveller.

He hopped to one side to make room for the book and peered at the pages.

Don't tell me he can read, too, Rosinda thought.

"I'm not really sure," he said slowly. "Flip through and look for something about animals, or thought-charms," he suggested.

"Well, you're not much help," Rosinda snapped at Traveller.

Jerrell hunched over his backpack, sorting through its contents again.

Rosinda began leafing through pages. *Planting and Harvesting Times,* said one page, and another read *Healing Herbs and Charms for Minor Wounds.* Next came a recipe for blueberry dumplings. "Nothing's in any kind of order," Rosinda complained. "I'll never find anything in this."

She passed a newspaper clipping with instructions for making hair dye, a spell for transplanting seedlings under a full moon, a list of autumn garden chores, and another recipe. She came to a section that seemed to be predominantly spells and charms and, by diligent searching, came upon one labelled, *For Divining the Thoughts of Sundry Creatures.*

She showed it to Traveller, reading the heading aloud in case he wasn't actually able to read it himself. He nodded.

"Sounds promising. Do you think you could cast it?"

Rosinda looked at him dubiously, her stomach tightening with sudden fear. "What if I do it wrong?"

"It just won't work," Traveller reassured her. "Nothing will happen."

"Okay." She picked up the book. "Let me read it over, and then...I guess I'll try it."

"Jerrell," said Traveller, "Could you round up the cat and bring her over here? Rosinda has some food for the creature if you need it."

Jerrell nodded, leaving his pack open on the damp grass.

"I don't know how to say some of these words," Rosinda said to Traveller. The crow hopped over to her. "This one, and this one right here."

While Traveller tutored her, Jerrell returned with Filara in his arms. The cat laid her ears flat when she got close to the crow, but at least she didn't hiss or spit at him this time. Jerrell stroked her fur and murmured to her.

They stood like that for a moment while Rosinda read over the spell again. She took a deep breath. "I think I'm ready," she said. "But I don't think this is going to work."

"Just give it your best shot," Jerrell said. "I'll hold the cat."

Rosinda hefted the book and held it open in the crook of her left arm, while she marked her place on the page with her right index finger. She began to read, twisting her tongue around the strange syllables.

"Ardilas omnimus emen, sigurlidas mensam onam." She reached out and patted Filara's head, and the cat jerked away

from the touch as if she'd received an electric shock. *"Filas severat minan,"* Rosinda finished hurriedly.

The cat shrieked and twisted in Jerrell's arms, and he struggled to keep her flailing claws away from his face. Filara leapt from his arms, flipped her body over and landed on her feet, then shot across the clearing in a calico streak.

Rosinda moaned and dropped to her knees as pain lanced through her head. She clutched the book to her chest as the world around her wobbled. She put one hand to her temple. "Oh, that hurts," she gasped.

"Oops," said the crow.

She glared at him through the pain. "Oops?"

"I forgot to mention the part about drawing power from the earth, so it doesn't have to come from within yourself."

"Kind of an important thing to forget," she complained, rubbing her head.

"I guess I thought it came naturally."

"Yeah, well, apparently not." Rosinda straightened and stared off where the cat had disappeared. "Did it work?" she asked Traveller.

The crow seemed puzzled. "I don't know. Are you getting any thoughts that might be hers?"

"Nothing. I don't feel a thing. At least since the pain in my head stopped." She fished in her pack and found the bag of kitty treats. She rattled the wrapping, but Filara didn't reappear. Rosinda felt a pang of guilt. "I'll feel terrible if anything happens to her," she said.

"Give them to me," Jerrell said. He took the treats and walked off in the direction Filara had fled, shaking the bag gently and making *psss-wsss-psss* noises.

Rosinda had to admit Jerrell had been right. He was proving handy to have around. Looking after him, she realized that already it was beginning to get dark. The short autumn day retreated into an early dusk.

"How much farther do we have to go this evening?" she asked Traveller.

He looked worried. Rosinda wondered briefly how he managed to convey so many different emotions on his non-human face.

"I don't know," he said. "That's why I was hoping we might find out something from the cat. It really depends on who—or what—is after us."

"*Psst!*"

Rosinda looked around to see Jerrell crouched down, backing towards them. In his outstretched hand he held a kitty treat, and Filara cautiously followed him, sniffing delicately. When Jerrell reached the stump, the cat continued past him, ignoring the treat, and came to stand at Rosinda's feet.

Filara sputtered, hissed, and coughed for a moment, and Rosinda took a step backwards. It sounded like a hairball might be coming up. But then, "Mrreeeooo *why* did you do that?" the cat asked with obvious anger.

Rosinda fought a sudden urge to giggle, and hastily turned it into a cough. Jerrell lost his balance where he still crouched beside the stump, and sat back on the grass. Traveller gaped.

"Bad enough you've allowed the Mistress to be taken, but now you have to drag me out into this *wilderness*," the cat said with particular venom, "and practice magic on me. And you're not even good at it. Really, it's enough to make me consider not helping you at *all*." Her voice had grown in strength and clarity throughout this little speech, and now Filara sat down on the grass and stared accusingly up at Rosinda with unblinking green eyes. The tip of her tail twitched in agitation.

"I—I'm sorry," was all Rosinda could think to say. "It's not what I meant to do at all."

"Well, yes, I *know* that," Filara said. She narrowed her eyes and glared at Rosinda. "And I'd give a good deal to know how it happened. But the important thing is, now that you have, what are you going to do about it? I have no desire *whatsoever* to continue speaking human. It is bad enough being able to understand it."

"If you can understand it, then you know why we attempted this," Traveller snapped. "Tell us about the disappearance of your mistress."

"Tell that *creature*," Filara said to Rosinda, her tail twitching faster than ever, "My kind does not speak to his kind."

Rosinda squatted down in front of the cat. "I'm sorry this happened," she said, "but can you tell us who took Aunt Odder? It's very important, because the same ones might be after us now."

The cat sighed. "Yes, of course. I did see them. Filthy creatures. A paw's-worth of humans, raggedy-looking ones from the Irylian Desert unless I miss my guess. Although I suppose from the look of them, they could have been Nangharen," she mused. "No, definitely Irylians. They had two dhangfoxes with them, vile things, sniffing around the yard and garden."

"A paw's-worth?" asked Rosinda, latching on to one of the many unfamiliar words the cat had just used.

Filara held up a paw and flexed each toe in turn, claws just flashing into sight before they disappeared back into the furry pads. "This many. A *paw's-worth*," she repeated, as if Rosinda were stupid.

"What's a *dhangfox*?" Jerrell wanted to know.

The cat didn't bother turning to look at him. "Bigger than foxes around here and a little smaller than one of your wolves," she said, "but with a double row of sharp teeth, and retractable claws like mine—but twice as long. They dig for small prey in the desert sands, and they can snap a sand hare in half with one bite. Some of the Irylian headmen keep them as companions."

She gave a delicate shudder. "They certainly aren't civilized."

"Wow," said Jerrell, "I wouldn't want to run into one of *those* on a dark night!"

"That's not likely to happen," said the cat.

"Oh, goo-"

"They hunt in packs."

"We'd best get moving," Traveller interrupted, "if it's Irylians and dhangfoxes we're running from. The cat neglected to mention their extremely keen sense of smell."

"I guess fairy rings are no good against that," Rosinda said, slipping Aunt Odder's book back into her pack.

"No good at all," said the crow.

"Where is he planning on taking you?" Filara asked Rosinda.

Rosinda looked at Traveller. "I don't know."

"When we started out I didn't know there would be pursuit, at least not so soon," the crow said. "Of course we have to go to Ysterad—"

"We do?" said Rosinda. "How do we even get there?"

"With that," said the crow, motioning with a wing to the emerald crystal that hung around Rosinda's neck. "But we need time to prepare you to use it. It wouldn't be safe to just—"

A long, eerie howl rose from the depths of the forest behind them. It was not the full-throated song of a wolf, but a higher, keening wail, and for a moment the cat and the crow let their eyes meet in a look of complete understanding.

Jerrell hefted his pack onto his back. "Let me guess. That was a dhangfox."

A cold finger of fear caressed Rosinda's spine at the sound. It was like before, the feeling that she was on the verge of a memory, but it swirled past her consciousness like a leaf in a stream before she could grasp it.

"You won't outrun them," the crow said flatly.

"You'll have to use the crystal," the cat said at almost the same time. "Everyone out of the fairy ring, or it won't work."

"But I don't know how! Traveller just said it would be dangerous!"

The howl sounded again, floating eerily in the lowering dusk. An image rose in Rosinda's mind, grey lips pulled back over glistening, sharp white teeth as the dhangfox threw its head back and howled.

"Maybe less dangerous than that," Jerrell said.

They raced to the outer edge of the clearing where the grass lightened just beyond the edge of the fairy ring. Traveller hopped close to Rosinda. "You must listen to me and concentrate."

"Can't you use it?" she asked, preparing to slip the cord over her head.

"No! It's bloodbound to your family. You're the only one here who can use it," Traveller said. "Don't take it off. *Never* take it off."

Her heart thudded painfully, but Rosinda lowered the cord around her neck again. She took the crystal in her hand and felt a wash of familiarity.

"Close your eyes," Traveller ordered. "Everyone else, stand close and touch her."

Rosinda closed her eyes, but it was difficult to keep them shut. She felt a soft touch on her foot—Filara's paw—and a brush against her other leg—the crow. Jerrell gripped the strap of her backpack where it hung from her shoulder.

"She can't go straight into the mainland," the cat said. "Her memories—"

"I know, if they all return at once—"

"And they will, if she doesn't go in gradually."

"I can hear you both," said Rosinda, "and you're not making this any easier."

"You can do this," Traveller told her.

"There is strength in everyone," said the cat.

"Just think of this name. Indos," said the crow. "Think of water—"

"And fish," added Filara.

"Warm sand and brightly colored birds," said Traveller. "Water as far as you can see."

"An island?" asked Jerrell.

"Yes. Rosinda, do you have that?" asked the crow.

"I—I think so."

"Now hold the crystal tightly and say your name—"

"My name?"

"Yes, your full name, and the words Indos and Ysterad." The crow pressed harder against her leg.

Memories of her last attempt at magic surfaced. "Do I have to draw power from the earth, or whatever you said last time?"

"No," the crow said. "The power comes from the crystal, not from you. Hurry!"

Rosinda's hands trembled. No, not just her hands; her whole body was tense and shaking. The comforting weight of Jerrell's hand on the backpack made her feel a little better. She was glad he was here. She squeezed her eyes tightly shut and said, "Rosinda Aletta Penyan. Indos. Ysterad."

The world shifted.

CHAPTER FIVE

Once, Aunt Odder had taken Rosinda to visit a friend of hers, a lighthouse keeper. Or rather, a former lighthouse keeper. Aunt Odder told her on the drive there that all the lighthouses in Cape Breton were now automated. No one lived or worked in them anymore. But the keeper, Cap'n Joe, had taken them out to the rocky promontory where the lighthouse stood. Rosinda stood at its sea-and wind-weathered base and tilted her head back to look up at the tiny balcony encircling the light far above them.

Perhaps sensing her interest, or perhaps because he wanted an excuse, Cap'n Joe had looked furtively around and produced a key from his pocket. He opened the door, and the three of them slipped inside. It smelled pleasantly of salt and wood with just a hint of fish.

A winding staircase curved around the inner walls of the lighthouse, and Rosinda climbed them eagerly. At the top the huge light winked on and off, even in the daytime, and Rosinda couldn't look directly at its brilliant eye. They went out onto the balcony.

While Cap'n Joe and Aunt Odder looked at the view out over the water, Rosinda watched a pair of gulls swoop over the waves, ever closer to the lighthouse. They coasted in on an updraft to alight on the rocks just below the tower in search of mussels, and Rosinda leaned over the balcony to watch them. The sight of the crashing waves so far below (seventy-two feet, Cap'n Joe proudly told her) had a strange, mesmerizing effect on her. She felt as if she were falling, even though she was aware of her feet still planted firmly on the weathered balcony decking and her hands gripping the cold metal handrail. Her head, though, felt as if it were spiraling down to shatter on the rocky beach. Aunt Odder gave Rosinda a little shake to break the trance, and they descended to the beach. She didn't really feel right again until the next morning.

That was how Rosinda felt now, spiraling, if the crow and the cat were to be believed, between two worlds. Physically, she could feel the crystal slightly warm in her hand, the light touches of Filara and Traveller and Jerrell as they maintained contact with her, the ground still firm under her feet. When she risked a peek through a slitted eyelid, she saw only inky black, and the sensation of falling persisted.

Then several things happened at once. The ground *squirmed* under her feet, changing into something softer and warmer. Light assaulted her closed eyelids, and she felt a physical jolt as if she had just walked into a wall.

"Oof!" Jerrell gasped, losing his grip on the backpack strap.

Rosinda's eyes flew open and she grasped at Jerrell, terrified he would be lost somewhere between the two worlds if he broke contact with her. But it was all right—he lay sprawled in the sand beside her, looking slightly disoriented but okay. Filara shook a paw distastefully, and Traveller spread his wings and ruffled his feathers.

"I *hate* sand," the cat said. "It gets in one's paws and is absolutely *impossible* to get out without a thorough washing. And when am I likely to get time to do that, I ask you?"

"So...this is Ysterad?" Rosinda asked, looking around. They stood on a sandy beach near an azure body of water. A warm, salt-scented breeze swayed the long, drooping fronds of trees nearby.

"A part of it," Traveller said, ruffling his feathers back into place. "This is the main island where the Selavine live. There are also a few smaller islands in the chain."

"Who are the Selavine?" Jerrell asked. He dug around in his backpack for a moment, pulled out a pair of sunglasses, and slipped them on.

"Hey," said Rosinda, momentarily distracted, "Why do you have sunglasses? It wasn't even sunny at home!"

Jerrell grinned. "I was a Boy Scout."

"I don't know what that has to do with anything."

"Their motto is, 'Be Prepared.' I was a very good Boy Scout," Jerrell added.

"Yeah, so you take all kinds of extra stuff to school with you?" Rosinda asked skeptically. "My backpack's heavy enough with books and scribblers in it. A digital camera, and now sunglasses?"

He chuckled. "No, this isn't my school backpack. This is my camping pack. When I saw you go into the woods, I ran home and grabbed this one. That's how you got ahead of me. I keep all kinds of useful stuff in it."

"Oh, okay." Rosinda realized she was sweating in her heavy jeans and hooded sweater. It had been cool, autumn weather back in Cape Breton, but here the sun beat down with a tropical intensity.

"So it's summer here?" she asked, unzipping the hoodie and stuffing it into her pack.

"Not in all of Ysterad, naturally. It's always warm here on the island, when it isn't raining. The Selavine don't really have to worry about seasons."

"Who are the Selavine?" Jerrell asked again. "What are they like?"

"They won't trouble us," Traveller said. "They're friendly folk, mostly fishermen, although there are some who raise—"

"Coconuts!" Rosinda blurted. "They...raise them in groves further inland...and trade them to—to—just a second." She squeezed her eyes closed and concentrated, frowning. "I've got it! The Horsetribes on the mainland." She put a hand over her mouth for a moment, her eyes wide. "I remembered!"

The cat flicked an ear. "It's because you're back in Ysterad."

"You mean my memories will start coming back just because I'm here?" Rosinda asked. "Why? And why didn't Aunt Odder bring me back here long ago?"

"Horsetribes?" Jerrell ran a hand through his hair. "Maybe I should start taking notes."

"If we're going to continue this conversation," said Filara, "We have to do it in the shade. It's *absolutely* too hot here." She turned and walked toward the nearby grove of trees, her tail high in the air.

Jerrell nudged Rosinda. "Did you really have to make her talk? That cat's got an attitude."

"I know it. Believe me, I would have been more careful if I'd understood the risks."

Once they reached the shade of the trees, Rosinda asked, "What about the Irylians, following us? They must be able to travel between the worlds, too. Will they find us here?"

"I think we're safe for the time being," the crow said. "They can't possibly know which part of Ysterad we've come through. We could be up north with the Hanjavi or down on the coast of the Burning Sea, or anywhere in between."

The cat twitched her whiskers. "Unless they're using magical means to scry for the girl," she snapped. "Which we ought to assume they are, since they've obviously had some sort of help already. Irylian shama don't have the world-crossing magic. So I'd suggest we don't get too comfortable here."

"Well, it was your idea to move into the shade," muttered Traveller, but Filara pretended not to hear him.

"I'm hungry," Jerrell said. "We missed supper. Although I don't really know what time of day it is here." He squinted up at the sun. "A little past noon, I'd guess."

Rosinda's stomach felt awfully hollow, too. "I have a little bit of food in my pack," she said, but her heart sank when she thought about how little it really was. Not enough to last two people for long.

"Save that for now," Traveller said. "There should be some berries in these bushes." He hopped into the undergrowth and called out a few moments later, "Come here, Jerrell."

Jerrell followed the crow into the brush and emerged a few minutes later, holding the hem of his shirt up to make a basket for the berries he'd picked. They were the color of peaches and the size of blueberries, but tasted like a cross between blackberries and pears. As hungry as she was, Rosinda would gladly have eaten them no matter how strange they tasted. They were very juicy, too, and sated her thirst.

As they ate, Rosinda asked, "Where do you think they've taken Aunt Odder? We have to find her."

Neither the cat nor the crow answered for a moment, and then the cat sniffed. "If they were Irylians, then I suspect they'd take her back to their desert, at least directly."

"So we should go to—Irylia?" asked Jerrell.

"Unless they're working for someone else," the crow said.

"In which case, we don't know where to go? We don't have any clues to find Aunt Odder?" Rosinda felt panic tighten her stomach.

"How big is this place? Ysterad, I mean," Jerrell asked.

"There are ten provinces," Rosinda said absently. "Well, eleven if you count The Hidden—wait! How did I know that?" She turned amazed eyes on the crow.

"Perhaps your memories surface naturally when you're not trying to force them," Jerrell suggested.

Filara twitched her tail. "That's what *I* was going to say," she said.

Rosinda frowned. "But...I can't think of their names."

"They'll probably come to you when you're not trying so hard," Jerrell assured her.

Filara cleared her throat. "*At any rate*, Irylia is as good a place as any to start. I wish it were one of the more open provinces, of course."

"Open?"

The crow explained. "Some of the provinces have grown rather...isolated. People tend to keep to their own kind, in their own province. They're generally suspicious of strangers. Only a few of the larger cities have very mixed populations. And it's grown much worse since—"

He broke off, darting a glance at Rosinda. Another memory, a darker one, floated to the surface of her mind, and she finished the sentence for him. "Since the king and queen were killed," she said slowly. It wasn't something she remembered clearly, more like something she'd read about in the news.

"And Prince Sovann disappeared," the cat added, watching Rosinda intently. "Without a proper monarch on the throne, the royal advisors have tried to keep things running. More and more, though, folks have come to rely on themselves and their local leaders for everything. And that's made people more apt to keep to themselves and mistrust others from across borders."

"How long ago did this happen?" asked Jerrell.

The cat and the crow shared a significant glance again. "Two years," the crow said.

"The Prince has been missing for so long?" asked Rosinda. "Where could he be all that time?"

"Your aunt might be able to answer that question," the cat said darkly.

"What does Aunt Odder have to do with it?"

"Maybe nothing. Maybe everything," Traveller said. "I think that's why she's been kidnapped. Someone thinks, rightly or wrongly, that she knows what happened to Prince Sovann and where he is."

"But why would they kidnap her? Why not just ask her?"

"Because...because there are some who would prefer the Prince never return to reclaim his throne," the crow said. "The ones who want him back, yes, they'd come asking, even pleading for any knowledge your aunt might have. I believe they may have done so in the past. Those who don't want him back, though, and want to *ensure* he doesn't come back...well, they wouldn't be so scrupulous."

Rosinda realized with horror what the crow meant. "You mean they want to make Aunt Odder tell them where the prince is—so they can kill him?"

"That's what I think."

"How old is he?" asked Jerrell.

"The Prince would be a little more than your age," the crow answered. "He is sixteen."

"So he's been in hiding all this time? What a terrible life for him."

"But a life, and one others would take from him," the crow reminded her. "And now, I believe we should begin figuring out a way to get to the mainland."

"By boat," Filara suggested sarcastically. "And I do *so* hate water."

"We must find someone with a boat who will take us across," the crow continued, ignoring the cat. "It's not a long crossing, but we should start looking. If we could catch someone going anyway, they might not look for much in the way of payment."

"That's good," said Jerrell, standing and hefting his pack onto his back, "because I don't think anyone here is going to be interested in the change from my lunch money."

"Jerrell," said Rosinda, as she stood too and stretched, "aren't your parents going to be worried when you don't come home?"

He shrugged. "It's just my uncle, and he's away working. He'll call to check in on me sometime in the next few days, but no one's going to miss me before that."

"You live practically on your own?"

"It's no big deal. He's gotta go where the work is, but it doesn't make sense to sell a good house and go live in an apartment somewhere. So I take care of things while he's away."

Rosinda thought for a minute. "What about while you're away, though?"

Jerrell shrugged again. "I guess I'll have to worry about that later."

"I'm sorry you had to get involved in this," she said.

He grinned. "I'm not. This beats math class any day."

•••

Despite her slowly returning memories, Rosinda was nervous about meeting someone from Selavine. Filara seemed confident they'd find help in the largest trading port, Indos. Rosinda couldn't remember what the people here looked like or what language they spoke, and although Traveller seemed confident they would easily find assistance, she wasn't so sure. She would have to do the talking, since Traveller and Filara assured her talking animals were out of the ordinary, even here.

They walked along the sandy beach for a mile or so, growing hotter with each step. When they came upon a small empty jetty, Traveller found a trail that led a little ways inland. It was cooler where the trail wound under the trees, but Rosinda's worries didn't let her enjoy it.

Finally the road curved back toward the shoreline again and opened onto a bustling wharf. Although her throat tightened nervously, another of Rosinda's recalcitrant memories returned.

All the Selavine wore wide grins, even while the short, sun-weathered folk haggled over merchandise or sweated to load and unload cargo. Rosinda and Jerrell hesitated, not sure where to ask for assistance. A woman in a brightly beaded sarong-style wrap strode over to them. Her feet were bare, her skin darkly tanned, and her hair curled into a magnificent mass on the top of her head. Tiny beach stones studded the curls.

"Looking for help?" she asked. "I'm Kathewatina, today's steward. Just arrived, or just leaving?"

"Just—just leaving," Rosinda managed. "We need to find a boat to take us across to the mainland."

"Hire or swap?"

Rosinda looked blankly at the woman.

"I mean, are you going to pay for your passage or barter for it?"

"Well, we don't have much money," Rosinda said. *None at all, actually.* "So I guess it will have to be barter."

"Goods or labor?"

Traveller hadn't prepared her for this. "What kinds of labor?" she asked.

The woman raised an eyebrow. "How'd you manage to get here, child, if you don't know that? It depends on the kind of boat you take. You could clean fish on a fishing boat, cook a meal, swab the deck, do laundry for the captain or the crew. The crossing takes about two hours. So whatever the owner wants done and you can squeeze in."

"I guess...we could do any of that," Rosinda said, although she had no idea how to clean fish and sincerely hoped it wouldn't come to that.

"Two of you?"

"Yes, and my cat," Rosinda said. Traveller had said he would find his own way across, although Rosinda thought two hours was a long time to have to fly without stopping.

The woman pursed her lips and looked down at Filara. "She might present a problem. Cats don't usually take to crossing water."

"She'll be completely well-behaved," Rosinda pleaded. "I'll guarantee it."

"Never saw a cat yet that did what a human wanted," the woman said, laughing, "But it's not me you'll have to convince. Follow me."

Filara made a rude sound but the woman didn't seem to notice it. Rosinda bent down and picked her up, stroking her fur as they walked after the woman. "Be good," she whispered.

"Humph!" the cat said, but she kept her voice low enough so only Rosinda heard it.

Beside her, Jerrell whispered, "What did she say?"

"Who, Filara?"

"No, that woman! I couldn't understand a word of what you two were saying!"

Rosinda looked at him. "We weren't speaking English?" she whispered back.

"Of course not!" Jerrell was staring at her as if she'd gone crazy. "I didn't know you spoke any other languages. Except in French class. And that sure wasn't French."

"I—neither did I," she stammered. How could that be? How could she speak another language she didn't even know she knew, without even knowing she was speaking it?

Unless it had something to do with Aunt Odder, and her magic, and the book that weighed down Rosinda's backpack.

They followed Kathewatina through the press of people, women carrying babies and parcels, and sometimes huge baskets on their heads; men toting bundles of goods or pulling small wicker wagons piled high. She stopped at a jetty where a small fishing boat bobbed on the water.

Oh, no, Rosinda thought. *It* is *going to be fish.*

Kathewatina hollered in the direction of the boat, "Sallah Dimwagetine! Do you have room for a couple of changas on this crossing?" She smiled back at Rosinda. "And a cat?"

A disembodied voice rose from inside the tiny cabin. "Will the cat eat my fish?"

Rosinda shook her head, and Kathewatina smiled.

"I am assured it is a most well-behaved cat," she replied.

A man's head appeared in the cabin entryway then, smoothly bald but covered with tattoos. They swirled over his head like a dark lace cap, and one ran down the length of his face and under his chin, a long vine of living art. The sun had turned his skin almost the color of milk chocolate, and his face was as wrinkled as a crumpled piece of tissue paper. He beckoned them over with a long, thin arm.

"Come on, then, come on. I've got a hold full of fish that can't wait to start filling Zaranian bellies!"

Rosinda turned to Kathewatina. "Thank you," she said. "I didn't know where to start looking, myself."

The big woman chuckled. "Just doing my job," she said. "Have a good crossing, now, and take good care of that excellent cat!"

"What did she mean by *that*?" Filara whispered as Rosinda followed Jerrell out onto the jetty.

"I'm sure she meant it as a compliment," Rosinda reassured her. "You will behave yourself, won't you?"

"*Phzzt!*" The cat turned her head away and refused to look at Rosinda, clearly insulted.

They climbed aboard the fishing boat, and Sallah Dimwagetine regarded them with twinkling eyes for a moment. "So you want to work your passage, do you? I'm afraid the fish are already cleaned and salted, so I can't put you to work doing that."

Rosinda tried not to let her relief show on her face.

"You, girl," the old man said, "Can you cook?"

She bit her lip. "A little," she ventured. "If you're not too fussy."

Sallah Dimwagetine laughed. "Not fussy at all, my girl. Come on into the cabin and see what you can rustle up from what's in here while I deal with the Earth-speaker. Then the boy and I can cast off."

Earth-speaker? The term seemed familiar, and Rosinda struggled to remember. The old man blew a short blast on a bone horn, and another woman strode down the wharf toward their little jetty. She was smaller than Kathewatina, wearing a headdress of feathers and tiny bones that chinked when she walked. Money changed hands, and she handed Sallah Dimwagetine a blue stone that resembled Rosinda's crystal.

It came back to her then. "Earth-speakers" were Indos magic users, and their magic propelled the boats on the waters around the islands. The jewel was a method for transferring the magical power, without actually having to have the Earth-speaker on board.

Rosinda started for the cabin then remembered something. She gestured to Jerrell. "He won't understand what you're saying," she told the fisherman, "Although if you show him things he'll catch on fast enough."

"Not from these parts, is he?" the old man asked, looking Jerrell up and down.

"N-No, he's travelled a long way," Rosinda said. She flashed a quick smile at Jerrell she hoped was reassuring, and stepped into the cabin.

Luck was in her favor. There was a little stove, which she managed to light with Filara's help, fresh water, vegetables, spices and fish, and it wasn't too difficult to throw all together in a pot for a fish stew. She was used to helping Aunt Odder in the kitchen at home, and it felt good to be able to stop and think while her hands did some mindless work.

Thinking of home made her lonesome...except supposedly *this* was her home, she reminded herself. It didn't feel like home. The little house in Cape Breton, just her and Aunt Odder and Filara—that's what felt like home, despite having no friends and always worrying about her parents. It was the only home she could remember.

She sighed as she sliced a long thin orange vegetable that reminded her of a carrot but tasted much sweeter. The name came to her when she tasted it. *Ollaroot.* She smiled in surprise, but her mind turned back to her worries. The car accident apparently hadn't happened at all. In spite of her concern about Aunt Odder, she realized she felt a little angry with her, too. Why hadn't she told Rosinda the truth? Did Aunt Odder think she was too young to handle it? That she'd worry too much? Although it was hard to imagine she could worry any more about her parents than she had, thinking they were invalids in a far-off country.

Perhaps her aunt hadn't trusted her to keep their secrets? Who would she tell? In Cape Breton, she was an outsider. Like Jerrell...

Rosinda dumped the chunks of ollaroot into the pot and started on something similar to an Earth onion. Jerrell. What was he really doing here? Had he simply been concerned about her, as he'd said? He was much nicer than he'd seemed at school if that was the case. Well, he *was* much nicer. And he was taking all of this much better than she was. Even though this was her world. She sighed again.

"The fish next," Filara prodded her, and Rosinda realized she'd stopped chopping onion and stood staring out the tiny porthole window. The cat's words reminded her of the last big thing she'd managed to mess up; the stupid spell Traveller had talked her into trying.

And that's enough thinking for now, she told herself, and put her mind and hands to work on the stew. Soon it was bubbling and fragrant, and she stuck her head outside the cabin door to tell Sallah Dimwagetine the meal was ready. The old man invited Rosinda, and Jerrell, who was washing up the tiny deck, to come and have something to eat.

Gratefully, they accepted the invitation to share the stew,

since the berries they'd had on the beach were now a distant
memory. They sat on low benches on the deck, bowls held
close to their chins, and slurped the stew from wooden spoons.
Rosinda was surprised at how well it had turned out, and both
Jerrell and the old man made appreciative noises.

"What's the name of this water we're crossing?" Rosinda
asked as they ate.

The old man raised an eyebrow at her. "What, you're not from
these parts, either? You sure speak the language well enough."

Rosinda swallowed. "I guess I'm good at languages but not
so good at geography."

He laughed. "This is the Silverflash Strait," he said, "Know
why they call it that?"

Rosinda shook her head.

"They say there are so many fish in these waters, you can see
the silver flash of their scales no matter where you look," he
explained. "Now, I don't know about that, but there are fish
aplenty, sure enough. Off to the northwest, on your left, that's
the Auroc Ocean, and if you went the other way far enough
you'd end up in the Burning Sea. Not," he added, "that you'd
want to go there."

Rosinda wanted to ask him why, but she was beginning to
squirm under the strange looks he gave her when she asked
something he thought she ought to know.

When they had finished, Sallah Dimwagetine went back to
start the boat moving again, telling Jerrell and Rosinda they could
relax for the rest of the crossing. Rosinda went into the cabin to
clean up the dishes and feed Filara the few scraps of leftover fish,
but she'd barely started when she heard a cry from Jerrell.

Through the narrow doorway, she saw Jerrell digging
frantically in his backpack. A huge bird swooped down toward
him, hooked beak wide and talons outstretched.

CHAPTER SIX

Rosinda screamed and ran out of the cabin as the giant eagle dropped toward Jerrell. She still clutched a long-handled metal ladle and brandished it over her head like a sword. An unfamiliar burning surged in her stomach and chest, and a red veil fell over her vision. She gripped the ladle tightly, swung it experimentally a few times, but felt annoyed. *The balance is all wrong. And it's too light.*

She stopped, confused. She had no idea why she was thinking these things.

Jerrell rolled away from his pack. Something bright and red flashed in his hand. The eagle screeched and raked the deck with its claws in passing, rocking the small boat.

"Get back inside!" Jerrell yelled to Rosinda, but she ignored him. Instinctively, she lunged with the ladle at the eagle, but missed. The bird wheeled up and around, turning to make another pass.

"What's happening?" Sallah Dimwagetine shouted from his steering perch at the front of the boat. The ship began to slow.

"No!" Rosinda screamed. "Don't stop! Keep going, faster if you can!"

The old man must have heard her but ignored her instructions. The boat continued to slow and Sallah Dimwagetine stormed around to the deck.

"What are you young rascals—" he started, but broke off, perhaps seeing the looks of horror on the faces of his two passengers. He turned to look up just as the eagle swooped low over the boat again and took an involuntary step backward. His foot hit the base of a bench and he staggered. Rosinda swung with the ladle again, trying to ward off the giant bird, but the weight and reach and feel were just *wrong*.

The eagle's outstretched talon caught the old man a glancing blow on the shoulder. Sallah Dimwagetine toppled backward into the water with a yell and a huge splash.

Rosinda gasped. The old man sputtered and splashed, making inarticulate sounds of rage. *Could he swim?* Rosinda scanned the tiny deck for a life jacket or rope.

Before she could do anything else, the eagle plunged at them again, screaming like a mad creature. Jerrell pushed Rosinda behind him into the cabin and put one hand up to his face. Rosinda couldn't see what he had in his hand, but her head pounded. This was *wrong*. She shouldn't be hiding behind someone else.

Then the piercing screech of a whistle split the air. Rosinda dropped the ladle and clapped her hands over her ears, the strange feeling that had gripped her shattered by the sound. It went on and on, stopping only for a brief second when Jerrell paused to draw breath. Quick, bright red flashes of light played over the deck and surroundings at the same time. Sallah Dimwagetine still splashed and hollered, sounds Rosinda was glad to hear. At least they meant the old man wasn't sinking.

The eagle screeched once more, and wheeled in midair away from the boat. Huge wings beat the air steadily as it gained the higher reaches of the sky. The whistle's incessant screech ended, but the light continued to flash around them. Rosinda watched the giant bird diminish until it was just a speck in the sky. Only then did she realize she'd been holding her breath. She let it out in a long sigh.

Jerrell grabbed a rope from under one of the benches and

threw one end of it to the old fisherman. It reached him on the second try, and Rosinda knelt beside Jerrell to help haul the man back onto the deck.

"What in the name of the Dark Moon is going on back here?" he demanded. When he'd caught his breath.

"We were attacked by a giant bird," Rosinda said hesitantly.

"Oh, is that all?" Sallah Dimwagetine blustered, waving his dripping arms in indignation. Drops of seawater flew in every direction, spattering both of them. "Could you tell me *why* you were attacked by a giant bird?"

"Um, not really," Rosinda said. "Maybe he was attacking you, not us."

The old man fixed her with a keen blue eye. "In sixty-five jihars, I've never been attacked by anything in making this crossing," he said, "not even a tiddlefish. Why would giant birds start attacking me now? No, it's you. One or both of you," he said, pursing his lips and nodding sagely. "You, not the boy, if I had to guess," he said to Rosinda.

Now it was her turn to be indignant. "Why me?"

"Because you've got a look about you. You're Kelton?"

Rosinda was tempted to say she didn't know, just to see what he'd have to say to that, but instead she said, "What if I am?"

"Then you're a Kelta, too, although you might not know it yet. And a fine Kelta you'll make, by the look of you swinging that ladle like milady's finest steel."

At her confused look, his face softened. "Ah, well, we're safe for now. The boy scared it off well and truly with those gadgets, which I see he's tucked away out of my sight, so I won't ask more about them. Fetch me the blanket from the cabin, girl, and we'll get back on course for the main. And mind you both," he said, wagging a wrinkled finger at them, "Keep an eye on the skies until we're safe in port."

Once the old man had dried off and headed back to the

wheelhouse with one last appraising glance at Rosinda, Jerrell turned to her.

"Are you okay?" he asked. "Did you see the *size* of that thing?"

Rosinda sighed. "I'm all right. That was really smart, the way you scared it away. Thanks."

Jerrell grinned. "I told you, I like to be prepared. And you have to think fast when a giant eagle is about to grab you!" He looked at her curiously. "What were you doing with that ladle? It was like you thought you had a sword or something."

Rosinda shrugged, not having an answer or wanting to talk about the strange sensation that had gripped her. "How come you have all that stuff in your backpack?" she asked evasively.

"My uncle and I go hiking and camping a lot when he's home," Jerrell said with a shrug. He held out something that looked like a small flashlight with a whistle in the end. "I have a lot of gadgets and stuff for that. This one's good for scaring bears, so I figured it was worth a try." He tucked it back inside his pack.

"Well, I'm glad you're so prepared. You didn't even have time to pack anything up. I did, and I didn't think of anything really practical."

"The crow said you brought food," Jerrell said. "That's pretty practical."

"Yeah, but it was his idea, and I don't have much of it," Rosinda answered gloomily. She looked up in the direction where the eagle had disappeared. "I wonder what that was about, anyway?"

Filara stepped delicately out of the cabin, avoiding the puddles of water on the deck and shaking her paw if it encountered a droplet. "Someone is looking for you, and now they know you're here," she said matter-of-factly.

"But I thought you said it was Irylians and dhangfoxes who took Aunt Odder," Rosinda said in a low voice so the old man wouldn't overhear. "You didn't mention giant birds!"

"I didn't say they were the *only* ones we had to worry about," the cat said. "There could be any number of folks who want the information they think the Mistress has. It's quite a while since we've been in Ysterad, so I don't know what's been going on here lately."

"I suppose a lot can change in a year," Rosinda said.

The cat made a snuffling noise Rosinda realized was laughter. "You've got a year's worth of memories of living in Cape Breton, but it's a good two years, or jihars, as the old man would say, since you and the Mistress and I left the castle at Sangera."

"What?" Rosinda said, confused. "It can't be. The accident— or whatever happened—"

"Happened two years ago, not one," the cat insisted. "The same time the Prince went into hiding. And believe me, if you're lucky, you won't get all of those memories back. There are some I wish I didn't have."

"But—you mean I'm missing a whole year even *after* the— after the attacks?"

The cat shrugged. "You don't remember anything before then either, what's another year?"

Rosinda felt like she'd been hit in the chest. She was suddenly so angry at the cat and her aunt, she couldn't speak.

"That's a rotten thing to say," Jerrell told Filara, looking like he was considering throwing her overboard. "She's already upset enough."

Filara must have seen the look on Rosinda's face, because she seemed to relent. "I suppose. Well, we didn't leave the castle and go straight to Cape Breton. We were in hiding, on the run—it was dangerous and frightening. Your aunt could have left you with those memories. But she wanted to make your life easier to bear for a while and protect you, so she blocked those, too. It wasn't an easy decision for her, but she was responsible for you.

She had to make the choices that seemed best at the time."

Rosinda didn't know what to say. She still didn't trust herself to speak, so she merely nodded, sat back on one of the benches, and turned her eyes to the cloud-studded sky. Everything seemed out of control, but at least she might be able to stop any more surprises like the one they'd just had.

●●●

A speck of land appeared on the horizon, growing steadily closer as the little fishing boat skimmed across the water. Before they knew it the boat was pulling up to a jetty at the waters' edge, and a bustling town rose beyond the wharves. "This is the port of Genia," Sallah Dimwagetine told them as they gathered their packs.

"I've never been here before," Rosinda said. She didn't know if that was true, but she wanted to know everything the old man could tell them.

He gave her an odd look, but said, "There are only a few towns in this part of Ysterad; the Horsetribes like to stay on the move most of the time. But they also like to trade with us and the Irylians and the Kelton, so we have to be able to find them sometimes."

"Do only people from the Horsetribes live in the towns here?" Rosinda asked, but the answer began to form in her mind even as the old man answered her.

"You'll find mostly Zaranians here, yes, although there'll be a few others in the mix, too. Not so much in Genia, but Zarab's a pretty big city."

When she stepped onto the jetty, Rosinda had to catch at Jerrell's arm for balance. The horizon seemed to tilt, and the world around her shimmered like the air above a hot roadway on a summer day. A surge of words and images rose in her mind like an onrushing wave and subsided back. The world steadied again.

Jerrell shot her a worried look, but she smiled and shook her head, letting go of his sleeve. She looked around at the land of the Horsetribes with a renewed interest.

Sallah Dimwagetine saw them off with a smile. "Some of the best fish stew I've ever had," he said to Rosinda, and then his face grew serious. "Take care, girl. I don't want to know any more than I do, but I suspect you need a little more good luck than some others might."

"Thank you, Sallah Dimwagetine," Rosinda said, giving him a quick hug. "I think you might be right."

Jerrell threw the old man a salute, and they hefted their packs and walked into the crowd with Filara at their heels.

"Any idea where we're going?" Jerrell asked in a low voice.

"Nope." Rosinda hoped to see Traveller appear somewhere close, but she didn't know if he would come right into the town. She looked around curiously. No one seemed to take particular notice of them. Most people, including the women, wore pants of a material very much like her denim jeans, and long-sleeved shirts, jackets, or woolen sweaters. Almost everyone carried some sort of parcel, or basket, or pack, so even their backpacks didn't set them apart too much.

Rosinda shivered. The air was cooler and drier than it had been on the island, even here at the ocean's edge. She stopped and pulled her sweater back on. Filara stood at her feet, tail agitatedly swishing the air.

"What's wrong?" Rosinda whispered, stooping down to pet her.

"There's a feeling here—I don't like it," the cat muttered. Rosinda could barely hear her over the noise of the crowd. "And look up there—those walls are new."

Rosinda followed the cat's gaze to a tall palisade rising beyond the low buildings of the wharf district. The tops of the pales had sharp, cruel-looking points, and while a gate stood open beneath them, four armed guards were very much in evidence.

The fortification did look new. A flag danced in the breeze above the gates; red, with silver-colored bars on the sides. In the center of the flag, in black, a sword and a river crossed in an X with a crow's head above and a horse's head below. Dark leaves and flowers traced their way along the silver bars.

"What flag is that?" she asked Filara.

The cat glanced up at it. "The Horsetribes have a new god, or possibly a goddess," she said with distaste.

Rosinda shivered, not from the cool air. "I don't like her flag," she said. The colors and symbols had a stark, angry feel.

Filara sniffed. "Looks like a war goddess to me. They like to instill a little fear in those who follow them—and a lot of fear in those who don't."

Rosinda didn't want to pass through that gate, under the scrutiny of the guards and the dark presence of a war deity's flag.

Fortunately, she didn't have to. A squawk sounded from the roof of a low building nearby, and Rosinda looked up to see a large black crow perched there. It looked straight at her and bobbed its head a couple of times. A wave of relief washed over her. *Traveller.* He launched himself off the roof and banked to the west, toward a wooded area.

Jerrell had noticed him, too. He caught Rosinda's eye and flashed a grin.

He's actually enjoying this, Rosinda thought, annoyed. Her Aunt Odder was in serious trouble, they were here in a strange world practically alone, and Jerrell was acting as if he were having the time of his life.

But as quickly as her anger rose, it dissipated again. She realized with a shock that she was—apart from the danger, of course—feeling better than she had in a long time. She was away from the school where she didn't fit in and the long hours of worrying about her memory loss and her parents. She was too busy dealing with life from moment to moment to have much time to think about those things. She was actually relaxed.

When I'm not terrified, she thought, but she smiled inwardly as she thought it.

No one seemed to notice or care as the two strangers with the calico cat left the wharves. They headed for the copse of trees outside the town. Traveller waited for them just inside the treeline.

"I'm glad to see you," he greeted them gravely, not looking at the cat. "Did you have a safe trip across the strait?"

Rosinda pursed her lips. "Well, we made it across in one piece, but we were attacked on the way by a giant eagle."

The crow gave an inarticulate squawk. "Were you hurt?"

She shook her head. "It didn't really come after me; it seemed to be after Jerrell. And the man who owned the boat was knocked overboard, but we got him out of the water and he was fine."

"After Jerrell?" the crow mused. "Interesting. What happened to it?"

"I scared it off," Jerrell said modestly. "It wasn't very persistent. And it might have gone after me because I was the only one out on deck at the time. Rosinda attacked it, too. Even if it was just with a ladle she thought was a sword." He grinned.

Traveller looked at her sharply, but all he said was, "Well, we'll have to find a place for you to spend the night. I don't think we have enough coin to put you up in an inn."

"I don't want to go into Genia unless I have to," Rosinda said quickly.

"We could camp," Jerrell said eagerly. "I have everything we need."

Traveller cocked his head at the boy. "Really? Why is that?"

Jerrell shrugged. "I believe in being prepared."

The crow nodded. "Let's go a little further into the woods. I'd rather be some distance away from the town before you settle in. You don't know who might be wandering close to the gates after dark."

Rosinda flashed a nervous glance over her shoulder as she and the others followed Traveller into the woods. No one seemed to take any notice of them, although she had the feeling of eyes watching her. A brief flash of movement drew her gaze to the top of the palisade, but it was gone too quickly to identify. She watched the spot for the space of a few heartbeats but saw nothing else. With an uneasy feeling she turned back to the path. Probably just a guard making his rounds, she told herself. But she couldn't shake the feeling of someone—or something—watching them.

CHAPTER SEVEN

The gods had gathered again, and it wasn't going well.

"You did what?" Morrigan asked, her voice cold and deadly.

Tyr shrugged. "I wanted to test her since she'd so neatly avoided Sekhmet's errand-boys," he said lazily. The one-handed god lounged on an intricately carved stone seat on his mountaintop. "Since the boy was with her, I tested him, too."

"I already have a watcher taking the measure of the girl," Morrigan spat. Her crow aspect was more in evidence when she was angered, and her black eyes glittered darkly. A cap of glossy black feathers overlaid her fall of red hair.

"Interfering idiot!" Sekhmet screamed, no doubt doubly irritated by Tyr's description of the men she'd sent to fetch the girl, and their failure. However, Sekhmet spent much of her time screaming. Tyr didn't seem much affected by it.

He shrugged. "No ill came of it, so what is all the shrieking about? We don't even know if the girl is important."

Gradivus intervened. "That's right, it is the hedge-witch—I mean the *Kelta*," he said with a nod to Morrigan, "that I want to know about, not a little girl. Where is she now, oh Lady of Pestilence?" He inclined a mock bow in Sekhmet's direction.

The Egyptian goddess settled herself more comfortably in her golden throne and looked smug. "They have arrived at my servant's camp," she said. "Even now preparations are being made to bring her here. My servant will mount a caravan."

"How long will it take?" asked Gradivus.

"They *are* on the other side of Ysterad," Sekhmet said

witheringly. "And unless our impetuous friend here wants to send a flock of giant eagles to scoop them up, they'll have to cross overland like everyone else."

"And hire ships to bring her here, from the Seafolk," mused Morrigan. "Even if we pooled our resources…"

"We don't have the power to bring the Kelta by any other means," said Tyr flatly. "Not yet."

"Tell your servant to watch for mine to arrive soon," Morrigan told Sekhmet. "I will instruct her to give an identifying sign."

"There isn't any need—"

"Mine will be there, too," Gradivus interjected smoothly. "The provinces are restless—thanks to us—and your people might need extra protection before they reach here. It would be unwise to turn down help when it is offered."

Sekhmet muttered something under her breath. Her slitted cat's eyes smouldered but she made no other protest.

Morrigan looked around at the others and felt like rolling her eyes. They were so fond of bickering. It was their nature, she supposed, but it annoyed her. She couldn't wait to get an actual war started so that she could treat these three as enemies.

"My watcher reports the girl seems to have some inborn ability for her Kelta powers, but they are undeveloped and unlikely to be useful to us," she told them in a businesslike voice.

"Does she know where to find the Prince?" Tyr asked.

"It's difficult to say. Someone has tampered with her memory, so there's no telling what may be locked away in there. She may know more than she realizes."

"Perhaps," Sekhmet said, licking her lips, "we could unlock her."

Morrigan looked at the other goddess with distaste. "I believe the girl will still serve our purposes best as a hostage," she said, "If the Kelta proves…difficult."

"Then should we send someone else to fetch her?" Gradivus

asked. Sekhmet said nothing, apparently sulking.

"No," said Morrigan. "I believe, whether she knows it or not, she will come to us on her own."

CHAPTER EIGHT

Traveller led them into the woods for about twenty minutes before he perched on a low-hanging branch. "This looks like a pleasant spot for a camp, and it should be far enough from Genia to keep anyone from stumbling upon us."

Rosinda looked around the forest in the deepening dusk with an uneasy feeling, but she was so tired she just didn't have the energy to argue. "It must be midnight or later back home," she said to Jerrell as she dug some bits of food out of her pack.

"One-thirty a.m., to be exact," he said, looking at his watch. "Still working fine."

"Why wouldn't it?"

Jerrell shrugged and grinned. "I don't know—I wondered if crossing the void into another world might affect it. I've never done this before, remember."

"Neither have—" Rosinda stopped. Apparently, she had. She just couldn't remember it.

She passed two slices of bread, a chunk of cheese, and an apple to Jerrell and took the same for herself. "What happened to my memory?" she asked Traveller.

The crow shook his head. "I don't know."

"Oh, right." Rosinda felt silly. She had come to rely on Traveller for answers to her questions, but she had to remind herself he didn't really know her. Only some things about her family.

"Well, *I* know the answer, if anyone cares," Filara said with a sniff. She had settled herself a little apart from the others and begun to clean her paws and face.

"Sorry, Filara. Would you tell me what you can?"

"As far as I understand it, the Mistress used her Kelta magic to seal off your memories," the cat said.

"Aunt Odder did this?" Rosinda's hand shook a little as she raised her apple to her mouth and nibbled it. Her stomach clenched. "But she knew how much it upset me, not being able to remember anything. She was always so sympathetic about it." It wasn't what she wanted to say; she wanted to scream it couldn't be true. Aunt Odder wouldn't have done such a thing. But she also didn't want to make a scene. Not in front of Jerrell, especially, since he seemed to take everything that happened to him in stride.

"She was sympathetic," the cat said reprovingly. "But she also thought it was for the best. Even though I couldn't talk back, at least not *then*, she often talked to me. When something worried her, she'd tell me about it. I think it helped her sort through things to say them out loud to someone, even if it was just a *cat*." Filara rolled her eyes.

"She never mentioned the prince, I suppose," said Traveller.

"No."

"What could be so bad she didn't want me to remember it?" Rosinda asked hesitantly. She was afraid to hear the answer.

The cat was silent for a few minutes, methodically grooming her coat.

"I don't know that I'm the one to tell you," she said finally. "Your memory is coming back on its own now that you're in Ysterad. There could be things I'll get wrong, or not remember right, or that I didn't fully understand at the time. Let's just say your family was involved in some terrible times and going into hiding seemed the best answer. The Mistress wanted to make it as easy for you as possible."

Rosinda quietly ate her supper while she thought about that, but Jerrell cast a faintly disgusted look at the cat.

"Why don't you look in your aunt's book," he suggested to Rosinda, "if no one else is going to tell you anything. I think you're better off knowing all you can, and the sooner the better. So you can be prepared."

Rosinda smiled. "Like a Boy Scout?"

"Exactly." Jerrell used a complicated-looking pocketknife to pare thin slices off his apple, carefully eating them off the blade.

"But she wouldn't write down everything that happened," Rosinda said glumly. "Not if she was trying to keep it secret from me."

"You never know. You said yourself there's a little bit of everything in that book. Why not take a look?"

Rosinda glanced around at the quickly darkening woods. "It's getting too dark to see, and I don't know if we should light a fire." She shivered. "It's going to get cold, though."

"Don't worry." Jerrell stuck his hand in his pack again and pulled out two flat, square packages. He opened one and unfolded a sheet of flimsy silver plastic. "Emergency blankets," he said with a grin, handing it to Rosinda.

She took it with a skeptical look. "This is going to keep me warm?"

"It'll retain eighty percent of your body heat," he said matter-of-factly. "Just wrap it around yourself. You'll be surprised. And here," he continued, passing something else over. "It's a book light. It'll give you enough light to read by, but it's not bright enough to attract attention."

Rosinda, feeling slightly bemused, pulled the blanket around her shoulders and found Aunt Odder's book in her pack. Her tiredness gave way to a strange excitement that bubbled up at Jerrell's words. What if he were right? What if the book held some of the answers she wanted? She carefully opened the cover and began to turn the pages.

She passed many of the pages she'd already seen when looking for the charm spell to read Filara's thoughts—how long ago that seemed! Rosinda glanced up to see what the cat was doing now, but she wasn't around. She must have slipped off to go hunting, or whatever it was that cats liked to do after dark. Jerrell had a small book of his own out, reading by the beam of his flashlight.

Halfway through the book, Rosinda turned a page and an envelope slid out. She caught it as it slithered down the side of her silvery blanket. The name *Rosinda* scrawled across it in Aunt Odder's writing.

"What's that say?" Jerrell asked, looking up at her sudden movement.

She frowned. "My name?"

"Really? Those are weird letters."

Rosinda stared at it. It looked perfectly clear to her. Intrigued, she opened the envelope and pulled out several folded sheets of paper. Something small and hard nestled in the center. She delicately separated the papers. There were two sheets of Aunt Odder's spiky handwriting, a handful of smaller papers, and on the crease lay three tiny items.

She examined them in the faintly blue glow of Jerrell's book light. A small heart-shaped crystal. A polished, round green stone. And an irregularly shaped fragment of purple gemstone. Rosinda cupped them in her palm as she read;

Dear Rosinda,

If you've found this, then several things are probably true. I am either dead or missing, you are in Ysterad, and trouble is afoot. Inside these pages, you should have found three items; treat them with great care. To be able to read any more of this letter, you must use the aventurine. That's the round green one. You must swallow it. It will work only for you.

The letter continued on, but it was true—Rosinda could

not decipher another word. The writing was not in a different language, or in code. But when she tried to focus on a word or sentence, the writing slid away from her gaze, the letters writhing and twisting, refusing to stay still long enough for her to read them.

She showed it to Jerrell. "Can you read this?"

He shook his head. "No, it's all gibberish to me, just like the writing on the envelope. It's like...a cross between Chinese letters and Egyptian hieroglyphics." He couldn't even read the first paragraph, although to Rosinda it looked like plain, everyday English.

Rosinda laid the letter down and picked up the green stone. It was no bigger than a small pea, and polished smooth. It would be no difficulty to swallow it, especially with a gulp of water. But she hesitated.

"What's wrong?" Jerrell asked her. "What's that for?"

"The letter is from Aunt Odder," she said. "I'm supposed to swallow this to be able to read it all."

"Cool. What are you waiting for?"

She stared at him. Even in the dim glow from their two reading lights, his face looked eager. How did someone get like that?

"Nothing, I guess," she made herself say. She wanted to read the rest of the letter, but she had a feeling that once she did, things were going to get more difficult. It was like taking a big step when you couldn't see where your foot was going to land. But Jerrell and Traveller both watched her silently.

With a sudden reckless determination, she pulled a water bottle out of her pack, popped the green stone into her mouth, and took a swallow. The stone went down as smoothly as the water, and it was done. "Do you feel any different?" Jerrell asked.

Rosinda considered. "Not at all," she said with a grin. She picked up Aunt Odder's letter and looked past the first paragraph. The words stayed put on the page. "But I guess it did the trick."

"Okay!"

Before she continued with the letter, she took the smaller pieces of paper and tucked them into her pocket so they wouldn't get lost. They'd brought back another memory, and it was a welcome one. Then she went back to reading, her heart beating faster. Despite the circumstances, Aunt Odder felt very close and comforting as Rosinda read her words.

Good girl! Now I must explain.

As you probably know by now, you are from Ysterad. Some of your memories have likely returned, but it's better if that happens slowly. Each place you visit will unlock more. If it becomes imperative that you remember everything, or something about a place that you can't reach physically, you may use the heart-shaped crystal to regain your full memory. But this is a potentially <u>dangerous</u> *course of action, and I do not recommend it! Only in the case of a real emergency. Don't swallow this one; place it in your ear and sleep with it there. When you awake, you will have your memories.*

Now to the trouble. When Prince Sovann's parents were killed, I managed to spirit him out of the castle and into hiding. Later, when more attacks came, I had to act quickly to get us to safety, and the safest place lay across the Worlds' Edge, on Earth. Prince Sovann was still safe at the time of this writing, but I don't know what time or events have passed since then. If you are in Ysterad and he has not been restored to the throne, it is imperative that you make contact with him.

Use the amethyst for this; it is a fragment of a stone that is bloodbound to his family. You must take it in your left hand at dawn and face the rising sun, press it over your heart and recite the charm for Calling the Lost. It is in my book, but I will also write it here for you;

Cordhan bel, cordhan treict
Althos creign al talthos mein
When he finds you (and it may take some time, depending on
where you are and where he is) he will have to—

Traveller swooped down and landed between Jerrell and
Rosinda, interrupting her reading.

"Someone's coming!"

Rosinda and Jerrell both extinguished their lights. Rosinda
leapt to her feet, but Jerrell fumbled in his pack for something.
It was almost full dark now, and two thin crescent moons
rode the sky high above them. They cast only a faint light into
the forest. Rosinda slipped the crystal and the amethyst into
the pocket of her jeans, dumped the book into her pack, and
stuffed the letter in on top. She nearly jumped when a voice
sounded nearby.

"Now, young ones, stand where y'are."

The voice held a thinly veiled hint of menace, and Rosinda
fought to swallow the panic that rose in her throat. It dissipated
quickly, replaced by the same burning she'd felt when the giant
eagle had attacked them on Sallah Dimwagetine's boat. She felt
her body shift into an alert stance, balanced on the balls of her feet,
arms hanging loosely at her sides yet tingling with anticipation.

A shape appeared out of the trees, and fire flared from a
torch. The shape resolved into a man, thin and hunched with
a narrow, pinched face.

"Nice evenin'," he said with an unpleasant grin. "Now what
would two young ones such as yerselves be doin' out here, all
alone together, hey?"

Rosinda caught his meaning and felt her backbone stiffen.
"Not what you think and none of your business," she snapped.
"And who are you, going around scaring people?"

The man chuckled nastily. "Got a bit of spunk, you do, girl.
Now both of you, unhandle those packs and move away from

them, while yer uncle has a look inside. It might be two against one, but trust me, yer no match."

Jerrell shot Rosinda a look she couldn't read, put his pack down and backed slowly away. With a pang of fear for Aunt Odder's book, she did the same. *Why hadn't she stuffed the letter into her pocket, instead of the pack?* She struggled to make herself back away. Her body was sending her signals to do something quite different.

As they backed off, the man moved forward, opening Rosinda's pack first and pushing things around inside. He pulled out the book.

"Now what's this?" he said. "Can't judge a book by its cover, I always say." He still held the torch in one hand, so he laid the book on the pack and rifled through it with the other hand. "There's a man in Gelang Street pays nicely for old books," he mused.

Several things happened at once. Traveller swooped down from a branch above the man's head and raked him with his claws. Filara pounced silently on his back and did some claw-work of her own. Jerrell motioned to Rosinda to back away and put himself between her and the man.

Rosinda's vision burned red. *This isn't right.*

The man howled under the combined attack of the cat and crow. He stumbled over Rosinda's open pack and almost fell. "Brats!" he shouted, turning to Rosinda and Jerrell fiercely, as if he blamed them for the actions of the animals.

He took only one menacing step toward them, however, when something seemed to snap in Rosinda's brain. She leapt past Jerrell, spinning a high kick that connected with the man's shoulder and knocked him backward a few steps. He held onto the torch, and Rosinda dropped into a crouch.

At almost the same moment, Jerrell raised the cylinder he'd concealed in his sleeve. He aimed it at the man and pulled a cord at the bottom. Bright red flame blossomed from the cylinder. Like a torch shot from a gun, the glowing sphere sped across the meagre space that separated them and burst against the man's other side.

He screamed and dropped his torch, beating frantically with one hand at the flames licking his coat. His left arm hung limp and useless from his shoulder.

Rosinda's scream echoed his. The torch had fallen on her open pack and flared brightly.

Jerrell rushed forward and dragged the pack away from the frenzied man. Flames danced from the top, and he quickly dumped the contents out and smothered them with the pack. Traveller and Filara launched a second attack at the man and this time he fled without another word. His inarticulate yelps of pain receded from hearing as he crashed through the woods.

Rosinda felt weak as the red mist cleared from her vision. The force that had taken possession of her body drained away. She dropped to her knees near the contents of her pack. Jerrell was at her side in a moment with a flashlight.

"Is everything okay?" he asked. "I put it out as fast as I could."

Rosinda slowly held up some charred sheets of paper. "Everything...except this," she said shakily. It was Aunt Odder's letter, and the bottom halves of both sheets, including what Rosinda had not yet read, had disappeared into ash.

.

CHAPTER NINE

"What was that thing?" Rosinda asked Jerrell as she gazed mournfully at the burned letter.

"Parachute emergency flare," Jerrell said. "That's not how you usually use it, but I didn't know what he was planning."

"You did the right thing," Rosinda said, still not moving.

"What about you? Where'd you learn to kick like that?"

She swallowed. "I don't know. I've been doing gymnastics a few times after school every week, and I'm pretty good at it, but we never do stuff like that."

"Did you ever take a self-defense course or anything like that?"

"I don't know," Rosinda said miserably. "Maybe."

"Oh, right. Sorry, I keep forgetting," he said awkwardly. "It came back to you when you needed it, anyway. But I was scared you were going to get in the way of the flare."

Rosinda simply nodded, feeling as though she couldn't say anything else. Tears threatened to overtake her, and she didn't want to cry in front of Jerrell. Her whole body felt limp and exhausted, drained by the effects of the fighting instinct that had possessed it and the effort of trying to control it.

Jerrell collected his pack and came back to her. "I think we should get out of here. I don't think he'll be back, but if he found us, so could others."

"I think he was watching us when we left Genia," Rosinda said. "I saw someone at the wall. But I guess you're right, we should move. I'm just so tired," she added. "What I wouldn't give to go home and sleep in my own bed!"

"Hey, could you do that? The crystal you used to get us here—if it's that easy to travel back and forth across 'the Worlds' Edge,' why not just go home, get a good sleep, and come back here tomorrow?"

Rosinda looked at Traveller. "Could I do that?"

The crow slowly shook his head. "Perhaps, but I wouldn't advise it," he said. "Crystals don't last forever, and I don't know how much power yours has in it. It could take you home and not get you back here again, and then you'd be stuck."

Rosinda shook her head. "I can't take the risk." She sighed, hefted her pack, and said, "Okay, we'll walk for another half hour, but then I'm getting some sleep."

Jerrell nodded and once again Traveller took the lead. Sometimes they came to a trail and followed it for a short distance before the crow took them into the woods again. Rosinda didn't like walking in the woods in the dark. Cobwebs tugged at her hair and stretched stickily across her face. Branches and bushes caught at her clothing, and roots seemed to rise up to trip her. The light from the two moons hardly made a difference in the forest. The undergrowth rustled with unidentifiable noises.

Finally Jerrell announced, "That's half an hour by my watch. Do you think it's safe to stop?"

Rosinda let her backpack slide to the ground. "It has to be. I can't go another step." When no one argued with her, she took out the thin, silvery blanket that Jerrell had given her and laid down on a mossy-looking spot.

Jerrell did the same, not far from her. Rosinda was almost asleep when he said, "Rosinda? It seems weird, but I'm really glad I'm here."

It *was* weird, but she didn't say that. "I'm glad you're here, too, Jerrell," she said, and fell asleep before he could say anything else.

•••

Hazy grey light filled the forest around her when Rosinda opened her eyes. For a moment she didn't know where she was, and then memory came rushing back—memories of yesterday, at least. She raised her head and looked around, surprised that the sun was not up yet. Last night she'd felt like she could sleep for a whole day.

She sat up, and the rustle of her blanket caused Jerrell to stir but not wake. As quietly as she could, she pulled the burned letter out of her pack and re-read what remained. The first page now ended with the words *"When Prince Sovann's parents were killed I managed to spirit him out of the castle and into hiding..."* Rosinda turned to the second page. It started with the words, *has kept him safe.*

Oh no. The instructions for what Prince Sovann had to do once he found her were gone, and she hadn't read them at all before the man had interrupted them. Fighting back tears, she continued to read.

Once this is accomplished, he must travel to the castle at Sangera, in the province of the Blood Clans. The way will be dangerous, as there will be those who will oppose his return. Safely in Sangera, his welcome should be assured by those who remain loyal to the throne, and the Tell of Ysterad will respond to his touch, proving that he is the true prince.

The second page had burned more than the first; after this first paragraph the entire right edge of the sheet was charred. Rosinda read what she could of it.

I hope that you have assistance in this venture, my d
perhaps your parents are with you. Your mother wi
Ysterad, and will no doubt be attempting to find you
are in their company then much of what I've told yo
writing this in case you find yourself thrust into peril
I would most deeply regret, for it will mean I have fa

In any case, you must be wary of the forces that s
ends. Ysterad and its people are vulnerable with the
Sovann so young, I did not trust those who might se
The situation had no good solution until Prince Sov
hope that time has arrived.
One more thing that it is important for you to kno
than mere mortals. I have sensed dark and powerful
have not yet reached their full potential. I am unsure

The fire had devoured the end of the page as well. Rosinda
stared at the remaining words, feeling like a giant vise had
clamped around her chest. *I can't handle all this*, she thought.
I'm not ready.

The insistent tears sprang to her eyes and she tilted her head
back, blinking them away. The grey, pre-dawn sky hung close
to the uppermost tips of the trees. The last clouds of the night
dissipated into tiny wisps, and among them the dark outline
of a moon flickered. It was bigger than the two she'd seen last
night, reflecting their pale glow into the forest. Faintly, on
its surface, Rosinda could make out shapes and outlines that
looked like a bird with outstretched wings. Another memory
slipped free of its bonds in her mind. *The Dark Moon. Or as
some called it, the Raven's Moon.* She'd heard Sallah Dimwagetine
swear by it, but the words had meant nothing at the time. Now
she remembered.

*She sat on a window seat on her mother's lap at just this time of
day, woken early by a bad dream.*

"What's that dark circle in the sky?" she'd asked.

*Her mother had smiled. "That's the Dark Lady of the Skies,
Rosie-posey. The Raven's Moon."*

*"Did it bring my bad dream?" Her mother laughed softly,
jiggling her. "I don't think so. Some folk don't like the Dark Moon
and think it brings bad luck. But it's important for Kelta magic,
so it must be a good thing. I think she's our nighttime guardian,*

shining her dark light into the shadowy places where normal moonlight can't go."

Staring up at the Raven's Moon now, Rosinda felt her fear fade. She wasn't alone in this. Jerrell was a useful companion, Filara knew a lot—if you could tease the information out of her – and Traveller seemed to know where they should be going.

She thought back to the ruined letter. *Use the amethyst to find Prince Sovann,* Aunt Odder had said. She could do that. Rosinda dug the small stone out of her pocket and turned her eyes back to the sky to get her bearings. Off in one direction a faint pink glow stained the horizon—that would be the sunrise starting. Now, what were the words she had to say...

Panic threatened to rise again; the words of the spell had been in the burned part of the letter. What had they been? She'd read them only briefly. They were in the language of Kelta magic, and if she knew it, it was still locked deeply away with her memories.

But wait. The letter said that the charm was in the book, as well. After a glance at the quickly brightening sky, she dug the book out of her pack, careful not to make any noise. Aunt Odder had told her to do this, and she had to try it. The memory of the last spell she had attempted rose with unsettling clarity, but she brushed it away. This one would work. She could take her time with the words, make sure she got it right. All this rolled around in her mind as she searched through the book's elderly pages. There it was: *Calling the Lost.* The words looked simple enough.

Grasping the tiny amethyst in one hand and the book in the other, Rosinda rose and walked to a spot where she had a clear view of the horizon to the east. At least she assumed it was east—the blossoming sunrise painted the sky pink and yellow.

Aunt Odder's instructions had gone something like, *take it in your left hand at dawn and face the rising sun, press it over your heart and recite the charm for Calling the Lost.* Mentally crossing her fingers, she clutched the stone in her left hand, then raised her fist to rest over her heart. It thudded under her hand as if she'd been running.

Kelta draw power from the earth, Traveller had said. How did they do that? Rosinda closed her eyes and thought about the ground she stood on, the web of life woven in and through and on and over it, water springing from deep within it, molten rock swirling at its core—

She felt a tingling in her feet that seemed to travel up through the bones of her legs and spread throughout her body. It was slight, like the vibration of a guitar string barely plucked, but it was something. She might have done it right. If not, she'd accept the headache.

She read over the words in the book, mentally working out the pronunciation and hoping she was right. Then she slowly recited, "*Cordhan bel, cordhan treict; Althos creign al talthos mein.*" Her voice sounded clear and strong in the misty forest.

Nothing happened—most notably, she felt no pain in her head this time. *So either I did draw power from the earth, or I completely messed up the spell,* she thought. She tried not to feel disappointed. The letter had said, after all, that it could take some time for the prince to find her. It wouldn't be reasonable to expect him to materialize in front of her.

"What are you doing?" Jerrell's sleepy voice sounded behind her. "Is something wrong?"

Rosinda closed the book and pocketed the stone then turned away from the rising sun. "I don't think anything's wrong," she said. "Aunt Odder left me instructions in her letter, and I was just doing what she asked."

Traveller flapped down to land on a branch just above Rosinda's head. "Instructions?" he asked. "What instructions?"

Rosinda carefully returned the book to her pack. "Instructions for finding the prince," she said.

"What?" Traveller and Jerrell said at the same time.

"With magic?" Traveller continued, eyeing her sharply.

She nodded, feeling defiant. Aunt Odder hadn't told her to ask anyone's permission or advice. She'd said it was important.

"That could have been dangerous," Traveller said. "If anyone's searching for you, they might sense you if you're using magic. You don't know how to do it quietly, yet. And anyway, I thought you didn't know anything about the prince."

"Well, I don't. Or I didn't. Only what Aunt Odder left in this letter for me."

"And this spell you cast—it will enable you to find the prince?"

Rosinda shrugged. "I think it will let him find me," she said. "If it works at all."

"When will we know?" Jerrell asked, looking around as if the prince might pop into view any minute.

"I don't know. Aunt Odder said it could take a while, depending on how far apart we are."

Filara stepped delicately across the dew-wet grass. "I hope you don't intend to sit around here waiting for him to turn up," she said. "I *hate* sleeping outdoors."

"How do you even know what we've been saying?" Jerrell asked her.

"*Please.*" Filara flicked an ear at him. "I could hear you if I were still back in Genia."

Jerrell rolled his eyes and scrambled out of his blanket, folding it deftly and stowing it back in his pack. He did the same with Rosinda's.

She found a couple of pears in her pack and handed one to Jerrell. "I guess this is breakfast."

"What's the plan for today?" he asked around a bite of the russet fruit.

Rosinda glanced up at Traveller, but he was quiet, perhaps

still considering the implications of her spellcasting.

"I think we have two choices," she said. "We can try to find Aunt Odder, but I don't know how to do that. We'd need help."

"There might be something in your aunt's book," Jerrell suggested.

Rosinda nodded. "There might, although I don't know if I should just keep doing—or trying to do—magic. I don't really know what I'm doing, and as Traveller says, it might attract unwanted attention."

"So what's the second choice?"

"Aunt Odder's letter said that the prince would have to go to the Blood Clans, and if the spell worked, he'll be heading in our direction," she said. "So if we start off for there, it might save some time."

Jerrell frowned. "What all did your aunt tell you in that letter? You sure seem to know a lot more than you did yesterday."

Rosinda smiled ruefully. "Not really," she said, but she gave Jerrell a quick synopsis of what the letter had said. Most of it, at least. The last section, that mentioned her parents and 'dark and powerful magics', she kept to herself for now.

"So what will it be?" Jerrell finished his pear and stood with his pack on his back, ready to set out at her word.

She looked to Traveller. "What do you think? Or is there a third option we should consider?"

He ruffled his feathers. "I don't see one. I suppose if the prince is found and takes the throne, that would also solve your aunt's predicament—whatever she knows about the prince would have no value then."

"So you think the kidnappers would let her go?"

Traveller shrugged. "Or kill her just out of spite."

Rosinda blanched. "What a terrible thing to say!"

The crow glided down from his branch to land at Rosinda's feet. "I just want you to realize the seriousness of the situation.

If the prince is coming to find you, that's wonderful, but we don't even know if the spell worked. I think we have to try to find your aunt before anything else. Even if the prince shows up, it's not going to be easy to get him into the palace at Sangera—not if it's controlled by those who want to keep him off the throne. Your aunt's magic would be useful."

Rosinda was disappointed in the crow's apparent lack of confidence in her spellwork, but she wouldn't let him see that. "Well, then, how do we find her? Filara said it was Irylians who took her—does that mean we should head for that province?"

He tilted his head to one side, considering. "I don't think the Irylians came up with that plan on their own. I think they must be working for someone else."

"So they'll be taking her to their employers," Jerrell said. "Who's that likely to be?"

"I don't know."

Rosinda felt heat rise up in her chest. "So we should find Aunt Odder, but you don't have any idea where we should look for her? Ysterad is huge! We can't just wander around hoping we'll stumble across her! That would take years!"

The crow had the decency to look uncomfortable at Rosinda's outburst. The cat had an answer, though.

Filara ceased cleaning a paw long enough to say, "It's obvious we need help. Why don't we go and *get* some?"

"Where?" Rosinda asked.

"Your aunt has a good friend in Whistler's Forest, up near Kiend. He's an enchanter. /he might be able to help."

"How far is it?" Jerrell asked, shifting his backpack on his shoulders.

"Kiend's a full day's flight, if I could do it without stopping," Traveller said.

"I don't know exactly how fast crows fly, but that's gotta be a couple hundred miles," Jerrell said. "We can't walk it."

Filara stretched her mouth in a yawn, displaying tiny white teeth. "Why is it that once you have a cat who can talk, you want it to do your thinking, too? Think about where we are."

Rosinda grinned, and let the insult pass. "The Horsetribes of Zara! We can buy horses!"

"Except we don't have any money," Jerrell reminded her.

"Ah, but we do," she said. She dug out the small pieces of paper she'd tucked in her pocket last night for safekeeping. "Aunt Odder thought of everything—or almost everything," she said. "These are Ysteradian notes. It's not a fortune, but it will keep us going for a little while." She handed half of the money to Jerrell, and at his quizzical look said, "I think it's safer if we each carry some."

He nodded and stuck the money into the pocket of his jeans.

"I guess the next question is, can you ride a horse?" Rosinda asked him.

It was his turn to grin. "Not yet, but I'm a quick learner," he said with confidence. "What about you?"

Rosinda shrugged. "I don't remember, but I think it's likely, if I'm really from here. Which is getting easier to believe. I recognized the money right away. I expect it's all going to come back to me at once."

"Then what are you waiting for?" the cat said in an exasperated voice. "All this standing around talking isn't getting me any closer to a feather bed."

•••

A huge wayfarer's stable sat just north of the gates on the main road, so that travellers could switch out horses without having to spend time wandering around the city looking for stables. The stabler eyed them curiously, perhaps thinking that Rosinda and Jerrell were a little young to be traveling on their own. But he seemed to decide that their money was as good as anyone else's, and he pocketed it without questions.

As soon as Rosinda began to look at the horses, she felt more confident. The knowledge she needed to pick out a couple of good, steady mounts and gear appeared in her mind when she needed it.

"Where you headed?" the stabler asked genially as he helped them saddle the horses. Rosinda had chosen a smallish, dun-colored mare with intelligent brown eyes for herself, and a stocky chestnut gelding for Jerrell. Jerrell's horse head-butted him in the chest and Jerrell stumbled back a few steps. Rosinda smothered a grin and answered the older man's question.

"Kiend," Rosinda said. "We won't ride them hard, though."

"A word of advice," he said with a grave wink. "The road through Irylian province is faster, but you'd be wise to head east into Kelton province and then turn north to Kiend."

"Is there trouble in Irylian province?" Rosinda asked curiously.

"Perhaps not trouble as such," the stabler said, "but they don't take as kindly to strangers as once was. It's a longer route, but safer. And stay this side of the River Puth once you're in Kelton province, too. I've heard the Nangharen are planning to claim the west end of the Nanghar, and they're even less happy to see strangers than they usually are."

"Seems to be a lot of folk unhappy these days," Rosinda said.

The stabler sighed, running a beefy hand over his face. "Not to say too much, but if they don't get things squared away in Sangera soon, it's going to get a lot worse," he said. "You two stick to the route I told you and be careful, all right?"

Rosinda thanked him for both the horses and the advice, and they climbed astride their new mounts. Jerrell was careful but confident, and his horse settled under his hands after a few tense moments. "This isn't as easy as it looks," he muttered.

"Just try to relax, and let him follow my horse," Rosinda advised him. "Once you have your seat you can ride next to me."

Filara settled herself on the strip of saddle blanket just behind

Rosinda's saddle, much to the amusement of the stabler. When they were out of earshot the cat said, "For goodness' sake, give me some *warning* if you're going to take this beast any faster than a trot. Bad enough that I have to perch up here, I have no desire to be pitched off onto the side of the road."

"Oh, you'd land on your feet," Rosinda said with a grin.

"That's not the *point*," the cat said haughtily.

"What was the guy at the stable telling you?" Jerrell wanted to know. "It's awfully hard, not knowing what people are saying. Do you think there's anything in your aunt's book that might help me understand?"

"I don't know if you'd really want me to try it, but I'll look when I have a chance," Rosinda promised. She recounted her conversation with the stabler as they rode.

The sun continued its climb into the sky, and by mid-morning Rosinda felt strangely at peace as they followed the trail. Despite the dangers, fears and unanswered questions that filled her mind most of the time, the rolling gait of the horse under her and the road stretching out ahead were soothing. For the first time in a long time, she felt as though the cup placed before her was very full. She intended to drink from it for as long as she could.

CHAPTER TEN

Morrigan sat beside the stream in her wooded palace, eavesdropping on the camp of Sekhmet's Irylian servant. His name was Dneb, a big man, robed in an ivory and yellow-striped garment to reflect the sun in the Irylian desert wastes. The goddess couldn't understand why anyone would want to live there, far from the cooling presence of trees and streams, but it seemed to suit these Irylians. And Sekhmet. Morrigan winced inwardly at the thought of the Egyptian goddess' hot, golden aura.

Morrigan found a beetle crawling up the side of the canvas tent and took over its tiny brain. She turned it towards the center of the tent so she could watch the meeting through its eyes, and made the scene appear on the surface of the water in front of her. Dneb sat on a thick pillow inside the multi-peaked tent, considering two others who sat facing him. One was Morrigan's servant, Banna, a Kelton woman with hair as red as the goddess' own. The other was a dwarf from the cold mountains of Ierngud, and Morrigan suspected he answered to Tyr.

"You acknowledge that our interests run parallel, then," Banna said. The flowing water rippled the images, but Morrigan almost felt like she was there in the tent with them.

Dneb tipped a goblet of something dark and red to his mouth. "I accept that your Mistress and mine have common goals at present," he replied. "And your Master," he added, inclining his head toward the dwarf.

"How do you propose to get the hedge-witch to the east safely?" the dwarf demanded.

Banna's eyes flashed. "Kelta are not hedge-witches."

"My caravan is well-equipped," Dneb answered, although his eyes narrowed.

"We're dealing with a former King's *Kelta* here," the dwarf said, emphasizing the word. He ran his eyes over Banna as he spoke. "Their powers can be...considerable."

"We're all here to lend our talents in whatever way might be most useful," Banna said. "We all want the same thing."

"Do you propose to speak for me and my Master as well, woman?" drawled a voice from the doorway. Dneb raised his eyes to the tent flap, and Banna and the dwarf turned to look at the newcomer. A tall man, Seafolk by the look of his long face and tanned skin, stood just inside. The gill-flaps on his neck were just visible beneath the curve of his jawline, and the hand holding back the tent flap showed translucent webbing linking the knuckles. A long, curved scabbard hung at his belt, although it was empty.

Dneb snorted. "If you've made it this far inside my compound, then you must be the one sent by the god called Gradivus," he said. "Therefore, yes, she must speak for your wishes as well. Sit, and tell us your name, since we are to travel together."

The man strode in on lanky legs and folded them elegantly under himself as he sat on one of the brightly embroidered pillows scattered on the canvas floor. "Kadli," he said, inclining his head.

"Imdayov," the dwarf offered gruffly, and Banna and Dneb introduced themselves as well.

"So where is this Kelta who can lead us to the prince?" Kadli asked.

Dneb sipped from his goblet again. "She is safe," he said, "and close by, in another tent."

"Has she spoken of the prince?"

Dneb shook his head. "As our friend Imdayov has noted, she is a former King's Kelta. It has been necessary to keep her quiet."

Banna frowned. "Do you mean she is being kept sedated?"

"Yes," Dneb said. "My lady Sekhmet wants the Kelta delivered unharmed to the Eastern Desolation, and that is what I have undertaken to do." He watched them with narrowed eyes. "Of course, you must all follow your own paths."

It was obviously a challenge, Morrigan thought. The big man felt that he was in charge, since he'd been the one to venture across the Worlds' Edge to fetch the Kelta, and the rest had arrived only later. The goddess nodded. She would tell Banna to let the Irylian continue thinking that way. If he thought he was in charge and the others were in agreement with that, he would be less suspicious of them.

She released the beetle and allowed the image of the Irylian tent to fade from view, then tried again to call up the girl. The clear stream clouded before her eyes, the water turning murky, choked with leaves and twigs. The goddess thrust her hand into it, frowning. The girl remained hidden from view. At first, Morrigan had blamed interference from the vast amount of magic expended for the girl to cross the Worlds' Edge. Now, though, the cloudiness persisted, and the goddess did not know why. She would have to touch the mind of her other servant, her watcher, and see if he had noticed anything that might explain it.

She trailed her hand in the cool water and sent her mind winging like a dark feathered creature across Ysterad.

CHAPTER ELEVEN

They met few travellers on the road that day, and those they did encounter passed with either a studied silence or a pleasant word. Rosinda didn't push the horses hard. She knew Jerrell would be sore enough at the end of his first day of riding, and she was enjoying herself for the first time in a long time. She wanted it to last. She was still concerned about Aunt Odder, but they were days from finding her and worry wouldn't hasten the search.

By the time dusk threatened, Traveller had flown ahead to scout and returned with news. They were only a mile from a hamlet that offered an inn. And no gates.

"We'll try it," Rosinda decided. A look of relief flashed across Jerrell's face. Rosinda smiled. They could both use a night in a real bed instead of on the ground, but she knew that Jerrell would never admit that he couldn't keep up with her.

The inn, when they finally reached it, was small but clean looking. The tiny but tidily swept front porch and freshly whitewashed door felt welcoming. Inside was even better. A fire crackled in a stone fireplace, and the smell of stew floated tantalizingly on the air. The pears they'd had for breakfast, and the bread and cheese from lunch seemed a long time past. They wasted no time in arranging for two beds in the common room and bowls of stew for supper. The apple-cheeked young woman behind the bar regarded them thoughtfully as they tucked into their stew, but Rosinda ignored it. She was simply too hungry to care.

They went out to the tiny stable after supper to make sure their horses were content for the night, but they needn't have worried. The stable offered clean straw, ample stalls, and sweet-smelling hay. Dark had just descended when they returned inside, and local farmers straggled in for an ale or two and some quiet conversation. Tired and not wanting to draw any extra attention to themselves, Rosinda and Jerrell, with Filara in tow, retired to the common sleeping room.

It was small, with six low bunks ranged around the sides and two windows on the northern wall. They seemed to be the only occupants. Rosinda warily inspected the beds, but the sheets, although well-worn, smelled freshly laundered. They slept in their clothes, with their boots and packs tucked into shallow baskets underneath the beds. When Rosinda laid her head down on the flattened pillow, the window showed her a patch of deep blue night sky, and just a sliver of a dark shape she knew was the Raven's Moon. *The dark light holds a power that feeds the land itself*, she thought as her eyes closed.

She snapped them open again. Where had that come from? It was like something she had known, but forgotten. It hadn't come back in a wash like her other missing memories. It was almost as if someone had said the words to her. But there was no one there except Jerrell and Filara, both already asleep. She almost thought the words had come from Aunt Odder, but she couldn't remember her aunt ever actually saying them to her. Sighing, she let her eyes close again.

When next she opened them, Rosinda was staring into the face of a wolf.

She yelped, sitting up in bed while trying to scramble backwards, and almost fell off the low bunk.

In his own bunk, Jerrell sat up as well. "Wha—?" They were still the only ones in the room, so apparently the inn wasn't having a busy night.

Rosinda couldn't find her voice, although she had realized by this time that the wolf wasn't getting any closer.

Filara opened one eye and twitched an ear. "It's *outside*," she said testily, and went back to sleep.

It was true. The wolf stood outside the ground-level window, staring in at Rosinda. She met his yellow eyes and he blinked, startling her. It was the first movement he'd made. Then he turned and was gone, silent as a shadow in the night.

"What is it?" Jerrell asked around a huge yawn. He wasn't always at the top of his form when he first woke up.

"Didn't you see it? A wolf. Staring in the window at us. At me."

"Really?" Jerrell sounded skeptical. "Wolves don't usually come around humans. They're very misunderstood animals. They're much more afraid of us than we are of them."

"Well, thanks for that, but I'm telling you he was at the window. Filara saw him," she added lamely, since the cat looked like she'd been asleep since they came in here after supper.

"Okay, whatever you say," he said, lying down again and snuggling into the blankets. "But it's not morning yet. Wake me if a pack shows up and starts attacking."

Rosinda pulled the blanket around her shoulders and crept to the window. The rough board floor was cold underfoot, and she shivered, glad they hadn't spent the night outside again. She put her face up to the uneven glass and stared out into the moonlit alley behind the inn. A small garden lay awash in moonlight, and a forlorn piece of laundry sprawled next to the wall. But no sign of anything living. The Raven's Moon had also gone, tracing its lonely path across the night sky in the wake of its silvery sisters.

She wondered where Aunt Odder could be—and in what circumstances. And where, in this strange world that was half terrifying and half familiar, were her parents? Feeling suddenly very alone, Rosinda crept back to bed.

•••

Morning dawned all too soon, and Rosinda felt a pang at leaving the little inn. They'd had a good meal and a good sleep, and now they faced the unknown again. They had to keep moving if they wanted to find Aunt Odder. Rosinda restocked the provisions in her pack before they left, and saw Traveller perched on the roof of the stable when they went to fetch the horses. Jerrell winced when he mounted the chestnut gelding, but said nothing.

With a wave to the young woman who ran the inn, they kept on through the village and soon found themselves on the wooded road. Traveller sailed in to land on the back of Rosinda's saddle, startling both the horse and Filara. The cat deftly stepped over Rosinda's leg and sat in front of her as Rosinda reined the horse in and calmed her.

"You're moving too slowly," the crow said from behind Rosinda. "It will take you weeks to get anywhere near Whistler's Forest at this rate."

Rosinda sighed. "I know that, but I don't know what else to do. We can't ride the horses too hard, and Jerrell isn't ready for that yet, anyway. We don't—"

Rosinda broke off and put a hand to her temple. A sharp pain had lanced through it, like the beginning of a bad headache, but there seemed to be a sound associated with it.

"What's wrong?" Jerrell asked, urging his horse up beside hers. "Did you hear something?"

He looked around. "No, only you and Traveller talking. And by the way, I'm okay. We can go as fast as you think—"

"Ouch!" The pain prodded her again. This time the sound was louder, low murmuring. She glanced around. The pain seemed to run straight through her head and behind her eyes.

Traveller launched himself off the saddle and flapped hard to gain altitude, circling overhead as he scanned the area.

"You really don't hear anything?" Rosinda asked Jerrell. He only shook his head, looking worried.

Grrrrosindaaaaaa? It started as a growl and turned into her name. Startled, she looked around again, but there was no one but Jerrell.

Filara, however, stood with her front paws on the pommel of the saddle, fur bristling along her spine. She hissed. Her eyes were fixed on a point ahead of them on the road, but Rosinda saw nothing.

Despite the pain, Rosinda urged her horse forward. She had to investigate.

Grrrrosindaaaaaa.

There it was again, although this time the pain had dulled. "Hello?" Rosinda called. "Who's there?"

"Shhh! Do you think you should advertise that we're here?" Jerrell hissed.

"Someone already knows we're here," she said. "And whoever they are, they know my name, too."

Her hands felt slippery on the reins, but she continued to walk her horse forward, scanning the road ahead and the forest on either side. A hundred feet down the road, a creature stepped out of the forest and stood watching their approach.

"A wolf!" Jerrell gave a low whistle and pulled his horse to a stop. "That's not something you see every day."

"It's him!" Rosinda recognized him. The wolf who had stared at her through the window last night.

"How can you be sure?"

Rosinda. The growliness had gone from the voice in her head, and now it was low and clear but not menacing. *Is that you?*

"I'm sure," she said. "He's communicating with me mentally." She reined in her horse and dismounted slowly, not wanting to scare the wolf.

"Are you sure this is a good idea?" Jerrell asked.

"I thought you said they were more afraid of us than we are of them."

"Yeah, but that's Earth wolves. I don't know about Ysterad wolves. Especially ones with psychic powers."

But Rosinda wasn't paying any attention to him or to the increasingly loud racket that Filara had set up when the wolf stepped from the trees. Traveller, too, swooped down, landing in the roadway between Rosinda and the wolf.

"What are you doing?"

"I'm going to talk to him," she said. "He knows me."

"He could be dangerous," the crow warned. "He could be sent by the forces that are allied against us."

Rosinda stopped and looked at the crow with narrowed eyes. "And what forces would those be?"

"The ones your aunt mentioned in her letter."

"I didn't tell you anything about that."

The crow ruffled his feathers. "I just want you to be careful."

"I will. And later, we need to have a talk. But first I'm going to see this wolf. You and Jerrell and Filara can keep an eye on me, but I'm going to be fine." Rosinda didn't know how she knew that, but it was as clear as the morning sun shining down on them. This wolf posed no threat to her.

He sat on his haunches as she approached, his yellow eyes intent. *Rosinda.*

"Yes," she said. "You know me. But I don't know you."

Kerngold, the voice in her head said. *Call me Kerngold. I do know you. I don't know how. I simply...knew you were here.*

She'd reached him now and squatted in the dirt in front of him, bringing her eyes to a level with his. The road and forest shimmered around them and she felt the wave of memory crest in her mind, but this time it didn't break free. It crashed against a breakwater and held firm. She knew more about this wolf, she was sure of it. The memories, however, remained locked up solid.

"We're looking for my Aunt Odder. She was the old King's Kelta," Rosinda said. "Do you know anything about her?"

The wolf blinked. *No. Yes.* He shook his head. *It is familiar. But vague.*

Rosinda thought of the words in Aunt Odder's letter— it had mentioned her parents. That they would try to help her. "I don't suppose my parents sent you?"

I don't think so, but I cannot be certain.

Rosinda sighed. She knew how he felt. Like everything else that had happened lately, this posed more questions than it answered. But it felt right, somehow, to be speaking with this creature. Impulsively, she reached out and touched the fur on his neck. An electric shock stung her fingertips. The wolf didn't flinch. The memory wave crested again in her mind, but something still held it back. There was a connection there, but Rosinda didn't understand it and couldn't access it. Not yet.

"You are coming with us, though," she said. It wasn't really a question. Somehow she knew he had to stay with them.

The wolf stood. *I believe I must.*

Rosinda nodded. "Come and meet the others."

They walked back toward the waiting group, the wolf padding easily at her side. Somehow, that felt *right*.

"Kerngold is coming with us," Rosinda said as they reached the horses. "This is Jerrell, and the crow's name is Traveller." Jerrell nodded gravely to the wolf in greeting, but Traveller stood stock-still.

Filara was still perched on Rosinda's saddle, her back arched and her fur up. Her lips drew back from her tiny pointed teeth. "And this is Filara," Rosinda said, lifting the cat from the saddle and holding her close. "Filara, this is Kerngold. He's not an enemy."

The cat twisted in her arms and leapt onto the dirt road. "I'll be the judge of that," she spat. She turned her back deliberately on the wolf and walked away with her tail held high.

"She's a little difficult," Rosinda said apologetically.

I can see that, the wolf answered. Rosinda thought she sensed a smile in his voice.

"So, you can hear Kerngold's thoughts?" Jerrell asked. "Is that how it works?"

Rosinda nodded. "But you can't, obviously."

"Nope, nothing."

"What about you, Traveller?"

"No. I advise against this, Rosinda. You don't know this creature at all."

She looked at Traveller. "I didn't know you, either," she said, "but I trusted you. Now you'll have to trust me. I know this is right."

The crow shrugged, his wings opening slightly as he lifted them. "All right, then. It's your decision, I suppose. Let's get moving. We've wasted too much time."

Filara wouldn't ride with Rosinda this time; she pointedly stood beside Jerrell's horse, saying nothing until he lifted her up and put her on the back of his saddle blanket. Rosinda rolled her eyes. She thought she knew why cats didn't naturally have the power of speech. Humans would have been driven crazy and wiped them out long ago.

Kerngold trotted beside Rosinda's horse, saying little. "How did you find me?" she asked finally.

The wolf glanced up at her. *I don't know,* he said. *I was hunting. The Raven's Moon still hung in the sky. Then I heard a voice. Your voice.*

"How could you hear my voice? I'd been asleep for hours before you came to the inn."

The wolf made a movement strangely like a shrug. *I do not know. I just know that I knew your voice, and that I had to find you.*

I feel as if I know you, too, Rosinda thought. *But if that were the case, Filara should recognize you."* She sighed. Once again, there were no good answers

They rode harder that day, and by nightfall the border between Zaranian province and Kelton province was within reach. They had swung slightly north, and while Traveller assured them that they were not going to pass close to the Irylian border, Rosinda felt uneasy. No convenient village with a comfortable inn awaited them tonight. She wished they could have made it into Kelton province before they'd had to make camp.

"I just think I'd feel more comfortable there," she said to Jerrell.

"Well, it makes sense. You're probably from Kelton province, right?"

"Maybe," Rosinda said. "Sallah Dimwagetine thought I was Kelton. I don't know how he could tell just by looking, though."

"Your Aunt Odder and your mother must be Kelton," Jerrell said, "since they're both Kelta."

Rosinda nodded. "That's true. Although I don't know for sure that I was born in Kelton province. Traveller said that my father's an Enchanter, so I don't know where we lived before the accident. I suppose it could have been anywhere here."

The words sounded strange, rolling off her tongue. *My father's an enchanter.* She could remember her father, or at least small bits about him, as she could her mother. Aunt Odder had somehow contrived, when she locked Rosinda's memories away for safekeeping, to separate her memories of her parents out from their surroundings. She could recall doing things with her mother, and things her mother had said, but they were without a context. Nothing pointed to Ysterad or the memories that would have made Rosinda think something was wrong. The same with her father. She could call his face to mind, but nothing in the memories suggested magic, or Ysterad. Or anything else in particular. Someday, she resolved, she would ask Aunt Odder how she'd managed that.

Kerngold veered off into the forest, then emerged onto the trail again. *There's a good campsite not far from here*, he told Rosinda. *A place to stake the horses and a sheltered spot for you and the boy.*

"Kerngold says he's found us a place to camp," Rosinda told Jerrell.

Jerrell looked rather dubious, but he didn't say anything. The wolf led them off the trail and into the woods for about ten minutes until they reached a small clearing, and even Jerrell couldn't complain. Plentiful grass awaited the horses, and an overhang of rock on the side of a low cliff would keep them dry if it rained. The two silver moons had just begun their slow climb into the night sky.

They ate a cold supper, not wanting to risk a fire. Filara stalked off in a huff after a biting little speech about having to sleep outside again.

"Doesn't she know she's a cat, for goodness' sake?" Jerrell asked.

Rosinda laughed. "I don't think anyone's ever told her. And I'm certainly not going to be the one to do it, are you?"

"Not on your life."

•••

In her dream, Rosinda walked beside a clear stream. The forest here was much like the one she slept in, except that the trees ran more to pine and spruce than the short deciduous ones in Zara province. All three moons rode the night sky above her, two silvery ones and their dark sister, the Raven's Moon. Rosinda carried a long, curved sword, perfectly balanced and gleaming with a polished glow in the moonlight.

She was searching for something.

A rustle of movement in the underbrush attracted her attention and she half-turned away from the running water to peer into the trees. A tall form flitted among the trunks, sometimes appearing human, sometimes birdlike, with glossy dark feathers and a sharply pointed beak. Rosinda couldn't get a good look at it in either form, and she kept turning back to the water, as if what she searched for waited there. Then the rustling noise would sound again and she'd be drawn back to the woods.

A sudden splash sent her spinning around, peering upstream and down for the source of the disturbance. In seconds, she saw it, a dark form that thrashed about in fear as the current swirled and eddied. "Stop!" she tried to yell, but as was so often the case in dreams, no sound emerged. "I'll save you," she shouted silently.

There was no way to cross the stream, and the figure swept along close to the other shore. Rosinda wanted to jump in, but her feet were bound to the earth. She couldn't move. She could only watch helplessly, sword hanging limply from her hand, as the figure drowned. Tears streamed down her face. Finally the body floated, face down, toward her, and a flash of moonlight revealed Jerrell's clothing. She felt her heart clench painfully in her chest. Just as it passed her, the body caught on a half-submerged branch and rolled over in the current, revealing a furred muzzle and lifeless, yellow eyes. Kerngold. Something even stronger gripped her emotions at the sight of his face and she screamed.

Rosinda woke, gulping for air against the sobs that shook her body. She struggled to sit up. The muscles in her arms and legs throbbed as if she'd been running for miles. It was almost dawn, the same time she'd woken the morning before last, and she looked up to see the Raven's Moon again. Jerrell still slept peacefully nearby, one hand cupped under his cheek. Kerngold raised his head from where he had laid it, close to her own feet.

Are you all right?

"I think so," she whispered, but she knew it was a lie. It had been the most vivid dream she'd ever had, and she knew it must mean something. Something very bad.

CHAPTER TWELVE

The bickering of the other gods made Morrigan weary. And their servants in Ysterad, travelling with the Irylian's caravan, were no better. They argued over whether they should move slower or faster, whether they should try to question the King's Kelta themselves, even when they should eat and sleep.

"I still believe the prince is dead," Tyr said, waving the stump of his right hand. "If he were still alive he would have come out of hiding by now."

"The brat lives," Sekhmet argued. "I would be infinitely more powerful if he were dead. I can feel the blood magic still protecting the land."

Gradivus chuckled, not looking up from the bronze shield he polished lovingly.

"Do you mock me?" Sekhmet screamed at the Roman god.

They had all become more or less immune to Sekhmet's rages, annoying as they were. He chuckled again, and shrugged. "No more than I mock all of us. Look at us. We're pitiful. Bringers of war, once mighty gods, now forgotten. Relegated to searching for places we can slip in unnoticed, stir up a bit of unrest and scrounge a few followers, hoping they'll love us or fear us enough to restore our powers. Bah!" He held the shield up, studying the way the light from Sekhmet's golden palace reflected off the metal. "It's not whether the boy is alive or dead that's keeping us weak, it's our own weakness. We're no stronger together than we were on our own."

"It's the boy," Sekhmet snarled. "If he were dead—"

"If it's just the boy then we're more pathetic than I thought," Gradivus said. "We can't even find him, let alone—"

"The Kelta will help us find him," Morrigan said in a quiet voice.

All eyes turned to her. "How can you be sure?" Tyr asked. "Our best information led to her, yes, but—"

"The girl," Morrigan said. "The Kelta left a letter for the girl, and it mentions the prince."

Sekhmet half-rose from her throne, like a cat readying itself to pounce. "Does the girl know where to find him?"

"No. But *he* may find *her*. A little more patience is required. Now we have two routes to the prince: one through the old Kelta and one through the girl. And once we have him, the war will not be far off."

"They're not a warlike folk, these Ysteradians," Tyr said. "I've been watching them. Except for a few pockets of disquiet, they seem to prefer peace."

"But with the prince dead, and the proof of it hanging from the castle wall at Sangera—"

"It still might not be enough," Gradivus interrupted. "Lady Battle Raven, the one-handed god is right. This isn't a matter of stealing a few cattle to rile up the farmers," he said condescendingly.

Morrigan's anger flared at that, but she held it back, not wanting to mirror one of Sekhmet's rages. "The prince is hardly a bull, Mars Gradivus. Once the blood magic is broken, once the people of Ysterad know for certain that their royal line is dead, they will begin to look to their own borders." She smiled. "And borders are what this war is all about. The fires will burn soon enough."

CHAPTER THIRTEEN

Rosinda slept fitfully after the dream. When she woke, a new worry wormed its way to the forefront of her mind. Why hadn't the prince found them yet?

Aunt Odder's letter had said it could "take some time" for him to show up, but two full days had passed since she'd cast the charm for Calling the Lost. Had she done it wrong? Was the prince in deeper trouble than Aunt Odder had anticipated when she wrote the letter? Was it possible that by casting the charm, Rosinda could have made things worse?

She sat quietly and absorbed these thoughts while they ate a meager breakfast and packed up the camp. Jerrell said little but finally asked, "Are you all right?"

Rosinda nodded. "I'm just worried that I might have cast the spell wrong, and the prince isn't coming. Or that maybe I did something bad by casting it." She glanced at Filara as she spoke. There was no telling what a spell might do if it were cast wrong, as they'd all found out already.

"He could have been far away when you cast it," Jerrell reminded her. "Look how long it's taking us to get anywhere."

"I know. I just can't help worrying," Rosinda said, and sighed.

"If you're so worried about being slow, why don't you take one of the Ways Under?" Filara asked in an exasperated tone. "Not that they're my favorite way to travel, with all that mud, but I don't imagine anyone's going to ask *my* opinion about that."

A memory flashed in Rosinda's mind: darkness and shadows and the dank, rich smell of fresh earth and rotting leaves. Then it was gone. She tried in vain to associate it with what Filara had said.

Jerrell sighed. "And what are the 'Ways Under?'" he asked the cat. "As if you didn't know that we were going to ask you."

The cat licked a paw and smoothed it over her face in a self-satisfied manner. "I don't know what you know or don't know," she said.

"Of course you do! You know that Rosinda's lost her memory, and I've never been here before!"

Filara continued to groom herself. "Yes, I do know that. But I don't know why *he* hasn't mentioned them." She twisted her head to glare up at Traveller, who pecked absently at something on the branch where he perched. He ignored her.

"Well, why don't you tell us," Rosinda cajoled. "I'm sure I know what you're talking about, but not quite. Remind me."

The cat sighed. "The Ways Under are magical routes of passage from one place to another. The only ones I know about are in Kelton province, but I think there are those that run to different places in Ysterad. I've only accompanied the Mistress a few times when she travelled them. But I know where several open into the earth."

"And it's faster than travelling in the normal way?" Rosinda asked.

Filara gave her a withering look. "Naturally. What use would they be otherwise?"

"They might be safer than the roads or good for travel in secret," Jerrell said. "Or if you didn't want to have to take any supercilious talking animals with you."

"Ha ha. Unfortunately, just because I can speak your language doesn't mean I appreciate your humor," the cat retorted.

Rosinda tried to steer the conversation back. "So, are there any of these Ways Under near here? Near where we'll go across the border into Kelton province?"

The cat stood, turned her back on Jerrell and faced Rosinda, and sat down deliberately. "I believe there is one. I can show it to you as soon as we get there, which I believe will be tomorrow. It may take magic to travel them..." She let the sentence trail off.

"And I'm not the best at Kelta magic," Rosinda finished for her. "I might be too afraid to even try it, but I guess I won't know that until we get there. Traveller, what do you—?"

The crow had left the branch, flapping his dark wings and gaining altitude. "Guess he doesn't want to talk about it," Rosinda said, frowning.

"Then let's get moving," Jerrell said, picking up his pack and hoisting it behind his saddle. "If there's any way to speed this up, frankly, I'm all for it."

"What I was going to *say*," the cat said haughtily, "was that I'm sure you can manage whatever is necessary. You simply have to learn to trust yourself a little more. That's all."

"Oh." Rosinda was startled. "Well, thank you, Filara. I'll think about that."

With the prospect of reaching Kelton province before them, they urged the horses a little harder than they had the previous day. The animals didn't seem to mind, keeping a steady pace without much coaxing. Kerngold loped along beside them, silently keeping pace with Rosinda's horse. When Rosinda asked Kerngold if he knew anything about the Ways Under, he merely shook his head. Rosinda worried at the memory fragment the words had triggered in her mind, trying to tease it into a full-blown recollection, but try as she might, she could not retrieve it.

•••

Rosinda's stomach told her it was time for supper when they crossed from Zaranian province into Kelton province. Rosinda didn't need anyone to tell her that she'd made the transition. It hit her like a wall and she almost fell from her horse. She gripped the pommel for balance and slumped forward.

Memories flooded into her mind, and for a moment she felt as if she were drowning, struggling to breathe against the mental onslaught of images, sounds and smells. They flashed past her almost too quickly to register, but a few stood out as they filed into place in her brain. She saw a place called Whistler's Forest, picking purple berries there with Aunt Odder. A wide road that led to the place where her mother was born. The sunny paddock where her father had taught her to ride a round-bellied bay pony.

Then—darker images, the things Filara had mentioned. The attack at the palace. Waking in the middle of the night to shouts and confusion, the thick acrid odor of smoke and a panicked escape. The pain of learning that her beloved king and queen, more like another aunt and uncle to her, were dead. The separation from her parents and frightened flight with Aunt Odder to a strange world.

"Rosinda! What's wrong?" Jerrell nudged his horse close beside hers, reaching out to steady her if she started to fall.

She raised her head as the landslide of images subsided. "Nothing. I'm okay," she said, blinking back sudden tears and forcing a smile. She looked around at the trees, which didn't look any different, but somehow were. "I'm home. We're in Kelton province."

•••

They spent an uneventful night under the shelter of a dense thicket of pines. No dreams disturbed Rosinda this time, which was good since she felt exhausted. In the morning she said to Filara, "How far to the Way Under you mentioned?"

The cat flicked an ear. "If you folks would *move* a little more quickly, we could be almost there by now."

Rosinda rolled her eyes and settled everything in her pack. It would be a sweet day when she or someone else put the cat back the way she used to be—quiet.

They'd been riding for perhaps an hour when Filara called a halt. They'd passed out of the thick forest and into a rolling, flat area. Rosinda knew it would turn into the steppes of the Nanghar if they continued east and crossed the river. The countryside here was unbroken except for small hillocks dotting the land. Filara pointed to one a short distance from the trail. Near it, a dead tree stretched its pale, twisted branches toward the sky.

"That's the one."

"The one what?" asked Jerrell.

"The one that the *path* lies under," the cat said with careful exaggeration. "Honestly, I wish people would pay *attention*. I don't know how you manage to accomplish anything *at all*."

"Oh, sure, like cats are the great movers and shakers of the universe," Jerrell retorted.

She blinked her green eyes at him. "You might be surprised, boy," was all she said. She turned her back on him and left the trail, stepping delicately into the longer grass of the field where the hillock stood.

"And *I* wish everyone would stop calling me 'boy'," Jerrell muttered as he turned his horse to follow the cat. Rosinda stifled a giggle.

The hillock stretched about forty feet wide and twice as high as Jerrell. It rose steeply from the flat grassland that surrounded it as if a giant hand underneath the earth had pressed it upward. While Rosinda walked around it, Jerrell scrambled up to the top, where Traveller was already perched.

"Nice view from up here," Jerrell called down, "but I can't see any way to get in."

Rosinda completed her circuit of the perimeter. "I can't either. Filara, are you sure this is the right place?"

The cat raised her face to the sky. "I *told* you, it takes magic.

Not just to use the Ways Under, but to find the doors."

Rosinda pulled her pack down from her horse's back. "So I need Aunt Odder's book?"

"Don't be too hasty with that," Traveller said, launching himself from the top of the hillock and gliding gracefully down to land in the grass near her feet. "You might be able to do it on your own."

Rosinda looked at him. "But the only magic I know is what's in the book."

The crow cocked his head at her. "I said before you've got Kelta blood running in those veins. It's worth a try."

"So what do I do?"

The cat spoke up. "Put your hands on the side of the hillock and try to feel the opening."

"Try to feel it?"

Filara fixed her with a glinting green eye. "I told you, you need to trust yourself more. Just do it, and you'll know how."

That sounded silly, but it was useless to argue with the cat. Rosinda sighed, dropped her pack to the ground and walked to the side of the hillock. "Okay, I'll try."

She pressed her hands against the short green grass that covered it, concentrating on the prickly mat of blades against her palms and the slight yielding of the earth beneath them. The air smelled of dust, sun, and growing things. Insects rustled nearby. She closed her eyes. *There's a way inside,* she told herself. *Where is it? If it's here, I should be able to find it. I have to find it so we can get to Aunt Odder before anything bad happens to her.*

She stood like that for a moment, feeling the quiet strength of the earth under her hands and feet, sending her mind around the perimeter she'd walked just a moment ago. When she saw it, she gasped. It was as clear as if she was looking at it with open eyes. *The western end of the hill.* It was open, if one only believed in it.

She opened her eyes. "I see it!" She walked around the hillock and pointed. "Right there. We can get inside right there."

Jerrell joined her. "It looks just like the rest of it to me," he said. "Do you mean we have to dig or something?"

Rosinda pursed her lips. "No. I think we just have to—to close our eyes and believe that we can walk in there. And it will let us through."

"We'll never get the horses to do it," he said.

Rosinda hadn't considered that. "No, I guess not. Unless we blindfold them! That might work. You can lead a horse calmly out of a burning barn if it's blindfolded, so the same thing might work here."

"Let's test it first," Jerrell said. He closed his eyes, stuck his arms out in front of him, and walked forward. He passed through the grassy side of the hill as if it weren't there.

Rosinda drew a sharp breath. *He really believed what I said.* It shocked and comforted her at the same time.

The next second Jerrell shot back out of the hillock as if giant arms had thrown him. He narrowly missed Rosinda, flew through the air for about ten feet and landed in the grass in a tumble.

"Gah!" He rolled onto his back and lay gasping for breath.

Rosinda rushed over to him. "Are you all right? What happened?"

"That thing tried to kill me!"

The cat wandered over to him and sniffed his hair with interest. Bits of mud and grass clung to him. "You say that as if it were a bad thing," Filara said.

Jerrell feebly waved an arm as if to swat her, but she stalked off again, stopping to stare at something crawling in the grass as if it were the most interesting thing in Ysterad.

"What does she have against me, anyway?" he managed.

Rosinda chuckled, relieved that he seemed to be all right. "I don't think it's just you. She doesn't seem to have much use for humans as a species," she said, holding out a hand to help him to his feet.

When their fingers touched it was as if she had grasped a live electrical wire. A vibration shot straight up her arm and jolted into her shoulder. Although it wasn't painful, it was more like a jolt of numbness. "Ouch!"

Jerrell hadn't seemed to notice anything wrong. "What?"

He still had a grip on her hand as the sensation subsided. She didn't want to jerk her hand away so she managed a grin. "Just got a shock," she said.

"Oh, okay." He got to his feet stiffly.

"What happened in there, anyway?"

He smiled lopsidedly. "Guess I was a little too quick. I made it through all right, although it's a weird sensation to walk through an earth wall. I ended up in a big room, kinda dark, but not totally black, and it smelled like when you dig a garden. Then this big hand slaps down on my shoulder, and a voice says, 'Kelta?'

"I turned around and there's this thing that looks like a skinny snowman, except made out of mud. I didn't get a chance to say anything before it roars, 'Not Kelta!' Then it picks me up and throws me out like I was a rag doll." He winced. "I don't think I'll ever make a snowman again."

Rosinda frowned. "So he didn't want you in there because you weren't a Kelta?"

"Of course," Filara piped up, even though she hadn't appeared to even be listening to the conversation. "Rosinda, you should have gone in first, and then the rest of us as your wards. The Ways Under belong to the Kelta, and the Urigm are their guardians."

"But I'm not Kelta either—not really," Rosinda protested.

Filara twitched the tip of her tail, a sure sign that she was annoyed. "Trust me, girl, you're Kelta enough," she said. "So are we going to go, or stand around here and wait for some other trouble to find us?"

Rosinda looked at the hillock. "I don't want to get thrown back out on my head."

"You won't," the cat assured her.

I believe the cat is right, Kerngold's voice told her. *You have the feel of a Kelta to me.*

Rosinda wanted to ask the wolf just how much previous experience he'd had with Kelta, but it would have to wait. She had to get them inside the hillock.

She and Jerrell fashioned blindfolds for the horses from their sweaters. With a last glance at the wolf for courage, Rosinda put her hands on the earth where Jerrell had passed through, closed her eyes and pressed, taking a few steps forward.

It was almost like walking through water, although as Jerrell had said, it smelled of earth and leaf mold, and something else indefinable. The transition took only five or six steps, and then she was through. The close press of cool earth gave way to cooler air on her skin. She opened her eyes.

Her vision adjusted quickly to a dim, yellowish light that emanated from fungus-like growths on the ceiling. When no large hand or other appendage clapped her on the shoulder, she relaxed a little, straining to see the chamber.

"Kelta?" The voice was soft and slurry in her ear. Rosinda jumped and turned. She found a mud-colored, skewed face close to her own.

She answered automatically. "Kelta," she said firmly.

It was the right answer. The mud-man's already soft features relaxed into what might have been a smile. He looked like something a child might have made out of clay, but man-sized. Jerrell was right; the creature's stacked round body parts and long spindly arms with twig-like fingers did remind her of a snowman. "All Kelta are welcome," he said, spreading his thin arms wide and bowing.

Rosinda worried that his sections would separate like a toppled snowman, but to her relief, he remained intact.

A brush of fur against her leg reminded her to move to make way for the others. The fur belonged to Kerngold, and she gave him a quick pat to show the mud-man—what had Filara called him? Urigm, that was it—that the wolf was under Kelta protection.

"I have friends," she said to the Urigm, pointing to the opening in the wall and hoping he would understand. To her relief, he nodded gravely, just as Jerrell stepped through, leading the two nervous horses.

Rosinda hurried over to take her mount and gave Jerrell a nod. Filara walked in casually with her tail high. Traveller flew in, completing the group.

The chamber under the hill resembled a cave dug out of earth instead of rock; the walls glistened in places where water had condensed, and root tendrils and stones clung to the soil. The hard-packed floor was mostly dry, although the whole room held an air of dampness. Rosinda shivered, pulled the sweater from her horse's eyes, and slipped it on. Several paths led off in different directions, all sloping down deeper under the ground before disappearing into darkness.

"So, which way?" asked Jerrell, looking around at the branching pathways.

Rosinda shrugged. "We want to go north, right? You must have a compass, Jerrell."

He grinned and reached into this pocket. "Naturally. If you think it will work here."

"I don't know," Rosinda said, "but unless someone else has a better suggestion..." She looked at Filara, Kerngold and Traveller, but they all shook their heads.

It's not the same as being above ground, Kerngold said.

"No, it certainly isn't," Rosinda answered, glancing around.

"What?" said Jerrell.

"Oh, nothing. Just something Kerngold said," Rosinda answered. "Sorry."

"Well, in that case," Jerrell said, looking at the compass, "I'd say it's this one." The path he indicated looked no different from any of the others. "They're all awfully dark, though."

Filara sniffed. "Kelta magic lights them when they're travelled, but not when they're empty," she said witheringly. "The Kelta don't believe in waste."

Jerrell ignored her. "Let's get moving, then," he said. "Just how do these things work to save time, anyway?"

"More magic, I guess," Rosinda said, before the cat had a chance to say anything else rude. "Exactly how, I don't know, but I expect the only way to find out is to use one." She turned to the Urigm, who still stood near the entryway, apparently taking no interest in the conversation going on around him. "Thank you," she said.

He inclined his head slightly by way of reply, but that was all.

Instinctively, Rosinda took the lead. A thousand butterflies seemed to spin around her insides, but since she was the closest thing they had to a Kelta, it seemed right. Her horse shied and whinnied at the dark, sloping path, but as they neared it, a dim glow emanated from inside, and the horse calmed. Traveller flapped up to sit in the saddle. Hoping the horse would take its cue from her, Rosinda walked firmly to the path and started down it. The light intensified so that she could see, if not a long distance ahead, at least a clear view of the tunnel-like Way around and just in front of them.

It arched overhead to a height of about eight feet, too low for riding, but high enough that the horses could hold their heads comfortably. At intervals, smaller paths led off to the right or left, but Rosinda kept to the main Way. Jerrell reassured her that they were still travelling in a generally northern direction, and that was good enough for her. They met no one, although once or twice Rosinda thought she heard rustling noises in one of the side tunnels.

They'd walked for perhaps half an hour when the tunnel began to slope upward and eventually opened up into another chamber much like the original one. Another Urigm (or it could have been the same one, for all the difference there was in their appearance) looked up at their approach but made no move to stop them. The northern tunnel continued at the other side of the chamber, and they hurried through.

Another half hour of walking brought them to a chamber bigger than either of the others they'd seen. As usual, an Urigm stood near one of the walls.

"I believe this is it," Filara said. She'd been riding on the saddle of Jerrell's horse for a time, although she still wasn't speaking to him.

"Already?" Rosinda had expected to walk at least the entire day, even though the Ways Under were a shortcut.

"You want to keep going? Be my guest, but don't complain to me when you come out on the Sea of Despair or somewhere in Ierngud," Filara said.

"I didn't mean that," Rosinda said placatingly. "I was just surprised."

The cat stood and shook herself. "I could be wrong, but it has the right feel."

"Well, I wouldn't want to argue with *that*," Jerrell muttered, but the cat continued to ignore him.

Rosinda wondered if they would have to blindfold the horses again to get them through the exit wall, but as she stepped close, it shimmered and grew transparent. Beyond it lay the thick, close growth of an old forest. If it turned out to be Whistler's Forest, as they hoped, she thought she'd slip a few kitty treats to Filara without Jerrell noticing.

CHAPTER FOURTEEN

Rosinda led them out of the Way Under and into late-afternoon sunshine. The "doorway" was set into the face of a cliff, and Rosinda took a moment to memorize the spot, in case they had to find it again.

A road ran close to the cliff face and disappeared into the forest. The trees here stretched long limbs toward the sky, their trunks thick with age and mottled with green and blue lichen. The whole forest emanated a feeling of ancient growth.

"What's the name of Aunt Odder's friend?" Rosinda asked Filara.

"Hmmm." The cat blinked slowly. "It's annoying, having to remember it in my own language and then work out what it would sound like in *yours*," she said in an exasperated tone.

Traveller squawked. "Don't tell me you've brought us all the way here, and you can't remember the man's name? What a waste of time!"

"It's not that I can't *remember*," the cat hissed. "I just have to work out how it *sounds*." She shut her eyes for a moment. "Qualla—no, Quill—no, *Quigsel*," she said finally. "Quigsel Danasson. That's it." She threw Traveller a look that clearly said *ha!*

"How do we find him?"

"Just follow this road into the forest," Filara said, "and ask anyone you meet along the way where you can find him. Quigsel is a well-known enchanter around here. Folk come from as far away as Deld to consult with him." Filara leapt easily to the stirrup of Rosinda's saddle and then up onto the blanket, settling herself with an unmistakably self-satisfied air.

"Then let's go," Rosinda said, mounting her horse and turning his head toward the road. Jerrell was right behind her, and Traveller took wing and flew on ahead.

Kerngold loped into the forest. *I will be near*, he assured Rosinda, but she felt a pang as she watched his silvery-grey coat vanish into the trees. *I should follow him. Keep him close.* With an effort, she kept to the road, the hoofbeats behind her creating a strange, calming rhythm.

They had the road to themselves; most folk were at home enjoying their evening meal. Rosinda's stomach growled at the thought of food. Despite the shortcut through the Ways Under, her body seemed to think that breakfast was a distant memory.

Luckily, though, there was little chance of missing Quigsel Danasson's two-story cottage. It sat in a small clearing, readily visible from the road with a finely hand-painted sign at the gate that proclaimed, "Quigsel Danasson, Enchanter." Smaller letters underneath read "Reasonable Rates." The well-oiled gate swung easily under Rosinda's touch, and the yard was trim and neat. Vibrant flower gardens lined each side with nodding blooms, resembling pink daisies, red roses and yellow dahlias.

Leaving Jerrell to hold the two horses, Rosinda steeled herself, walked over and knocked on the bright green door. It opened almost instantly.

"Hello!" The man in the doorway offered a friendly smile. The enchanter had a long face and wore his straight, greying hair down to his shoulders. He wore plain black, except for a heavy canvas stain-spotted apron. What surprised Rosinda, though, were the partially webbed fingers on the hand holding the door open, and the closed, gill-like ridges on the sides of his neck. So he was Seafolk, not Kelton.

"Here for a potion?" the man asked.

"Hello, er, no," Rosinda said. "We're here for—um—a

consultation. If it's convenient."

The man peered more closely at her as she spoke, and a strange expression flashed across his face. The smile came back immediately, and he swung the door wide. "Of course, please come in. And your friend? Is he coming in, too?" he asked, looking into the yard where Jerrell stood with the horses.

"Yes, please," Rosinda said, motioning to Jerrell. He looped the horses' reins over a post and swung his backpack over his shoulder. Rosinda suddenly realized that she should have hers with her as well, but Jerrell pulled it down and carried it over to her. Filara followed behind him, but Traveller had seemed to disappear. Rosinda took her pack with a grateful smile and followed the enchanter into his home.

The room they stepped into occupied the entire bottom floor of the house. Tables and counters crowded the floor space, their surfaces covered with things that bubbled and hissed, smoked and simmered. In one corner, a tall apparatus of tubes and wires stood to some unimaginable purpose. Bookcases lined the walls, fairly groaning under the weight of leather-bound tomes, stacks of parchment and untidily rolled scrolls. A set of stairs led to a railed loft tucked up under the rafters.

As soon as the door closed behind them, Quigsel swept Rosinda into an enormous and unexpected hug. "Rosinda! What a relief to see you!"

Despite her surprise, Rosinda returned his hug; he smelled almost like Aunt Odder's book: herbs and earth. But something else lay underneath that she couldn't place for a moment. Then it came to her. The crisp, salt smell of the sea.

He released her and held her at arm's length, studying her face as he rattled off questions. "How are you, girl? What are you doing back here? Where's Oddeline? And what news of the Prince?"

Rosinda fought back tears for a moment. Here, finally, was someone who *knew* her, understood her situation and could tell her things. She swallowed a sob and said, "I'm fine, but I came here for help."

"Here, sit down, sit down," he said, leading them to a slightly less cluttered corner of the room. A small round table held a silver tea set, and a group of comfortable looking chairs clustered around it. An ornate mirror hung on the wall behind the chairs. Lamps with fringed shades cast a low, pleasant glow. Rosinda lowered herself into one of the well-worn but plush chairs.

Quigsel turned to Jerrell. "You too, my friend."

Jerrell looked blank, and Rosinda hurried to explain. "This is my friend Jerrell, but he's not from Ysterad. He can't understand what you're saying."

Quigsel raised an eyebrow. "Would you—and he—like me to fix that?"

"Oh, that would be wonderful, if you could," Rosinda said.

"One moment." He crossed back to the "laboratory" part of the room and rummaged around for a few minutes. He came back with a book, a vial, and a sheet of paper covered with handwriting. He handed the vial to Jerrell. "Tell him to drink it," he said to Rosinda. He winked. "Doesn't taste too bad."

"He says you should drink it," Rosinda told Jerrell. She was a little surprised when he immediately did.

At the same time, Quigsel crumpled the paper in his hand and read a strange-sounding phrase from the book. The paper disappeared as Jerrell puckered his lips, frowning. "Ugh!"

"Let's try again," Quigsel said to him. "I'm Quigsel. Or Quig if you like. Good to meet you, Jerrell."

"Same here," he said with a nod, still working his mouth to get rid of the taste. "Blech. That tasted awful. But hey, I understood you!"

"Excellent." The enchanter set down the book, took the teapot from the table and poured them each a cupful of steaming liquid. He added a dollop of thick cream to each one and handed them over. Then he sat down and looked from one to the other. "So, who's going to start?"

Jerrell took a hesitant sip from his cup and rolled it around his mouth, looking relieved.

Rosinda took a deep breath. "Is it safe to...talk about things here?" she asked.

Quigsel grinned. "Built inside a fairy ring," he said. "Ha! Most enchanters don't think of that. There'll be no scrying on my customers."

"That's a relief," Rosinda said. "Well, I guess it all started when Aunt Odder was kidnapped—"

"What?" Quigsel almost leapt from his chair, clutching the arms. "How in the world did that happen? Who took her?"

"I don't know. I was at school." Rosinda proceeded to tell Quigsel a brief version of how they came to be on his doorstep. She didn't mention her memory loss or Kerngold.

When she finished, he reached down and stroked Filara's head. "Good girl to think of coming here," he said to the cat. "So you can talk, now, can you? Why didn't you say hello to me, then?"

"Just because I *can* talk, doesn't mean I *want* to talk," the cat said witheringly.

Quigsel laughed. "Too bad more folk wouldn't think that way."

"So, what should we do next?" Rosinda asked.

Quigsel gave her a strange look. "That's an odd question, coming from you," he said.

"Why? What do you mean?"

He chuckled. "I'm not saying this is a bad thing, but you're not generally one to ask for advice. You're more apt to just give orders or go out and do what needs to be done."

Rosinda frowned. That didn't sound like her at all. "I don't understand."

"King's Keltas are not exactly known for their retiring natures," Quigsel teased.

She smiled. "You're thinking of Aunt Odder. I don't really take after her much."

Quigsel fixed her with a hard stare. "Rosinda, do you really not know what I mean?"

She bit her lip. "I didn't mention that my memory was—not erased, but closed off, I guess you could say. Filara says Aunt Odder did it to protect me, but it's turning out to be a problem."

The enchanter raised his eyebrows. "So you don't remember your training in Ysterad?"

"No."

"Hmmm." He was quiet for a long moment, studying her.

"My memories have been coming back slowly," she said. "Bit by bit."

He nodded.

"Aunt Odder left me a charm in case I needed to get them back all at once, but she said it might be dangerous."

"She's right."

Rosinda felt exasperated. "Well, are you going to tell me what I was doing before? One more memory won't hurt, surely?"

"What?" He shook himself. "Oh, yes, I'll tell you. I was just deciding the best way to go about it."

"Um, just say it?" Jerrell suggested.

"I think I'd rather show it," Quigsel said. He stood and touched the mirror on the wall. It turned slowly black, then brightened again, revealing a picture in place of its silvered surface. Figures in the picture moved. Rosinda and Jerrell stood, left their chairs, and moved closer for a better look.

"That's you!" Jerrell said.

Rosinda stared. It certainly looked like her, although the clothes were strange, and she never wore her hair that way, in one long braid down her back. The strangest part, however, was what she was doing.

"This can't be right!" she gasped.

The Rosinda in the image was fighting—a mock-fight, since her opponent and she both wore protective padding, but a serious fight nonetheless. She kicked, punched, and threw her opponent in a series of martial-arts-type moves that astounded her. Even as she watched, though, she found herself following the engagement, anticipating what each of them would do and assessing each move.

"I thought you took gymnastics!" Jerrell said, "Not tae kwon do!"

"I do—I did," said Rosinda. "I don't remember this." Yet even as she spoke, she knew that in a way, she did. She didn't remember this particular fight, but a certain part of her brain knew it could tell her body to do this, and it would work.

The scene switched abruptly from an outdoor courtyard to a stone-walled chamber. It looked a little like Quigsel's room, cluttered with the same magical paraphernalia. Rosinda and Aunt Odder bent over something on a table. Rosinda's heart gave a lurch. She looked so real, her blonde hair flyaway as usual and her eyes intent as she gave Rosinda instructions.

"Magical training, too?" Jerrell asked, but Rosinda could only shrug.

The images faded, and Rosinda sat down heavily in her chair. She apparently had more skills than she'd ever dreamed.

"Did any of that seem familiar, Rosinda?" Quigsel asked. "I didn't want to get into too much..."

"I can sort of remember doing some of those things," she said slowly, "but it's more like someone else is remembering them and not really me." She looked up at Quigsel, and he nodded.

"But I can't remember *why*," she added. "Kelta training?"

Quigsel raised an eyebrow. "Not just Kelta training," he said. "You were assigned to Prince Sovann. You're the Prince's Kelta."

At the enchanter's words, more images flashed free in Rosinda's mind. Winning an important competition. A scene in a castle, blurry, smiling faces surrounding her. And a boy—a boy for whom she felt a fierce loyalty, but he was nothing but a vague shape in her memory, no face or features she could grasp or recognize.

"Rosinda." Quigsel's voice broke into her thoughts. "Are you sure—now that I've told you that much—do you know where the prince might be?"

Rosinda closed her eyes. "No. I don't. I wish I did." She couldn't take it all in at once. The vague bits of memory that shaped in her mind told her that it must be true, and yet—the Prince's Kelta? How could it be? If she were blood-bound to protect him, how could she not know where he was? And how could she have messed up so badly when she cast the charm to find him?

With that thought came another realization even more startling. Someday, when the prince became king, she'd be the King's Kelta.

Just like Aunt Odder.

"I think I'd like some more tea, Quigsel," Rosinda said shakily. "I hope there's lots in the pot."

CHAPTER FIFTEEN

"She's an actual Kelta?" Sekhmet shrieked.

"That's what my source tells me," Morrigan said evenly. "And not just any Kelta: the Prince's Kelta."

"What?" That jolted even Gradivus out of his usual equanimity. "Then she must know where he is."

Morrigan shook her head. "No. If she has that knowledge, it's locked well away with the rest of her memories."

"Then as I said before, we need to unlock her," Sekhmet said with a snarl.

"Don't be so impatient, Eye of Re," said Tyr. "We already know she is heading our way. And there is no doubt she will try to rescue her aunt."

Sekhmet glared at him. "Why wait when we don't have to? *You* may enjoy days of doing nothing but contemplating your losses," she said, looking pointedly at the Norse god's truncated arm, "but I would prefer to be in battle."

"Prince's Kelta or not, we still don't know if the girl has any knowledge of his whereabouts, and she's protected by a charm that I cannot penetrate," Morrigan said, knowing it cost her some pride to admit it. "The older Kelta has that knowledge, and she is on her way here."

When Sekhmet opened her mouth as if to argue further, Morrigan cut her off. "We still have to conserve our strength," she blazed. Her aspect shifted to that of the carrion crow, and her auburn hair became a fall of glossy black feathers. Yellow eyes pierced the Egyptian goddess. "Each of us has at least one servant already in Ysterad, and whatever priests and prophets we can find trying to rally the folk to our banners—are you telling me you have the strength to do more? Because I don't believe it. You're as vulnerable as the rest of us."

Sekhmet lounged back in her golden throne, two cats winding around her feet. Her rage of a moment before faded as quickly as it had flared. "I'm sure you'd like to measure my strength, Child of the Forest," she drawled. "But you'll have a chance to do that in due course. Perhaps I should take your words as a sign that your own powers are already overextended. If you can't scry the girl—"

"The girl is protected from me—that should give you pause. Who foresaw that necessity? Did someone sense our coming? Does someone know or suspect our plans?"

The other gods were silent and Morrigan turned back to Sekhmet. "My servants are providing us with useful information," she snapped, "what are yours doing?" She knew she was unreasonably annoyed with the Egyptian goddess, probably because Dneb was giving her own servant, Banna, a hard time elsewhere in Ysterad. The Irylian baited the Kelton woman constantly, testing her loyalty. Morrigan was tired of Sekhmet's posturing and rages, when they were all on edge from waiting. A powerless god is an irritated god.

"Mine have their own tasks," Sekhmet said sweetly. "And of course I'll share any information they provide me."

Another lie, Morrigan thought, but she was out of patience with the goddess already. "You'd be wise to do so, and one of their tasks should be cultivating followers," she hissed, "if you want to have any hope of defeating me in the final battle. If you betray this trust, I'll see you back in your pyramid, alone without even your cats, until the end of time."

"We shall see who's alone at the last," Sekhmet sneered, and she and her golden palace disappeared.

"You really shouldn't bait her like that," Tyr said to Morrigan, frowning. "We're going to need her for a time yet, and her servant has control of the King's Kelta."

"I know." Morrigan sighed and let her crow visage slip away. "She knows things she isn't telling us. She's too sure of herself."

Gradivus shrugged. "You have your woman and the other one gathering information; she must have more than that oaf, Dneb. She's just not sharing."

"But not more than one other. She isn't that strong," Morrigan insisted.

"My eagle saw a cat with the girl," Tyr offered. "Perhaps it's a servant of Sekhmet."

"I don't know. I think I would have felt that, but perhaps not," Morrigan said thoughtfully. "If that is the case, Sekhmet knows everything we do."

"She bears watching," Tyr said.

Morrigan nodded. "That she does, Son of Hymir," she said. "That she does."

CHAPTER SIXTEEN

Rosinda lay in a big comfortable bed in Quigsel's loft, a thick quilt pulled up to her chin and Filara nestled in a warm ball at her feet, but sleep would not come. She couldn't get Quigsel's words, or the images he'd shown her, out of her mind.

The Prince's Kelta.

"You're certain?" Quigsel had asked her again. "You don't know where he is? With the bond you two share, you might have some feeling, some sign...?"

Rosinda had shaken her head and sighed. She told Quigsel about her failed attempt to use Aunt Odder's spell to call the prince to her. "Surely he'd have found me by now, if it had worked?"

Quigsel had reluctantly agreed. "Probably. But don't give up hope," he said. "Your aunt is a shrewd woman. She could have hidden him away anywhere. He might have a long way to travel."

"Well, he'd have to be back on Earth not to have arrived by now," Rosinda had said bitterly. "And how will I even know it's him if he does find me? I can't remember what he looks like."

Quigsel sighed. "I'm sure your aunt would have thought of that."

"You sure put a lot of trust in her," Rosinda said.

The enchanter nodded. "Yes. Yes, I do."

Rosinda thought about that as she lay wakeful in the silvery light of the two sister moons. She'd relied completely on Aunt Odder for the past year, and she'd felt as Quigsel did—that she could put all her trust in her aunt. It seemed harder to do that now. However good her intentions, Aunt Odder had tampered with Rosinda's memories, kept important secrets from her, and who knew what else? Confronted with all that had happened, Rosinda felt ill-prepared to deal with it. She was very alone in this situation, despite the companionship of Jerrell and Traveller and Kerngold—even Filara. She valued their help, but none of them was in her position.

Rosinda squirmed around in the bed, trying to fall asleep. Her mind squirmed around, too, and focused on another worry. If she found the prince, would she know him? She scoured her memory, but she couldn't bring his face into her mind. She couldn't even settle upon his height or the color of his hair. Maybe he'd recognize her, but could she trust that alone? She didn't think Aunt Odder would expect her to. Surely there would be some kind of sign. A code that would unlock more of Rosinda's memories? A secret signal she'd recognize? A shock of recognition if they shook hands?

Rosinda sat straight up in bed, disturbing Filara, who growled in her sleep. Hadn't she gotten a weird, inexplicable shock just yesterday when she touched someone's hand?

Jerrell.

Could Jerrell possibly be the missing Prince Sovann?

Rosinda left the comfortable bed and crossed to the window, staring out at the moonlit forest. The chill of the rough board floor bit into her bare feet, but she needed to be sure she was wide awake. The idea seemed crazy. But if Jerrell were the prince, it would explain why Aunt Odder's spell hadn't worked. It hadn't needed to, since he was already there. It would explain the times when Rosinda had felt an urge to protect him. It might even explain why he'd followed her into the woods the day she had to flee from home. It would explain the shock.

It would be just like Aunt Odder to keep him close enough to watch over, but not close enough to put him in danger.

Did Jerrell know? Rosinda's feet were getting too cold, so she went back to the bed and sat, pulling the quilts up again. Filara opened one eye, and Rosinda almost blurted out what was on her mind, but decided to keep it to herself for now. The cat might not even know.

Rosinda turned to face the window, where the soft, dark curve of the Raven's Moon came into view. The sight of it calmed her. *Because I'm a Kelta, I suppose.* She made up her mind to ask Quigsel tomorrow if there was any chance Jerrell was the missing prince. And although it was the last thing she expected, Rosinda fell asleep.

•••

"I doubt it," Quigsel said the next morning, shaking his head.

"But you're not sure," Rosinda countered.

The enchanter stirred his tea and carefully set the spoon down. "No. We're talking about your aunt here, so I can't be sure. He could be disguised." He grinned. "She's quite a remarkable woman."

"I know." But Rosinda wasn't going to be distracted. "If he is—"

"If who is what?" Jerrell asked, coming into the corner of the big room that Quigsel called his kitchen. Jerrell had slept in one of the big comfortable chairs in Quigsel's workroom, and Rosinda had asked the enchanter her question when Jerrell went outside to check on the horses.

Quigsel and Rosinda looked at each other, and the enchanter shrugged.

"I was asking Quigsel if he thought there was a chance..." Rosinda's voice trailed away.

"A chance of what?"

"A chance that you might be Prince Sovann," she finished in a rush.

Jerrell looked at her as if she'd lost her mind. "Me? Of course not! Why would you even think that?"

"A couple of reasons." Rosinda proceeded to lay out her thoughts of last night.

"I didn't feel anything when you helped me up yesterday," he said, obviously puzzled. "And anyway, I can remember my whole life—well, most of it. And there's definitely—definitely!—nothing in it about being a prince."

Patiently, Rosinda said, "I know, but think about it. Aunt Odder locked away my memories so I wouldn't ask questions. Maybe she just gave you different ones for the same reason."

"You mean everything I remember is just made-up, it didn't really happen?" he asked skeptically.

Rosinda nodded.

Jerrell shook his head. "I don't think so. If that was the case, how come my own memories aren't coming back now that I'm in Ysterad, the way yours are?"

"I don't know. Maybe it's a different spell." "Wouldn't somebody recognize me?" Jerrell turned to Quigsel for support. "Don't you think you'd know if I was the prince?"

The enchanter answered carefully. "I honestly don't think you are, but how could I be sure? If Oddeline used magic to change your appearance—"

"Well, isn't there some spell you could use to find out?"

Quigsel laughed. "Me? Cast a spell to see through one of Oddeline's charms?"

Rosinda sighed. "Okay, so we're no further ahead. Let's forget about that for now. What do we do next? I get more and more worried about Aunt Odder every day. Quigsel, isn't there something you can do?"

The enchanter frowned. "Let's take our tea over here and sit down."

They made their way to the comfortable chairs once again, and Quigsel said, "Honestly, Rosinda, I'd like to help. I just don't think my talents are up to the tasks that you face."

Rosinda felt herself slump in disappointment, and Quigsel must have noticed it, because he went on.

"To tell the truth, you're much more powerful than I am. If you had your full memory, of course."

"What?"

He nodded. "It's true. Kelta magic is more powerful than enchantment, and you've had training beyond the usual. But since you can't access it yet, you need another plan."

"Do you think I should use the stone Aunt Odder gave me? I could get everything back with that."

"No. Your aunt was right to tell you that it was too dangerous. If more time passes, and more memories return slowly, on their own or triggered by being here, you'll get to a place where you could manage to have the rest come back all at once. But I don't think you're there yet."

"So what else can we do? We can't take on Aunt Odder's kidnappers."

"Find your mother."

Her mother? Rosinda's mind whirled. Why hadn't she thought of that before? Events had been moving so quickly since she arrived in Ysterad, there hadn't been time to think—

"Aunt Odder's letter!" Rosinda said suddenly. "I just remembered—" She ran upstairs and fetched the remains of the burned letter from her pack. "I didn't get to read all of this before it burned," she said, showing the charred pages to Quigsel, "but there was this part. Something about my mother trying to find me here in Ysterad. Do you think—"

One look at Quigsel's face betrayed the answer. "What's wrong?"

"I'm afraid that although your mother might be aware that you're in Ysterad, she's not able to try and find you," he said. "Both your parents, as far as I know, are in prison."

Rosinda gasped. "In prison? Why?"

"They were accused of aiding in the disappearance of the

prince—not to save him, but to eliminate him," Quigsel said. "At first the accusations were brushed aside, but they grew in strength. Finally, it was decided that they should be held in the Ierngud Mountains until the evidence could be properly deliberated."

"And when will that be?" asked Jerrell. Rosinda seemed too shocked to speak.

Quigsel sighed. "That's the problem. With them locked away in Ierngud, and your Aunt Odder gone...they've sort of fallen by the wayside."

"You mean they've been forgotten?" Rosinda asked. "Well, why aren't you doing something about it?"

"I've tried. But the voice of one man—it's not loud enough."

"Then I'll do something," Rosinda said. "Where should I go? Who should I talk to?"

Quigsel held up a hand. "You can't do it that way. If you advertise who you are, you could be locked up as well."

Tears sprang to Rosinda's eyes, but she angrily blinked them back. "I can't just stand by and do nothing!"

"I know, but listen. The best way to help them would be to return the prince to the throne, which you're already working on. There'd be no grounds to hold them any longer if the prince showed up alive and safe."

Rosinda interrupted him. "But just a minute ago you said I should find my mother!"

He nodded. "I meant you should find her mentally, make contact with her so that she can guide you. Your Kelta training might return faster than ever, and you'll be strong enough to help Oddeline."

Rosinda blew her breath out in a long sigh. "So how do I do that? How far away is Ierngud?"

"A long way, I'm afraid." Quigsel went to the mirror again, and a map shimmered into view on its surface.

"We're here," Quigsel said, pointing to a spot in the western half of the largest landmass. "Ierngud is here, in Nordas." He moved his finger to the far north of the continent.

He was right; it was a long way. As Rosinda looked at the map, another trickle of memory seeped out from behind whatever mental wall had blocked it in. "I recognize this," she said with quiet happiness. "This is Selavine, where we started, right?" She pointed to the biggest of a chain of islands that trailed off the southwestern coast.

Quigsel nodded encouragingly.

"And here's Irylia, where we think they took Aunt Odder first." The desert-like region lay west of their current position in Kelton province. Rosinda moved her finger around the map. "Blood Clans, Nang, Deld, Hanjavia, Seafolk...it's all coming back to me," she said.

"Well, that's good, isn't it?" said Jerrell.

She nodded. "Yes, it is. But it also makes me realize how much territory we have to cover to do anything."

"You've only got to go into the Nanghar to contact your mother," Quigsel said hesitantly.

"The Nanghar! The tribes there are not exactly welcoming to any but their own—" Rosinda started, and then looked surprised. "How did I know that?"

"I expect it's the map. Also, didn't Sallah Dimwagetine say something like that?" Jerrell said.

"No, it was the stabler outside Genia," Rosinda said. "Well, however I knew it, it's true. Why do we have to go into the Nanghar?"

"The Crypt of a Thousand Voices is there," Quigsel said, "and you will find a fountain inside—your aunt described it once— that lets you communicate mentally with anyone in Ysterad."

"Anywhere?" Rosinda asked in disbelief. "Ierngud is hundreds of miles away from the Nanghar."

Quigsel shrugged. "I know, but that's what your aunt told

me, and I'm inclined to believe her. She's not one for boasts, your Aunt Odder."

"Can you come with us?"

The enchanter looked uncomfortable. "Sadly, no. I don't travel quickly any more, and you're probably safer without me. I'll only draw attention to you, and the Nangharen and Seafolk—we don't exactly mix well."

"I get the impression that the Nangharen don't mix well with anyone," Jerrell said.

Quigsel nodded. "You're right. But Seafolk least of all."

"So when we get to the crypt—" Rosinda started, but a loud squawking and thumping at the door interrupted her. They ran to open it, and a disheveled Traveller flew in and settled himself on one of the tables.

"I found out—" he squawked harshly, then shook himself and started again. "I found out where they're taking your Aunt Odder," he said.

"What? Where?"

"East," the crow said. "To the Eastern Desolation."

CHAPTER SEVENTEEN

Jerrell asked, "What's in the Eastern Desolation?"

"Not much," Filara drawled. "That's why they call it a *desolation*."

"So why are they taking her there?" Jerrell retorted.

"So there's no one around to catch them?"

Jerrell aimed a mock kick at the cat. "I wasn't asking you, I was asking Traveller," he said. "Rosinda, why did you ever give this creature the ability to talk?"

Rosinda ignored that. "Why are they taking her there?" she asked the crow, "And how did you find out?"

The disheveled crow smoothed his rumpled feathers with his beak. "To meet whoever sent the Irylian to get her," he said. "Where do you think I've been for the past day? I went looking for them."

The cat wrinkled her nose in apparent disbelief. "And you just *happened* to find them? Irylia is only half as big as Kelton, but still—"

"I had help," the crow said shortly. "Do you think I'm the only crow in the world?"

"No, more's the pity," the cat muttered, and stalked off to sniff around the kitchen floor for dropped tidbits.

"Um, excuse me?" Quigsel said politely. "I don't believe we've met, but you must be Traveller. Rosinda has told me about you."

The crow turned and inclined his head graciously toward the enchanter. "Enchanter Quigsel. I apologize for bursting into your home—"

Quigsel returned the bow. "No, no, it's quite all right. We're all anxious to hear what you've learned."

Traveller turned to Rosinda. "They're not in Irylia anymore, anyway. They've crossed into Kelton, headed toward the Nanghar. They had already crossed the River Puth when I found them."

Rosinda crossed to the table where Traveller had perched. "Thank you," she said and reached out to smooth the feathers on his back. She had the impression that he almost cringed away. When her fingertips made contact with his back, though, she felt a surge of electricity through her hand.

She jerked it back. "Well, this is getting ridiculous!" she sputtered.

"What is it?"

She rubbed her shocked hand. "Almost everybody I touch in this place gives me a shock," she complained. "First it was Kerngold—"

"Who's Kerngold?" Quigsel asked, but Rosinda continued on. "Then Jerrell, and now Traveller. What's going on?"

"I don't know. Is it always the same type of shock?" Quigsel asked.

"A shock's a shock," Rosinda snapped, but then she relented. "Sorry. I don't know. They didn't happen all at the same time, so it's hard to compare them."

"But you didn't get one when I hugged you," Quigsel said.

Rosinda shook her head. "No, not then."

"Hmmm. Well, it could be something that your aunt put in place," he suggested. "Some kind of signal...or something."

"Well, it's not much good if I don't know what it means."

"Does this mean you don't think I'm the prince anymore?" asked Jerrell.

Traveller stifled a squawk. "You think Jerrell is the Prince?"

"I don't know. I considered it. But we don't have time for that now," she said. Getting angry seemed to have shaken something loose in her, or shaken something into place. She felt energized and filled with the need to start doing something. She turned back to look at the map, staring at it with her hands on her hips for a moment. "We need to make a plan. Everything else can get sorted out later."

She turned back to the others and caught a look that passed between Jerrell and Quigsel. "What?"

Quigsel grinned. "Oh, nothing, really. I was just thinking that you sounded more like the Rosinda I know. The Prince's Kelta."

Rosinda took a deep breath. "Well, let's hope she keeps showing up. I have a feeling that we're going to need her."

• • •

They stayed one more night with Quigsel. He offered them so many provisions that eventually Rosinda had to tell him to stop, their horses would be too loaded down to walk in the morning. With the caravan already in Kelton, Rosinda struggled with a wild urge to set out immediately to try to catch them, but the others had talked her out of it.

"There's no sense in catching them yet," Quigsel said. "You're not strong enough to confront them."

"Yeah," added Jerrell, "and don't you think you should talk to your mom first? It's east, and they're going east."

Rosinda finally agreed. That evening, though, while Quigsel and Jerrell discussed what to pack and what to leave, she went out for a walk alone in the woods behind Quigsel's house. She hadn't been there long when she heard the voice she sought.

Rosinda.

"Kerngold?" she answered, and the wolf padded out of the forest.

Such a surge of joy overwhelmed her at seeing him that without thinking she ran over, dropped to her knees on the mossy forest floor, and threw her arms around his furred neck. This time there was no shock. Instead, she felt a wild mix of emotions; relief that he was safe, anger at him for staying away for so long, and underlying it all, a strange peace.

She pulled back and cupped his muzzle in her hands, looking into his yellow eyes. "I think my Aunt Odder or my mother must have sent you to find me," she said. "Are you sure you're not a familiar or something? I feel like you're part of my family."

The wolf chuckled in her mind. *I don't have any memory of that, but you could be right. Much of the past seems hazy to me. I don't like to stray too far away from you now. I've been right here in the woods the whole time, but the hunting leaves much to be desired.*

"Quigsel says we have to go into the Nanghar," Rosinda told him. The enchanter hadn't asked again who Kerngold was, which had left Rosinda strangely relieved. For some reason, she didn't want to tell him about the wolf. "And Traveller says they're taking Aunt Odder into the Eastern Desolation." She felt a strange fear of asking the next question, but she had to know. "Will you come with us?"

Kerngold rubbed his muzzle along her arm. *Yes. I don't feel I have a choice.*

They sat like that for a long time, saying little, until the sister moons rose and Quigsel called Rosinda to come to supper. "See you in the morning?" she asked.

I'll be here, the wolf told her. *You can count on it.*

•••

Leaving Quigsel's house was the hardest thing Rosinda had done since leaving her own. She'd been able to relax here for the first time since she'd met Traveller on the road on the way home from school, and she'd begun to feel not quite so alone. Going back to just her, Jerrell, and the animals felt lonesome.

However, the morning was bright, and they were well-supplied. Quigsel had presented her with a parchment map that mirrored the one he'd showed her on the wall. He'd marked the location of a couple of entry points to the Ways Under, although he confessed that, as an enchanter, he didn't know them all.

"Only the ones I've travelled with Oddeline. This one, though, leads into the Nanghar." He showed her the entrance. "It'll mean a lot less travelling time above ground, and that's what you want."

Once they were underway, Jerrell asked what the enchanter had meant by that.

Rosinda was silent for a moment, trying to recall some memories of Nang, but Kerngold's thoughts slid into her head and she merely repeated them for Jerrell.

The Nangharen are a wild folk, living by their wits and weapons in the steppes of the Nanghar, he said. *They live in tent cities, and interact as little as possible with the other peoples of Ysterad.*

Jerrell pursed his lips. "They don't sound very...welcoming," he commented.

However, if once a Nangharen feels indebted to you, they are loyal for life, and will fight to the death for you, Kerngold continued. *They are a proud and strong race, and their dishvas rival even the horses of Zara for speed.*

"And *dishvas* are?" Jerrell asked, when Rosinda had finished.

"Filthy animals that look like a cross between a camel and an antelope," Filara piped up, revulsion evident in her voice. "They always smell like a wet dog, and *they eat cats.*"

Rosinda managed to stifle her giggles, but Jerrell burst out laughing, earning him a glare from the cat. Their good mood lasted until they reached the Ways Under entrance that Quigsel had marked.

Sparse forest growth and empty clearings surrounded them. The trail they'd followed wound in an easterly direction, and led straight to the River Puth and a ford across it. They weren't to cross the ford, however, according to Quigsel's instructions. A footpath led along the bank of the river, and they followed it for a short distance until they came to a forked tree whose roots stretched across the path and down over the bank into the water. Quigsel's instructions were to wade into the water between the roots, then turn and walk straight into the bank. At Jerrell's skeptical look, he'd sworn that he'd done it with Aunt Odder, and that (apart from getting a bit wet) it was as easy as any other.

They found the place with no difficulty, although getting the horses into the water and then blindfolded took a bit of maneuvering. Filara perched atop one of the horses, absolutely refusing to get her paws wet. Rosinda turned and faced the bank, although she led her own horse this time; leaving both of them for Jerrell wasn't practical. The bank looked solid and unyielding, but Rosinda closed her eyes, stretched one arm out in front of her, and walked forward. After a few steps, water streamed away from her legs. She kept walking, to make sure the horse was entirely through before she stopped.

When she opened her eyes, she stood in the middle of a room that held the same moist, just-turned earth aroma, but with added scents of fish and lakeweed. The walls glistened darkly, and the pervasive trickle of running water filled the air. An Urigm, as muddy and round as his brethren, stepped forward and made her an odd salute.

"All Kelta are welcome," he said, as the other one had. "But the Prince's Kelta brings joy to the guardians."

Unexpected tears stung Rosinda's eyes. *I hope I can live up to this*, she thought, but all she said was "Thank you."

In a moment, the others had joined her and they turned to a southeast passage. Rosinda asked the Urigm, "Is this the way to the Nanghar?"

The mud-man nodded reassuringly, and Rosinda wondered why she hadn't thought to ask them for directions before. If anyone knew their way through the Ways, surely it would be these quiet guardians. She'd have to remember that if they got lost.

The Way to the Nanghar felt more oppressive than the other Way they'd travelled, narrower and dimmer. It was still easy to see where they were going, though, and the horses did not protest. No one spoke much. Rosinda spent the time worrying about what she would say to her mother if the Crypt of a Thousand Voices actually worked. And more importantly, what her mother might say to her.

They emerged into another crossroad room and opening to the surface. Rosinda knew they must pass through this one and keep going. The first hint of something wrong was the absence of an Urigm.

Rosinda stopped and looked around. Something tingled in her mind and made the hairs on the back of her neck stand up. Always in these rooms, an Urigm stepped forward immediately to make sure that she was permitted. But here, no sign of a mud-man, no sound but the trickling of water on the walls. Four other side routes exited the main chamber, all black-shadowed and forbidding.

"What's wrong?" Jerrell whispered from behind her.

"I don't know," she whispered back and stepped slowly into the room.

A scream split the thick air, and a shape bounded out of the northwest passage, straight toward Rosinda.

Her horse whickered in fear and rose on its hind legs, thrashing out with its hooves at the attacker. Rosinda dropped the reins and felt her body take over. She glanced around for something, anything, that she might use as a weapon. Behind her, she heard the sound of Jerrell's pack slithering down from the saddle. Kerngold rushed past in a blur of brown and grey fur and launched himself at the creature. A pang of fear for him lanced her heart.

She spied a broken root on the floor, perhaps three feet long and as thick around as her wrist. It wasn't much. She dove for it, snatched it up and in one fluid motion faced the creature, the root held in front of her defensively.

The thing stood almost as tall as a man, though spindly and crooked. Tattered pants covered its legs, but its feet and upper body were bare. Mottled, greenish skin with a sickly sheen stretched over a skeletal framework of bones and tendons. As it turned toward her, she saw a face that was mostly mouth, filled with sharp teeth. Kerngold's jaws clamped around the creature's left leg.

Rosinda swung the root at the creature as it lunged toward her. At the same moment, Traveller flew low over its head, raking with his claws. It hissed and backed off a step or two. Rosinda heard a metallic clink from Jerrell's direction, and he stepped out from behind the horse, wielding a small, long-handled shovel. He swung it experimentally a couple of times.

The creature lunged at Rosinda again, seemingly oblivious to Kerngold's grip on its leg. She swung the root, but this time the creature whipped up a long-fingered hand and caught it, twisting it out of her hands. Traveller swooped in again, and the creature flailed at him with the root, knocking him out of the air. He hit the ground with a wet thump.

The follow-through of the swing connected with the side of Kerngold's head, and the wolf yelped and let go. A reddish fog clouded Rosinda's vision, narrowing her focus to the creature. Anger bubbled like volcano lava inside her. This thing had attacked her *friends*.

Jerrell leapt to Rosinda's side and swung at the creature with the shovel, but missed. The creature retaliated with the root, catching Jerrell on the wrist.

Jerrell yelped in pain as the shovel fell from his numbed fingers and thunked into the dirt at Rosinda's feet. Again she felt the sure, angry knowledge that she should be protecting the others, not the other way around. She snatched up the shovel and stepped in front of Jerrell, gripping the shaft like a sword. She swung at the creature's head, wishing desperately for a shtava—a Kelton sword.

Suddenly the shovel *was* a sword, blade flashing silver in the dim yellow glow of the chamber, slicing through the air to connect with bone and muscle. The creature screamed and swung at her with the root. Rosinda effortlessly blocked the blow then shifted her weight and sliced upward, taking the creature in the ribcage. Her blade bit deeply this time, and the creature gave a wet, sickening gasp and fell forward onto the dirt floor.

For a moment, the only sounds in the chamber were the nervous whickering and shifting of the horses. Then Jerrell said, "Where did you get *that?*"

Rosinda tore her eyes away from the dead creature on the floor and looked down at the sword she held. "I—I don't know," she stammered. "I think it was your shovel."

"Okaaaaay. You can keep it now," he said, shaking his hand to revive it. "What happened to it?"

"Magic?" Filara suggested, jumping lightly down from the saddle of Rosinda's horse. "Although I've never seen Kelta magic work quite that way," she admitted. "Transformation— that's more like enchanter magic. Not within the realm of Kelta powers as far as I know."

"But—but I didn't draw power from the earth or anything," Rosinda protested. "And I don't have a headache. And I don't even know how to do that!"

Filara sat and twitched an ear. "Perhaps you know more than you think. Your memories, remember?" She eyed Rosinda strangely. "Your father's an enchanter. That could account for it, although—"

"That's what I'm told," Rosinda said crossly. She was getting very tired of not having her own memories, and not knowing what she might be missing.

"It would be very strange," Filara finished. "Very strange indeed. But you certainly did *something*."

Kerngold clambered slowly to his feet, and Rosinda dropped to her knees beside Traveller. He still hadn't moved. She stroked the crow's feathers with one hand and spoke to the wolf at the same time. "Are you all right?

Except for the horrible taste in my mouth, he said wryly. *That was awful.*

Jerrell joined Rosinda beside the crow. "Is he all right?"

"He has a heartbeat," Rosinda said, pressing gently on the crow's side. "He must have been knocked unconscious, that's all."

Filara walked over and sniffed at the unmoving bird. "I don't like the smell of him," she said. "More than usual, I mean. You might have to use some healing."

"I don't know—" Rosinda began, but then she stopped. Half the time she said that, she turned out to be wrong. "I'll get the book," she said instead. Her horse had calmed, but it stood as far as possible from the dead creature, breathing through wide-stretched nostrils. She pulled the book out of her pack and tossed her sweater to Jerrell. "Would you wrap him up in that?"

While Jerrell carefully cradled Traveller in the sweater, Rosinda leafed through the yellowed pages of the book. A *Potion for Enhanced Affections,* a recipe for tea biscuits. *How to Remove Warts and Boils. Notes on planting vegetables,* half a dozen other potions and charms, and then, finally, *A Healing of Hidden Injuries.* It sounded promising, and didn't require any special herbs or implements. Just a laying-on of hands and a simple incantation.

She settled herself beside the crow after reading through the charm a few times. Earlier, she'd needed Traveller to help her with the pronunciations, but now as she read the words they echoed in her mind. *I can do this.*

Rosinda closed her eyes and laid her hands on Traveller's body, focusing on his warmth through the soft covering of his feathers and his steady heartbeat, so much faster than her own in his comparatively small body. At the last moment, she remembered the power. She mentally probed the packed dirt beneath her feet and felt the life force of the world pulsing through it. She imagined herself as a siphon, drawing a little of that power off to help Traveller. Then she spoke the words of the charm.

Traveller's body twitched, but his eyes remained closed.

"Did it work?" Jerrell whispered.

Rosinda nodded slowly. "I think so. It felt right. Maybe he just needs to rest for a while." She got to her feet, cradling the crow in her arms, still wrapped in the sweater. "If you can handle both horses for a while, I'll carry him."

Jerrell nodded. Kerngold brushed up against her leg. "Are you all right now?" she asked him.

Yes. You were very brave, Rosinda.

She shrugged. "I didn't really think about it. It just happened."

I am very glad we are together, Kerngold told her. He made a circuit of the chamber while Jerrell loaded the packs back onto the horses, sniffing both the air and the ground. He stopped at one of the pathways and moved a few steps down the tunnel. *The Urigm is here*, he said to Rosinda. *It is dead.*

Reluctantly, Rosinda went to look at the body of the Urigm. It seemed to be already seeping back into the earth, returning to the mud. She guessed the same creature had killed it. "What will happen to this gateway?" she wondered aloud, turning away from the dead Urigm and coming back into the main chamber.

"I expect another one will turn up to take his place," Filara said somberly. "They seem to come when they are needed."

For a moment, Rosinda stared down at the body of the

creature she had killed. "Does anyone know what this was?"

Kerngold came over and sniffed the body. *I believe it is a creature from the mountains of Nordas*, he said. *It should not be this far from home.*

"Do you think someone sent it after us?" Jerrell asked.

"If they did, it won't be going back," she said. It surprised and frightened her a little that she felt no remorse. She had done what was necessary to protect herself and those in her care. She couldn't regret that. Still cradling Traveller, she bent and picked up her sword. It felt right in her hand, balanced and responsive. She thrust it through a ring on the saddle and handed Jerrell her horse's reins.

"Are we ready?" she asked, looking around at the others. They all nodded. "Then let's keep going," she said, and led the way across the chamber and into the next tunnel.

CHAPTER EIGHTEEN

"Your young Kelta is resourceful," Tyr said to Morrigan. He'd shown up in her forest, minus his usual mountaintop backdrop, looking thoughtful and slightly out of place. "As is your servant."

"What have you learned?" she asked him, more harshly than she'd intended. Her failure to scry the girl irked her. The young Kelta had become much more than simply a source of information.

Tyr lounged against the trunk of an elm, his handless arm folded across his chest. Morrigan met his gaze and felt the Norse god's wild grey eyes taking her measure.

"I sent them a visitor," Tyr explained. "Not a human. I didn't expend my resources that much. A creature from the coldlands, transplanted into an underground place it did not understand." He shrugged. "It did not need to. Its instincts were enough for my purpose."

"I cannot see her yet," Morrigan confessed grudgingly. "Neither in my stream, nor through the eyes of my servant. When he is with her, his mind and senses are closed to me."

"Did you instruct him to reveal where they are taking the older Kelta?" Tyr asked.

"No. Did he do that?" Morrigan frowned. "I don't understand why you are able to see her, when I am not. The Kelta are closer to me than to you, even if they worship neither of us."

"It was a wolf, Fenrir, who took my hand off long ago," Tyr said thoughtfully, holding out his stump. "And they say a wolf's cousin will be my death at Ragnarök. So perhaps wolves and I are attuned. Sometimes, with luck, a wolf's mind will open to me. I gain, briefly, the ability to see where others' eyes cannot."

Morrigan didn't think he was taunting her. "And are you going to tell me what you saw, or do you plan to keep your own counsel like the Egyptian goddess?"

Tyr laughed, although even smiling he seemed grave. "I hope I am nothing like Sekhmet," he said drily. "The girl's memories are seeping back, and what was buried drifts ever closer to the surface. The young Kelta worked some interesting magic, perhaps by accident. She turned a low piece of metal into a blade that would have kings eyeing it with greed. Then she worked a more commonplace charm to heal your servant, injured by my creature. I apologize for that," he said quickly, as Morrigan's eyes blazed. "I did not seek to harm what was yours."

"I did not sense his distress," she said. "That alone gives me cause to worry. Is he well now? Did the Kelta heal him?"

"I believe so," the one-handed god said. "They travel further east, since your servant pricked them into more incautious action. The window has closed, now, however. I cannot see them any longer."

Morrigan studied the Norse god for a moment. "Why do you tell me this?" she asked. "I was at a disadvantage before you came to me."

Tyr shrugged. "We four have come together for our own purposes, and I know that the day is not far off when we will stand against each other. For now, I'd rather have you at my back than the Egyptian. And if a time came for alliances..." He let the words trail away.

"It will all be for naught if we cannot find the prince," she said tiredly.

"I know." Tyr smiled. "Ragnarök may come sooner for me than expected. But if this is my last chance to hold it at bay, I'd sooner do so with you at my side than ranged against me, Lady of the Forest." He touched the stump of his arm to his brow in salute and disappeared.

Morrigan's felt certain that the Norse god looked to his own fortunes in coming to her, but that was all right. She'd rather know what he was thinking and doing than wonder what he was plotting with Sekhmet behind her back.

She turned her mind to what he had told her, trailing her hand in the chill water of the stream. So her servant had acted on his own initiative to get the girl moving more quickly toward them? That was good—but strange. She wondered why he hadn't consulted with her. Then he'd been injured, presumably protecting the girl. He would assume that Morrigan wanted her kept safe for now, but it was also unexpected that he'd put himself in mortal danger to do it.

She wondered. Yes, she very much wondered.

CHAPTER NINETEEN

They'd passed through two more crossroad chambers, each properly manned by its Urigm. "The next one is the one we take to the surface," Rosinda told the others.

"We'll be in the Nanghar then?" asked Jerrell.

Rosinda nodded. "Not far from the Crypt of a Thousand Voices if Quigsel's map is accurate."

"Did Quigsel tell you what you have to do when you get there?"

Rosinda sighed. "He found some instructions in a book. When I asked him, he said he'd never been there himself. But he thought I'd know what to do."

"Well, that's reassuring. Not."

"Mm-hmm. That's what I thought."

"Think we'll run into any of the Nangharen?"

"I certainly hope not," said Rosinda.

"How's Traveller?"

"Still sleeping." She didn't want to say "unconscious."

The tunnel ahead brightened, and within moments they reached the chamber. The Urigm nodded to her, and the doorway to the surface opened on the southern wall. Beyond its strange barrier lay a flat plateau studded with yellow grasses and clumps of dense brush. A thin line of sky hung above the end of the plateau, which seemed empty of any other life.

"Are you going to wake him before we go out there?"

Rosinda shook her head. "I think I'll let him sleep. We have the map, so we should be able to find the crypt. And if we get into trouble..." She didn't finish the sentence. If they ran into trouble with the Nangharen, it wasn't likely that one little crow would be able to help them.

She should have expected it, but the rush of returning memories when she stepped out onto the Nangharen plateau took Rosinda by surprise. Of course—they'd now crossed another border. The yellow-tinged landscape shimmered around her, and she almost missed her footing on the rocky ground. Images of sun-bleached, tattooed and leather-clad men riding strange-looking beasts filled her mind; women with long pale hair braided and twisted into intricate knots, and long, low tent-dwellings that rustled and flapped in the dry, ever-present breeze.

Jerrell stepped out beside her and pulled a deep breath. "Fresh air at last!" he said. He squinted against the yellowish light and looked around. "Geez, there are places even more desolate than this?"

"Don't let the Nangharen hear you say that," said Filara with a sniff. She pawed at a dry spot on the ground and shook the dust from her fur. "They think it's the most wonderful place in Ysterad, and they're just as likely to kill you as argue the point."

"Then what are we doing standing around?" he retorted. "Let's find that crypt and do what needs doing, and get the heck out of here."

They mounted up, Rosinda still carrying Traveller. She tied the sleeves of her sweater together and slung them around her neck, making a sling to support the sleeping bird. She handed the map to Jerrell. "I'm sure you're better at reading this than I am, even if it is familiar to me."

He took it with a grin. "I like to be helpful," he said. After looking at the map for a moment, Jerrell turned his horse's head to the east and spurred it forward.

The expanse of the Nanghar stretched out on every side, flat plateaus building one upon another like a giant's stepping-stones, short blackish scrub and stunted evergreens standing fast against the dry wind. Some patches, like oases, were more verdant than others. When they got close enough to one, Rosinda and Jerrell spotted a thin stream winding through the steppes and, once or twice, a good-sized lake nestled in a depression. They saw a few small gopher-like creatures and a long-eared hare in the distance, but for the most part, they were alone in an eerie silence.

"We must be close," Jerrell said at last when the sun had sunk halfway down its descent toward the horizon. They'd stopped at a small lake to allow the horses to drink. "Seems like we're right on top of the X that Quigsel marked."

They'd been climbing gradually for the past hour or so. "Maybe over the next rise," Rosinda said. "Quigsel said if we stayed on the trail, we couldn't miss it."

She turned out to be right. Over the next flat-topped steppe was a wide plain, covered with stubbly grass and dotted with ragged clumps of brush. A single edifice rose from the flat land, looking small and lonely.

"That's got to be it," Jerrell said, and Rosinda nodded, urging her horse into a trot. Now that they were here, she felt an overwhelming urge to get the next part over with before anything else could go wrong.

The building, when they neared it, was almost a ruin. One toppled column lay in pieces next to the entryway, and harsh weather had left the stone of the crypt pitted and worn. It looked big enough inside to hold five or six horses and riders. The doorway stood open. The overhanging roof allowed little light to find its way inside, and darkness shrouded the interior.

"I hope you're coming in with me," Rosinda said to Jerrell as they both dismounted.

He looked unsure. "Do you really want me to? I mean, you're going to talk to your mom, right? I thought it might be...you know, private."

Rosinda smiled briefly. "Jerrell, I don't know what to expect. I might need you there, so if you don't mind, I really want you to come inside with me."

"Okay. The horses?"

"We should take them with us. It's big enough. And that way there's nothing to advertise our presence."

"Good thinking."

With one more glance around the empty plain surrounding them, Rosinda stepped into the crypt. The darkness closed around her like ebony wings, but she wasn't prepared for the voices.

It really did sound like a thousand voices whispered in Rosinda's ears. Just a soft susurration with no identifiable words standing out from the others. A steady, relentless hum of speech thickened the air until Rosinda felt that she could hardly breathe.

"Do you hear them, too?" Jerrell asked, his own whisper rising slightly above the others.

Rosinda jumped at his voice. "Yes. I guess I know where the 'thousand voices' part comes from."

"No kidding. This place gives me the creeps," Jerrell said, looking around.

Inside, the crypt was smaller than it had appeared, and lighter once Rosinda's eyes adjusted. Pale light crept in through two skylights, limning the room with a dim grey glow. They barely fit inside, because the walls were thick—thick enough to house the tombs that lined them. Many of the slots had once borne name plaques identifying their occupants, but the metal had long since corroded away. Rosinda had an eerie mental image of the whispers themselves eating away at the names, but she shook it out of her head.

At the furthest end, an open stairway descended into total blackness. "We don't have to go down there, do we?" Jerrell asked.

Rosinda gulped and turned to him. "According to Quigsel, I do. You can stay up here with the horses. I don't mind." It was a lie; she would much rather have company, but she didn't want to make him go down into that darkness if he didn't want to.

I will go, Kerngold said.

At the same time, Jerrell said, "I'll go. It's okay."

"Kerngold said he would, so you can stay here with the horses."

"Are you sure?"

She nodded.

"Do you need anything out of the packs?" Jerrell asked.

"I could use a flashlight," she said, as she passed Traveller's sleeping form over to Jerrell. While he fetched one, she drew her new sword from where it hung on her saddle. Then before she could think about it anymore, she started down the stone steps. Kerngold padded comfortingly beside her.

The voices grew louder as they descended the stairs, swirling around them like ghosts. Whether or not they were malevolent spirits, Rosinda couldn't tell. She hoped not.

At the foot of the stairs she switched on the flashlight and to her great relief saw exactly what Quigsel had told her to look for: a stone basin set on a pedestal rising from the center of the floor. A silvery liquid filled the basin, emitting a faint light that reminded Rosinda of the Raven's Moon, illuminating places where the other two moons couldn't shine. The glow felt inviting, and she walked over without hesitation.

She needed a free hand for the next step, so she stood the flashlight on the floor beside her, pointing up. It threw weird shadows around the room but still gave her enough light to see. She wasn't about to put down the sword. She glanced at Kerngold, and he nodded encouragingly. She plunged her free hand into the basin.

The water, or whatever the liquid was, was surprisingly warm, not the cold shock she had expected. The crowd of voices vying for her attention silenced immediately. She closed her eyes and concentrated on her few memories of her mother, willing the kind and beautiful face she hadn't seen for a year or more into her mind. Hot tears welled behind her eyes, but she fought them back, concentrating on her task.

To start, she thought of the conversation she'd recalled not long ago, talking to her mother about the Raven's Moon. Other memories followed: reading together, her mother showing her a needlework stitch, walking together on a windswept cliff or tower. They were all good memories, and Rosinda was glad to have a reason to stop and focus on them for a moment.

From a long distance she felt a stirring, as if she were trying to wake someone from a sound sleep. *Mother?* She sent the word out tentatively, not sure what to do.

For a long moment nothing happened, and she brought her mother's face into clear focus in her mind and mentally said the word again.

Mother?

Rosinda? The voice was confused, unbelieving. *Rosinda, is that you?*

Relief flooded through her. It was working! *Mother, it's me. I'm okay, but I need your help.*

Rosinda, where are you? Her mother's voice sounded completely awake and alert now. Rosinda pictured her sitting up straight somewhere, eyes closed, focused on her daughter's words.

Reluctantly, Rosinda said *I'm in the Nanghar, at the Crypt of a Thousand Voices.* She felt sure that would only make her mother worry. The inarticulate gasp she heard her mother make only confirmed that theory. She couldn't hide the rest of it, so she rushed on, *Aunt Odder's been kidnapped and I only have parts of my memory. I need to know what to do next. I do know about being the Prince's Kelta, but not much else,* she added.

Her mother was quiet for such a long time that Rosinda began to worry that their connection had been broken. The other voices from the crypt didn't return, so she stilled her mind and waited.

Did Oddeline leave instructions for getting your full memory back? her mother finally asked.

Yes, but she said it could be dangerous, and I should only do it in an emergency.

There was a sound as if her mother chuckled a little. *Honey, you're alone in the Nanghar and Aunt Odder's been kidnapped. I think that qualifies as an emergency.*

Okay, Rosinda said. *I'm not quite alone, but I'll do it tonight.*

Wait. Can you get back to Cape Breton?

I think so. The weight of the bloodbound crystal was heavy on her neck, a reassuring presence. *I don't know how much energy is in the crystal, though.*

There was another silence. Then her mother said, *I think you should chance it. It will be much less dangerous if you regain your memory away from Ysterad. There's power in the earth there that will help to protect you.*

What if I can't get back here? Rosinda felt a panicky lurch in her stomach at the thought.

With your memories intact, it shouldn't be a problem, even if the crystal is not strong enough. There are other ways. Do you have Oddeline's book?

Yes, Rosinda said. *But I'm not very good with it.*

I'm sure you're fine, her mother said. *But you should bring something back with you.*

What is it?

In the woods behind the house, there's a clearing with a fairy ring, her mother said.

Rosinda grinned. *I've been there!*

Good. Her mother sounded like she was smiling. *That's a*

very special ring, and there's great power in the earth there. Bring some back with you.

I can do that.

Try to find a weapon, maybe after you've gotten your memory back—

Would a sword do? I have one of those.

This time her mother definitely laughed. *Are you sure you need my help at all?*

Rosinda smiled. *Just a little.*

Take your sword with you to the fairy ring. Do it after you have your memories back, and you'll know what to do.

Okay. It was all very vague, but she didn't know how long she'd have to ask questions. *Are you all right, Mother? Is there anything I can do to help you? Is Dad with you?*

Her mother fell silent again for a moment. *We're doing all right—your father's sleeping. Just stay safe, Rosinda. Find the prince if you can, get him to Sangera. Most of all, try to help Aunt Oddeline. That's the best way you can help us, too.*

"Rosinda!" Jerrell's voice reached her in a harsh whisper from the upper floor.

"Just a second!" she whispered back. *Mother, I have to go. Give my love to Dad, okay? Tell him I wanted to talk to him, too, there just wasn't time.*

I will, honey. Be careful. I love you.

"Rosinda!"

I love you, Mom.

She pulled her hand out of the basin, and the thousand restless voices fell upon her ears again, their force redoubled. Jerrell's voice reached her again as she bent to retrieve the flashlight.

"Someone's coming!"

Rosinda ran back up the stone steps, her heart pounding. The voices around her seemed to saturate the air. "How do you know someone's coming?" she hissed to Jerrell.

At the top of the stairs, she had her answer. Two men and a woman with forbidding faces stood just inside the doorway of the crypt, weapons drawn.

"Because they're here," Jerrell said, and he didn't sound happy about it at all.

CHAPTER TWENTY

"What are you doing here?" one of the men barked in a harsh tongue.

She strode forward, brushing past the horses and Jerrell before she had time to think about it.

"I have business here," she said to the man who had challenged them. She stopped a few feet in front of him and drew herself up to her full height, resting the point of her sword on the ground, her hands draped casually on top of the hilt.

The man frowned. "We guard the crypt of our ancestors," he said. "It is not a place for *children* to play."

Rosinda's heart quailed at the sneer on his face, but she couldn't back down now. "Kelta do not play," she sneered back. She wasn't about to mention the prince, since she didn't know where the Nangharen loyalties lay, but naming herself as a Kelta seemed like it might lend her a bit of credibility.

"We are not here to play games," the man replied. "You must leave the crypt immediately."

"Fine. I have completed my business," Rosinda said. She was acutely aware of the bloodbound crystal resting heavily on her chest now. If she could get everyone gathered close enough to touch her, she could have them all safely in Cape Breton and away from here in a matter of seconds. She glanced around when she turned to take her horse's reins from Jerrell, trying to judge if they were all close enough together, but she didn't see Kerngold. He mustn't have followed her back up the steps.

Rosinda took her horse's reins and led the way out of the

crypt past the Nangharen who stood to the sides to let her pass. The odd light of the steppes made her blink when she emerged out into it again. A dozen or more Nangharen waited for their comrades outside the crypt.

They all looked much the same as those inside, the women with their pale hair intricately twisted, as Rosinda had envisioned them when she set foot in the Nanghar. Men and women alike had white-bleached skin and clothes of soft, supple-looking leather dyed bright colors. The creatures they rode, the dishvas, were as Filara had described them—part camel, part antelope, with a broad, humped back for riding and strong, hoofed feet, but a long, slender neck and curving horns atop the head. An elongated muzzle tapered to a mouth filled with sharp teeth. Mottled brown fur furrowed into horizontal stripes on their legs. One sniffed the air with interest. Rosinda realized that it had fixed Filara with a heavily lidded eye.

The others followed her out of the crypt, and the Nangharen formed an intimidating circle around them. The three from inside mounted their beasts. No one spoke. They seemed to be waiting for something.

"May we go now?" Rosinda finally asked with as much confidence as she could muster.

"You will wish to speak to the Durnstad, Kelta," said the man who had spoken to her inside. It was a statement, not a question, and Rosinda remembered that the durnstad were the shama of the Nangharen. To visit without paying respects to the local durnstad would be a high insult. At least he had called her Kelta, and he didn't seem to be making fun of her.

"Of course," she said. Without hesitation, she swung herself up into the saddle. "We will be honored to do so." Jerrell took his cue from her and did the same, still carefully holding Traveller in his sling. Filara had been sitting on the saddle blanket on Rosinda's horse, but climbed over Rosinda's leg and settled herself in front.

"Filthy creatures," the cat whispered. Rosinda hoped that no one else had heard her. She stroked Filara's back reassuringly, hoping the cat would keep her mouth shut.

The Nanghar turned their dishvas as one and headed to the east. Rosinda and Jerrell followed, although some of the riders stayed back to ride next to the horses. Rosinda threw one casual glance back over her shoulder at the crypt as they rode away. The wolf was not there.

•••

They hadn't been riding long when Jerrell caught her eye and looked down at Traveller. When Rosinda glanced at the crow, his eyes were open again. Traveller closed and opened one at her in a grave wink. Relief bubbled up inside her. She hadn't realized how much she'd relied on the crow until he'd been knocked unconscious. Even though her own confidence grew as her memories returned, she still felt nervous depending on her own decisions without the crow's guidance.

"How far do you think they're taking us?" Jerrell asked in a low voice.

She shrugged. "I don't know, but we're still going in the right direction, so we might as well go along."

Jerrell looked back over his shoulder and then at Rosinda, raising one eyebrow in a silent question, *where's Kerngold?*

Rosinda shrugged again. *I don't know.* Perhaps Jerrell had been hoping that the wolf was communicating with Rosinda mentally. She wished he'd been right.

They rode for the better part of the afternoon, keeping in an easterly direction. None of the Nangharen attempted to speak to either Rosinda or Jerrell again, although from time to time Rosinda would catch one of them looking at her. They'd usually smile when their eyes met, but it was a difficult smile to interpret.

Dusk had deepened the shadows in the steppes when they crested a rise and saw a city of flat-topped tents erected along the shore of a small lake. Thickets of scrub and low pine trees dotted the surrounding area. A few fires pricked holes in the lowering darkness and the aroma of roasting meat wafted to them on the breeze, making Rosinda's stomach rumble urgently.

The Nangharen rode to a pen where other dishvas crowded and sniffed the scents of the new arrivals. Rosinda didn't feel comfortable putting their horses inside. Not with the mouths full of sharp teeth that she'd observed on the creatures. Instead, she tied her horse to a small, scraggly tree that pushed its way doggedly out of the earth nearby, and Jerrell did the same. She opened her pack and tucked Filara inside before the cat could protest, then slung it over her back and took her sword in her hand. The tall Nangharen, who was the only one who'd spoken to them so far, nodded for them to follow and strode off toward the center of the tent city.

Rosinda walked with her head high as they wove their way through the tents and around cooking fires, ignoring the curious stares they garnered but keeping her own face pleasant. Inside, she was a bundle of nerves, but she reminded herself that they were not being treated as prisoners. Once they'd paid their respects to the durnstad, they could probably leave. Part of her, primarily her stomach, hoped they'd be invited to have supper first.

Eventually the Nangharen stopped outside a tent that was much smaller than most of the rest. "Driasch awaits your company," he said formally, and then gave Rosinda one of those enigmatic grins.

She swallowed and said, "Thank you," then pulled aside the tent flap and entered, with Jerrell close on her heels.

Inside the tent, the air was thick with a heavily scented haze of smoke. Rosinda blinked and stifled a cough. In the backpack, Filara sneezed once. A low fire, just embers really, burned in a metal bowl full of holes like a colander. Beyond that, a figure sat hunched under what seemed to be a huge pile of furs. Two bright blue eyes peered out at Rosinda and a pale-skinned, claw-like hand wormed its way out of the furs and beckoned them in.

"Come in, young Kelta," said a voice, high and cracked. *Male? Female? Impossible to tell.*

"Greetings, Wise One," Rosinda said as she stepped closer to the fire. The proper form of address bubbled up from somewhere in her mind.

"Sit," commanded the voice. "The boy, too. Have you come to tell me that the prince from the Blood Clans lives?"

Rosinda's heartbeat quickened. What did this shaman know about the prince and her connection to him? She lowered herself to sit cross-legged on the floor, and Filara wormed out of the backpack and settled herself in Rosinda's lap. "No," she said quietly. "I'm not certain of that answer myself."

"And how does a Prince's Kelta explain the lack of that knowledge?" the shaman asked.

Rosinda fought to keep her rising alarm under control. "That is a long story, Wise One," she said lightly. Deciding to take a risk, she added, "Would it please you to hear that he is alive?"

The blue eyes squinted at her. "The prince is all that stands between Ysterad and a bloody war that would raze it to the very bones of the earth," the shaman said. "I would be so pleased to hear of a living prince that I might get up and dance around this fire."

The prospect of that seemed so unlikely that Rosinda couldn't quell the smile that pulled at her lips. The shaman chuckled as well. Then Driasch sobered again.

"You're young, Kelta, to be meddling in the affairs of gods, no matter what blood oath you took to the prince."

"Gods?" Rosinda asked before she could stop herself.

The blue eyes narrowed, studying her. "You didn't know, did you? No. That knowledge is well-hidden. But the bones tell, young Kelta. Always remember that the bones tell. They told me you were coming and who you are."

Rosinda nodded, although she didn't have a clue what the shaman meant. She wasn't left to wonder long. The skinny hand stretched out from the furs again and pointed to a flat piece of smooth, polished wood to one side of the fire. A collection of small bones, perhaps from birds or rodents, apparently randomly scattered across its surface. She bent toward it for a closer look.

"Don't bother," the shaman said. "The magic of the tellbones does not speak to Kelta. But I will tell you what they say." The hand gestured over the bones, and as Driasch spoke, Rosinda could begin to see patterns in the way they lay. "Four gods," Driasch said, "with blood in their eyes and their fingers poking about into Ysterad. The only thing that makes me believe that the prince is still alive is the fact that the wars haven't begun yet. While he lives there is some protection, but without him..."

"But I thought it was just—just people who wanted to see the prince dead," Rosinda said. "Some people." Her hands wanted to shake, but she stroked Filara's fur to keep them still. Politics, she could understand. The desire for power or a changing of the ways. People wanted those things at different times and for different reasons. That's what she'd thought was behind Aunt Odder's kidnapping and the attacks on her parents—everything. Just people fighting. If *gods* were involved, though, how was she supposed to do anything against that?

"Some people, yes," Driasch said, nodding. "And some people who wouldn't think about it much one way or the other if it weren't for the gods." The shaman gestured to the bones again. "War gods, all of them, lovers of blood sacrifice and strife. Their names I do not know; they are not of Ysterad. Our own gods are weak with no one of Ysterad blood upon the throne; they cannot stand against these usurpers."

"Can you see anything else about them?" Rosinda asked, her eyes intent on the bones.

The shaman pointed out shapes in the scattered bits. "A burning goddess, with cats coiled around her feet. A proud warrior sprung from a seafaring folk. A goddess of forests and streams—"

"And a one-handed winter god," Rosinda finished absently, seeing the sign in the bones as plainly as if it were written out. Filara's ears twitched. Rosinda looked up at the shaman's sharply indrawn breath. The blue eyes peered at her with more intensity than before.

"A Kelta should not see that," Driasch said in a low voice. "Not even the Prince's Kelta."

Rosinda looked at the bones again, and plainly saw the signs of the four gods, although something made her wish she could not. She turned to Jerrell. "Can you read anything in these bones?"

Jerrell peered at them for a long moment then shook his head. "They just look like bones to me."

"Why can I read them, then?" Rosinda demanded of the shaman. "And I couldn't at first—only when you started to explain them."

The head swathed in furs shook from side to side slowly. "That is not for me to say. These are hard times. In hard times, sometimes—only sometimes—something extraordinary happens."

It wasn't an answer, but Rosinda sensed it was all she would get. "If you can read things like this, can you tell me where the prince might be? I cast a charm to call him, but he hasn't shown up yet. I may have done it wrong," she added.

The shaman sat silent for a long time. "I could attempt a soul-walking," Driasch finally said. "I have not done one for many years. They are better undertaken by the young and strong. They involve the strongest of the shaman magic."

"What would it tell you, a soul-walking?" Rosinda asked.

Driasch shrugged. "If the prince is alive, for one thing. And whether he is close, what he is thinking." Under Rosinda's gaze the shaman added, "I could have done one before this, yes, but the need to know if the prince was alive was not as pressing. I could not help him. You, though..."

What can I do? Rosinda wanted to ask, but she kept quiet. If the old shaman could tell her something important, she would play along as best she could.

"I will do it tonight," the shaman said suddenly. "The moons are not at their best, but it will do. Now send my son Iander in to me, and I will instruct him to feed you and see you settled for the night. In the morning I will tell you what, if anything, I have found."

Rosinda had many more questions, but it was obviously a dismissal, and she didn't want to push her luck. So she merely said, "Thank you," and she and Jerrell went back outside. The man who had led them to the tent still stood there, and Rosinda said, "The Wise One is asking for Iander." She didn't want to admit that she still didn't know if the shaman was a man or a woman. He nodded and slipped inside.

The dusk had given way to full dark now, and Rosinda went to pull her sweater out of her pack. She soon realized that it was still doing double duty as a sling for Traveller, but Jerrell handed her an extra one from his own pack. She slipped it over her head.

"Do you think he'll like us any better now?" Jerrell whispered, his breath rising in cloudy puffs.

"I don't know, but at least we should get supper," she whispered back.

They did. Iander emerged from the tent a few moments later and led them to another tent about the same size as the shaman's. A fire burned in a small ceramic basin in the center of the floor, and a system of pulleys had opened smoke flaps in the ceiling of the tent. Iander picked up what looked like a small stack of slatted boards, and with a strange twist of his hand, the boards transformed into an elegant chair. He did the same with another one, and produced a small table in the same way.

"That's amazing!" Jerrell exclaimed.

Iander merely smiled and said, "Good for folk who like to travel." On either side of the tent lay a long, low wooden box, and Iander moved to those next. With the press of a button, the top of each one opened and he pulled out blankets and furs; in a moment what had looked like plain boxes had been transformed into comfortable-looking sleeping pallets. He bade them wait inside for a few moments. "I'll return with your supper," he told them.

As soon as the Nangharen left the tent, Jerrell was down on his knees examining one of the chairs, running his hands over it in a search for hidden buttons and mechanisms. Rosinda rolled her eyes. Any kind of gadget, mechanical or electronic, riveted Jerrell's attention. She could admire the craftsmanship and ingenuity of the furniture, but she didn't feel an overwhelming need to know how it worked.

When Iander returned, he carried two servings of stew in smoothly polished wooden bowls and a basket of warm, dark bread. With a bow, he left them alone to eat. The stew was hot, spicy, and filling. After a day when they'd eaten almost nothing since breakfast, it was heavenly. While they ate, Rosinda told Jerrell what her mother had said.

The tall Nangharen didn't return. Traveller finally shook off the comforting folds of Rosinda's sweater, stood and stretched, then walked around the inside walls of the tent, "working out the kinks." Filara dozed by the fire, and Jerrell emptied his pack and neatly repacked it all. Rosinda thumbed through Aunt Odder's book, looking at anything interesting, but her mind was actually churning over what the shaman had said, and what she herself had seen in the bones.

"How are you feeling?" Rosinda asked Traveller when he'd completed his circuit of the tent and settled near her.

"I'm fine, I think," he said. "A bit stiff. Jerrell told me that you healed me. Thank you, Rosinda."

She felt a flush warm her cheeks. "It wasn't anything, really," she said. "I just used a charm from the book."

The crow looked at her with a bemused expression. "Yes, but you did it correctly without anyone to coach you on the pronunciations and without any memory of having done it or anything like it before. That's quite remarkable."

She didn't know what to say to that, but Filara saved her from having to think about it. "Rosinda's just *full* of remarkable talents, crow, or haven't you noticed?"

"Filara," Traveller began, but the cat cut him off.

"No, I mean it. It's time we thought about this. Kelta can't *do* transformation magic. Rosinda turned a shovel into a sword. Kelta can't *do* divination magic. Rosinda read the shaman's tellbones. What's next? Talking to the dead like a necromancer or mind reading like a thaumat? Maybe she's already been doing that with that wolf."

"I'm not doing that!" Rosinda protested.

Traveller ignored her. "I'm sure there's a perfectly—"

"*Logical* explanation," the cat finished. "Well, I'd like to know what that is. I've lived with a Kelta—a *King's* Kelta—for a long time, and I know what she can and can't do. A Prince's Kelta should have even fewer talents!"

"Excuse me, I'm sitting right here," Rosinda said crossly. "Would you mind not talking about me as if I'm in another room...er, tent?"

"Are you going to use the travelling crystal to go back to Cape Breton after we find out what the shaman has to tell us in the morning?" Jerrell asked her.

"I guess so. I'm just worried about Kerngold," Rosinda said, glad of the change of subject. "I don't want to abandon him." She didn't mention that just the thought of leaving the wolf behind made her head pain and her stomach clench. She'd been feeling worse and worse ever since he'd separated from them at the crypt. She didn't know if the two things were linked or not.

"Maybe he'll show up in the morning," Jerrell said, then yawned hugely. "I think I'm going to get some sleep."

The yawn was contagious, and Rosinda did the same thing. "Me, too. I think Kerngold is just staying away from the Nangharen, so once we leave them he'll come back. At least I hope so," she added, but only to herself.

•••

Rosinda realized that she was dreaming, but she couldn't make herself wake up. The Nangharen tent and the warm pile of furs were gone, replaced by cold ground. She felt lost and confused. She'd tried to make a place to sleep by nestling underneath a stunted pine tree, but the wind nipped at her and made it impossible to relax. Her mind would not settle. It bubbled with unanswered questions, memories that taunted her, but would not reveal themselves. Feelings pushed and pulled her in all directions. She lifted her head from the thin mat of pine needles and looked at the night sky. The two silver sister moons rode high above a cloud bank, but the dark orb of the Raven's Moon floated low in the sky, an all-seeing eye that pierced her soul with its eerie dark light. Rosinda had never felt so alone. She threw her head back and howled...

•••

Rosinda sat up, startled.

"What?" Jerrell yelled. He sat up on his pile of furs, barely awake. A thin sliver of moonlight trickled in through the open flap in the ceiling, casting a pale silver glow around them.

Rosinda was about to tell him about her nightmare when she heard the noises outside the tent. Shouting and yelling filled the air, feet pounded near the tent, and—could it be the clash of weapons? Her confusion cleared.

"The camp is under attack," she said to Jerrell. "Gather everything. We're getting out of here."

They hastily threw everything into their packs then drew the tent flap aside just enough to look out. Pandemonium reigned in the camp. Fires flared on some tent walls. Everyone was running.

"What do you think it is?" Jerrell whispered.

"I don't know, but it's nothing to do with us. We should get out of here. Can you remember where we came into the camp—where the horses are?"

Jerrell nodded.

"Lead the way, then, but carefully—no, wait," she ordered. "I'm going to check and make sure the shaman is all right."

Jerrell opened his mouth as if to argue, but Rosinda just shook her head at him. "Get to the horses. I'll meet you there. If I'm not there in five minutes start riding east, and I'll catch up." Jerrell might have said something else, but Rosinda looked him in the eye and she saw him give up.

"Five minutes," he said, and then he was off, running in a low crouch through the forest of tents. Traveller launched himself into the air and flew after Jerrell.

Rosinda waited while a family ran past her tent, then headed for the shaman's. The door still hung closed. Rosinda quickly pushed it aside and ducked inside. The fire burned very low, just a red glow in the coals, and the shaman lay on the floor in a heap of furs. Rosinda crossed to Driasch and gently shook the shaman's shoulder. There was no response.

For a terrible moment Rosinda thought the shaman was dead, but then a twitch and moan told her otherwise. It seemed the Wise One was asleep, or perhaps in the midst of the soul-walk. Rosinda hesitated to interrupt that, but she simply couldn't leave the elder here with no protection. She glanced around. With a swift movement she scooped up the shaman's scrying bones and dropped them into her pocket then, as gently as she could, crouched and lifted the sleeping shaman over her shoulder. It wasn't as difficult as she had feared, because the old shaman was little bigger than a child. Still, Rosinda wished she'd brought Jerrell with her instead of sending him for the horses.

Well, she thought, *this is my first rescue mission. I can't think of everything.*

When she left the tent again, the noise seemed to have moved further from the animal pens. She hurried as much as she could under the weight of the shaman. She heard a shout behind her, but it didn't sound close. She kept going, weaving through the tents, not sure if she'd been seen or not. Within a minute she reached the animal pens. Jerrell waited, holding the reins of both horses. Traveller was perched on one saddle and Filara on the other.

The shout behind her sounded again, closer this time. Others joined in. "What are you doing?" Jerrell hissed at her.

"I couldn't leave him—her—whatever," Rosinda panted. "There was no one else there. Help me get him onto my saddle." Together they lifted the still-unconscious shaman up and steadied him while Rosinda climbed awkwardly up behind.

Thunk! A black-fletched arrow bit into the ground near Rosinda's horse, and the animal shied.

"Quick!" she yelled, and Jerrell tried to clamber onto his own horse. The creature was spooked, though. She shifted and danced away from him when he tried to get a footing.

Rosinda looked up to see two groups running at them. Iander led one knot of men. The others were not Nangharen. Their coloring was different, and their clothing was of woven cloth, not leathers. As they ran, they unleashed a volley of arrows at the Nangharen and at Rosinda and Jerrell. A few narrowly missed them, and one of the Nangharen with Iander fell.

Barely thinking, Rosinda reached up and tugged the bloodbound crystal from inside her shirt. It made her sick to think of leaving Kerngold behind. She didn't know if she could make herself do it, but they were as good as dead if they stayed here.

"Jerrell! Never mind! Just come here," she yelled, and Jerrell turned. He must have seen the crystal and realized what it meant, because he made a lunge to touch her leg. Traveller, too, pushed off into the air and landed behind her on the saddle's cantle.

I am coming. A silvery streak burst from between two of the burning tents and rushed toward them.

Rosinda could have cried with relief. Iander had almost reached her, shouting at her even as his companions rushed toward the strange warriors. She shook her head at him. She couldn't wait. Kerngold made one spectacular leap past the milling, bleating dishvas in the pen and bounded to her, leaning against her leg on the opposite side from Jerrell. Rosinda closed her eyes and thought as desperately as she could about the little house in Cape Breton.

"Rosinda Aletta Penyan," she said. "Cape Breton."

The flaming, noisy, threatening world around them winked out.

CHAPTER TWENTY-ONE

In her woodland glade, Morrigan looked up, startled. Her servant had crossed the Worlds' Edge again, this time without her knowledge or permission. She didn't like being cut off from him. Although at one time, she'd held considerable power in that other world, it had been mostly erased long ago, swamped by the onslaught of new beliefs.

She rose and paced the length of the clearing, pausing to lean against the grey standing stones at one end. Even though the girl was hidden from her, it had been a comfort to know she was in Ysterad. Now Morrigan suspected the girl had also gone back across the Edge, and the goddess felt even less in control.

Should she tell the other gods? Not yet, she decided. They might be back at any moment, and the caravan continued eastward with the older Kelta. Could she afford to let the girl go? The magical shroud that functioned to confound her scrying efforts irked the goddess. As did some of the reports her servant had sent.

She trailed her hand in the clear water of her stream, considering, then reached deeper in and pulled out the palm-sized travelling crystal she had hidden there. Its amber depths sparkled wetly in her palm. She'd kept this to herself, but perhaps the time had come to make use of it. When the other gods found out, they would probably be angry. Especially Tyr after his offer of a tentative alliance. But she couldn't worry about that now.

She had enough power to get it to her other servant. If she

sent Banna across the Worlds' Edge after the girl, it would leave the older Kelta in the hands of the others for a time, but she didn't think any harm would come from that. It would be a coup if her servant could return with the younger Kelta also. The girl seemed more of a threat now than she had at the beginning. Morrigan wasn't sure they could continue to wait for the girl to come to them.

She sat down on a mossy stone to contemplate her options. After a while, she sent a messenger winging to Banna, with new instructions, and an amber crystal gripped tightly in its claws.

CHAPTER TWENTY-TWO

Fortunately, they didn't come through inside Aunt Odder's house, since Rosinda still sat astride the horse. That would have made for an uncomfortable landing. When the sense of emptiness around her faded and Rosinda opened her eyes, they stood in the yard near the back door, dusk gathering around them.

Jerrell staggered a few steps away but didn't fall. "Whew!" he said. "I wonder if you'd ever get used to that?"

"I doubt it," Rosinda answered. "Help me get the shaman down from here, Jerrell, and we'll all go inside."

"Girl?" said a weary voice from the bundled-up form of the shaman. "Where have we—what have you done, girl?"

Rosinda leaned forward. "It's all right. Someone attacked your clan, but I brought you here with me to keep you safe. We're going back to Ysterad soon."

"Back to Ysterad?" Driasch sat up straight, and pushed away the bundled furs. "We've travelled across the Worlds' Edge?" The shaman looked around, bright eyes alert.

"Ye-es," Rosinda said hesitantly. "I'm sorry, but it was the only thing I could think of to do."

"And you brought me with you. Well, well." The shaman's head shook in amazement as Jerrell took the weight in getting down from the horse. "No, boy, it's all right, I can walk. I never thought to cross the Edge in my lifetime. It's Kelta magic, not something a shaman could ever hope to attempt." Driasch sniffed the air like a dog. "Smells like a Kelton forest," the shaman said. Rosinda saw the shaman's eyes widen at the sight of Kerngold, standing patiently beside the horses.

"Don't worry," Rosinda said quickly. "He's a friend."

"If you say so," the shaman said. Glancing around at the small group, the boy, the girl, the cat, the wolf and the crow, the shaman added, "You have an interesting collection of friends."

"Let's get inside where we can sit down and think for a minute," Rosinda said. She took her key out of her pocket and unlocked the door, wondering how it could seem so long since she'd been here when in fact it was only a few days. Although it was still as cozy and welcoming as ever, the house held a chill, as if something was missing. With dismay, she realized that it felt like a place she had only visited, never really lived. *Ysterad*, she thought. *It really is my true home.*

"There's a strong Kelton aura here," Driasch said, following her inside and looking around interestedly. "Not only in the house, I mean, but in the earth here."

Rosinda thought for a moment. "Yes," she said finally, "I know what you mean." She thought she understood why Aunt Odder had chosen this place to hide. Cape Breton felt like Kelton more than any other place she'd ever been, more than anywhere else she'd been in Ysterad.

"Would you like a cup of tea?" she asked automatically. She didn't know if the shaman would like "tea" from this world, but it seemed important to be welcoming. "And please, I don't mean to insult you, but are you...are you...male, or female?"

The shaman laughed, and threw back the furred hood. For the first time, the shaman's entire face—wrinkle-mapped pale skin, twinkling blue eyes, curling grey hair and a small, smiling mouth—were revealed. "Certainly, I'll have some tea, and I'm not at all insulted. Iander calls me *umma*—mother."

With a sigh of relief, Rosinda put the kettle on to boil. The shaman sat on a chair and pulled furs close around her. "Did you see my son?" she asked after a moment.

Rosinda nodded. "He saw me taking you, but he was in the middle of a fight—or about to be—and I didn't think he could protect you. I didn't have a chance to explain, so I think he's angry with me."

The shaman smiled. "He won't stay angry when we return unharmed. That is—we are going back, aren't we?"

"Oh, yes. I have some things to gather here, and we'll stay the night just to be on the safe side, and then..." She didn't want to say they'd try the crystal and hope it worked. She didn't want to mention getting her memories back, in case that didn't work either. "And then we'll head back," she said with more assurance than she felt. What had her mother said? *With your memories intact it shouldn't be a problem, even if the crystal is not strong enough. There are other ways.* Of course, there hadn't been time to tell Rosinda what those ways might be.

She had to get her memories back. It had to work.

After they ate, Rosinda declared that she was taking advantage of the opportunity to take a shower and change her clothes. Jerrell said the same thing and left for his house with a promise to be back in an hour. Without bothering to explain herself, Filara went with him. Kerngold settled on a braided rug in the kitchen, and the shaman said she was perfectly happy to wander around the house looking at all the strange things in it. Rosinda locked the doors and went upstairs. She felt like she could stay in a hot shower forever.

This time she chose her clothes carefully, looking for things that would be inconspicuous, things she could layer for warmth. She slipped thick socks on her feet and planned to wear her sneakers tomorrow. When she dried her long hair, she braided it into one thick braid down her back, the way she'd been wearing it in Quigsel's mirror. It felt right. She went downstairs, feeling renewed.

Jerrell was back, and he'd obviously chosen his clothes in

the same way. His pack bulged more than ever, and he stifled a huge yawn. Rosinda caught it and yawned too. Their last sleep had been rudely interrupted, but when she went to sleep here, she planned to use Aunt Odder's crystal. When she woke, all her memories would return—if it worked. She wanted that, of course, but the thought made her nervous, too. She wasn't quite ready yet.

"Let's sit and talk a while," she said. She was curious about the shaman's trance-like state when Rosinda had found her.

They settled in the comfortable living room. "Were you soul-walking when I found you in the night?" she asked Driasch. "You were so deep asleep that I couldn't wake you, and you seemed to be having a nightmare."

The shaman nodded. "I was trying to find the prince," she said, "And I thought I had. But it didn't really make sense."

"What do you mean?"

"It had the right feel in one way, but not in another. I should explain. Soul-walking is like dreaming, but for a short time it's seeing through the eyes of the person whose soul you're 'borrowing.' I thought I'd found the prince, but then I realized it couldn't be. Instead, I'd found an animal, a troubled creature trying to squeeze in a nap under a little pine tree. But its mind was unusually active for an animal. I remember looking up at the moons and feeling a terrible loneliness. Then I lost that soul, and I drifted for a long time, dipping into this soul and that, searching for the right one. I never did find him, which worries me..." The shaman's voice trailed off.

Rosinda barely registered the last few things she'd said, however. The shaman's words had thrust her back into her dream from the night before. It was as if she'd been describing Rosinda's experience!

"Driasch," she asked hesitantly, "Do Kelta have the soul-walking magic?"

"Not that I've ever heard," she said, shaking her head. "That's shaman magic. Why?"

Rosinda pressed her lips together, not sure if she should tell the old woman or not. "You just described the dream I had last night," she said, "And I must have been dreaming it just about the same time you were."

"That's very strange," the wizened shaman said. She regarded Rosinda with narrowed eyes, stroking her chin in thought. "Hmmm. You read the bones, too. Have you ever done anything else outside the realm of Kelta magic?"

Filara snorted. "She did transformation. And possibly telepathy, although that could be something else."

Driasch stared at the cat for a moment. It was the first time she'd heard the animal speak. To her credit, though, she didn't remark upon it, simply swallowed once and went on. "Rosinda, have you ever heard of a magister?"

Traveller ruffled his wings, as if the mere mention of the word made him agitated.

She sighed. "Not that I remember," she said. "But many of my memories, especially of Ysterad, are not...available to me." She almost added, *ask me again in the morning*, but she was too worried that the whole crystal thing wasn't going to work.

The shaman stared into the distance as she spoke. "There hasn't been a true magister in Ysterad in many, many years," she said. "Some folks don't even believe that they existed—or that they could again. A magister is someone who can access the powers of all the different types of magic users—Kelta earth magic, shaman scrying magic, necromancy, thaumaturgy, enchantment—all of it."

"You think Rosinda might be a magister?" Jerrell asked, leaning forward in his chair.

"No," Rosinda protested. "That's crazy." A million butterflies started fluttering in her stomach at the idea. She didn't want to be a magister. She wasn't even sure if she wanted to be a Kelta, although she didn't seem to have much choice at this point.

The shaman shrugged. "I don't know—it's just a thought. But it would explain some things." She sighed. "And it would be a great thing for Ysterad to have a magister again, in these troubled times."

"I'm not one," Rosinda said flatly.

"What's wrong with your memories?" the shaman asked, changing the subject.

"My aunt brought me here for protection when our family was attacked," Rosinda said, keeping the details vague. "I think she must have thought I'd worry less if I didn't know the truth."

"If she suspected—" the shaman said, but bit off the thought abruptly and yawned. "Well, I don't know about the rest of you, but I'm ready for that comfortable bed you promised me, girl, even if it is still the middle of the day here. My brain says it didn't get enough sleep last night." Rosinda yawned again, too. "Jerrell, do you want to bunk here on the couch?" He nodded and Rosinda closed all the blinds, darkening the room. "Driasch can have my bed, and I'll sleep in Aunt Odder's room." She led the shaman upstairs and saw her comfortably settled. Then she went into Aunt Odder's room, closed the curtains, and sat down on the side of the bed.

The room smelled like Aunt Odder, that same herb and garden and fresh-cut grass scent that the book held, although here the aroma of flowering lavender underlaid the others. Rosinda dug in her pocket and found the tiny, heart-shaped crystal that she'd transferred out of her other jeans. The words from Aunt Odder's letter rose starkly in her mind: *this is a potentially dangerous course of action.* However, her mother had said it should be safer outside Ysterad.

Feeling a bit silly, Rosinda tucked the tiny crystal into her ear and lay down. The pounding of her heart seemed intensified, and she wondered how she would ever manage to fall asleep. It was still quite light in the room, even with the curtains closed. Her mind skipped from thought to thought like a Ping-Pong ball. In the distance, a dog barked a few times then fell silent. Would she be able to get them all back to Ysterad? She suddenly wondered what day it was here. Time seemed to run at a different pace—it was never the same time of day when they crossed from one world to the other. She wondered if Jerrell had thought to check on that. Was he actually the prince, regardless of the arguments against the possibility? It would still explain why her charm had not seemed to work...

•••

When she woke, it was fully dark in the bedroom. She had a long moment of disorientation, not sure where she was. Then the scent of lavender tickled her nostrils and she remembered. She was in Aunt Odder's room. The glowing red numerals on the bedside clock read 2:27 a.m. The house lay in silence.

Rosinda rolled over, and something small moved in her ear and fell out, down into the bundle of bedclothes. The crystal. Rosinda sat up, adrenaline suddenly pricking her arms and legs. She should remember now. Had she slept long enough?

Tentatively, she probed her mind. Her mother—yes, there were more scenes of her mother there now, in familiar surroundings that Rosinda recognized as their house in Ysterad. Hot tears welled up in her eyes, and she felt weak with relief. Her father was there, too, and Aunt Odder—of *course* she was the King's Kelta, how could Rosinda ever have forgotten about that? That was the feeling as each memory leapt to the forefront. *How could I forget that?* She felt angry with herself and angry with Aunt Odder. With an effort, she let those emotions slip away. It was just good to be back.

Ysterad returned to her with gleaming clarity—even places she hadn't visited, only seen pictures of. It was all there like a geographical photo album just waiting for her to thumb through it. The ice-covered mountains of Nordas, where the dwarf-like Nordans toiled in their mines and ice caves. The busy, bustling towns of the Blood Clans, who traded anything and everything. The verdant Seafolk, a jewel set between the Duroc Ocean and the Burning Sea. It all came back with an almost overwhelming clarity. Even being in Ysterad had not given her such a feeling of being *home*.

Now, the magic. She had to go through that in her head, familiarize herself with what she could and couldn't do. Maybe there would be some answers about her apparent abilities, the ones that seemed to get Filara in such a tizzy. Mentally, she reached—

There was nothing there.

Rosinda blinked. She pulled the covers up around her again. The cool air, or possibly fear, raised goosebumps on her skin. She recalled the training she'd seen herself receiving in the images in Quigsel's mirror.

No. The memory of watching it at Quigsel's house was intact, but there was no memory of actually having done it. The panicky feeling rose again in Rosinda's chest. *Something's gone wrong.* She felt around in the tangled sheets and blankets until she found the heart-shaped crystal. Maybe she needed to replace it and go back to sleep? Maybe it just needed more time to complete its task?

She held it up to the sliver of moonlight that crept in through the curtains and realized it had turned blackened and dull. Its magic was spent. For a moment she couldn't breathe, and her stomach churned.

Her mother's words came to her. *Take your sword with you to the fairy ring. Do it after you have your memories back, and you'll know what to do.* Maybe her mother understood the process better. Maybe everything would be unlocked at that magical spot. A slim hope, but Rosinda grasped at it and held on.

She slid out of bed and slipped her clothes on, shivering in the chilly darkness. No sound came from anyone else in the house, as she tiptoed down the stairs, but Kerngold had stretched himself out on the kitchen floor near the doorway and raised his head when she tried to sneak past.

You're not going anywhere alone, I hope.

"You can come with me, if you want," she whispered. "I'm going to the fairy ring."

The wolf didn't question, just got to his feet and stretched. Rosinda collected an empty preserve jar from under the sink and tucked it into the pocket of her sweater, picked up her sword where it stood next to the door, and let them out into the night, carefully locking the door behind them.

Her horse whickered from where Jerrell had tied it next to the garden, and Rosinda gave it an absent pat on the nose as they passed. It was a bit of a walk to the fairy ring but not a good trail for riding. The woods were dense in some spots and hung low over the path. When they reached the edge of the woods, she glanced up into the sky, searching for the Raven's Moon. She felt silly when only Earth's single moon peered down at her. This travelling back and forth between worlds could be confusing at times.

Then they were in the woods, walking briskly, Kerngold keeping comfortable step beside her on his quiet, padded feet. Rosinda tried to settle her mind, concentrating only on the trail, the almost silent forest, the comforting weight of her sword and the presence of the wolf beside her. She found it surprisingly easy. There was something very *right* about being here.

In a surprisingly short time the path opened up into the clearing that she recognized—only days ago she'd been here with Traveller and Jerrell and Filara, trying to keep up with a breakneck course of events that didn't make any sense.

Rosinda half-smiled. She wasn't sure they made any better sense now.

She moved to the center of the fairy ring and took the glass jar from her pocket. Carefully, with the sharp tip of her sword, she dug up a chunk of grass and earth and filled the jar, screwing the cap back on tightly. When she straightened up, Kerngold sat on his haunches, calmly watching her.

What's that for, again?

Rosinda grinned. "I have no idea, but at this point I think it's wise to do whatever people I trust tell me to do," she said. She tucked the jar back into her pocket and stood with the sword hanging easily from her hand, glancing around the clearing. "However, I still don't know what I'm supposed to do next."

Kerngold shook his body like a wet dog. *Maybe you need to just close your eyes and see what comes to you,* he suggested.

Rosinda pursed her lips. "That sounds kind of lame."

Don't you trust me? he teased.

"Okay, then." She obediently closed her eyes and tried to relax her tense shoulders. With an effort, she cleared her mind of all the thoughts and worries that tried to crowd in, and concentrated on simple things. The heavy balance of the sword in her hand. The feel of the ground under her feet. The cool night air on her face. When a flow of power from the earth began to prickle her skin, she was surprised, but forced herself calm. It felt the same as when she'd drawn power for the charm in Aunt Odder's book, the one to call the prince.

This time, though, she wasn't actively trying to do this— it was happening on its own. And this power didn't have the same...*taste.* That was the only way she could explain it, although even to her it sounded strange. It felt Kelton, in a way, but not quite the same. It was old, as old as Kelta magic, but it hadn't originated here; someone had carried it on a long and dangerous journey to bring it from another place.

Her recent magical failures and mistakes tried to push their way into her mind, but she ignored them, bringing her attention back to the feel of the power. Now it seemed familiar, not frightening or strange.

Rosinda?

Kerngold's voice seemed to come from far away. She didn't want to open her eyes and answer him. The power coursed through her, warming her, erasing the night's chill.

Rosinda!

Her eyes flew open as she registered the concern in Kerngold's voice. Although she hadn't been aware of moving, now she held her arms stretched out before her, elbows locked and hands clasped around the sword's hilt. The blade pointed straight up to the blue-black sky. An aura of silvery light surrounded it and her, flickering like flames eager to devour fuel.

She remembered.

Thrust. Feint. Parry. In her mind, her body moved in the complex ballet of attack and block and defend, assessing risks and reading when to take chances. The memories flowed through her like a wave, replacing what was lost, making her whole again.

ROSINDA!

She whirled around this time, broken out of her reverie by the panic in Kerngold's voice. She saw a flash of brown and silver fur, and heard a female voice that she didn't recognize. Something struck her back. She fell to her knees and winced in pain as the sword hilt crushed her fingers against the ground.

CHAPTER TWENTY-THREE

Rosinda's reflexes kicked in. Her new memories surged. She rolled aside, still gripping the sword hilt. In seconds, she was back on her feet.

A woman she didn't recognize struggled to dislodge Kerngold's teeth from her calf. She was tall, with flashing eyes and dark red hair. She looked Kelton to Rosinda, but that wasn't what drew her attention. She sliced down at Kerngold with a short, curved blade.

Instinctively, Rosinda growled and lunged at the woman. Her vision clouded with a crimson fog of anger; her sword was an extension of her own arm. One thought sang in her mind. *Protect Kerngold. Protect the wolf.*

Kerngold yelped and tumbled sideways, struck by the woman's blade. Rosinda attacked, the tip of her sword flicking past the woman's blade and biting into her arm. With a snarl, the woman pulled her attention away from the wolf and turned toward Rosinda, swinging the flat of her sword at Rosinda's head.

She doesn't want to kill me, Rosinda realized. *She just wants to disable me. Knock me out.* She parried the blade easily and tucked the knowledge away. That would make things easier for her. Rosinda realized with cold detachment that she could easily kill this woman if she tried again to harm Kerngold. The thought should have been frightening, but with the red cloud in her eyes, it was as if this was happening to someone else. Someone cold, and strong, and purposeful.

Kerngold struggled to his feet, and Rosinda lunged at the woman again, their blades clanging in the still night air. The woman was capable, but her fighting was blunt and predictable, without style. She telegraphed every move with her body before she made it. Rosinda had no trouble keeping her at bay. In fact, she thought the woman was tiring.

"Stand down," Rosinda said in her most commanding voice. "You are no match for a trained Kelta. I do not wish to shed more blood."

"Arrogant...little...witch," the woman growled, and attacked more wildly.

Rosinda easily avoided the blade and spun around. A backhanded thrust sliced through the woman's loose breeches and into the flesh beneath. She grunted in pain, and Rosinda was surprised to feel nothing. Whatever she did in the protection of Kerngold, she would neither hesitate nor regret.

The woman suddenly stepped back out of range of Rosinda's blade, and although she stood ready to defend herself, she stopped attacking. "The Lady of The Forest bade me fetch you, young Kelta" she said, obviously annoyed. "I doubt she knew what that entailed. Morrigan may punish me for failing, but I don't think she's ready to kill me, yet. I sense you have no qualms in that area." She pulled a cord that hung around her neck, drawing from inside her shirt a crystal much like Rosinda's own bloodbound stone, though a light amber in color. She grinned and backed away, out of the fairy ring. "We'll meet again in Ysterad. Things might go differently then."

Kerngold barked and made a leap for the woman, but she grasped the crystal that hung around her neck, muttered a few words that Rosinda didn't quite catch, and disappeared. The wolf landed in the spot where the woman had stood only a heartbeat before.

Why didn't you try to stop her?

Rosinda didn't answer for a moment. The red fog silently faded and her vision cleared. She felt overwhelmed—her arms and legs trembled. She let herself sink to sit on the dew-wet grass, not caring that her jeans soaked up the moisture. She stared at the wolf. "I—I didn't realize," she said slowly, but she wasn't really answering him.

We could have tried to find out who sent her, and why, Kerngold said.

"She said the Lady of the Forest," Rosinda said absently, "Morrigan. That must be the name of the forest goddess Driasch saw in the tellbones." Rosinda wasn't focused on the woman, or the goddess she served, though. She stared at the wolf with eyes that suddenly knew exactly what they saw. What they'd been looking at without really *seeing* ever since the night she'd worked Aunt Odder's charm for calling the lost. The one person she was bound to defend and protect no matter what— even if, at the moment, he did inexplicably look like a wolf and seem to have no recollection of his true identity.

Prince Sovann.

Rosinda, what's wrong? Kerngold padded closer, putting his muzzle close to her face, staring into her eyes.

Rosinda shook herself and blinked. She didn't think the wolf could read all of her thoughts at will, but she didn't want to take any chances just now. She had to consider this more before she could share her suspicions.

"We should get back," she said suddenly. She patted her pocket to make certain that the bottle of soil was still intact, gripped her sword hilt, and turned back toward the house.

Are you sure you're finished here now? the wolf asked.

Rosinda nodded, walking. "I think so. Now I just want to get back and make sure the others are still safe."

Kerngold bounded up beside her and shot her a sideways glance. *All your skills are restored?*

She flashed him a quick grin. "It felt like it, when I was fighting that woman."

And your memories?

Rosinda nodded, then frowned. "Yes, except...the magic. That part of my mind still seems pretty blank, except for the things that have seemed to just happen on their own, or when I had instructions to follow."

Perhaps when you return this time to Ysterad. You will have gone full circle then.

Rosinda shrugged. "Maybe. I'll just have to wait and see."

The house lay quiet and sleepy when they returned, but Rosinda was in no mood to go back to bed. She made another pot of tea and sat quietly in the kitchen, sipping it and thinking. Kerngold dozed at her feet. She looked down at the sleeping wolf and considered the revelation that had come to her in the forest.

She could see it clearly now, that he was the missing prince. It all made sense. He had indeed heard her call when she cast the spell according to Aunt Odder's instructions. It had taken him a few days to find her, but he'd come in response to the spell. He'd been safe all this time because no one would think to look for the prince in the guise of an animal. Her blood oath explained the fierce protectiveness she felt toward him. Even in her dreams!

As she drained her cup and the first hint of dawn played on the curtains, Rosinda considered her two newest problems. The first was how and when to tell Kerngold that he was Prince Sovann. The second was how to turn him back into a human. She felt quite certain that he would not be welcome to the throne at Sangera while he was still a wolf.

CHAPTER TWENTY-FOUR

"Do you think it's safe to go back now?" Rosinda asked Driasch as the shaman finished off tea and a thickly buttered roll for breakfast.

The tiny woman shrugged. "If I had my scrying bones, I might be able to tell. But without them..."

Rosinda grinned and dipped her hand into her pocket. The bones were still there, where she'd dropped them after scooping them up with the shaman last night. She scattered them around the old woman's teacup with a flourish. "Ta-da!"

The bones didn't lie still where she dropped them, however. They twitched and wriggled for a moment as if they were alive then settled on the tablecloth. Driasch gasped.

"I'm sorry," Rosinda said quickly. "I didn't mean to—"

Driasch stopped her with a raised hand. The shaman leaned forward, scanning the shapes of the small bones on the table. Then she leaned back and eyed Rosinda keenly.

"It's all right, girl. I know you meant no harm, but in future keep in mind that a shaman's scrying bones are...a personal possession. If you want to cast futures with them, you'll have to collect your own set."

Rosinda felt her cheeks burn, even though the old woman's words were kind. She started to stammer another apology, but Driasch pointed at the bones.

"Have a look. Can you read what you've cast?"

With curiosity overcoming her embarrassment, Rosinda leaned over to look closely at the tiny scattered bones. Clear shapes were evident, and their meanings obvious.

"The battle is over..." she said slowly. "The attackers were driven back." She gulped and looked up at the old woman. "Many were injured. I think...I think Iander was among them."

The shaman's mouth tightened, but she merely nodded her head. "I was afraid of that. I would like to go back as quickly as possible, Rosinda. I have healing skills that my people need."

"Yes, of course." Rosinda jumped up from the table and went into the living room. Jerrell stirred, and she put a hand lightly on his shoulder. He opened his eyes.

"Time to go," she said. "If you're coming back. You really don't have to, you know."

He grinned. "I thought I was the prince in disguise," he said. "If I am, I have to go back, don't I?"

Rosinda shook her head. "I think you were right about that. You're not the prince." She smiled. "Are you disappointed?"

Jerrell pushed himself up on his elbows and snorted. "Not at all. I never thought I was. But what convinced you?"

She looked around. There was no one else in the room. Even so, she bent down and whispered to him. "I think I know who the prince really is. But don't say anything yet."

Jerrell's eyes grew round. "But you're going to tell me who it is, aren't you?"

Rosinda bit her lip. "I will," she said slowly, "but not yet. I have to figure some other things out first." Jerrell looked disappointed and she added, "It's for safety—not just the prince's, but yours too."

He nodded. "Okay, if you say so. But don't try to stop me from coming back with you."

"Your uncle is still away?"

"Yes, but I called him last night just to check in. I said I was going camping with friends for a few days so he wouldn't worry if he didn't hear from me."

Rosinda had to smile. Everything Jerrell did—it seemed so easy for him. Suddenly curious, she asked, "Jerrell? What made you come after me that first day?"

He glanced away, studying the intricate, swirling patterns on the quilt he'd slept under, then looked up at her again, his eyes thoughtful. "I don't know—well, I suppose I do. I always thought...you know...that we had a lot in common. Not just being outsiders at school. I knew you liked to read, and that you didn't go in for a lot of the stuff other girls seemed to like. I thought we'd get along." He grinned at her lopsidedly. "If I could ever get up the nerve to talk to you, which I couldn't."

Rosinda sat down on the couch beside him, and he scooted his legs to the side to make room for her. "I didn't know that," she said simply. "I'm sorry."

He shrugged. "It doesn't matter. I know now why you never noticed. You kind of had a lot on your mind."

She smiled. "I guess I did."

"Anyway, I think somehow I got the feeling that—I don't know, that someone should be looking out for you." Jerrell ran a hand through his hair, leaving unruly spikes behind. "That's why I always let you get ahead of me walking home from school. So that I'd know you got home safely."

"Guess it would have been nice of me to slow down sometime so we could walk together," Rosinda said ruefully.

Jerrell smiled. "Well, it worked out anyway. When I saw you that day, I just knew I had to go after you. And I'm glad I did."

"Me too," Rosinda said, and she realized how much she meant it. She didn't want to sound too mushy, though. She grinned. "You did turn out to be handy to have around. Once or twice."

"Haha. You're welcome."

Rosinda sighed. "Seriously, though, are you sure about coming back to Ysterad? This is your chance to get out of it. I'll understand if you want your life back now."

"Oh, no," he said, scrambling out from under the quilt and getting to his feet. "I have to see how this turns out. And I might come in handy again yet, you know."

She shook her head and stood, too. "Just as stubborn as ever. Well, let's get going, then. We have to find Aunt Odder and get her free. I don't know what else we can do without her."

"You can't do that, Rosinda," said a voice from behind her.

Rosinda turned to see the tiny shaman standing in the doorway, her brows drawn together in a frown.

"I meant after we take you back to see to Iander," Rosinda said.

"It isn't that," Driasch said. "I just cast the tellbones. Only a magister can defeat the powers that threaten Ysterad now. And that magister is you."

•••

Rosinda didn't waste time arguing with the elderly shaman, but she firmly believed that if there was a magister loose somewhere in Ysterad, it was someone else. The whole idea seemed ridiculous. So what if she'd been able to do random bits of magic? Who knew what else Aunt Odder might have done besides blocking off her memories? Maybe her abilities had something to do with that.

If anyone were a magister, Rosinda thought, it must be Aunt Odder. A little voice in the back of her head whispered that if that were true, Aunt Odder probably couldn't have been kidnapped in the first place. Rosinda ignored that and concentrated on preparations to make the trip back across to Ysterad.

They gathered in the back yard near Rosinda's horse, and Rosinda locked the door again. This time the key seemed to click with a horrible hollow sound, and Rosinda felt as if she were locking the door on the life she'd had here with Aunt Odder. She put the key back in her pocket and turned resolutely to the others.

"Driasch, you should get up in the saddle," she said to the elderly shaman. "We don't know for sure what we'll find on the other side, and you'll be safest up there. And you can get away quickly if you need to."

The shaman looked as if she might argue for a moment, then shrugged and clambered up into the saddle with Jerrell's help.

"Gather close, everyone," Rosinda said. She picked Filara up and tucked her under one arm. Traveller flapped in to perch on the cantle of the saddle behind Driasch, and Jerrell laid a hand lightly on Rosinda's shoulder. Kerngold padded over and leaned against her leg. She pulled the bloodbound crystal from inside her sweater and held it tightly, taking a deep breath and envisioning the Nangharen camp in her mind. Then she said, "Rosinda Aletta Penyan. The Nanghar, Ysterad."

The crystal twisted against her palm and grew hot. Rosinda had to fight the urge to drop it. The world around them dimmed slowly, not tumbling into blackness as it had the other times she'd traveled across the Worlds' Edge.

It's not working. The crystal's not strong enough. She heard the shaman begin a low, barely audible chant, words that fizzled in Rosinda's brain but made no sense. Somehow she knew that the shaman was trying to help.

Her mother's words from the Crypt of a Thousand Voices came back to her. *With your memories intact, it shouldn't be a problem, even if the crystal is not strong enough. There are other ways.* But her memories were not intact! She hadn't recovered the magical knowledge that she needed. Frantically, Rosinda sifted through her brain again.

"Rosinda?" Jerrell asked hesitantly. His hand tightened on her shoulder. "This isn't the way I remember it."

"I know. I'm trying," she said. The crystal's heat was just bearable. The world around them consisted of a thick grey fog, too dense to see further than a foot or two away. Rosinda had no sense that they'd moved anywhere. The horse shifted its hooves and whickered uneasily.

Rosinda squeezed her eyes shut and tried to draw power from the earth to boost the crystal. The odd taste was there, but she felt energy trickle into her. Desperately, she brought the image of the Nanghar camp into her mind as vividly as she could, trying to invoke every detail. Beside her, on the horse, the shaman still chanted, and Rosinda felt her thoughts fall into the rhythm of the words. She recalled the smells of the campfires and animal pens, the sounds of the tent hides moving in the breeze, the feel of the hard-packed earth thudding under her feet.

Eyes still closed, she felt the world *shift*. The smells and sounds of the Nanghar camp were no longer only in her mind.

They had arrived back in Ysterad.

Rosinda opened her eyes and looked down at the bloodbound crystal in her hand. The intense heat faded quickly, and a spiderweb of dark lines now marred the emerald-green gemstone. She knew instinctively that it would not work again. She quickly dropped it inside her sweater before the others saw.

The sun climbed high overhead and the sound of running feet signaled a response to their arrival. Driasch held up a commanding hand as three Nangharen rounded the corner of a tent. They pulled up short when they recognized the tiny shaman.

Driasch spoke quickly to them in a low voice and moved to sidle off the horse at their hurried replies. "Rosinda, come with me, please. The attackers are gone, but there are wounded to attend."

"Iander?" Rosinda asked, remembering the signs she had read in the shaman's tellbones.

The shaman nodded briefly as she scurried away, and Rosinda handed the reins of her horse to Jerrell and followed.

A large central tent, presumably used by the tribe for gatherings, now served as a sickroom. The floor held a dozen or more pallets where the wounded lay, some groaning, others forebodingly silent. Driasch moved quickly to kneel beside one of the silent ones.

"Help me," she said quietly to Rosinda.

Rosinda swallowed, her throat suddenly thick. Iander lay on the pallet, pale and unmoving except for the painfully slow rise and fall of his chest. A sudden terror gripped her. Could she help—or would she simply mess up again?

She hadn't even realized that Jerrell had followed them, but he put a hand on her shoulder and spoke quietly into her ear. "You healed Traveller when he needed it. Just get out your aunt's book and do the same as you did then. I know you can do it."

Rosinda nodded, unslung the backpack and pulled out Aunt Odder's book. Bits of blackened paper fluttered out when she opened the cover—the remains of Aunt Odder's letter. Rosinda stared at them for a moment. It seemed like so long since the night she'd started to read it. If only she'd been able to finish it! She might know so much more now. Tears pricked her eyes, but just then Iander stirred and moaned. Rosinda shook the tears away resolutely, putting the paper back inside the front cover. That would have to wait.

She knew now where to find *A Healing of Hidden Injuries*. Rosinda knelt beside the Nanghar warrior. Unfortunately, his injuries were horribly evident, and his already-pale skin now looked greyish. As she'd done before, she read the spell twice, fixing the words of invocation in her mind. Then she put a hand on the man's shoulder. His skin felt chill and damp, and she was acutely aware of his unsteady breathing. Now to call up the power.

She sent her mind searching the hard-packed Nangharen earth beneath them. Another "flavor," different from the Ways Under or the fairy ring back in Cape Breton. Still, the life-force was there, waiting for her call. She opened her mind to it, pulling it into herself to channel it into Iander, and recited the spell.

Like a wayward lightning strike, the power coursed through her and into the unconscious man. Iander's body arched and convulsed, the way Rosinda had seen people do on television when paramedics tried to restart their hearts with a defibrillator. Rosinda gasped and dropped the book, snatching her hand away from Iander's shoulder. Driasch cried out and fell back on her heels in a tangle of furs.

Rosinda's entire body trembled from the amount of power that had coursed through her. She felt bruised, her bones ached, and she drew a long, deep breath to try to calm her rapidly beating heart. *I've killed him!* she thought in horror. *There was too much power—I didn't know how to control it!* Rosinda looked fearfully over at the shaman as Jerrell helped her up. She didn't know what the old woman would do now.

Miraculously, she heard Iander's voice. "*Umma?*" he said, and his voice sounded strong, if bewildered. "Where did you come from? Are you all right?"

Driasch chuckled. "Am *I* all right? I'm not the one lying on a pallet on the floor!"

Iander sat up then, stretching his arms and twisting his back. "I...I was wounded..." he started, then caught sight of Rosinda. "You!" he growled. "What were you thinking—"

"Iander!" Driasch said in a low voice that was nevertheless commanding. "Mind how you speak to the young magister who may have saved my life. And just saved yours as well."

Rosinda shook her head. "I couldn't have—I didn't know what I was doing—"

"And yet you did," the shaman said with a smile. "Your powers are wild yet, that's all. You need to learn control." She glanced around at the other wounded warriors. "Now, do you think, with my help, you can do the same for these others?"

The image of Iander's convulsing body rose in Rosinda's mind, and she felt the blood drain from her face. "It's too dangerous," she whispered. "I don't know what might happen. Can't you heal them? You're a shaman."

Driasch leaned across Iander and placed a gnarled hand on

Rosinda's shoulder. "My powers are nothing compared to yours. Nothing. This time I'll help you, Rosinda. It won't be the same. You'll know what to expect, and you'll know how to handle it."

Someone across the room cried out suddenly in pain, and Rosinda felt her heart twist. How could she refuse to help if she had the ability?

Suddenly, there was another hand on her arm, and Jerrell whispered again. "You can do it, Rosinda, I know you can. You have to try." He squeezed her arm.

Their faith buoyed her up. Despite the frightening amount of power that had flowed through her body, Jerrell was right; she had to try. Not trusting herself to speak, she nodded to the shaman.

Driasch hovered over Rosinda as she knelt beside the next pallet and began to chant. The words sounded similar to the ones she'd used when Rosinda struggled to bring them across the Worlds' Edge. Jerrell was a comforting presence at her side. When Rosinda concentrated, she could control the amount of power that she drew from the pulsing force deep in the ground. She also improved at sensing where the injuries were, and directing the healing power to that spot in particular. A sword-slashed leg here; the next was a nasty stomach wound.

Rosinda lost track of time. Driasch had to tell her twice that they were finished before the words made sense to her. Her own body was one huge ache, and she could hardly keep her eyes open.

"Tired," she managed to say, but her voice sounded far away. She felt a strong arm help her to her feet, and turned to see Iander supporting her. Her legs felt light and weak.

"She's done too much," a voice snapped from near her feet. Filara, Rosinda realized. She wondered briefly where the cat and the other animals had been since they'd arrived back in Ysterad. "You've pushed her too far, *Durnstad*. She may well be a magister, but she's too young and inexperienced to channel that much power for so long."

Rosinda glanced up and saw the shaman purse her lips. "You may be right. I only thought—well, it's done. Iander, bring her to my tent. She'll sleep until suppertime at least."

Rosinda tried to take a step, but the Nanghar warrior swept her up easily and carried her out of the big tent before she could protest. It felt undignified, being carried like a baby, and yet it was so much easier than doing anything else. She had a brief impression of soft furs under her cheek as Iander lowered her onto Driasch's bed, and then fell into a deep, dreamless sleep.

CHAPTER TWENTY-FIVE

"You did *what?*" Sekhmet screamed.

Morrigan rolled her eyes, although she was careful not to let the Egyptian goddess see the expression. "The girl left Ysterad, so I sent my servant after her with instructions to bring the girl back if she could."

"Which, it turned out, she could not," Tyr said tersely.

Morrigan sighed. "No, it seems the young Kelta is more capable with her sword than we believed. My servant came back empty-handed."

Sekhmet sneered. "She gave up too easily."

"She tells me the girl would have killed her. With ease," Morrigan said.

"*I* would have killed her myself if she were my servant and failed so simple a task," the Egyptian goddess said.

"I don't care to waste my servants," Morrigan snapped. "They are in short enough supply as it is."

"You have a travelling crystal," Sekhmet said. It was not a question as much as an accusation.

Morrigan didn't bother to reply. Obviously she had one since her servant had used it. She sensed Tyr looking at her, but she didn't return his gaze.

Gradivus looked up from polishing his bronze shield. "The most important thing is to find out where the girl is now."

"Back in Ysterad," Morrigan replied. She'd felt the return of her other servant earlier, although he had not been in contact with her yet. That fact left her slightly unsettled, but she didn't mention it to the other gods. "If she was able to best my woman with a sword, then she has obviously regained much that she'd lost. I'm not so sure we can ignore her any longer."

"Surely a little girl can't be much of a threat," Tyr said.

Morrigan stared at him now. None of them seemed to understand why this was important. "This is no ordinary 'little girl.' She's the Prince's Kelta. We had some advantage while her memories were blocked, but now..."

"Does she know now where to find the prince?" Gradivus asked.

"I don't know."

"How much longer until the old Kelta reaches us?" Sekhmet asked. With her long, slender fingers, Sekhmet stroked the fur of one of her cats as her golden, cat-like eyes fixed far off in the distance.

"A few days," Tyr said with a shrug.

"Once she does, it is simple. We send a message to the young Kelta, telling her the old one is in our hands. She will have no choice but to come to us herself. When she does, we will have them both."

"I still think you underestimate her," Morrigan said.

"Then she can be your responsibility," Sekhmet rejoined with a smile that lifted the corners of her mouth but did not touch the rest of her face. "If you are so worried about her, you take care of her. If you need help, of course, you have only to ask."

The Egyptian goddess' mocking tone was not lost on Morrigan, but the Celtic goddess ignored it.

"If I need help, it will be the worse for all of us," she said. "And I will not hesitate to say, 'I told you so.'"

CHAPTER TWENTY-SIX

Filara woke Rosinda later. She didn't employ any of the usual methods cats use to wake someone—purring, pawing gently at the sleeper's face, rubbing along the sleeper's arm. She simply said, "Rosinda, I think it's time you got up, now. I have something for you."

Rosinda immediately woke, although it took her a moment to remember where she was. The shaman's tent held only dim light. She could just make out Filara's green eyes as the cat sat on the floor next to the pile of sleeping furs, intently watching Rosinda.

"What time is it?"

"Supper time, I believe. The Nangharen are preparing a meal in the meeting tent. You should probably eat, given your earlier exertions."

Rosinda remembered the blur of healing she'd performed with the shaman's help. "How are they—all the Nangharen warriors?"

"They're fine. You did a good job."

Rosinda pushed herself up on one elbow. "Did you say you had something for me?"

The cat nodded and gestured with a paw. Rosinda saw two small dead animals lying next to the sleeping furs.

"Eewww! What are they for?" she said, wrinkling her face and edging away from the small bodies.

Filara snorted. "You need your own tellbones, as Driasch said," she answered huffily. "I took the liberty of getting you some."

"But those aren't just bones," Rosinda protested. "They're still...still—"

The cat sighed. "Driasch will show you how to prepare them," she said. "What did you expect me to do, gnaw all the flesh off them first?"

"Argh! Stop it!" Rosinda cried, covering her ears. "I'll talk to Driasch about them, but you don't have to be so...descriptive." Grimacing, she gingerly picked up the creatures and wrapped them in a scrap of cloth. One was a mouse-like animal with a long snout, the other a small brown-feathered bird. *Sorry about this*, she said to them mentally. Aloud she said, "Um, thank you, Filara."

"Humph!" the cat said. "*That* sounded sincere. Come on, you'll miss supper."

Most of the tribe had already gathered in the large tent when they arrived. Rosinda spotted Driasch and Iander right away and made her way toward them. Jerrell already sat cross-legged on the floor, eating from a wooden bowl. The whole tent smelled delicious, and Rosinda's stomach growled. After receiving a quick hug from the shaman, she found a spot on the floor beside Jerrell and had soon cleaned her own bowl.

Driasch motioned Rosinda over to sit beside her. "You did well today, young Kelta," she said with a smile. "Thanks to you, not one of the tribe was lost."

"Who attacked you? And why?" Rosinda asked.

The shaman's lips tightened into a thin, hard line for a moment. "Nanghareem, our cousins from the east," she said slowly. "Long ago, a rift split our people, but for the most part, we've left each other alone. But lately..."

"Lately?" Rosinda prompted when the shaman did not continue.

The elderly woman sighed. "There have been rumors that the Nanghareem follow a new god, a god of war and the sea."

"One of the gods we saw in your tellbones?"

Driasch nodded. "I think so. There's been so much unrest in Ysterad since the old king was killed and the prince disappeared. And it's getting worse."

Rosinda felt her heart thump excitedly in her chest. Maybe what she knew...or suspected...about Kerngold could solve everything. "If the prince were found and restored to the throne, what do you think would happen?"

The shaman sighed and looked off into the distance for a moment. "I think," she said finally, "There would be a war anyway. It's been such a long time, and there are many who don't want the prince returned. They've gotten a taste of power in his absence, and they won't want to give it up easily. And these war gods—they won't go away without a fight, now that they have a foothold here."

"So even if the Prince were back in Sangera, it wouldn't help?" Rosinda's elation drained away.

"Oh, it would help," Driasch said. "It would make the problem of choosing sides a lot easier for many people. If the prince were here, they'd support him. I just don't think it would make all the problems disappear."

Rosinda sat quietly for a moment. One of the elders had begun to tell a story at the other end of the tent, and most of the tribe had gathered around to hear. Even Jerrell had scooted closer and wasn't paying any attention to Rosinda and Driasch's conversation.

In a low voice, Rosinda asked the shaman, "Do you know anything about transformation magic?"

The shaman looked curiously at her. "No. Transformation of inanimate objects is enchanter magic. Shapeshifting for living things is related, but that's Kelta magic. They're not within my realm. Why?"

Rosinda felt tears prick her eyes, and the words came out in a rush. "I think...I might know where the prince is, but I need magic to be sure...and my memories didn't all come back—not the magic. I think Aunt Odder left instructions for me in her letter, but it got all burned up before I could read it all—"

"Letter?" Driasch looked interested.

Rosinda nodded and explained, "It only half-burned, really, but the terrible thing was, I didn't have a chance to read it all first."

"Do you still have a piece of the letter?"

"What's left of it is in my book—I mean, Aunt Odder's book."

Driasch tapped a gnarled finger against her lips. "I might be able to do something with that."

"What do you mean?"

"Bring it over to my tent, and we'll see," Driasch said mysteriously.

They left the others listening to the storyteller and made their way to Driasch's tent. Before she took out the letter, Rosinda showed the shaman the "presents" that Filara had brought her. The shaman laughed.

"We'll fix those up for you, no trouble," she said. "I won't even make you skin them, although you'll have to do a few minor things to bind the bones to your second sight."

"Er, okay," Rosinda said uncertainly. She wondered if she really needed or wanted her own tellbones in the first place. But that was another question for later. She pulled the book out of her pack and fished out the remains of Aunt Odder's letter.

Driasch read over the legible parts carefully and nodded. "I think you're in luck," she told Rosinda. "I should be able to see what's missing."

"See it?"

The shaman nodded. "It's a little like the soul-walking...a related skill, at least. You'll have to be ready to copy down what I tell you, though, because I can do it only once. When I can see the letter in my mind, I'll read it out loud to you."

Rosinda took out her journal and pen, glad that she'd kept

them in her pack when she'd repacked it. "Try to go slowly, okay? I'm not a fast writer."

Driasch smiled. "I'll see what I can do." She settled herself on her sleeping furs and threw a few pinches of herbs into the low fire that still burned in front of her. The tent filled with a lovely, smoky-sweet scent that made Rosinda want to sneeze until she got used to it.

The shaman gathered all the pieces of the letter in her cupped palms and closed her eyes, chanting in a low voice. Rosinda held her pen ready. The familiar words of the first part of the letter came from the shaman's lips, although her eyes remained closed. Rosinda didn't bother writing those parts down. She'd read them over so many times she knew them by heart. However, when the shaman reached the part about contacting the prince, Rosinda began to scribble the words down as the shaman spoke them.

Use the amethyst for this; it is a fragment of a stone that is bloodbound to his family. You must take it in your left hand at dawn and face the rising sun, press it over your heart and recite the charm for calling the lost. It is in my book, but I will also write it here for you;

Cordhan bel, cordhan treict

Althos creign al talthos mein

When he finds you (and it may take some time, depending on where you are and where he is) he will have to swallow the amethyst stone to remove the enchantment that has kept him safe.

Rosinda gasped aloud when the shaman spoke these words. The amethyst! Did she still have it? She searched her memory, heart pounding, even as she kept writing. What had she done with the tiny amethyst when she'd finished performing the charm, away back on that hilltop outside Genia? She couldn't remember. She put the thought aside, concentrating on the shaman as she recited the words of the letter.

Once this is accomplished, he must travel to the castle at Sangera, in the province of the Blood Clans. The way will be dangerous, as there will be those who will oppose his return. Safely in Sangera, his welcome should be assured by those who remain loyal to the throne, and the Tell of Ysterad will respond to his touch, proving that he is the true prince.

I hope that you have assistance in this venture, my dearest Rosinda, and that perhaps your parents are with you. Your mother will have felt your arrival in Ysterad, and will no doubt be attempting to find you from that moment onward. If you are in their company, then much of what I've told you here won't be necessary. I am writing this in case you find yourself thrust into peril on your own, which circumstance I would most deeply regret, for it will mean I have failed you.

In any case, you must be wary of the forces that seek to turn Ysterad to their own ends. Ysterad and its people are vulnerable with the throne empty, but with Prince Sovann so young, I did not trust those who might seek to stand as his regent. The situation had no good solution until Prince Sovann reached an age fit to govern. I hope that time has arrived.

One more thing that it is important for you to know: there is more to be wary of than mere mortals. I have sensed dark and powerful magics gathering in Ysterad, powers that have not yet reached their full potential. I am unsure what this means, but surely it is not good for Ysterad or any who live there. I hesitate to guess the extent of this danger. It would not surprise me to discover that it stems from a being or beings of enormous power. You must do everything you can to help Ysterad, but please be careful. I only wish I were there to help you. And I hope you will understand that everything I have done, I have done in the hope of keeping those I love safe.

Your loving
Aunt Oddeline

The shaman fell silent and sat with her eyes closed for a moment more. Rosinda read over the entire letter quickly, making sure she could read her own hastily scribbled writing. When she glanced up, Driasch was looking at her.

"Did it work?" the shaman asked quietly.

Rosinda nodded and burst into tears. It was suddenly too much, reading her aunt's words. They held so much love, yet also imposed such a heavy burden. The old shaman's arms went around Rosinda in a tight hug. For the first time since she had met Traveller on the road home from school, Rosinda simply let herself cry.

After a few moments, though, she gulped a deep breath and wiped at her eyes. "I'm all right," she managed to whisper.

"You will be," Driasch said kindly. "Now I'm going to make us a hot drink, and we can sort out what you have to do next."

While the old woman measured herbs and water into a pot, Rosinda glanced down at the letter. She had to remember what she'd done with the amethyst. Rosinda thought back to that morning when she'd cast the charm, the sun just coming up on the horizon. She'd clasped the stone, put her hand over her heart and spoken the words...but then what? Jerrell had woken up and asked her what she was doing...she was sure she hadn't thrown the stone away. It seemed most natural that she would have just put it back in her jeans pocket. She'd changed to clean jeans back in Cape Breton, but she remembered switching the Ysterad money to the new ones, so hopefully...

Rosinda closed her eyes, and reached into her jeans pocket. Yes! Her fingers met the tiny, smooth shape of the amethyst, down in the very corner of the cloth, past the crumpled Ysterad notes. The relief lifted some of the burden that had felt so heavy just moments before.

"So it worked. The question now is, did it help?" Driasch asked.

"I think so," Rosinda said. "But if I'm wrong about something...it's going to be embarrassing, or worse."

"None of us are right all the time, my girl," the shaman said briskly. "Sometimes we just have to trust ourselves and hope for the best. What's your worry?"

Rosinda hesitated only a moment before telling the shaman. "You know Kerngold, the wolf who was with us in Cape Breton?"

"How could I forget him? First wolf I ever saw that would cheerfully travel with humans. Or cats," she added thoughtfully.

Rosinda straightened her back and swallowed. "Well, I think...I think he's Prince Sovann. In disguise."

The elderly shaman's eyebrows rose so high Rosinda thought they might fly off her head. After a moment she said, "What makes you think so?"

Quickly Rosinda told her about how the prince had never appeared in response to her charm, but Kerngold had turned up soon after. How her worst nightmares lately had all involved something bad happening to the wolf. About the fierce protectiveness she felt toward him—how sure she'd felt when they fought Morrigan's warrior. "And...we can communicate mentally," she added. She hadn't been anxious to tell the shaman about that because—

"Mind reading? That's telepathy, Rosinda. The realm of the thaumats," Driasch said excitedly. "You see? More proof that you're the magister!"

Exactly why I didn't want to mention that little detail, Rosinda thought. "I don't think it's me doing it," she protested. "I think it's him—he's the only one I can communicate with that way, and he started it when we first met. I seem to be the only one he can talk to. It seems more likely that it's linked to Aunt Odder's spell."

Driasch rolled her eyes but said nothing more about Magistera. "So...disguise the prince as a wolf," she mused. "It's clever, I'll say that. Do you think he knows?"

Rosinda shook her head. "No, I'm sure he doesn't."

"So how are you going to find out for sure?"

Rosinda told the shaman about the instructions in Aunt Odder's letter. Driasch had no recollection of what she'd read but assured Rosinda that the spell usually worked that way.

When Rosinda was finished, Driasch nodded. "Well, there's only one way to tell for sure—get him to swallow the amethyst. If you're wrong, we'll only have to wait a few days before it... reappears, and we can try it on someone else."

Rosinda wrinkled her nose at the thought. "I don't think it will come to that. I feel so certain. But if it's not him, I won't know what to do next."

"Well, when do you want to try it?"

Rosinda stifled a yawn. "In the morning. I'm just too tired to go through it all again tonight. And if it works—"

"There'll be a lot of other things to think about," the shaman finished, nodding. "I think you're right. Let's do something simple tonight, like preparing your tellbones."

Rosinda felt like grimacing again, but she didn't want to hurt the old shaman's feelings. "Okay," she agreed, "but I'm expecting you to do most of the work."

They both laughed at that and turned their attention to the task.

•••

Rosinda woke early the next morning, rested but nervous. The air felt charged, as if everything in the world held its breath, waiting to see what would happen next. Rosinda was just as curious.

She woke Jerrell with a gentle shake. "Driasch invited us to have breakfast with her."

"Okay," he said groggily.

Breakfast was herb tea, sweet cakes, and a fruit that tasted like a cross between blackberries and cherries. Rosinda remembered having them occasionally as a child, although they grew only on the highest points of the Nanghar steppes and were a delicacy in the rest of Ysterad.

Traveller seemed agitated while the others ate breakfast. "Rosinda," he finally said, when she asked for more tea, "we have to get moving again today. Your aunt is getting further and further away."

"I know," Rosinda said, her mouth suddenly dry despite the tea. "But there's something else we have to do first."

The others looked up in surprise, but she ignored them. "Kerngold, this is about you. Would you come here?"

The wolf rose and padded over to her without question.

She took his muzzle in her hands and looked into his eyes. "If I asked you to do a simple thing for me without asking any questions, would you do it? Even if it seemed rather strange?"

His reply came immediately. *Absolutely.*

Rosinda fetched a deep breath and dug the small amethyst out of her pocket. "Would you swallow this for me?"

Filara made a tiny sound in her throat. Rosinda ignored her.

The wolf chuckled in her mind. *More magic? This is getting to be a habit with you.*

Rosinda smiled. "I think it already was a habit. Just one I'd forgotten about."

The wolf's soft tongue licked her hand, and the amethyst was gone. He swallowed once, and Rosinda held her breath.

It didn't take long. A strange look came into Kerngold's eyes. With a sudden sigh, he lay down on the soft dirt floor of the tent.

Rosinda? His voice sounded confused.

A sudden pang of fear lanced through her. *What if I'm wrong? What if it's dangerous for someone who isn't the prince to swallow the stone?* She put a hand on his head. "Are you in pain?"

No, he said. *I just feel so...strange...*

Rosinda swallowed hard. A sick feeling rose in her throat at the thought that she might have hurt Kerngold without meaning to.

The air around the wolf shimmered like heat waves on a sunny day. His fur began to *slide* into something smoother and lighter in color. Driasch gave a sudden, startled cry, echoed by Traveller. Rosinda watched the wolf's face, fascinated. His muzzle shortened and disappeared, his eyes changed shape, and his ears shrank and slid down the sides of his head. Where fur had been a moment before, he now had a shaggy mane of dark hair.

The rest of his body slid through the same kinds of changes, too, and he jerkily pushed himself to a sitting position with hands that had only a moment before been paws. The shimmer intensified for the space of a heartbeat and then disappeared altogether. Kerngold was gone.

In his place sat a young man, quite naked, staring into Rosinda's eyes with a look of enormous confusion.

CHAPTER TWENTY-SEVEN

Driasch moved quickly to wrap a blanket around the young man. He absently thanked her, but his eyes never left Rosinda's face.

"I know you," he said slowly, the hint of a frown puckering his brow.

Rosinda couldn't speak for a moment. Seeing Prince Sovann's face in person had unlocked all of her memories of him. Training, court attendances, pranks they'd played together growing up, all washed through her mind in a flood. She realized that in the time before all this had happened, he'd been her best friend—like a brother. It seemed terrible, unthinkable, that she could have forgotten him.

Finally, she nodded. "I know you, too," she said quietly. She was afraid to say too much, too soon, recalling the overwhelming sensations of her own memories returning. It seemed safer to let him ease into it.

He flashed a sudden smile, and his eyes lit up. "Rosinda!"

"Sovann," she replied.

He seemed to become suddenly aware of his surroundings and glanced around the tent. "I hope *you* know what's going on here," he said. Apart from being confused, though, he didn't seem worried.

He thinks he must be safe, because he's with me, Rosinda realized. Considering how unsure she felt about everything herself, it was a sobering thought.

"How much do you remember?" she asked tentatively.

He frowned. "My brain feels...foggy...like I've been asleep and dreaming for a long time," he said. "Lady Oddeline was there, and we were running from some kind of commotion—the castle! The castle was attacked," he almost shouted. Sudden pain bloomed in his eyes. "My parents—"

Rosinda felt tears well up. She knew what he had remembered. However hard it had been for her when the memory returned, it must be a thousand times worse for him. He looked around at the others again, uneasily this time. She put a hand on his arm, to steady him.

"Rosinda, who are these people, and where are we?"

"They're friends, Vann." The nickname rolled off her tongue so easily it surprised her. "Better friends than you can imagine. Driasch, would you make some fresh tea? I'll tell you everything I know, but it's a long story. We'd all better get comfortable."

●●●

At least an hour passed in the small tent. Jerrell and Driasch between them came up with a set of clothes for the prince. Everyone had been introduced, including Filara and Traveller. Prince Sovann gravely gave his thanks to each one. Rosinda had, with the help of reminders and interjections from the others, told him all that she knew.

She had a bad moment during the introductions when she looked for Kerngold, then realized suddenly how silly that was. Although her relief at having Sovann back was huge, the loss of the wolf sat like a cold stone in her chest. It was as if Kerngold had died. Although she had seen with her own eyes that his body had actually been Sovann's body in disguise, he'd had his own personality, his own spirit—or so it had seemed. It was very confusing, and the ache in Rosinda's heart did not subside.

Sovann himself had only vague memories of being a wolf. "It's like I was dreaming all that time," he said again. "You say two years have passed since...since then?" He took a deep breath and looked at Rosinda. "What is the state of Ysterad? I should be in Sangera," he said.

She nodded. "I know. And I have to get to Aunt Odder. Things are not well." She told him about Aunt Odder's letter and showed him the parts she'd transcribed. It felt right to share it with him.

He looked up from her notes with a troubled face. "If you can get me to Sangera safely, there are many who'll recognize me. The Tell will remove any last doubts that I'm who I claim. Then we can send an armed force after Lady Oddeline's kidnappers."

Before Rosinda could answer, Jerrell spoke. "I don't mean to speak out of turn here, but I don't think there's time for that," he said.

"I have to agree," Filara said. "They must be only days from catching a boat across Connar's Strait to the Seafolk. By the time we straggle all the way up to Sangera—"

"Even if we use the Ways Under to get there—" Jerrell interjected.

The cat shot him a look. "Yes, as *I* was going to say, *even if* we use the Ways Under to get there, my mistress will be in the Eastern Desolation long before any force sent from the Blood Clans can catch her. And with what I suspect..." the cat let her voice trail off, glancing at Rosinda.

"What you suspect is probably the same as what I suspect," Rosinda said firmly. "The powers that Aunt Odder mentions in her letter are behind her kidnapping. And if she's being taken to the Eastern Desolation—"

"We need to get her free before she gets there," Jerrell finished.

It seemed everyone held his or her breath then, waiting for the prince to speak. Although he'd only been himself again for a short while, he was still the prince.

"If I can get to Sangera, I should be able to have your parents freed very quickly, Rosinda," was all he said.

"I know." Rosinda abruptly stood and paced the confines of the tent. Obligations tugged at her from all directions at once. Her blood oath to the prince told her to follow his decisions, keep him safe and get him to Sangera if that was his wish. Concern for her parents weighed in on that side, too—Sovann could rescue them from their imprisonment in icy Ierngud.

But Aunt Odder—how could Rosinda simply turn in the other direction and hope that someone else would rescue her aunt in time? After everything she'd done to protect Rosinda— and the prince himself? No, she couldn't do that. There had to be a way to accomplish it all.

And there might be. But first, she had to ask the prince a question. She stopped pacing and stood before him. "If you command me to take you to Sangera, you know I can't refuse. My blood oath as your Kelta binds me. Are you going to invoke that?"

The prince got to his feet to face her. "Only a very foolish ruler disregards the wisdom of the Kelta. Your understanding of the situation is far greater than mine, so whatever you advise, that's what we'll do."

Rosinda took a deep breath. This was the hardest thing she'd had to do, yet. "Then I must ask you to release me from my blood oath," she said.

Prince Sovann looked shocked. "What?"

"It would only be temporary. My oath forces me to put your welfare first," she said gently. She reached out and grasped his arms. "But right now, I think I have to put the welfare of Ysterad there. I have to be able to look at all the options and choose the one with the best chance of success. And I need a free mind and heart to do that."

The prince looked at her, frowning, for a long moment. Then his face relaxed. He grasped her arms in return. "Much as I hate the thought of losing my Kelta again so soon after finding her, I believe you're right. Rosinda," he said, the words spilling out quickly as if he were afraid he might change his mind, "I, Prince Sovann of Ysterad, release you from your oath to me and free your blood from my service, from this day forward."

Rosinda gasped, feeling as if someone had thumped her on the back. For a moment her body fell limp, as blood oath magic released her from its grasp. "Vann!" she whispered, when she could speak again. "You didn't have to do it so completely! I said temporary would be enough!"

A faint smile curved his lips and he nodded sadly. "Yes, I think I did. You need to be free to make the decisions you think will be best for us all, not only now, but for the future. *Entirely* free. But," he added, clasping her hands, "I'm still going to need a Kelta later on, so I'm hoping you'll take the oath again."

"I will," she replied. She knew in her heart that it was true. She wasn't going back to the little house in Cape Breton, and she wasn't going back to her life there. Her future, whatever it held, lay here in Ysterad, her true home. "When this is over, I'll be your Kelta again."

Her heart was so full that her throat clenched, and she felt tears prick the back of her eyes. She blinked them away and turned to Driasch.

"I have an idea," Rosinda said. "We could use your help, but I'll understand if you can't offer it. You have your own troubles with the Nanghareem."

"The Nangharen are fine warriors," the old shaman said with a touch of pride in her voice, "and we owe you a debt, Rosinda...several debts, in truth. You thought to save me during the Nanghareem attack, and you saved Iander's life and many others afterward. If we can help, we will."

Rosinda nodded. "What if a clutch of warriors, perhaps led by Iander, escort the prince to Sangera, while I and the others go after Aunt Odder? An army, the kidnappers would see coming, but the four of us might just be able to take them by surprise." She turned back to Sovann. "If that's acceptable to you, too, of course."

"I've said I'll be guided by your advice," he said. "I can't in good conscience leave the Lady Oddeline in the hands of kidnappers. You're correct; we have to accomplish both things at once if we are to have any chance in this. To do that, it's obvious we have to split up." He smiled at Driasch. "I couldn't wish for better protection than Nangharen warriors."

Rosinda breathed out a deep sigh. "It's settled, then. Our paths must separate for a while. But," she added, trying to infuse a note of confidence into her voice, "when this is over, we'll all be together again."

She hoped with all her heart it was true.

•••

Things moved quickly after that. Driasch sent for Iander and explained the situation to him. He glanced appraisingly at the young prince, then bowed his head once. "Give me an hour to gather my men and pack supplies, my lord," he said. "We'll see you safely to Sangera." Jerrell took the prince to the meeting tent to find something more to eat, and Filara went with them. Driasch offered to pack some supplies for the others. Rosinda and Traveller went to check on their horses.

The crow had been strangely silent ever since the prince's transformation. Rosinda felt a little hurt that Traveller hadn't said a word about her figuring out the prince's identity. As she checked over their saddles and packs, she finally turned to the crow where he perched on the fence railing and asked, "What's wrong with you, Traveller? You haven't said a word in ages."

He ruffled his feathers, not looking at her. "I'm worried."

She stopped what she was doing and tried to meet his eyes. "About the prince?"

"I think it's a good idea for him to go with the Nanghar," the crow said.

"About us, then?"

"I'm not sure what's for the best," Traveller said vaguely.

"We have to rescue Aunt Odder," Rosinda said. "Just this morning you thought we had to get back on the road after her as quickly as possible!"

"I know what I said."

Rosinda glared at him in frustration. "What is it, then? Is there something you're not telling me?" It seemed the crow was always either telling her something she didn't want to hear, or making her think he was keeping secrets from her.

His golden eyes met hers. "Yes."

Rosinda waited, but he didn't continue. "Well, are you going to tell me, or not?" she asked impatiently.

"I have to leave you," the crow finally muttered.

"What?" Rosinda was bewildered. "Why?"

He ruffled his feathers again. "I think it may be safer for you from now on if I'm not around."

Rosinda felt like someone had punched her in the stomach. First Kerngold was gone, and now she would lose Traveller, too? That would leave only three of them to rescue Aunt Odder. "How could it be safer? You've been such a help all along. I couldn't have made it this far without you!"

The crow agitatedly shook his feathers. "Don't! This is already hard enough."

She clenched her teeth together and forced her voice to remain calm. "Then you have to explain to me what you're talking about," she said.

"You'll hate me."

"I could never hate you!"

The crow regarded her sadly. "Even if I told you I'm the servant of your enemy?"

The words didn't make sense. "What are you talking about?"

"I'm bound to Morrigan," the crow said, spreading his

wings. "And now that I've betrayed her, she's going to kill me sooner or later. Probably sooner. I don't think you should be around when she comes looking for me."

CHAPTER TWENTY-EIGHT

Traveller flapped his wings and began to lift off the railing. Still stunned by his words, Rosinda acted instinctively. She raised her right hand in a grasping motion, drew a little power from the ground beneath her feet, and said, "*Onthande!*"

The crow tried to twist away, but he hovered, held in place by a giant, invisible hand. Rosinda knew the charm would only last long enough for her to reach out and gently catch the immobilized crow to keep him from falling to the ground.

"I'm sorry, but I don't think this conversation is finished yet," Rosinda said. Her mind reeled, but she tucked him under her arm and ran to the shaman's tent. She needed help with this. Driasch would know what to do.

She passed Jerrell. The prince was no longer with him. When he saw Rosinda, he broke into a run toward her, and they arrived at the shaman's tent together.

"What—" he started, but Rosinda shushed him with a look.

"Inside," she said.

The tent was empty. Rosinda placed the crow down on the floor. The charm had faded, and he stretched his wings, looking affronted, but made no move to try to get away again.

"You didn't have to do that," he said sullenly.

"What's up?" Jerrell asked.

"Traveller just told me he's been working for Morrigan."

At the stunned look on Jerrell's face, which quickly slid into anger, she added hastily, "Now he says he's betrayed her, and we'll be safer if he leaves us."

Rosinda hadn't noticed Filara with Jerrell, but the cat leapt to stand in front of the crow, fur bristling, staring at him.

"You feathered swine," she hissed. "If you've endangered Rosinda or my mistress—"

Rosinda cut her off. "I'll handle this, Filara," she said, in a voice so strong she surprised herself. "You need to give me some explanation, Traveller. Or whatever your name is," she added.

The crow didn't answer for a moment. Rosinda felt her anger pulsing hot and bitter, even as she tried to control it. Just as she was about to ask him again, he spoke.

"Morrigan gave me the task of getting you to Ysterad. Safely," he said. "She knew there might be others who would look for you, but she thought it easiest to let you come to her."

"And why would I do that?" Rosinda asked coldly. A detached, rational part of her mind had taken over. The part of her that wanted to cry had retreated behind a thick wall.

"Because of your aunt," the crow said.

"So it's a trap," Jerrell accused.

"It's the Lady Oddeline they wanted," the crow said. "They knew she was the old King's Kelta. She's the one they thought could lead them to the prince. You were just...insurance."

"To make Aunt Odder talk," Rosinda flashed.

The crow nodded. "My mistress—Morrigan—thinks you're more important now that she knows you're the Prince's Kelta. Or were," he added. "But the others aren't convinced."

"You've been spying on us from the very beginning," Rosinda said. "Reporting everything to this Morrigan."

The crow simply nodded. "I'm sorry."

"So how have you betrayed her?" Jerrell asked.

Traveller sighed. "I haven't been in contact to tell her I know where the prince is, and I'm not going to. Other things she might forgive, but not that."

Rosinda knelt down in front of the crow, puzzled. "Why

aren't you going to tell her, if this is what you've been working toward from the very beginning?"

The crow hunched his shoulders and pulled his head down. "Because I think it's wrong," he said, "and I don't want to hurt you, Rosinda. I didn't know—when this all began—and then you saved my life and healed me...we became..." His voice trailed away.

"Friends," Rosinda finished for him. She rocked back on her heels. This was all so confusing. She wanted to believe Traveller, and yet he'd lied to her all along! Was he even telling the truth now?

"I say we kill him," Filara said suddenly.

"Filara!" Rosinda was shocked. "How can you even say such a thing?"

The cat shrugged elegantly. "He's a bird, I'm a cat. It's not that difficult. We'd know for sure that he's not running off to Morrigan with any tales. If you don't want to do it," she said, extending her claws and flexing them, "I can."

"No," Jerrell said seriously. "Not yet, anyway. Look, you might as well tell us everything about Morrigan and the rest of them, whoever they are. Then we'll know you're serious about helping Rosinda."

"We're not killing him," Rosinda insisted. "Traveller, will you tell us what you know?"

The crow sighed. "Of course. But once Morrigan discovers that I've closed off my mind to her, I don't know what she'll do. She might well come looking for me. I thought it would be best if I were far away from you when that happened."

"Jerrell, would you run and get Prince Sovann and Driasch?" Rosinda asked. "I think they should be here for this."

He returned moments later with the other two in tow. They looked puzzled.

"Traveller has some things to tell us," Rosinda said. "I'll explain how that came to be later."

The crow took a deep breath. "The gods," he began, "that the shaman saw in her tellbones and Rosinda's aunt mentioned in her letter—they're not from Ysterad. I imagine they've been many places in their day, but they've all had followers on Earth at one time or another. They're all war gods. Their names are Morrigan, Sekhmet, Tyr, and Gradivus. Gradivus was called Mars by the ancient Romans."

He twitched his wings. "They heard of or sensed the unrest in Ysterad when the king and queen were killed, and no one took the throne. Any place in political trouble is a place where they might get a foothold. The thing about war gods is, they *like* war. They're happiest when everyone's fighting. This looked like a place that was ripe for that.

"However, gods get their power indirectly, by having followers. If no one's praying to them or worshipping them, they can't do very much. These four concocted a plan to pool their powers for a time, try to exert some influence over Ysterad and gain some followers in the various provinces. At the same time, they'd work to keep stirring up the political unrest that was already here, until the provinces were ready to go to war against each other."

"That's horrible," Rosinda said in a low voice. Driasch sat very still, listening, with her lips pressed in a straight line.

"When their followers clash, the gods will clash as well," the crow continued. "That will be the end of their alliance. The winner will hold sway over all of Ysterad."

"How strong are they now?" It was the first thing Prince Sovann said since he entered the tent. His voice sounded like stones grating together.

"Not very," the crow said. "They've gained followers in different parts of Ysterad, but none of them have more than a few really dedicated servants yet." He paused and looked at Prince Sovann. "The fact that you're still alive is keeping them weak."

The prince's eyebrows rose slightly. "So that's why they want to find me? To kill me?"

The crow nodded. "That would do two things. It would weaken the blood magic protecting Ysterad, and it would feed the unrest in the provinces."

"But if Sovann gets to Sangera—"

"It will help our cause, but it won't stop them—or the war," Driasch said. "There's been too much disagreement and fighting over the past two years. Look at what happened right here with the Nanghareem. Some folks will calm down if the prince is back on the throne. But many will not."

"What if these war gods were gone?" Rosinda asked. "If they weren't making things worse?"

Driasch considered. "Without their influence and with the prince back on the throne making concerted efforts to bring the people of Ysterad together again...yes, we might be able to avoid a war. It would be close, but it might be possible."

"But the gods were not behind the deaths of my parents?" Sovann asked Traveller.

The crow shook his head. "No, they only came after that. I don't know what precipitated that."

The prince breathed out a long sigh. "So defeating the war gods may not solve all our problems."

"But it's a place to start," Filara said. She still hadn't taken her eyes off the crow.

"Then we have to get rid of them," Rosinda said.

The others stared at her.

"How are we going to do that?" Jerrell asked.

"I don't know yet," Rosinda said determinedly, "But we can't let them start a war here. We have to stop them."

"And I must get to Sangera even more urgently than before," Sovann said. "Maybe their power will be even weaker if I'm officially recognized by the Tell."

"What is the 'Tell', anyway?" Jerrell asked.

Sovann said, "It's a statue—"

"An *ugly* statue," Filara interjected.

The prince quelled her with a stare. "It's a statue of a...a person—"

"Or some sort of creature," the cat said.

"Well, I think it's a person," the prince said, continuing to glare at the cat. "She's holding a book in one hand and a chakram in the other—"

"What's a chakram?" Jerrell asked.

"It's a ring-shaped throwing weapon," Rosinda said. "Hey, I didn't know I knew that!"

"*Anyway*," continued the prince, "The book that she's holding is said to contain the names of all the rightful rulers of Ysterad, past and future. If someone whose name is in the book puts his hand on the chakram, the pages of the book glow for a few seconds."

"Couldn't someone just look in the book for the name?"

"It's a *statue*," the prince answered. "Carved from stone. It's not a real book with pages and a cover."

Jerrell opened his mouth to ask something else, and the prince cut him off. "I don't understand how it works, if that's what you're going to ask. It's magic, that's all. There's no way to fool it. If it recognizes you as a ruler, no one questions it."

Rosinda drew a deep breath. "So we'll just stick to the original plan," she said. "Prince Sovann will go to Sangera, and we'll go after Aunt Odder. But," she added, turning to the prince, "as soon as you're recognized by the Tell, you have to send us whatever help you can."

Sovann shook his head. "Now I think you should come with me. This changes everything. You can't do it alone."

"I won't be alone," Rosinda said. "I'll have Jerrell and Filara... and Traveller...with me."

Filara hissed. "You can't bring that traitor along! He's likely to tell the gods exactly where to find us!"

Rosinda frowned. "I don't think so. I can't think of any reason Traveller would have confessed to this if he weren't on our side. Can you?" When no one answered, she continued, "If he comes with us, he can keep proving himself to you by helping us even more. Will you do that?" she asked the crow.

He tilted his head and looked at her. "I'm still concerned that I'll make it more dangerous for you."

Rosinda half-smiled. "More dangerous than facing four war gods? You've got to be kidding."

The crow nodded. "I suppose you're right." He lowered his head toward Rosinda until his beak touched the hard-packed dirt floor. "If I can help you, Rosinda, I will."

Sovann still looked worried, but he said, "I released you from your oath, and I can't take it back. You must choose your own course."

Jerrell shrugged. "You're the boss, Rosinda."

Filara snorted. "She's a fool, boy, and so are you. As if I didn't have my paws full before, babysitting the two of you...now I have to keep the reins on that two-faced feathered creature..." She stalked out of the tent, muttering.

In other circumstances, Rosinda would have laughed, but the task before them weighed heavily on her heart. She thought of all the people—her parents, Aunt Odder, all of Ysterad—who were depending on them in one way or another and took a deep breath.

"Okay, everyone," she said, squaring her shoulders. "Let's get back to what we were doing. There's no more time to waste."

CHAPTER TWENTY-NINE

"We'll have to go back to the Ways Under," Rosinda said as they set out from the Nanghar camp on horseback again. They'd said goodbye to Prince Sovann, and Iander had gravely shaken hands with Rosinda.

"I'll get him there safely," he'd promised with a steely look in his eye.

Driasch had sent them on their way with hugs and instructions.

"Don't be afraid of being a magister," she whispered to Rosinda. "The power is there, within you. Use it."

"Even if I don't know how?" Rosinda whispered back. "My memories for using magic haven't come back."

The old shaman took her by the shoulders. "I have a theory about that," she said. "I think that maybe those memories are gone for good."

She must have seen the panic Rosinda felt at her words, because she continued earnestly, her blue eyes boring into Rosinda's. "It's because they're no good to you now. Before, you had some Kelta magic. Now you're a magister—you have access to all the realms of magic, and you'll use them together, in different ways than you would have before. Those old memories would just confuse you."

"But I don't know how to be a magister," Rosinda said finally, her voice sounding very small and shaky.

"You will," the shaman said. "When the time comes, you will."

Rosinda wished she had the old woman's confidence.

Driasch spoke to Jerrell in a low voice after Rosinda mounted her horse. Rosinda saw the shaman press something small into Jerrell's hand. He slipped it into his pocket before she could see what it was.

Now they were finally underway with Traveller perched on the pommel of Rosinda's saddle while Filara rode wordlessly with Jerrell. Considering how well those two had gotten along at the beginning, Rosinda found this quite amusing.

"Are you sure it's safe to go back underground after that thing we met the last time?" Jerrell asked.

Rosinda shook her head. "No, I'm not. But we're running out of time, so we have to risk it."

"At least you'll have your sword this time," Jerrell said. "You won't need to transform anything else first."

"Hopefully," Filara said, breaking her frosty silence. "I suppose you never know what a magister might do."

"What do you think Aunt Odder will say when she finds out you can speak?" Rosinda asked, mainly to turn the conversation away from this magister talk. It still made her uncomfortable to think about these supposed powers.

"I was hoping the matter might be remedied before then," the cat sniffed. "I really don't know what she'll say."

Jerrell grinned. "Don't worry, Filara. I'm sure Rosinda's aunt will be only too happy to fix things for you," he said. "As quickly as possible."

"There are a few other things I wish she could fix as easily," the cat retorted, flicking an ear as if a fly were annoying her.

Rosinda reined in and scanned the area. Steep cliffs and plateaus rose from gouges in the earth here, as if giants had scratched at the soil and stone. "Over there," she said, pointing to a strange rock formation. "The next entrance to the Ways Under should be there. I remember being here once with—well, I'm not sure. Either my mother or Aunt Odder. I can sense it."

Filara looked at her with narrowed eyes. "That's new."

Rosinda ignored her. She could almost see the word *magister* forming in the cat's mouth and urged her horse into a trot before the cat could say it.

"Where does this one lead?" Jerrell asked, dismounting as they drew close to the rock formation. It was a tall, wind-carved crag, which looked like a gnome with a crooked hat, or a rabbit drinking from a glass, depending on where you stood.

"All the way to Pheyla's Crossing, I think, on the coast of Connar's Strait, if we don't come up before then," Rosinda said. "From there we'll have to hire a boat to take us over to Seafolk."

Filara shuddered. "I'd face an army of those troll creatures rather than take another boat."

"Don't any of the Ways run under the water to Seafolk?" Jerrell asked.

Filara made an exasperated noise but Rosinda said, "No, none of the Ways run under water. You can't get to any of the islands that way."

"Or to the Eastern Desolation," Filara added. That silenced them all, and they went through the now-familiar motions of finding the hidden doorway and coaxing the horses through.

The room inside the entrance looked and smelled the same as any of the other Ways they'd been in, and, as usual, an Urigm stepped forward to check them.

Rosinda chose the path that would lead them to the coast and they started down it, the horses following them placidly through the earth-scented tunnel. Filara and Traveller stayed on the mounts. They walked in silence for a few minutes when Jerrell suddenly spoke, startling Rosinda.

"I miss Kerngold," he said.

Rosinda's eyes brimmed with sudden tears. "I know," she gulped, trying to keep her voice from cracking. "So do I."

"It's weird," Jerrell continued. "I don't feel like Kerngold *turned into* Prince Sovann, even though I saw it happen. It's as if he was a different...person. Even though he was a wolf. And he didn't speak to me like he spoke to you. I don't know. It's weird," he repeated.

"You're right," Rosinda said, turning to look at Jerrell. "He talked to me, right inside my head, and it wasn't the same...like you said. Not the same person as Sovann at all."

Jerrell shrugged. "I guess it's because you didn't remember Sovann then."

"I guess. But even when I realized it had to be him in disguise...he wasn't familiar, even a little bit. It's like Kerngold was a different personality completely." Rosinda's eyes filled with tears again. "I guess that's why I miss him so much."

Awkwardly, Jerrell slipped his arm around Rosinda's shoulders and gave a quick squeeze. For once, neither Traveller nor Filara said anything.

They continued in silence after that, except for the occasional warning about hazards underfoot or brief discussions about the route. Rosinda was glad when they reached the last entryway and emerged into the sunlight again. The dark and gloomy underground path had intensified her sadness.

The exit point was in the trunk of a huge, ancient oak tree this time, and Rosinda turned to watch Jerrell lead his horse out of it. The sight made her blink at its strangeness. They stood in a small clearing, hemmed with trees and low brush on all sides, but the air held a salt tang that told Rosinda they had reached the coast.

"Mid-afternoon," Jerrell proclaimed, squinting up at the sun.

"We'll stay in Pheyla's Crossing tonight and book passage on a ship headed for Seafolk tomorrow," Rosinda said. "I wish we didn't have to waste half the day, but I doubt anyone's setting out from the docks tonight."

They urged the horses along the trail out of the clearing,

and within minutes the bustling port town sprang into view. Rosinda noted with relief that no forbidding flags flew over the gates; no sense of foreboding hung in the air as it had at Genia. The two guards at the gate looked amiable and ready to assist travellers rather than intimidate them.

They quickly found an inn with rooms for the night and a delicious-smelling common room. The innkeeper was neither Nanghareem, Nangharen, or Seafolk; he had pale, fine hair that grazed his shoulders, and the blackest eyes Rosinda had ever seen. He heartily welcomed them and promised that supper would be ready by the time they settled their horses. For now, Filara and Traveller would wait in the stables, too. Rosinda promised to open their windows later for the cat and crow to join them. She felt nervous about leaving the two together, but since they weren't speaking to each other, she didn't see how they could get into a fight.

Rosinda and Jerrell enjoyed a delicious meal of stew and dumplings in the common room. They sat finishing a plate of berries for dessert and tried to decide if they were too tired to go searching for a boat to hire tonight, when a man in a dark green cloak stopped and stood beside their table. Rosinda looked up, startled, but she recognized the face half-hidden in a hood immediately.

"Quigsel!" she exclaimed, and jumped up to hug the startled enchanter.

He looked pleased and returned her hug, and then his face grew serious.

"Shhh! I thought you were never going to get here!" he whispered. "Have you taken rooms for the night?"

Rosinda nodded.

"We have to get somewhere quiet, to talk," Quigsel said, glancing around the half-full common room.

"What are you doing here?" Rosinda asked, recovering

from the shock of seeing her aunt's friend where she least expected him.

The enchanter put a finger to his lips. "I'll go and talk to the innkeeper for a minute while you two finish," he said. "Then we'll catch up."

When he moved over to the bar, Jerrell said with a grin, "Wouldn't he be less conspicuous if he didn't go around all covered up in that cloak, shushing people?"

Rosinda stifled a giggle. "You may be right," she said. "Oh, let's hurry. Maybe he has news about my parents!"

They gathered their things and collected Quigsel from the bar, where the innkeeper winked at Rosinda and bowed his head slightly. She wondered what the enchanter had told him about her. When they'd reached the privacy of the room, Quigsel threw back the hood of his cloak.

"That feels better," he sighed, releasing the clasp of the cloak and draping it over the back of a chair before he sat.

Rosinda opened one of the windows of the ground-floor room, and it wasn't long before both Traveller and Filara joined them. The chill that still hung between the animals was almost strong enough to make the room feel colder.

"So, why so secretive?" Rosinda asked, sitting cross-legged on the bed.

"I told you, remember? Seafolk don't get along well with Nangharen."

"But these are Nanghareem," Rosinda protested, remembering that Driasch had pointed out the difference, "There's a big difference, right? And the Nangharen are really nice people... well, once you get to know them," she added, thinking of Iander's stern face when she had first encountered him in the crypt. "Anyway, they must have a lot of dealing with Seafolk, with all the shipping and travel across Connar's Strait."

"Not that much," Quigsel said. "The Nanghareem who

work on the docks know the Seafolk who sail the ships, and vice versa. Travellers take a few set routes and pass through Nanghareem as quickly as possible. Everyone else is suspect."

Jerrell frowned. "That's stupid. If you don't mind my saying so," he added quickly.

"I don't mind," the enchanter said, smiling. "I think it's stupid, too. Why do you think I live in Kelton province? It's gotten worse in the last couple of years, too, with the prince gone. Speaking of the prince," he said, turning to Rosinda, "is there any news of him?"

Rosinda grinned. "Some. He's on his way to Sangera, protected by a troop of Nangharen warriors."

The enchanter's eyes grew wide. "Really? You found him? Have you found Oddeline, too?" He looked around the room, as if they might have hidden her somewhere.

"No, but we know where to look." Rosinda sighed. "In fact, we're on our way to try and rescue her. The news about the prince is the only good news we have. The rest is all pretty bad." As briefly as she could, Rosinda told him everything—or almost everything—that had happened since they'd left his cottage in Kelton province. How long ago that seemed! So much had happened in the interim, it took longer to tell than Rosinda expected. She said nothing about Driasch's belief that Rosinda was a magister, and hoped the others would keep quiet about it as well.

"War gods? That's bad," Quigsel said when Rosinda got to that part.

"Agreed. But we have to get Aunt Odder and try to stop them—at least keep them occupied until Sovann reaches Sangera," Rosinda said.

"You didn't mention the traitor among us," Filara said coldly, her tail lashing the floor behind her.

Reluctantly, Rosinda told Quigsel what Traveller had told

her. The enchanter looked at the crow with narrowed eyes.

"I could enspell him so he'd have to tell us the truth from now on," Quigsel offered.

"No!" Rosinda crossed her arms. "I trust Traveller. He's on our side now."

There was an uncomfortable silence, which Jerrell finally broke.

"Why are you here?" he asked Quigsel. "And how did you find us?

The enchanter grinned. "At the request of Rosinda's mother, I came to help."

Rosinda's eyes grew wide, but Quigsel held up a hand.

"No, I regret to tell you that she isn't freed yet," he hurriedly explained. "She used magic to contact me, and it must have been difficult—" He broke off suddenly.

"Why? Tell me!" Rosinda exclaimed.

Quigsel sighed. "I believe she's being kept in a place with magical shielding around it," he said. "It sounded like it took a great amount of energy for her to contact me at all. And we didn't have very long before she was too tired to continue."

Rosinda frowned. "It was easier than that when I spoke with her."

"Maybe because you were using that thing in the crypt," Jerrell suggested.

"Or maybe because Rosinda is a magister," Filara said.

Quigsel looked momentarily stunned. Rosinda glared at the cat.

"That's what *some people* think," she said. "Personally, I don't believe it."

The enchanter peered at her with uncomfortable intensity. "There hasn't been a magister in Ysterad in hundreds of years," he said slowly.

"So I've heard," Rosinda said.

"Why do they think you might be one?" Quigsel asked.

"And who thinks so?"

It seemed like Filara had been waiting for the question. She held up a paw and flicked a claw out for each item she named. "She's done Kelta magic, transformation, and tellbone reading," she said, "and possibly telepathy when the prince was disguised as a wolf."

"That wasn't me, that was Kerngold," Rosinda protested. "I mean Sovann." She shook her head. "It had to be a spell, some of Aunt Odder's magic. I wasn't trying to communicate mentally with him, it just happened. And I can't read any of your minds."

Quigsel looked skeptical. "I don't think it could be anything to do with your Aunt Odder's spell," he said. "As this extremely intelligent creature points out," he continued, bowing to Filara, "the communication of mind to mind is not within the realm of Kelta magic. So unless Oddeline had a thaumat to help her with the spell, which I doubt, considering how quickly she would have had to do all this, it seems more likely to have come from your own abilities."

Filara looked intensely pleased with herself, smugly glancing at Rosinda. Jerrell made a fake gagging sound, which the cat ignored.

"Well, whatever," Rosinda said, exasperated. "I'm not going to argue about it. What's important now is figuring out how we're going to rescue Aunt Odder. Quigsel, do you have a plan?"

The enchanter looked blank for a moment. "No," he finally admitted.

"Do we know where they are now?" Jerrell asked. "Or where they should be?"

"Once we arrive in Seafolk tomorrow, I should be able to determine if they're still on the island or not," Quigsel said.

"Could we send Traveller to find them?" Jerrell asked. "He did that before, right?"

"I wouldn't advise it," the crow said slowly. "If I get too close to Morrigan's other servant, my former mistress will sense me. And then she'll be able to find you," he added.

"How convenient," Filara said coldly. "Are you sure it's not just that you're chicken, crow?"

Rosinda fought down an irrational urge to giggle. "Quigsel, can you help us find passage to Seafolk, first thing in the morning?"

The enchanter grinned. "Already arranged," he said. "We've just been waiting for you to get here."

"How did you find us so quickly?" Jerrell asked suddenly. "I wondered about that."

"You might have noticed that your innkeeper is neither Seafolk nor Nangharen. We outcasts stick together," he said mysteriously.

Rosinda opened her mouth to thank him, but it turned into a huge yawn. She realized just how very tired she was.

"That's wonderful about the boat. Thank you," she said. "We'll look for Aunt Odder in Seafolk. If they've already moved on, then we'll follow."

Jerrell caught the yawn and put a hand up to smother one of his own. "I really want to know more about the Eastern Desolation," he said, "but I think I can wait one more day."

We can all wait one more day to think about that. All Rosinda wanted now was a good solid sleep. The problems would still be there in the morning.

●●●

Pre-dawn light filtered in through the window when Quigsel rapped on the door. Rosinda woke groggily and stumbled across the chilly floor to let him in. Jerrell, as usual, woke a little more slowly when the enchanter shook him.

No fire burned in the inn's common room yet, but Quigsel had used his friendship with the innkeeper to secure bread and fall apples for breakfast. They munched hungrily as they made their way to the docks. Even with dawn staining the horizon pink and gold, the docks bustled with burly men struggling crates and trunks up gangplanks and bleary-eyed travellers seeking the proper dock. The salt tang of the sea filled their lungs, and huge seabirds wheeled overhead. Rosinda noticed Filara sniff the air distastefully and delicately walk around the small puddles that littered the ground.

Quigsel led them without hesitation to a docked ship with three tall, stepped masts. The ship itself was long and low, built for speed rather than cargo, and the name *Jessara's Lyre* adorned the prow in flowing letters. Bright blue paint covered the hull. An intricately carved figurehead of a mermaid strumming a lyre sat at the top of the bow, long curls of her hair sweeping back along the sides as if blown by a strong wind. A slender man stood on deck at the top of the gangplank. He wore a double-breasted coat with two rows of shining brass buttons running down the front, and a tricorne hat. A sword scabbard hung from a belt slung low on his slim hips.

"Captain!" Quigsel called, and the figure on deck bowed.

As they hurried up the gangplank, Rosinda studied the captain's face. He was younger than she'd expected. His complexion was similar to Quigsel's, so Rosinda thought he must be Seafolk. When they reached the top of the gangplank and stood next to him, she saw the telltale gills on the sides of his neck, almost hidden by the loops of golden earrings he wore. Now he seemed even younger, almost as young as Jerrell, with a smooth face that looked like it never needed shaving and dark, merry eyes.

Quigsel smiled. "Rosinda and Jerrell, meet Captain Steffen, the owner of *Jessara's Lyre*."

"Pleased to meet you, sir," Jerrell said first, and stuck out his hand.

The captain's lips quivered, as if fighting back a grin. With one hand, he shook Jerrell's, but with the other he reached up and pulled off his tricorne hat, sweeping it low into a bow. Two long dark braids of hair slid out of their coils under the hat and fell almost to the captain's belt.

"Very pleased to meet *you*, Jerrell," the captain said in a very feminine voice. "But it's 'Ma'am', if you please, or my crew will be laughing behind my back. Again," she added.

Rosinda recovered quickly from her surprise and offered her own handshake with a smile. "Thank you for taking us across the strait, ma'am," she said warmly. The captain's features had seemed young and boyish when Rosinda had thought they belonged to a man, but now she realized that the captain was probably in her early twenties. Still young to be a captain, Rosinda thought.

"Welcome aboard *Jessara's Lyre*," she answered. Her handshake was warm and strong. "Now, if you'll excuse me, I'll spur my crew to get us underway now that you're here. Uncle, you know where the bunks are." She gave Quigsel a quick hug and turned on her heel, calling to a woman high up in the rigging. A man in the crow's-nest shouted a question, and she answered him with a wave. Jerrell watched her go with a slightly glazed expression.

Rosinda raised her eyebrows at the enchanter. "Uncle?" she asked.

Quigsel half-smiled. "My brother Harro's girl. Harro's a sailor too, of course, but he's gone up the coast with a load of passengers to Ell's Landing." He led them to a narrow hatchway that disappeared below decks.

"What does the name of the ship mean?" Jerrell asked, peering around as if hoping he'd catch another glimpse of the lovely captain.

"Her first name's Jessara, and playing the lyre is her other great talent," Quigsel said. "Harro had this ship built for her when she turned twenty, because he said she could play the sea with a ship as skillfully as she plucked the strings of a lyre." He looked at Jerrell's absent stare. "It means she's a fine captain, Jerrell."

"Yes, I'm sure she is," he agreed automatically.

Quigsel grinned. "My niece has this effect on young men sometimes. Half the male crew is in love with her, I think—at least when they first sign on."

They had climbed down into a wide passageway lined with small berths on either side, and cargo stacked toward the stern. It was empty of other passengers. "We'll be in Emeroc by day's end, so we won't need to sleep," Quigsel said, "but you can rest down here if you'd like, or leave your packs."

The ship rolled gently under their feet and Rosinda clutched at an upright beam to steady herself. "We're underway," the enchanter said with satisfaction. "Jessara doesn't waste time."

"That's good," Rosinda said. She sank down on one of the small beds. "Do you think we'll catch them in Seafolk?" It felt, finally, as if Aunt Odder might be within reach. It was a relief, and yet a pit opened up in Rosinda's stomach at the thought. How would they rescue her?

"We've had no indication they're using the Ways," Filara said. She'd been quiet since they'd left the inn that morning. "Otherwise they'd be much further ahead of us."

"There's a Kelton woman with them," Traveller said, "Morrigan's other servant. But she must not be a Kelta."

"We've met," Rosinda said briefly, remembering her encounter with the woman in the fairy ring clearing back in Cape Breton. "She didn't try any magic on me then, so she must not be. That's good to know."

"Weren't you in the fairy ring when you fought her?" Traveller asked.

Rosinda nodded.

"That's a dead magic area, remember? She couldn't have used magic anyway."

"But I did," Rosinda protested. "At least, I didn't actually *do* any magic, but before she arrived I had my sword out, and I could feel the power flowing up from the ground..."

Filara looked at her and cocked her head. "Do I *have* to say 'magister' again?" she asked.

"Anyway," Rosinda hurried on, ignoring the cat, "the woman stepped out of the fairy ring before she used the crystal to go back to Ysterad. She could have used other magic if she'd wanted to."

Filara turned to Traveller. "When you saw the caravan before, how many people were there?" It was the first time she'd addressed him directly in days.

The crow paused a moment, thinking. "The man who seemed to be in charge, and five of his people, all from Irylia, by their appearance. Three others; the Kelton woman, a Seafolk man, and a dwarf, probably from Nordas. And of course, Rosinda's aunt. That's all I remember seeing."

"Five of us, against nine? Those aren't good odds," Jerrell said.

Not to mention that two of those five are a cat and a crow, Rosinda thought. *What good will they be against armed warriors?* She said nothing aloud, however.

"We do have two magic-users, though," Quigsel said, looking at Rosinda, "and they may not have any. That will give us an advantage."

"I hardly count—" Rosinda started to say, but broke off as footsteps sounded in the hatchway.

It was the captain, her head now wrapped in a brightly colored bandanna with the long braids looped together and swinging down her back.

"We're out of port and there's a fair wind," she reported. "We should make good time to Emeroc. And Uncle," she said, turning to him, "I have word on those travellers you asked about. One of my crewmen heard that such a group took passage from Pheyla's Crossing just yesterday on a Nanghareem ship, Captain Lynnet's *Dancing Mermaid*."

Quigsel nodded. "Yesterday? That's not so bad."

Captain Steffen cocked her head. "There's a strange rumor to go with the news, as well. They didn't want passage to Seafolk. They wanted to go straight to the Eastern Desolation."

"Is the *Dancing Mermaid* taking them there?" Rosinda asked breathlessly. The kidnappers would be there long before them if they didn't have to pass over the island of the Seafolk.

The captain shook her head and laughed, her loops of golden earrings tinkling. "You'll not find a Nanghareem sailor who'll willingly go near the coast of the Eastern Desolation," she said. "Not many Seafolk, either, although there are a few. None of them happened to be in port when your friends were looking, though, so they had to settle for passage to Emeroc. They may have other arrangements past that."

"Rosinda," Jerrell said suddenly. "Do you still have that map of Ysterad? The one Quigsel gave you?"

"It's right here," she said, and dug it out of her pack. "Why?"

Jerrell unrolled it. "I was just thinking..." he said slowly. He knelt down and spread the map out on the plank floor so that they could all see it. "Look. They always seem to keep one step ahead of us. What if, instead of putting into port at Emeroc, we went southeast down along the Seafolk coastline and kept on around to Olim? Would it be faster than going overland? We might get ahead of them, whether they're going across the island or trying to book passage on something else from there."

Rosinda frowned. "Are there any Ways Under on Seafolk? I assumed if there were—"

Quigsel was shaking his head. "No, it's a long story, but there aren't any—now. Legend says that there were, a long time ago. But during Godrin's War they...disappeared."

"So it's got to be faster to go around?" Jerrell turned to Captain Steffen. "Could you do it? Take us to Olim instead of Emeroc?"

The captain held up her hands, laughing a little, and backed away a step or two. "Whoa, hold on there. I need more information, if you're asking me to take the *Lyre* that far to the southeast. The south coast of Seafolk is too close to the Burning Sea for comfort. The ships that regularly sail to Olim have reinforced hulls and other...specializations."

Quigsel shook his head and snorted. "Not that any of them ever actually encounter anything out of the ordinary," he said.

"True," the captain agreed. "But sailors are a suspicious lot. And there are enough tales about the waters near the Eastern Desolation..."

"Rubbish," Quigsel said, but his niece shrugged.

"It's important," Rosinda said, standing up from her bunk. She didn't want Quigsel to be the one to convince the captain to do this. It was her battle, and her responsibility. "Captain Steffen, I'm Prince Sovann's Kelta—or at least, I was, and hope to be again when this is over. We're trying—" she took a deep breath. "We're trying to stop a war that will affect all of Ysterad. I know how that must sound," she went on hurriedly. "There are so few of us. But it's the truth, and we need your help. Jerrell is right. If we can get ahead of these people, we stand a much better chance.

"If it's dangerous—if you don't want to risk your ship—I understand," Rosinda concluded. "But if you can help, well, we'd appreciate it."

Jessara Steffen studied Rosinda for a moment, and Rosinda felt those dark eyes taking her measure. Then suddenly the captain hugged her.

"I never believed those superstitions anyway," she said. "We'll get you there. Although," she added, turning to Quigsel, "it probably won't hurt if you stay up on deck, Uncle. In case your particular talents are needed."

She threw a wink at Jerrell and headed for the hatchway again. Rosinda thought that Jerrell looked a bit like a puppy gazing after her, but she kept it to herself. They heard the captain reach the deck above and shout new orders to her crew. Rosinda drew a deep breath.

"So, I guess we're going to Olim," she said. "Any ideas about what we'll do when we get there?"

CHAPTER THIRTY

The crossing to Olim would take much longer than the one to Emeroc, so they spent the night in the narrow berths. They were more comfortable than Rosinda expected. The ship flew before the wind, all three sails unfurled to their fullest to catch every scrap of air, but the sea lay calm and the only motion below decks was a gentle, rhythmic roll. The ship's cook had wisely laid out only a light supper for them, so no one suffered any ill effects. Except perhaps Filara. She barely spoke except to snap at someone and didn't eat anything that Rosinda saw. She seemed quite content to do nothing but sleep at the foot of Rosinda's bunk.

The next morning, a shout from the hatchway woke Rosinda.

I wonder if I'll ever get to sleep in again? she thought, dragging her eyelids open and struggling to sit up.

"What?" she called blearily. Only a trickle of pale yellow light filtered down through the hatchway, but she could see that Jerrell hadn't even moved in his bunk across the narrow corridor.

"I said, the crow's nest reports another ship ahead," Captain Steffen repeated. She clattered partway down the hatch stairs and peered in at Rosinda.

Does she ever sleep? Rosinda wondered. Aloud she said, "Is it the *Dancing Mermaid*?"

"Too soon to tell," the captain said. "But I wouldn't be surprised. Looks like the shape of her sails. How your friends managed to convince a crew of Nanghareem to come this close to the Burning Sea, though..." She trailed off and shook her head.

Rosinda's heart sank. So much for Jerrell's idea to get ahead of them. "They're definitely not our friends. Can we catch them?"

The captain pursed her lips. "She's a ways off, but the *Lyre* is definitely the faster ship. Depends on how much time we have to overtake her. I'll ask Mr. Giles what he thinks. They may put into Olim before we've a chance to catch up."

Rosinda nodded. "Okay. I'll wake the others, and we'll join you on the deck as soon as we can."

A few hurried moments later, they gathered on deck. Traveller flew up and perched high in the rigging. The rising sun painted the sky in rosy swaths, but Rosinda had eyes only for the small dark shape on the water far ahead of them. If the captain's information was correct, Aunt Odder was aboard. *Right there.* A shiver prickled the skin on Rosinda's back, only partly caused by the chill dawn breeze. Excitement and fear, in equal parts, were responsible, too.

This was the closest Aunt Odder had been since Rosinda had last seen her in Cape Breton the morning of the day she'd met Traveller. She peered at the ship riding the waves ahead of them. Without conscious thought, Rosinda concentrated on the ship, trying to feel her aunt's presence. Her eyes began to water from the strain as she stared. It seemed that if she were there, Rosinda would know it somehow.

Then it felt as if a spark flared in her brain. *Aunt Odder.* For a moment Rosinda could—feel? sense?—she didn't even know what to call it. But her aunt's presence was there. Aunt Odder was on that ship.

"It's the one," she breathed, but no one heard her.

Jerrell gulped down a yawn, perked up and stood straight when Captain Steffen strode over to them.

"She's riding further off the coast than I'd expect," the captain said. "If we keep close to the coastline, I'd almost think we could still make it to Olim before they do."

"They're not going to Olim," Rosinda said. She didn't know where the words had come from, but she knew they were true.

The captain turned to her with a frown. "What do you mean?"

"That's why they're so far out from the coast," Rosinda said. "They're heading straight for the Eastern Desolation."

"On a Nanghareem ship? Not likely," Captain Steffen said skeptically, shaking her head. "As I said, I'm surprised they even talked Captain Lynnet into taking them to Olim."

"You said no Nanghareem would *willingly* go near the Eastern Desolation," Jerrell said. "What would it take to make them go there against their will?"

Captain Steffen raised an eyebrow and pursed her lips. "Not money," she said. "Magic, or threats, maybe. They would have to be serious threats. The Nanghareem aren't easily intimidated."

"If there are only nine passengers, that's probably not enough to pose a serious threat to the crew. So there must be at least one magic wielder among them," Quigsel said. He rubbed his hands together, almost as if he were enjoying the prospect. "What type of magic; that's the next question."

"No, I think the next question is, will you take us after them?" Rosinda said to the captain. "I know this isn't what we discussed earlier. But we have to catch them."

The captain didn't answer for a long moment, and Rosinda could sense her inner struggle. The gills on her neck fluttered and flared as she thought. *There was no doubt that following the other ship could be dangerous; there was no way of knowing what would happen if they did manage to catch it. But she wanted to prove that Jessara's Lyre was fast enough to do it, and the captain had a taste for adventure that wasn't altogether satisfied shuttling passengers and cargo back and forth between Seafolk and the mainland.*

Rosinda blinked. It felt like she'd been reading the captain's thoughts for a moment. What she'd been thinking had been so obvious. The blue sky wheeled around the ship, and she put a hand on a nearby barrel to steady herself. She felt disoriented.

"The crew won't like it," the captain finally said, still hovering on the edge of uncertainty.

"But they'll do it if you ask them to," Jerrell blurted.

Because I would, Rosinda heard him think. She shook her head. *Stop it!* she told herself. This was strange and uncomfortable, these voices in her head, not at all like when she'd communicated with Kerngold.

The captain grinned at Jerrell. "You're right, they probably will," she said. "But you shouldn't have figured that out so soon. Next thing, you'll be asking to join the crew."

While Jerrell blushed furiously, Captain Steffen turned to Rosinda. "I'll change course," she said, "but I want to be clear on this. You want to overtake them if we can. Then what?"

Because I don't mind getting you there, but I don't want my ship boarded. Rosinda blinked again. She should not be so certain what the captain was thinking. "If they're going to go ashore, you can let us do the same. You don't have to get dangerously close to the *Dancing Mermaid.* I don't want any harm to come to your ship."

The captain nodded once. "All right then. I'll give the orders. Hang onto your hat, Uncle. We're about to fly." She strode off toward the quarterdeck, shouting orders as she went. Rosinda heard her thinking, *I'll show them what the* Lyre *can do.*

"I don't even have a hat," Quigsel said dryly. *I love Jessara dearly, but she can be a bit of a show-off sometimes.*

"Stop it!" Rosinda hissed, pressing her hands to her temples.

"What?" asked Filara. Her thoughts were not as clear as the others' were, jumbled together in a mixture of human and cat languages, but Rosinda plainly heard the words *silly girl, complaining,* and *magister.* Also *fish,* although that was probably only because the cat hadn't eaten anything since the day before.

"I'm hearing everyone's thoughts, and I don't want to!" Rosinda said in a rush. "It's terrible! I want it to stop!"

Quigsel immediately thought, *telepathy* and *magister*, and Jerrell stifled a quick thought about that being embarrassing. Filara leapt up onto the barrel next to Rosinda and commanded, "Rosinda, look at me!"

Rosinda focused on the cat. Filara's mind was a labyrinth of strange sounds, scattered with familiar words here and there. The cat continued to talk, her green eyes boring into Rosinda's as she spoke.

"Rosinda, you have to concentrate. You're the only one who can control this. If you want it to stop, you have to do it yourself. Do you hear me?"

Rosinda nodded. It was a little easier to keep the other thoughts out of her mind while the cat kept talking. "I don't know how, though."

"I want you to imagine that there's a door inside your head that you can close. When it's closed, you won't hear what anyone is thinking. Only what they're saying. Can you see that door? Can you picture it? I want you to tell me what color it is."

"What color?" Rosinda was confused. What color was an imaginary door? "Um...it's green, I guess. How is this helping?"

"Never mind that, just do as I tell you. Now I want you to imagine that this door is very thick, and very tight. It is only through this door that you'll be able to glimpse other people's minds, and only when it's open. There are no cracks. There's no space underneath it. There's no keyhole. All right?"

"All right," Rosinda said uncertainly. Strangely, as the cat spoke, she could begin to see the door forming in her mind. A solid-looking door, like the door of her bedroom back in Cape Breton. She'd always felt safe in the sanctuary of her room behind it. She could close out all the unfriendly kids and all the concern about her parents, the accident, and Aunt Odder's worried looks if she wanted, and lose herself in the comfort of her books.

"Is the door open or closed?" Filara asked, still intently staring at her.

"It's...it's open a little bit," Rosinda answered. The more she concentrated on it, the more real it seemed. The grain of the wood showed faintly through green paint. A brass handle gleamed on one side. She almost felt like she could touch it.

"Now close it, Rosinda, and close it tightly," Filara instructed. "You can open it again when you want, just a little or all the way, but for now I want you to close it tightly. Lock it if you must. You'll have the key if you need it."

Rosinda had been staring into the cat's green eyes all this time, but now she closed her own to concentrate on the door. A few words still slithered through the opening, but they were faint and she didn't know where they originated. She imagined grasping the brass handle, pulling the door toward her. It closed all the way with a solid *clunk*. The sounds stopped. Slowly, she opened her eyes. They all looked at her expectantly.

"Well?" asked Quigsel.

"The door's shut," Rosinda said and let her breath out slowly. "That was...weird."

Traveller came flapping down from the rigging and landed on a crate next to Filara's barrel. "What's wrong?"

"Oh, Rosinda's thaumat abilities just kicked in," Filara said. "What were you doing, Rosinda, trying to read the captain's mind to see if she was going to agree?"

"No," Rosinda said, "I think it started before that. I was looking at the other ship and trying to...it's hard to explain... *feel* if Aunt Odder was there. Then I knew she was, and then I started hearing what you all were thinking. It wasn't like before, though, with...with Kerngold." She bit her lip as she spoke her lost friend's name. "It was...kind of horrible."

Filara looked at them all with a superior tilt to her head. "Does anyone still have any doubts that Rosinda is a magister?"

She turned her gaze on Rosinda. "Even you?"

Rosinda sighed, feeling defeated. "Maybe you're right, Filara. I guess I don't have any other explanation. I just don't know how it can *be*."

Quigsel put a fatherly arm around her. "Your parents...your family...there's a lot of magical ability in your blood, Rosinda. It's part of who you are."

"Surely I'm not the first person to be born with an enchanter and a Kelta for parents," she protested.

"No, I suppose you're right. I'm afraid I can't explain it, either. Just—stop thinking of it as a bad thing," the enchanter suggested. "Ysterad is in danger. Maybe your abilities are needed to save it."

Rosinda huffed. "Maybe. That's what Driasch said, too. But it would make a whole lot more sense if I knew how to use them."

"When you need to, you will," Traveller said gruffly, echoing what the shaman had said before.

Rosinda wished she had half as much confidence in herself as others had in her.

There was no time to dwell on it now. Captain Steffen had unfurled the sails to their fullest, billowing breadth and width, and the *Lyre* leapt through the waves like a bounding cat. Below decks, some of the crew shifted cargo around as the captain sought the configuration that would lend them the most speed. She stood up on the quarterdeck, her hands on the wheel, the wind whipping the tails of her colorful bandanna out behind her. Her eyes were fixed on the ship that rode ahead of them, but a grin tugged at the corners of her mouth.

"She's having the time of her life," Quigsel said, seeing Rosinda looking up at his niece. "She's exactly where she belongs."

Rosinda felt a pang. The last ten days had taken her sense of where she belonged and turned it upside down and inside out. Even the feeling of being home she'd finally had in Ysterad hadn't entirely solved her sense of being adrift. *When this is over,* she thought, *that's what I'm going to do next. Find out for certain where I belong.*

But that would have to wait. She turned her eyes back to the ship ahead of them. What mattered now was catching the *Dancing Mermaid* and rescuing Aunt Odder.

Rosinda climbed the short flight of steps leading to the small deck at the front of the ship. She thought she'd heard Captain Steffen call it the "Fo'c'sle." She stood at the rail with the wind whipping tendrils of her hair around her face. Spray from the waves stung her eyes and wet her cheeks, but she pulled her mind away from those distractions and thought about the door in her mind, the one that Filara had just helped her to create. With a deep breath, she imagined it opening, and pictured her Aunt Odder standing just on the other side.

Can you hear me? Aunt Odder?

Pain pierced Rosinda's temple, and she quickly shut the door, realizing that she hadn't tried to draw any outside power to fuel the magic. She looked over the rail at the dark, seething waves below the ship. They were a long way from land. Could she draw the energy of the world through the water?

She concentrated, searching for that pulse of the world's energy that she'd been able to tap into before, and found it. Again, it held a different flavour here than on land, but she thought she could use it just the same. She drew some off, opened the mental door, and called to Aunt Odder again.

No pain this time. There were no words, no coherent thoughts, but Rosinda caught a hint of a response, a breath that felt like her aunt. Muted, though, as if she slept a deep, deep sleep. Her aunt must be mentally restrained in some way, through drugs or magic, to keep her unconscious. Rosinda had suspected something like that—otherwise she was sure her aunt would have been able to escape from her captors long before this. She was the King's Kelta, after all; her powers were strong. If they had been able to keep her captive for this long—

Jerrell came and stood by her side. He gripped the rail with both hands and stared at the ship they chased, not looking at Rosinda. "Are you okay?"

She nodded. "I'm all right. I was just trying to reach Aunt Odder with this new 'power' of mine and I can't. I can feel that she's there, but her mind—it's as if it's asleep. That's bad."

"Like Quigsel said, they must have someone who can use magic."

"Someone strong," Rosinda agreed.

Jerrell was silent for a moment, watching the other ship. "I think we're gaining on them," he finally said.

Rosinda looked. He was right. She could make out more of the other ship's shape now, and the bright mermaid on the flag that flew atop her mast.

"What will happen when we catch them?" Jerrell asked her.

She turned to look at him. "I don't know," she said. "But I hope you've got some interesting stuff in your backpack this time."

He grinned at her. "No worries," he said. "They'll be no match for us."

"I hope you're right," was all she said, and went back to watching the ship riding the waves ahead of them.

CHAPTER THIRTY-ONE

"They're *where?*" Sekhmet screamed. "Stop them!"

Tyr rolled his eyes. "*Will* you stop that? We're all right here! We can hear you!"

The Egyptian goddess ignored him, leaping up from her golden throne and pacing to the edge of her illusory environment. "I want that witch here without any further interference from the girl! I want her here now!"

"Then use your powers, if you're so much stronger than the rest of us," Morrigan told her in a voice cold enough to freeze water. "Do you think we'd be sitting around doing nothing if it were that easy?"

"My energies are tied up in getting the old Kelta here," Sekhmet growled. "Surely the rest of you could manage to deal with the other ship!"

Tyr waved his handless arm in the air. "Oh, yes, let me sink it for you, shall I? Oh, dear, it didn't work."

"Idiot!" Sekhmet hissed.

Morrigan felt her temper snap. She left her cool stream and strode over to the Egyptian goddess, stopping directly in front of her. The brightness of the desert aura nearly made her cringe, but she stood her ground. "The only way—the *only* way—we have any chance of salvaging this situation is to work together. Really work together, not pretend to cooperate while we're doing things in secret and hiding information from each other."

"And just what have you been hiding, Battle Raven?" Sekhmet asked, her voice suddenly dangerous and low. "What

has your feathered servant told you lately about the girl Kelta?
I haven't heard you sharing anything with the rest of us." She
looked pointedly at Tyr. "Or at least, not with all of us."

"I have had nothing to share," Morrigan said bitterly. "The
girl has done something to my servant, bewitched him or turned
him or magicked him somehow. He is closed off from me."

"And none of the rest of you?" Sekhmet turned to the others.
"None of you are watching them?"

The one-handed god shrugged. "Not really. I had a chance
glimpse through an unknowing creature's eyes once. Nothing
since then. I cannot find him anymore."

Gradivus sat polishing his armour as usual. He didn't bother
to look up at the goddess. "Spying is not my concern," he said.
"Finding new followers and readying myself for battle, those
are the things I deem important. I lent a servant to help protect
the old Kelta and bring her here. I listen to your rages. I wait."

Sekhmet glared at him, then turned back to Morrigan and
Tyr. "I cannot wait to kill the prince," she said with a snarl,
"so that I may wield my full power. You will all be begging
for my mercy then."

And that's supposed to make us want to help you? Morrigan
thought. She had realized before this that the Egyptian goddess
was insane, even by the standards of war gods. The last task
Morrigan, Tyr, and Gradivus would probably cooperate on
would be destroying Sekhmet. Then they would wage war
against each other through their followers, to see who would
rule Ysterad. None of that could happen, though, until the four
worked together to remove the prince. Morrigan concentrated
on making her voice calm and reasonable.

"Perhaps if we focused our collective will, we could call up
a storm to slow them down? Or summon a creature from the
depths of the sea to attack the ship? Their speed is their only
advantage. If we can foil that—"

"My uncle," Gradivus interrupted her in a quiet voice, "was Neptune, god of the sea." He held the gleaming breastplate up to the light and inspected it for dull spots. "If you want to stop a ship, the easiest way is to becalm it. Stop the wind, and you stop the ship."

The others stared at him for a long moment, but he didn't take his eyes from the armour. Finally, Tyr shrugged.

"Well, ladies, shall we take our learned friend's advice?"

Sekhmet tossed her head. "I have better things to do than play with *weather.*" She strode back to her throne and winked out of view.

Morrigan nodded slowly to the Norse god. "It should take less power than calling up a storm."

Gradivus continued to burnish his armour as Morrigan and Tyr put their heads together and set about taming the wind.

CHAPTER THIRTY-TWO

When the wind suddenly abated, Rosinda didn't notice right away. Her focus was on the ship ahead, her mind a jumble of half-formed rescue plans. She only realized there was trouble when Filara paced along the rail and stopped in front of her.

"Time to go to work, magister," Filara said, although this time her tone was serious, not teasing.

"What? We haven't caught them yet—"

"No, and we won't anytime soon," Filara replied. She sat on the railing and motioned her head upwards. "Someone's noticed us."

Rosinda looked up to see the sails fall slack, where only moments ago they had strained at the seams in the full wind. She could feel the ship slowing.

"Magic?" she asked.

Filara shrugged elegantly. "Specific weather control—like this—is not generally in the realm of any single one of the types of magic," she said. "It could be the result of several magic talents working together, or—"

"The gods," Rosinda finished for her.

"I really don't know," the cat said. "But I do know that you and that enchanter had better come up with something to get us moving again, and quickly. I notice that the wind continues to fill the sails of the other ship."

"I hope Quigsel has some ideas, then, because I certainly don't," Rosinda said. She turned away from the rail to go in search of the enchanter, and found him striding across the deck toward her.

"Got any ideas?" he asked.

"I was going to ask you the same thing."

Filara walked up behind them and sat down to wash her face. "If you don't mind my bluntness," she observed between licks, "you two are pathetic."

Quigsel frowned, but Rosinda knew how to handle the cat by now. She squatted down on her heels beside Filara. "What do you think we should do?" she asked.

"I can't tell you how to use magic," Filara said, diligently washing her ears, "but I can see what needs doing. You either need wind to push the sails, or something in the water to move the boat itself."

"How would you suggest we do that?" Quigsel asked, taking his cue from Rosinda.

The cat gave him a scathing look. "You're the magic experts," she said. "I'm just a cat. But," she added, "I've heard there are some very large, very *unusual* creatures in the Burning Sea." She rose and walked away toward the hatchway, presumably in search of another nap, as if she hadn't a care in the world.

Quigsel watched her go, shaking his head. "Surely she can't mean what I think she means," he muttered.

"What?" Rosinda had pulled Aunt Odder's book out of her pack and leafed through, looking for any spells related to ships, sailing, or weather control. So far, she hadn't found much.

Quigsel knelt down on the deck beside her. "You won't find anything in there. The cat's right, although I hate to admit it. If we work together— or maybe you could even do it alone—we might be able to summon one of the blink whales."

Rosinda stared at him. "Blink whales? Now I'm sure I've never heard of those."

"Huge creatures, live in the Burning Sea, mostly," Quigsel said. "They have inherent magic that lets them travel very fast—it's like they blink out of one place and into another."

"How does that help us?" Rosinda sat back on her heels and looked up again at the limp sails.

"They have an aura," the enchanter said. "Anything in the aura, close to the whale when it blinks—well, it blinks, too. Ships, people, other fish."

Rosinda nodded. "So if we could call one of these whales, get it close to the ship, and then get it to move toward the other one—"

"Right. We'd move, too."

She looked skeptically at him. "How hard is it going to be to do all that?"

The enchanter shrugged. "No idea. If you can summon one, I might be able to charm it into wanting to help us."

Rosinda went back to the book, searching for a summoning spell. "I'll try it," she said. "I'll try anything. We can't let them get away from us, not when we're this close."

Rosinda quickly found the spell she wanted. In fact, when she came to the right page and read it over, she realized that the words were already in her mind. She just hadn't trusted her memory. *I guess I have to start doing that more,* she thought. *Trusting myself.*

"You'll have to describe the blink whales to me," she told Quigsel. "I have to picture them for the summoning spell to work, but I've never seen one."

"Me, neither," Quigsel admitted. "But surely one of the crew has." He ran to speak to Jessara, and in a moment was back with a confused-looking sailor in tow.

"Aye, I've seen a blink whale before," he said. "I'd hoped never to see one up close again, though. The feeling when they move, and you go with them—" he shuddered. "It's not pleasant. Not pleasant at all."

"Could you describe it for me—the whale, I mean?" Rosinda asked. She didn't think it was wise to tell him why she wanted to know.

He shrugged. "Big—almost as long as the *Lyre* from tip to tail, the one I saw. White, with blue-black stripes running the length of her...not in straight lines, but wavy, like she was covered in strands of seaweed. Blunt-nosed. A blowhole, like any whale, but in front of that and a little bigger, a sea-gem. The one I saw, hers was a blue-green color, but I hear that's not the case with all of them."

"What's a sea-gem?" Rosinda asked, frowning.

The sailor pursed his lips. "Can't say that I know, exactly. It looks for all the world like a jewel, cut and set there in their head. Glows when they're about to blink-move, so you might have a chance of getting away in time if you're fast and the wind is with you. It's not a real jewel, though. If you kill a blink whale, or come across one already dead, you'll find the 'jewel' is just a part of the flesh, soft like skin. Sad to say, a terrible number have been killed for a gem that doesn't exist."

Rosinda thanked the man, and he returned to his post. She'd built an image of the whale in her mind as he spoke, although she hoped the color of sea-gem she imagined wouldn't matter for the spell.

"Ready?" she asked Quigsel.

He had one of his own books out and open and a pearl the size of a marble in one hand. "Ready."

Rosinda drew power from the ocean, brought the image of the blink whale to the forefront of her mind, and recited the words of the spell. She concentrated on the whale for a long moment after the words had been spoken, hoping it would carry the summoning through the water until it found a whale.

"I hope we're not too far from the Burning Sea," Quigsel fretted. "I don't know how far north they usually come."

Rosinda looked at the ship ahead of them, still pulling away with her billowing sails. "Let's hope there's one exploring near here," she said. "We can't afford to wait very—"

The swell of a huge wave rocked the *Lyre* sideways, and Rosinda grasped at the rail to keep from sliding across the deck. Quigsel lost his footing and skittered into a nearby crate. Somehow he kept hold of the book, but Rosinda heard the pearl drop and roll across the planks. A tremendous splash sounded off the port side, and a mournful-sounding wail filled the air.

Rosinda ran to the side and looked over. Alongside the ship swam one of the most beautiful creatures she'd ever seen, lithe and graceful in the water, its back and sides painted with irregular dark bands. An intelligent eye swivelled to look up at her, and a bottle-green spot sparkled like a gem in the center of its head, high above its eyes.

"It's here," Rosinda breathed. "It worked. Quigsel, it worked," she called in a low voice, not wanting to startle the creature. "Quick, you have to charm it."

"I can't find the pearl," he answered in an agonized voice. "The spell won't work without it."

"Look harder!" Rosinda turned back to the blink whale. The sea-gem on its forehead began to glow brighter as she watched. "I think it's going to blink away again," she cried.

That could be disastrous. If the whale blinked itself back to where it had been, they would be even further away from the ship that carried Aunt Odder. Without stopping to think, Rosinda opened her imaginary door spoke to the whale.

Please, wait. We need your help! she implored.

The creature's mind came into focus, disjointed and difficult to read. It was like looking at words in a foreign language, but Rosinda knew she had at least caught its attention.

We need to go north and east, and close to the shore, she thought at the whale, picturing in her mind the coastline that was hazy on the horizon. She thought of the Eastern Desolation on Quigsel's map, although she didn't know how much sense that would make to a whale. *Can you take us there? Please?*

Although there were no words that Rosinda could identify, she could feel the mind of the great creature like a soft, blue haze. It seemed to flow into her own mind through the open door, but it wasn't intrusive, the way the thoughts of the others on board the ship had been. It felt for a moment as if her whole brain was gently sifted and evaluated. There was no answer to her question, not in words, but she felt the benevolent nature of the whale envelop her mind. It seemed to be saying *yes*. The sea-gem brightened.

"Hold on, everyone!" Rosinda turned and yelled to the others. For a moment she wondered if she'd done the right thing. The sailor's words came back to her: *It's not pleasant. Not pleasant at all.*

The whale blinked.

When Rosinda had crossed between the two worlds, everything had gone black around her, and she'd had the sensation of falling. Travelling with a blink whale was nothing like that. The world did not go black; in fact, the blue light of water and sky intensified to an almost painful brightness, making Rosinda squint. A sudden, nauseating rush of movement pushed them forward. Sailors screamed, men and women alike. Sea and ship blurred together like a watercolor painting in the rain. Rosinda felt wind and sea spray pass *through* her body, and then the shoreline materialized in front of them, frighteningly close. They had landed so close to the *Dancing Mermaid* that Rosinda could see people moving about on the main deck.

"Drop sails!" Captain Steffen roared, and the huge cloths thundered down. If the wind freshened while they were this close to shore, they'd be dashed against the rocks or run the hull of the ship aground.

"Ugh," Jerrell groaned. "What was that?"

"A blink," Quigsel said slowly, still clutching the book to his chest. "That sailor was right. Not pleasant at all."

Again?

Rosinda was still trying to recover from the blink when the question formed in her mind. It took her a moment to realize it came from the whale.

"No!" she cried out loud, then concentrated on focusing her thoughts. *No, thank you. This is wonderful. Thank you so much for your help.*

Warmth spread through her mind, a last touch of the whale's consciousness, and then she felt it withdraw from their connection. Rosinda looked over the ship's rail to see the silvery flash as it dove away from the ship. Her legs wobbled at the thought of what she had managed to do, and she wanted desperately to sit down for a moment.

A sudden shout from the sailor in the crow's-nest tore her attention away from her own weakness.

"They're going to run aground!"

Rosinda, with Quigsel and Jerrell behind her, ran to the starboard side rail and watched in shock and horror as the *Dancing Mermaid,* sails belling in the stiff wind, raced at full speed toward the rocky shore.

CHAPTER THIRTY-THREE

"What are they doing?" Jerrell gasped.

Rosinda's heart pounded painfully in her chest. She couldn't breathe, couldn't draw enough air into her lungs. What would happen to Aunt Odder if the ship grounded on the rocks?

Captain Steffen ran down the steps from the quarterdeck two at a time. "Something's wrong!" she shouted. "Captain Lynnet would *never* deliberately ground his ship. They're in trouble."

"Don't take us any closer," Rosinda said, amazed that her voice didn't shake. She could hardly hear herself over the throbbing of her heart. "I don't want you in danger. Can you put the ship's boat over the side, and we'll row to shore from here?"

"I'll send some of my crew with you," the captain said. "The folk on the *Mermaid* might need help."

"They might need more help than we're able to offer," Quigsel muttered, but not loud enough for his niece to hear as she set about ordering the keelboats lowered.

"What do you mean?" Rosinda asked him.

He shook his head. "Two possibilities." He held up a finger. "The kidnappers have incapacitated the crew—which means I don't know what will happen to them when the ship runs aground and breaks up on the rocks." He held up a second finger. "Or they've already—dealt with them in some other way. As Jessara said, the captain would never willingly ground his own ship."

Rosinda gulped. Quigsel's words brought home to her with sudden clarity the type of people they were dealing with. Not simply kidnappers following orders, but cutthroats who would stop at nothing to achieve their goals. And Aunt Odder had been in their clutches for over a week now.

Cold anger replaced her fear. "We'll deal with whatever we find," she told the enchanter. "Some men from the *Lyre* might come in handy. Let's move and see how quickly we can get to shore."

The ship's boat touched the surface of the water. Rosinda and the others scrambled down a swaying rope ladder. As Rosinda neared the end of the ladder, a tremendous crash reverberated through the air. The *Mermaid* had hit the rocks.

Rosinda looked over in time to see the ship heel crazily to the port side, sails still straining with the wind. The force pushed the ship over even further, and crates and barrels that had stood on the main deck slid dangerously down the tilted planks to crash against the rail. Eerily, Rosinda heard no sounds of shouting or cries for help. As she watched, one of the figures on the main deck slid toward the smashed rail and over the side, splashing into the water without making a sound.

"Something's wrong," she breathed, and dropped the last few feet into the ship's boat.

"Everything's wrong," corrected the sailor who caught and steadied her.

She turned to see the man who'd told her about the blink whales. "No cap'n would run his ship aground on purpose," he said, shaking his head.

"I'm sorry about the blink whale," Rosinda said sheepishly. "You were right. It wasn't pleasant."

He grinned briefly. "No, it wasn't. I warned you. But what's life without a little adventure?"

The sailors from the *Lyre* began to row with strong, quick

strokes toward the shore. Quigsel pulled a long spyglass out of his cloak and trained it on the *Dancing Mermaid.*

"They're putting a ship's boat down, as well," he announced.

"Let me see," Rosinda said, and he handed the glass to her. Through its round eye, the deck came into clear focus. A few men lowered the boat, while others stood awkwardly on the sharply canted deck, staring vacantly either at the dark water below them or up at the sky. They didn't seem the least bit alarmed at their situation or the predicament of their ship.

"They must be enchanted," Rosinda said, still watching them.

"No question about it," Quigsel replied. "If we can get close enough, I might be able to snap them out of it. The ship's a loss, though. I can't magic it into being seaworthy again."

Rosinda drew a sharp breath as three more figures appeared on the deck, near where the ship's boat hung over the side. A man and a red-haired woman, dragging another woman between them. She appeared as unconcerned and vacant as the rest of the crew, but Rosinda would have known that flyaway blonde hair anywhere.

"Aunt Odder," she whispered. The two kidnappers struggled to carry her down the rope ladder to the boat waiting below. She did nothing to either help or hinder them. It was as if she were sleepwalking. The image in the spyglass went blurry and Rosinda had to lower it to wipe tears from her eyes.

"Take heart," the enchanter murmured to her, easing the spyglass out of her hand. He raised it to watch the activity on the other ship. "We'll have her out of there in no time."

There was a hard, cold edge to his voice that Rosinda hadn't heard before. It seemed to steel something in her. She squinted at the other ship, not needing the spyglass to see the other kidnappers swarming down the rope ladder. None of the regular crew left the boat.

"We'll give them time to get to the shore," she heard herself say. "Once they're well away from the *Mermaid*, try to get her crew back in the real world. Once we're on land, this crew can head to the *Mermaid* and help as they can."

The *Lyre's* crew still strained at the oars when the other boat's occupants clambered onto the sandy beach. The *Mermaid* had grounded herself close to the shore, so they had a head start. It surprised Rosinda that none of the kidnappers attempted to use any magical means against them.

"I thought I'd have to shield us before this," Quigsel agreed, clutching his spellbook close to his chest. "We know they must have a magic-wielder with them. Why haven't they done anything?"

"I'm sure we'll soon find out," Filara observed tersely. She sat in the absolute center of the small boat, as far as possible from any stray splashes of water.

As they rode the waves toward shore, Rosinda studied the landscape of the Eastern Desolation. The name fit. No trace of green showed anywhere, and the sand on the shoreline was a patchwork of sickly greys and burnt-looking browns. The shore sloped up away from the water to a low rise, where scrub bushes provided some ground cover, but even the few leaves they sprouted were not green, but a pale yellowish-brown. Further in the distance, striated rock formations rose in twisted and blasted shapes toward the sky. Even the sky overhead looked strange, its normal blue tinged with orange and grey. Rosinda shivered.

"What's wrong with this place?" Jerrell asked.

"Magic misused," Quigsel answered. "A battle here long ago practically destroyed the land."

"People must have been much more powerful, then," Jerrell said. "I haven't seen any magic since I came to Ysterad that could do all this."

"You're right. There were many...magistera then," Quigsel said, not looking at Rosinda.

Rosinda felt a tightness in her chest. "Magistera did this?"

The enchanter was silent for a moment. "Yes, Rosinda, they did. Unfortunately, controlling that much power makes some people only want more."

"I don't want it at all," Rosinda said, her throat tight.

"I know." Quigsel reached over and squeezed her hand. "That's why you're a safe person to have it."

It didn't make her feel much better.

They drew closer to the shoreline, and the kidnappers scuttled up the sloping beach toward the line of scrub. The red-haired woman and one of the Irylians propelled Aunt Odder between them, while two more, one of them the dwarf Traveller had mentioned, followed. They seemed to have trouble walking on their own, and one of the Irylians supported each. The remaining three men walked backwards, watching the second boat approach. Two carried bows, but they were still too far out of range to bother firing.

"Rosinda." Filara climbed up onto her lap, staring up at her with serious green eyes. "It's time for you to use those powers."

"What?"

The cat stared intently at her. "You can find out where they're going, what their plans are. Open that door in your mind and invite their thoughts in."

Rosinda pulled back from the cat, flinching. "It's so... horrible. You don't understand."

"We all have to do things we don't like, Rosinda. Ease into it, if you must. This is one of our only advantages. We have to make the most of it."

Reluctantly, Rosinda nodded. She knew in her heart that the cat was right. Any information they could get would help them plan their next move, and the shoreline loomed closer.

She took a deep breath, clenched her hands in her lap, and focused on the biggest of the three men who watched their approach. She drew power from the dark waves beneath the boat, then focused on him, opening the green door in her mind just a crack, for the stream of his thoughts to seep in.

It wasn't easy. She knew the power did not work both ways, that he could not read her mind unless she allowed it. But she still felt invaded, as if someone were pawing through her things. The man's thoughts were a jumble, swirling with dark images and horrible notions. It felt repulsive and ugly, like walking down a dark alleyway filled with slippery mud and spiders. After a long moment of letting his thoughts pour into her mind, she didn't think she could take any more. Fighting down a rising pain and churning in her stomach, she closed her eyes, closed the door in her mind, and slumped forward, exhausted.

Jerrell helped her straighten up and put an arm around her shoulders to support her.

"Well?" asked Filara.

Rosinda nodded, grimacing. "It worked. I got into the mind of the biggest of those last three men. He's working for a goddess named Sekhmet. She's promised—" Rosinda broke off. She didn't want to mention some of the things the goddess had promised him. "She's promised him he'll rule all of Irylia for her, and possibly the Horsetribes as well."

"What's wrong with Oddeline?" Quigsel wanted to know.

"The two men who are following her—the ones having trouble walking on their own—they're thaumats, followers of two of the other gods. They're using magic to keep Aunt Odder's mind...muzzled. At first, it was just one of them, and the other was controlling the crew of the *Mermaid*. Now it takes both of them to keep her controlled. Dneb—that's the big man's name—he's disgusted with them, thinks they're weak. But I think she must be fighting them," Rosinda said, feeling both pride and fear for her aunt well up inside her.

"So there are two thaumats, both pretty weak," Quigsel

said, "and the Kelton woman—but you don't think she's Kelta, right?"

"No, I didn't get that feeling from her in Cape Breton, and there was nothing in Dneb's thoughts about it."

"Any indication of other magic users?" the enchanter asked. Rosinda shook her head.

"Then we should be able to overcome them and get Oddeline out of their clutches," Quigsel said excitedly. "Between the two of us, we outmatch them magically."

"I know," Rosinda said slowly. She hated to tell them the other information she'd learned on her dark visit to the Irylian's mind. "But that's not all."

The others looked expectantly at her.

"They're on their way to meet the gods," she finally told them. "And there isn't much time. It sounded like they'll be here any minute."

CHAPTER THIRTY-FOUR

"They're coming!" Sekhmet's strident voice intruded into the solitude of Morrigan's cool green forest grove. Morrigan had just received the same message, delivered much more calmly by her servant, Banna, along with the news that the young Kelta was right behind them.

"I will see you at the Gathering-Place," she told the Egyptian goddess, and mentally shut her out.

Morrigan gazed into the water of the stream. Things were finally happening, and yet she felt a strange emotion...was it sadness? Events would progress quickly now. They'd find out from the old Kelta where the prince was and deal with him. Their followers could be urged to all-out war. The uneasy alliance of the four gods would end.

She'd be glad to part ways with the Egyptian goddess. And the Roman, Gradivus—he was too single-minded, too wrapped up in his armour and strategies, to be good company. In a word, boring. The Norseman, Tyr—she had enjoyed his company, in a strange way. It would be more difficult than she'd expected to go to war against him.

There was also the worrying development with the crow-spirit. Banna thought he still travelled with the young Kelta, but he had closed his mind off to Morrigan. She'd have to investigate that. Had he made a choice to betray her? Or had the girl twisted his mind against her?

The Celtic goddess stood, brushing leaves from her skirt with a sigh. It was time to go and face all these things. She glanced once more around the glade she'd created for herself. It had felt tedious and lonely here at first, as she daydreamed about the glory of the battles soon to come. Now she felt strangely hesitant to leave it.

She shook herself out of her reverie. What was she thinking? Of course war and followers were much preferable to sitting alone in the woods. Soon she'd be back where she belonged, worshipped and loved and feared by fierce warriors, commanding troops on the battlefield.

But even as she gathered her strength to move to the Gathering-Place, she felt as if the sad, grey eyes of the one-handed god were watching her. What message they held, she could not be sure.

CHAPTER THIRTY-FIVE

When Rosinda felt the hull scrape the shore, she gathered Filara in her arms and climbed over the side. Two of the sailors from the *Lyre* leapt out and held the boat steady for Quigsel and Jerrell. Traveller took wing and sailed low overhead toward the beach.

"Go to the *Mermaid* and see if they need help," Rosinda told the sailor nearest her. The crew of the wrecked ship seemed to have regained their senses once the thaumats were away from them; shouts and other signs of life rose from the ship. Without magic or weapons, the crew of the *Lyre* could do little to help Rosinda and the others now. They might as well lend a hand where it would do the most good.

Rosinda held Filara with one arm and put the other hand on Jerrell's shoulder. "You can go with them, if you want," she said. "Without magic, I don't know—"

He grinned at her. "Leave now, and miss all the fun? I don't think so," he said, although his eyes were serious.

"I don't want you to get hurt."

"I know," he said, hitching his backpack higher up on his shoulders. "Don't worry. It'll be okay."

He splashed away from her, following Quigsel. Rosinda sighed. She would have been relieved—but sadder—if he'd gone out to the other ship. But Jerrell had done what he wanted since the day he'd followed her into the woods, so he wasn't likely to change now. She followed the others to shore, trying to splash as little as possible. Filara complained all the way.

Once on the beach, they followed the tracks of the kidnappers. The trail led straight to where they had disappeared over the top of the rise and into the scrub. The sand burned, hot and scorched, underfoot.

"Do we have a plan yet?" Quigsel asked.

Rosinda squinted ahead. "They know we're right behind them. Do you have any spells that might incapacitate any of them? If we can take out a few, I'm just going to try to fight my way to Aunt Odder. It's taking two thaumats to keep her under control. If I can get her free, she'll be able to help us from there."

"I've got a flare gun in my pack," Jerrell offered. "I took it out of my uncle's camping gear when we were home, but there were only three flares, and they may not make great weapons. I'll try for the two at the back, with the bows. It should distract them at least, especially if their clothes go afire."

"The thaumats are weak and their full attention is on Oddeline," Quigsel said, panting slightly as he trudged through the sand. "I think I could hit both of them with a sleeping spell. It would never work if they were fully alert, but their minds are occupied. Under the circumstances, I think it will do."

"That leaves four Irylians and the Kelton woman," Rosinda said. Her voice was steady, but her heart quailed. *Five people? How could she deal with five enemies on her own? Even with her Kelta skills and whatever magic she might manage, that seemed impossible.*

Jerrell must have realized how it sounded. "But by then your aunt should be free, at least mentally. She'll be able to help."

They had almost reached the line of scrub. The land flattened out beyond it, but they were still on the low side of the rise and couldn't see their quarry yet.

Rosinda shrugged. "Maybe. We can't count on it though."

Filara picked her way through the sand, obviously annoyed at the feel of it in her paws. "Don't forget about me. I'll be distracting one of those brutes." She paused to shake sand out of her claws.

"And I," Traveller said. He'd been hopping along behind them, keeping silent up until now. "I'm going to see if I can see them," he offered, and flapped into the air.

Rosinda said carefully, "So if everything goes according to plan, there'll only be three for me to worry about." It still sounded scary, but she concentrated on the image of the kidnappers herding Aunt Odder up the beach. If she kept the anger burning, she wasn't as frightened.

"Get down!" Traveller dropped back down to the beach as quickly as he had taken off. He'd barely gotten above their heads. As he spoke, two arrows whistled overhead, *thunking* into the sand just a few feet beyond them.

"This is it. They're not waiting for us to get any closer," Jerrell said, his voice thin with excitement. He hauled two flares out of his pack and a silver lighter from his pocket.

Wait, Rosinda thought frantically, *I'm not ready!* But already her Kelta instincts reacted, her hand going automatically to the hilt of her sword. She raised her head, trying to see over the rise. They were still too low, their attackers too far away. She crept forward, closer to the bushes, and peered through. She felt, more than saw, Jerrell ease up behind her.

"Can you see them?"

Rosinda nodded. "The last three have stopped. I can't see the others. Two of them have their bows nocked to fire again, but they're just waiting."

Jerrell inched up beside her. He had one flare in his right hand, ready to load into the gun, and the other tucked into his belt. "Are we ready, then?"

Rosinda nodded. "Quigsel?"

"Ready." The enchanter's voice was right behind her.

"Then let's do it!"

Without another word, Jerrell pushed a flare into the gun, stood up, aimed and fired. The shot sounded unnaturally loud in the still surroundings, and Rosinda's heart thumped. The report echoed back from the rocky cliffs. Jerrell ducked down quickly as an arrow snaked overhead.

One of the men screamed as Jerrell stood again and fired the second flare. Then Rosinda stood and ran toward the third man, pulling her sword from its scabbard as she went. The red fog coiled and spilled down over her vision, but her mind was clear and calm.

Both bowmen were down. One flailed and rolled on the ground in an attempt to smother the flames that licked at his clothing. The other lay ominously still. The third man had drawn a long, curved sword and stood watching Rosinda's approach.

When she was within a couple of sword's-lengths of him, she stopped. "I have no wish to harm you," she said calmly. "Put down your sword and you may yet live."

He grinned, a wide, toothy grin that had no humour in it. "So this is the little girl my mistress has waited for," he said. "You are brave. I admire that. However, you must be the one to put down the sword, and come along with me. The Lady of Pestilence is eager to meet you."

Her Kelta training controlled her now, the red fog urging her on, strengthening her resolve, planning her attacks. "I must decline your offer," she said politely, and lunged in to attack.

Surprise slowed his hand for a split second. He managed to parry her blow and tried to twist his blade to force hers out of her hand. She dodged, too fast for him. He lunged, she defended, and the battle was on.

Part of Rosinda felt as if she watched the fight from the sidelines. Her "Kelta brain," as she'd started to think of it, directed her movements and planned her attacks. It studied her opponent, quickly learning his strengths and weaknesses. Her world had narrowed down to the clang of steel on steel, the pulse of the world-energy under her feet, and the face of the man she fought. She wasn't sure yet if he was trying to kill her. She thought not.

She lost track of how long they moved across the hard-packed bare ground in a complicated dance of lunge and parry, attack and defend. Finally Rosinda sensed a change in her opponent. The man was tiring. Her blade had touched him more than once, and blood flowed freely from cuts on his arms and a shallow slash across his midriff. His own blade had not touched Rosinda.

Kelta brat!...Goddess will kill me...interfering...skilled for one so young...tired—

The words appeared in her mind unexpectedly. In the single-mindedness of the battle, her concentration on the "door" in her mind had slipped for a moment. Her opponent's thoughts, so intent on her, flowed through unchecked.

Rosinda knew that his fatigue would soon lead to a mistake. She still felt alert and only slightly winded from the duel. Once he made that mistake, she would have him. It made her angry. Why was he being so stupid? He had realized by now that she was a match for him. Would he really keep fighting her until it meant his death?

If you're so tired, why don't you just go to sleep? she thought angrily. *I don't want to hurt you or kill you. I just want Aunt Odder back—*

Her thoughts broke off in amazement as the man suddenly froze. Rosinda had to check her sword thrust or she would have run it straight through him. His eyes fluttered closed and his sword dangled from limp fingers. Then he collapsed in a heap. A gentle snore broke the stunned silence.

"Excellent!" Jerrell was on the man in a second, tying his hands behind his back as the Irylian slept on. The red fog of battle receded and Rosinda gradually became aware of her surroundings. Jerrell and Quigsel had dragged the two bowmen a little distance away and tied them up as Rosinda and the third man fought.

Filara sniffed at one of the trussed-up Irylians, then crossed to investigate Rosinda's opponent. "No magic here," she said, wrinkling her nose. "They were clearly outmatched."

"You can *smell* magic?" Rosinda asked, surprised.

"Oh, yes," the cat casually replied. "That's one of the reasons I first suspected you were a magister. You practically reek of magic."

"Thanks a lot. I was happier not knowing that."

"You're welcome."

Rosinda turned to the enchanter. "You shouldn't have used your sleeping spell on him. I thought you were going to save it for the thaumats! He was tiring. I could have—"

Quigsel held up a hand. "I didn't do anything. I still have my spell."

"Then what—" But even as she spoke, she knew. *Why don't you just go to sleep?* she'd thought at him. And he had. Rosinda swallowed hard. "Then I guess—I guess I did it."

Quigsel pursed his lips. "Mentally?"

Rosinda nodded.

The enchanter stared at her. "I don't know what you can or can't do anymore, Rosinda. I have no experience with magistera." He grinned. "But I'll take anything. Let's find the others before they get too far away!"

Despite her misgivings, Rosinda nodded. Aunt Odder was the first priority. There'd be time to figure it all out later, she hoped.

The others were no longer in sight, but their options were limited. Two tall, twisted rock formations reached into the sky a few hundred meters away, forming an opening into a narrow pass. After a quick study of the ground, Jerrell said that they had travelled in that direction.

Traveller hopped to where Rosinda stood. "The gods approach," he said in a low croak. "I feel Morrigan's presence. If we hurry, we might be able to get your aunt and be gone before they arrive."

"We're moving," Rosinda said. "Come on, everyone. This is it."

They followed the rock-strewn trail to the narrow pass. Traveller flew ahead, checking for a possible ambush. He wheeled back to them almost immediately and reported that the coast was clear.

"It turns inside," the crow said, "I couldn't see all the way in. But no one waited just inside."

"And you believe him, I suppose," Filara said.

"Yes," Rosinda replied. "I do."

The crow turned and spoke directly to the cat for the first time in a long while. "Do you love Rosinda?"

Filara blinked. "Of course I do," she said indignantly.

"Then why is it so hard for you to believe that someone else might, too?" Turning away, he flew off ahead of them again, to the opening in the rock.

For once, the cat seemed to have nothing to say.

Rosinda entered the narrow pass first. She let her mind make a quick search, probing for nearby thoughts. She felt no one but her companions, so she closed the door again. They passed between the tall stone columns.

A passageway wound ahead of her like an underground tunnel, but open to the sky far above her head. It seemed to be a natural feature, the cliff walls rough and uneven, not smoothly cut by hand. Rosinda led them through the tunnel warily but quickly. Knowing that Aunt Odder was so near hastened her steps. The others followed close on her heels.

The passageway widened into a huge open canyon, surrounded on all sides by striated walls of rock. The kidnappers came into view, still moving away from them.

"Now!" Rosinda hissed.

Quigsel nodded, already reading the words of his spell from the book. Rosinda took off at a run towards the kidnappers. Filara bounded easily beside her, and Traveller flew low over her head.

The red-haired woman Rosinda had encountered back in Cape Breton released her hold on Aunt Odder, leaving her to slump against the remaining Irylian. Morrigan's servant turned back to meet Rosinda, sword drawn and eyes flashing. Just as Rosinda reached her, the two thaumats collapsed to the rocky ground. Without meaning to, she grinned. That should mean Aunt Odder was free of their mental control.

"Don't look so pleased," the red-haired woman growled. "There's nothing here you should be happy about." She struck out at Rosinda confidently. Apparently, she expected things to go better for her now that they were in Ysterad.

You couldn't be more wrong, Rosinda thought. Beside her, Filara and Traveller attacked the two Irylians who had been in charge of the thaumats. She defended against the woman's attack, but did not strike offensively yet. She backed away a few steps. "All I want is my aunt," Rosinda said calmly. "Release her to me, and we'll leave."

The woman smirked. "You won't be leaving here, any of you, until my mistress and the others are finished with you," she said. "And then you might not be leaving here at all." She came at Rosinda quickly, and the red fog washed down over Rosinda's vision once again. Her mind became cool and detached. Her body moved with a will of its own in the graceful and deadly dance of battle.

She realized quickly again that the red-haired woman's goal was to disarm her. Her orders must be to deliver Rosinda in one piece. However, she was very skilled at defending herself. Rosinda began to grow annoyed. She wanted this fight over with, so she could see to Aunt Odder. She could risk only quick glances away from her attacker, but she didn't think that Aunt Odder had moved, even with the thaumats' control gone. The last Irylian still supported her.

Parrying a flurry of quick thrusts, Rosinda opened the door

in her mind, seeking a way into the woman's mind. Perhaps she could simply put her to sleep, as she'd done with the big Irylian. But this time, she heard no thoughts from her opponent. Either the woman's mind was unusually strong, or she'd been trained to resist such mental attacks.

And then, after a particularly agile block, the red-haired Kelton woman froze in place like a statue. Rosinda checked her sword in mid-swing and held her own attack.

"Excellent!" she heard Quigsel say from behind her. It must have been a spell from the enchanter that had ended this fight, and Rosinda didn't mind at all. She looked around. The man whom Filara had attacked lay on the ground with his hands bound behind him. She suspected Jerrell had something to do with that. Another sat sullenly clutching his arm, his face scratched and his hair matted with blood. The sleeve of his shirt was blood soaked and in tatters, no doubt where Traveller's claws had raked him. Jerrell stood close to him, pointing the flare gun unwaveringly.

The last man standing still supported Aunt Odder's limp form. Rosinda took a step toward him.

"Lower her down gently and step away," she ordered. "You must see that it's the only intelligent thing to do."

Before he could answer, a rushing noise filled the canyon, as if a thousand birds had all flown low overhead at once. A woman's voice sounded, coming from everywhere and nowhere.

"Actually, the intelligent thing would be to bring her here, to us," the voice said. It sounded hot and feverish, but sent a cold chill down Rosinda's spine. "And since the alternative is certain death, I think our friend here is going to agree with me."

CHAPTER THIRTY-SIX

Just beyond Aunt Odder and the Irylian, strange things happened. Four large thrones appeared out of nowhere, arrayed in a straight line on the rocky floor of the canyon. They were each of a different material; hammered gold, polished grey marble, rough mountain stone, and intricately carved wood. Their size was remarkable. Three humans could have sat in any one throne.

There was little time to study them, because their owners appeared, seated in them. In the golden throne sat a woman with the head of a lion. She wore a crimson sheath that reminded Rosinda of the ancient Egyptians. She was three times as large as a normal human, and held a long golden sceptre. Two cats, house cats in appearance but the size of cougars, sat docilely at her feet. Rosinda heard Filara hiss behind her. The woman's lion-eyes seemed almost to glow as they took in the scene. Rosinda felt certain this was the woman who had spoken.

The man next to her, in the marble throne, wore brightly gleaming bronze armor and a twined wreath of coppery leaves on his head. A polished shield rested against the side of his throne, and a sharpened lance leaned close to his hand. His face was smooth and handsome. He looked, surprisingly, rather bored.

The occupant of the stone throne wore a ragged fur tunic, and his face was craggy and worn. His left arm ended in a stump rather than a hand. Greying hair fell almost to his shoulders, and his eyes, too, were grey and knowing. He cradled his handless arm in his lap, and leaned in his throne toward the last in line, the wooden throne.

In this last one sat another woman, with long, glossy auburn hair that fell past the seat of the throne and spilled over the front of her green brocade gown. Rosinda blinked. Viewed directly, she looked human, but in Rosinda's peripheral vision, she seemed to have the head of a crow. Like the others, she was huge.

The Irylian holding Aunt Odder hadn't moved yet, probably paralyzed by fear and shock as much as the red-haired Kelton woman remained paralyzed by Quigsel's magic. He seemed to come out of his trance then, however, and moved just a step toward the gods.

Instinctively, Rosinda put up a hand and spoke the same spell she'd used to stop Traveller from flying away. *"Onthande!"*

The Irylian froze in place.

The lion-headed goddess leapt from her throne and took two quick paces toward Rosinda. "Stop that!" she screamed, in a voice that rattled the very stones on the ground. "Interfering little brat! I'll teach you to counter my wishes!"

She raised a hand quivering with rage, and Rosinda instinctively pulled energy from the earth beneath her feet. She had the odd sensation that it was laced with whispered words, the way the air had been in the Crypt of a Thousand Voices. The words of a spell to create a protective shield rose in her mind, and she spoke them mentally, not aloud as she had with the other spells. There simply wasn't time.

No dramatic bolt of lightning or beam of light erupted from the goddess's hand. Rosinda felt the force of the goddess's magic ripple through the earth around her, but it didn't touch her. It was as if Rosinda stood under a giant invisible umbrella that reached to the ground.

The goddess's cat-like eyes burned bright with rage and she shrieked, no doubt ready to launch another attack. A hand caught her arm from behind and swung her away from

Rosinda. It was the bored-looking god.

"Sekhmet. Don't expend your energy," he calmly told her. "The child's not worth it. Let's just find the prince so the real battles can begin."

While the goddess was distracted, Rosinda opened the door in her mind and searched for her Aunt Odder's consciousness. What she found almost destroyed her hope. She touched her aunt's mind with tender mental fingers, but found only a deep chasm of unconsciousness. Aunt Odder had been so exhausted from her long mental battle with the thaumats that, released from their hold, her mind seemed to have collapsed. It was not sleep, from which Rosinda could have woken her. It was deeper than that, and more frightening.

Rosinda hurriedly closed the mental door. There would be no help coming from Aunt Odder. All Rosinda could do was try to protect her and the others.

The goddess turned back to her for a moment, a sneer curling one side of the cat-like mouth. "Perhaps you are right, Mars Gradivus," she said. "I will deal with this one later, at my leisure."

As she spoke the words, Rosinda saw through them. *She's too weak to do much to me, and she knows it.* Rosinda's spell had been quick, but the goddess had wanted to frighten her more than anything else. Moreover, she was desperate not to let the others know.

"Wake the old woman, then," the Egyptian goddess ordered no one in particular. "Let us find this prince."

Rosinda thought she saw the rough-faced god roll his eyes, but he raised his left arm towards Aunt Odder.

The familiar crimson fog gathered at the edges of her vision. The pounding of the earth-power under her feet felt like a giant heartbeat, strong enough to topple her over. *This probably means I'm about to do something stupid.*

She said loudly, "She doesn't know! She is injured. Leave

her alone."

The red-haired goddess narrowed her eyes at Rosinda. "Our information says that she does know. That she is probably the *only* one who does."

"Your information is out of date," Rosinda said coldly. Her heart raced so hard it felt like someone pounded on the inside of her chest with two fists. "She did know, but not now. The situation has changed."

"Which means that you must know, Kelta-girl," drawled the one-handed god. "And probably your friends, too." The threat in his words was easy to read.

The red-haired goddess spoke again, although she did not leave her throne. "Crow-spirit," she said suddenly, "come forward."

Traveller hopped along the uneven ground to stand next to Rosinda, although he did not move any closer to the goddess. He said nothing.

The goddess, whom Rosinda had already realized must be Morrigan, leaned forward slightly on her throne, her auburn hair spilling forward like a waterfall around her face. "You have not kept contact with me, or have been kept from doing so. Do you have anything to tell me about the prince?"

"No," he answered in a quiet voice.

"Have you been enspelled to disobey or mislead me?"

"No," he said again. "I chose."

The goddess sat back on her throne, her face suddenly hard. "Then I release you back to the spirit world," she said, and waved a hand at the crow.

He fell over as if pushed, his feathers just brushing against Rosinda's leg. With a gasp, she knelt and picked him up, but at a touch she knew the truth. Traveller was dead. She could not heal him.

Rosinda cradled his body for a long moment, her thoughts in a jumbled whirl. She wanted time to spin backwards, wanted this not to be true. If only she'd realized what the goddess was going to do! But there'd been no warning. They hadn't even fought! She should have made Traveller stay behind her, where she could have protected him. She should have—

The lion-headed goddess, Sekhmet, interrupted her thoughts. "There, you see how useless it is to withhold information from us? As Tyr said, one of your friends will be next, or perhaps you, if you do not tell us where the prince is."

"Traveller *was* my friend," Rosinda said. The words seemed to scratch her throat. As she spoke, she pulled a measure of throbbing power out of the earth and extended her protective umbrella over all of them; Quigsel and Jerrell and Filara behind her, and Aunt Odder, the Irylian, and the still-paralyzed Kelton woman in front. The energy thrummed with the susurrant voices again, still unintelligible. No one seemed to notice what she had done, least of all the gods. It was so quick, and she did it with only a thought. She knew that should have frightened her, but it didn't. For the first time, she was glad, so glad to have her power. She bent and softly laid Traveller's body back down on the parched earth.

"No," she said as she straightened, just as Traveller had. "You will not find the prince. You will not bring Ysterad to war. You will leave here and not return." She lifted her sword and pointed the sharp tip at the golden-eyed Egyptian goddess. "*You are not wanted.*"

That brought the goddess screeching from her throne, hurtling forward as if she would throw herself on Rosinda and crush her. The goddess's clutching hands, now adorned with lion's claws, could not reach her. The protective wall slowed and stopped them, mere inches from Rosinda's face.

It was difficult not to flinch, and harder to maintain the barrier under the onslaught. Rosinda hid the effort. She merely stood her ground and channeled earth-power up through her body, pouring it into the shield as the frenzied goddess tried to break through, shrieking and clawing. Dimly, Rosinda sensed Quigsel and Jerrell move to stand close behind her, but they said nothing. Which was a good thing, because with so much power flowing through her, the murmuring, sibilant voices were louder than ever. She realized with a start that they were the words of spells, a thousand spells chanted together in an incoherent jumble of magic.

Suddenly the goddess's lion-like eyes dilated and she froze in place, still staring at Rosinda. Her shrieks cut off in mid-scream. She stood unmoving, as if a switch had been flipped. In slow motion, she turned away from Rosinda to face the line of thrones. Rosinda saw with horror that the long lance, the one that had leaned against the Roman god's throne, now protruded from the goddess's back. Blood poured from the wound, spreading a darker red stain down the back of the crimson dress.

Tyr and Morrigan glared at Mars, more in annoyance than anything else. The handsome god shrugged.

"I just couldn't take it anymore," he said to them. "I know the two of you together have the power to undo this. But honestly, wouldn't it just be easier to finish it now?"

"She'll still heal over time," Morrigan said, glancing at the lion-headed goddess, her lip curling slightly with distaste.

Tyr shrugged. "But by then she'll be someone else's problem. I'd prefer an end to the constant screaming, myself."

Morrigan's eyes flicked to Rosinda. "We might yet need her."

"I want a war as much as anyone, but frankly, if we need her to do it, it's not worth it," Mars said. With a twist of his finger, his lance appeared back in his hand.

"Agreed," said the one-handed god.

"Agreed, then," said Morrigan. The gods did nothing that Rosinda could see, but the golden throne and the Egyptian goddess simply disappeared. She hadn't had a chance to say another word.

Rosinda struggled for a moment to push the pulsing earth-energy back down to a manageable level. She felt as if she might burst into flames if she let it continue coursing through her at such a rate.

"Now," said Morrigan, "we can proceed."

"I'm still not going to tell you anything about the prince," Rosinda said stubbornly.

"You stood fast against Sekhmet, it's true," Morrigan said, "but she had very little imagination. I have other...ideas."

She waved a hand, and the ground split and crumbled where Aunt Odder and the Irylian stood. The man pinwheeled his arms, fighting to keep his balance as the earth slid away underneath him. Aunt Odder fell, landing heavily just to the side of a gaping wound in the earth. Jerrell leaped past Rosinda as she called to mind a spell to stop the erosion, and Aunt Odder would have rolled into the chasm if he had not been so quick. He caught hold of her arm and pulled her away from the edge just as the ground gave a final shudder and stabilized. The Irylian was not so lucky. He slipped with a scream into the gap just before it stopped shaking.

"Can your shield keep out the elements?" Tyr drawled. He waved his handless arm in a circle and a hot wind sprang up, lifting a fine layer of sand and dust from the ground and swirling it into their faces. The god was right; the protective shield was not dense enough to stop a million tiny particles from sliding right through it.

Rosinda raised an arm to protect her eyes. The stinging sand was distracting, but she managed to keep the shield in place. Jerrell had dragged Aunt Odder all the way back to Rosinda and rolled her to face away from the dust storm.

"Is this going to take much longer?" Mars asked. Then

without warning, his voice sounded inside Rosinda's head, painfully loud. It was as if he had flung open the green door and shouted, *WHERE IS THE PRINCE?*

Startled, Rosinda almost answered, but she mentally slammed the door shut in the god's face before she could think the word *Sangera*.

So this will be their plan of attack now, she thought, *keep throwing things at me, keep me off-balance, until I make a mistake.* That seemed inevitable, even with the enormous amounts of power the earth here seemed to offer. She could still only concentrate on so many things at once.

Something tugged at her jeans. It was Filara, sitting close to Aunt Odder, helping to protect her mistress from the flying dust.

"She's saying something," the cat murmured.

"What?" Rosinda didn't dare open her mind to her aunt's, not with the three gods seeking a way in. She bent down close to Aunt Odder's face. "What did you say? Aunt Odder, I'm here. What?"

"...*banish...*" the word was just above a whisper. "...*you're... Prince's Kelta...power to...banish...*"

A banishing spell? Rosinda searched her mind for it. It wasn't there.

"I don't know it, Aunt Odder," she said urgently, but close to her aunt's ear. "I can't find it."

A tiny frown creased her aunt's brow. "...*must know it...*" she said. "...*Prince's Kelta always—*"

In a flash, the problem came to Rosinda. "But I'm not the Prince's Kelta at the moment," she whispered. "He released me so that I could come and rescue you. Do you know the spell?"

The frown deepened, then smoothed away. Aunt Odder still didn't open her eyes, but the corners of her mouth twitched. "...*not anymore...fine pair...we are...*" she whispered. "...*King's Kelta with no king...Prince's Kelta with no prince...*"

With a crackling sound like electrical wires sparking, something erupted out of the ground behind Rosinda. She whirled, sword at the ready. Two of the troll-like creatures they had encountered in the Ways Under clambered out of the ground and rushed at her. She cut one down with a few deft strokes. Quigsel cast a spell that dealt with the other, but the encounter distracted her, and she felt the protective barrier around them waver. Of course, that was the gods' intent. Hurriedly, she pulled more power from the earth and strengthened it again. The voices grew louder, clamouring for attention. She caught a word.

banish

Spells. She'd already realized that the words spilling out of the earth were spells. Now it came to her in a flash. One of the voices was speaking the words of the banishment spell. Bolstering the barrier as much as she could to shield her mind as well, she opened the imaginary green door and sought Aunt Odder.

Can you hear me?

Rosinda? What's this?

She could hear the confusion in her aunt's mind, but there wasn't much time to explain. *I'm—I might be a magister, Aunt Odder, but I need to know something—I hear voices speaking spells when I draw on the earth's energy here. I think one is the banishment spell. If I can figure it out, can I use it?*

Aunt Odder's thoughts swirled in confusion for a moment, then cleared. *A magister...but not a Royal Kelta...I don't know. It might work. I'm so weak...but I'll try to support you as much as I can. Try, Rosinda. Just...try.*

It was all the encouragement Rosinda needed. She drew Quigsel and Jerrell close for a moment. "I'll hold the shield, but you have to keep the gods busy for a minute. Just long enough for me to try something. Keep them from distracting me. I may not be strong enough, but—"

"Do it," Quigsel said, flipping open his spellbook.

Jerrell bent down and picked up a rock, then, without saying a word, hurled it at the gods. It bounced harmlessly off something invisible, but not before Morrigan flinched. She looked annoyed.

"Go for it," Jerrell told Rosinda. "You'll be strong enough when the time comes." He bent to pick up another rock and unslung his backpack at the same time. Rosinda hoped he had a few surprises left inside.

She turned her attention to the only two things that were vital. Siphoning enough energy to keep the shield strong and stable, and sifting through the voices for the spell she needed. Some of them lined up in neat rows when she concentrated on them. Others were as slippery as eels.

A commotion erupted outside the barrier. She heard Quigsel intoning the words of a spell. Resolutely, she kept sorting through the voices, chasing that one elusive word.

banish

banish, banish

Finally she had it, grasping the words like slippery fish. After a bit of mental juggling, they fell into place. She had the spell. Now she had to cast it.

She turned and strode toward the three thrones, to the limit of the barrier. Mars, the smooth-faced, handsome god, did not look bored any longer, simply angry. Not so much at her, as at the other two gods.

"Such a waste of time," he spat, "playing games with children when we could be immersed in the glory of the battlefield!"

Tyr and Morrigan ignored him, their eyes on Rosinda. She didn't give them a chance to say anything else.

"I told you before, you must leave Ysterad," she said in a ringing voice. "And you will have no choice." She closed her eyes to focus, and allowed the earth-energy to flow freely into her body. It was like being back in Nanghar, healing the wounded warriors, only ten times as strong. The force almost knocked her off her feet, but she steadied herself, opened her eyes, and began to recite the spell.

At first the gods merely stared at her, but as she began the incantation the second time they showed discomfort. They began another barrage of attacks, seeming to forget about the barrier, or suddenly too distracted to consider it. Fat drops of rain pelted down from the sky. Wind howled around the canyon. Flocks of birds appeared, screeching and battering themselves against the barrier. Some attacks got through, others met the resistance of the magic barrier. The gods seemed to simply throw whatever came to mind.

Rosinda continued to recite the spell, over and over. Her voice wavered once, and she felt a faint boost as Aunt Odder, weak as she was, poured her own almost-depleted energy into it. Rosinda accepted the help gratefully, but in her heart, she knew it would not be enough. Neither of them was a Royal Kelta any longer, and not even magistera shared the same bond with the land.

She felt another boost a moment later. Jerrell stood beside her, and pulled something from his pocket. "A gift from Driasch," he said seriously, and tossed a small, smooth stone up into the air. It did not fall back to the ground, but caught in midair just above his head, then began to circle slowly around him. He stiffened, and his face blanked. He added his voice to hers, chanting low and rhythmically.

Rosinda felt a different kind of power flow from him and into her. She recognized the source. The chant was the same one Driasch had used twice before to enhance Rosinda's powers. The shamanic force swirled around and through her. Rosinda felt her bond with the earth strengthening.

A soul-stone? Aunt Odder sounded delighted. *You've been making friends, Rosinda.*

The gods struggled visibly now, hurling everything they had at the barrier. A barrage of rocks. Jagged strikes of lightning. Monsters dragged from the darkest of nightmares, trailing dark streamers of smoke. The barrier glowed yellow and hot, pulsing with energy as the powers clashed.

Still not enough, Rosinda thought. She repeated the words of banishment feverishly, layering the spell over and over upon itself. Perhaps with enough repetitions—but she didn't really expect it would be enough. She felt shaky, weak. Her hands trembled. Sweat trickled down her spine. Her body was wearing out, channeling this much energy for so long. If the gods broke through or she collapsed, the others wouldn't have a chance.

Her legs wobbled and she locked her knees, willing herself not to fall. And then something changed. The earth-power leapt once, as if in joy, and then the *feel* of it was different. Stronger, richer, not so painfully hot burning through her but at the same time, subtly more powerful. Rosinda came to the end of the spell and started it again. She stopped in mid-word as she realized what the change signified.

Sovann was in Sangera. He had touched the Tell of Ysterad. The world's magic had acknowledged him as the true ruler and the very earth was changed.

The gods glanced at each other—a look of consternation— and Rosinda knew that they must have felt the change as well. If Sovann had been right, perhaps they were weaker now. The look that passed between them seemed to say so.

When she picked up the words and completed the spell, she saw the red-haired goddess frown. Her words must have had gained strength, as well. *So close...*but still, still something was missing. She let her knees go soft, knelt to ask Aunt Odder what else—anything—she could do. She felt a heavy bulk in her pocket.

The bottle of soil from the fairy ring.

Rosinda's mind whirled. These gods...all had once held sway on Earth. Could this be the final key? Rosinda fumbled the container out of her pocket and loosened the lid. Shakily, she dumped the soil at her feet, dark and rich on top of the dry red earth of the Desolation. She spread it out with her fingers, mingling the essence of the two worlds. Then she stood and took one step forward, standing on it, searching for whatever power · it held. The ancient magic responded, surging up through her bones. Rosinda thought her knees might buckle under the force of the energy she channeled now. She recited the spell again, almost breathless.

This time all three gods flinched visibly. Morrigan turned to Tyr, speaking in a low voice. Rosinda heard her clearly, the words carried on the murmuring sibilance of magic that still surrounded her. "The girl is stronger than I thought. We should not have let Sekhmet go so easily."

Tyr nodded. "The prince is back on the throne, and with only three of us now...it's possible this could go badly."

Possible? Rosinda thought. *Only possible?* She felt ready to break in half, or melt, or shatter, from the currents of magical energy flowing through her. They vibrated through her bones, rattling her to her core. And still it was not enough? There had to be something...something she was not thinking of...if only her memories of how to use magic had come back...

No. She shook her head. What had Driasch said to her about her memories? *They're no good to you now. You're a magister— you have access to all the realms of magic, and you'll use them together, in different ways than you would have before. Those old memories would just confuse you.*

I'm a magister. The thought came effortlessly, and for once Rosinda did not fight it or brush it aside. What if that was the missing piece of the puzzle? What if it was her stubborn refusal to accept her true nature?

If I'm a magister, I can use all of this together, she thought. *I just have to see how it fits.* She closed her eyes and visualized all the energies coursing through her.

With a concerted effort, she let the earth-energy of the two worlds flow through her, raw and swift, weaving them together the way she had mixed their soils with her fingers. She mingled it with the Kelta power emanating, weak but pure, from Aunt Odder, and swirled in Driasch's shamanic energies, streaming from the soul-stone through Jerrell and into her. Then she bound it all together with her own power, the power of the bonds of friendship she'd formed, the power of the promise she'd made to Vann, and the power of her own acceptance. *I am a magister. This is where I belong.*

She felt white-hot. As old as the stones under her feet. As unmoving as an ancient tree. As strong and solid as the mountains. As fluid and unbreakable as water.

She was going to get these meddlesome gods out of Ysterad.

And she was going to do it now.

Rosinda threw her head back and her arms wide, and recited the words of the spell one more time in a clear, ringing voice.

Her protective barrier exploded outward, blasting shards of pulsing light over the three remaining gods. Mars turned his head away, shielding his eyes from the blast. He muttered something in an ancient tongue. Without a glance at the other two gods, he kicked over his lovingly polished shield like a petulant child, shook a fist at Rosinda, and vanished.

In the seconds before the other two gods also disappeared, Rosinda thought she saw something strange. Tyr reached out quickly with his good hand and caught at Morrigan's arm. She turned to look at him, wincing against the power still emanating from Rosinda, and he bent toward her and spoke urgently. She looked bewildered, then smiled hesitantly. The one-handed god turned his craggy face toward Rosinda as his hand slid down to clasp Morrigan's, and, unbelievably, he winked. The goddess also caught Rosinda's eye, bowed her head in graceful defeat, and then the two were gone. Something small and round fell to the ground where Morrigan's throne had stood.

After a moment, Rosinda heard another voice. "I think," it said weakly, "that you can stop now, dear."

Rosinda blinked and let her arms fall to her sides. She'd barely been aware that she was holding them out toward the gods—or where the gods had been only moments before. Jerrell's voice had ceased its chant, and the shamanic magic slowly ebbed away. It took what little strength Rosinda had left to stop the flow of earth energy through her, and when it disappeared, she dropped to her knees. It felt like the magic had been the only thing holding her up.

She realized that Aunt Odder was sitting up, propped heavily against Quigsel. Weak, but awake, and grinning.

"Now what's all this," she said, "about you being a magister?"

"Ask your cat," Rosinda said, and toppled sideways.

CHAPTER THIRTY-SEVEN

It seemed like no time at all had passed before they sat in Driasch's tent, back in the Nanghar again. Aunt Odder told Rosinda that this was because she'd slept for three entire days after their encounter with the gods, half-waking only enough to swallow a little soup before drifting back to sleep again. She hadn't had a chance to thank Captain Jessara personally for all she'd done, but she resolved to get back and do that before too long.

Driasch had enfolded her in a huge bear hug when they arrived. "I knew you could do it," she whispered. "You just had to trust in yourself."

Rosinda smiled. "And have a lot of help from my friends," she said.

Driasch *tsk-tsked*. "Still being too hard on yourself! Well, I expect your duties will soon knock that out of you." But she was grinning as she said it.

The old shaman hugged Jerrell, too, praising him for knowing exactly when to use the soul-stone to do the most good. "Although you caught me right in the middle of dinner," she said. "The others thought I was having some kind of fit when I dropped my bowl and started chanting for no apparent reason."

They'd had to tell their story bit by bit in the meeting-tent, while the Nangharen, young and old, sat around them, entranced. The only thing Rosinda left out was what she'd seen pass between the two gods at the very end. She wasn't sure what to make of it, so she kept it to herself.

She also hadn't mentioned the gem that the gods had left

behind, the one that seemed to have fallen from Morrigan's throne. Jerrell had picked it up, but Rosinda had a vague memory of shaking her head at him.

"Leave it," she'd told him drowsily. "I don't trust anything that belonged to them. Leave it here, where no one comes."

Jerrell shrugged and dropped it back onto the hard-packed ground. It winked redly in the sun, almost beckoning, but Rosinda turned away from it.

Back in the Nanghar, Rosinda had been able to contact Sovann through the Crypt of a Thousand Voices. She'd been escorted there by an honor guard of Nangharen, quite a different experience from the first time they'd led her away from the crypt. He'd had good news.

"Your parents are free," he told her. "They're on their way down from Ierngud under royal guard, and they'll be here when you get back. You're coming soon, aren't you?"

She'd assured him that she was. "I just have to take care of a few things first."

With Aunt Odder's help, she charmed a travelling-stone for Jerrell. "If you want it," she'd said when she offered it to him, feeling oddly shy. "I know you'll be going back to Cape Breton, but this way, if you want to come back..."

Jerrell took the sparkling amethyst stone eagerly, turning it over in his hands with the enthusiasm he usually reserved for gadgets. He looked up and met her eyes. "Thank you," he said seriously. "I have to go back—I couldn't leave my uncle not knowing what had happened to me—but I don't want to leave Ysterad forever. There's a lot I'd like to do here. I wonder, do you think I could learn to sail a ship?"

Rosinda grinned. "Like Captain Steffen? Maybe she'll take you on as a cabin boy, if you ask her nicely."

Jerrell blushed, then looked sheepish for a moment. He reached out and took her hand. "Mostly I want to come back to see you, Rosinda. Remember when I told you I always thought we'd get along? Now I know it's true. I don't want to lose that."

Rosinda almost couldn't speak. She shook her head. "No, and I don't want to lose my best friend," she told him, and stepped forward to wrap her arms around him in a tight hug. She'd barely known his name when it all started, but now she couldn't imagine getting along without him. He'd been there from the beginning, had stuck by her through all the craziness and the danger. He and Traveller.

They'd brought the crow's body back with them, and the shaman buried him in the tribe's burial-ground. "He was a fine warrior," she said. Rosinda's eyes had filled with tears. Traveller had started her down the path of this whole re-awakening, the seventh crow and his secrets. It seemed too cruel that he'd died for his loyalty to her. Whatever his reasons had been in the beginning, there had been no doubt of his devotion in the end. Even Filara, although apparently she'd decided to hold on to the power of speech for a little while longer, had attended the burial in solemn silence.

Traveller and Kerngold, Rosinda thought as she looked around Driasch's tent at the others, laughing and eating. *The rest of us are going home, but not those two.* She still grieved for Kerngold as a separate person, not just a part of Sovann. She didn't understand it, but she knew what she felt.

She realized someone had spoken her name.

"Rosinda?" It was Driasch. She stood beside the door-flap of the tent. "I have a surprise for you."

She smiled at the shaman. "Not more tellbones, I hope," she said. "I'm still learning to use the first set."

The shaman grinned. "No, something that will keep you company a little better than old bones." She pulled aside the flap and a silver-grey bundle of fur tumbled in and rushed over to Rosinda.

"A—a puppy?" A bright pink tongue licked Rosinda's hand.

"A *wolf* pup, to be exact," the shaman corrected. "Abandoned by its mother. Seems to like people, though. I thought of you right away."

Rosinda cupped the pup's muzzle between her hands and gazed into his eyes. Golden eyes with green flecks, that knowingly gazed at her.

Rosinda!

Her heart fluttered as the voice sounded inside her head. She couldn't believe she'd heard it.

Rosinda?

"Kerngold?" she whispered in amazement, and turned her face up to the shaman. "How—?"

Driasch sat down beside her and stroked the pup's fur. "Do you remember when Prince Sovann changed back to human form, right here in this tent?"

Rosinda nodded. How could she forget that?

"During the change, I felt a spirit loose in the tent. Displaced, and confused. I opened up my mind to it—or maybe my soul, who knows how these things happen—and it found a place to stay, at least temporarily. Turned out to be your friend Kerngold. I told him we'd keep an eye out for a more permanent home for him. When this pup turned up—well, it was perfect."

"But how could that be? That Kerngold could have his own...spirit, or whatever." Rosinda was confused. "Kerngold was Sovann."

Aunt Odder cleared her throat. "Um...I might be able to explain that."

All eyes turned to her.

"When I cast the spell to turn Sovann into a wolf to hide him, I knew I'd have to cover his memories of who he was, or he'd go crazy—a human in a wolf's body, with no way to get back. There would also be a greater chance that he'd be discovered if his mind was open. So I...I sort of copied the brain patterns of a wolf that was nearby. I didn't intend—or expect—it to persist after Sovann was changed back. In fact, I didn't even know that could happen. But I was in a hurry, and I was making things up as I went along—"

"So you cast a spell that had unexpected consequences?" Rosinda grinned. She looked pointedly at Filara. "Well, I'm glad to know that it can happen to the best of us sometimes."

The cat flicked her whiskers. "Don't flatter yourself, girl. You're still not half the Kelta your aunt is."

"I think I could fix that problem I caused for you now, though," Rosinda said, her heart full as Kerngold curled up in her lap and went to sleep. "You must be so tired of speaking human by now."

Filara stood and walked casually to the door-flap. "Oh, you don't have to worry about it just now," she said. "I imagine I can hold out a bit longer. There may be more I need to tell you, or the mistress, before we get home." She slipped out through the flap, tail in the air.

It was just as well. She wouldn't have been amused by the laughter that erupted behind her.

THE END

Sherry D. Ramsey is a speculative fiction writer, editor, publisher, creativity addict and self-confessed Internet geek. When she's not writing, she makes jewelry, gardens, hones her creative procrastination skills on social media, and consumes far more coffee and chocolate than is likely good for her.

Her debut novel, *One's Aspect to the Sun*, was published by Tyche Books in late 2013 and was awarded the Book Publishers of Alberta "Book of the Year" Award for Speculative Fiction. The sequel, *Dark Beneath the Moon*, is due out from Tyche in 2015. Her other books include *To Unimagined Shores—Collected Stories*, and an urban fantasy/mystery novel, *The Murder Prophet*. With her partners at Third Person Press, she has co-edited five anthologies of regional short fiction to date. Her short fiction and poetry have appeared in numerous publications and anthologies in North America and beyond. Every November, she disappears into the strange realm of National Novel Writing Month and emerges gasping at the end, clutching something resembling a novel.

A member of the Writer's Federation of Nova Scotia Writer's Council, Sherry is also a past Vice-President and Secretary-Treasurer of SF Canada, Canada's national association for Speculative Fiction Professionals.

You can visit Sherry online at www.sherrydramsey.com, find her on Facebook, and follow her on Twitter @sdramsey.

If you enjoyed *The Seventh Crow*, please take a moment to review it where you purchased it!

We're always happy for you to come by the site, let us know what you think, and take a look at the rest of our science fiction and fantasy books.

DreamingRobotPress.com

Or email us at books@dreamingrobotpress.com

Continue reading for a sneak preview of *Coyote's Daughter* by Corie J. Weaver.

Coyote's
Daughter

Corie J. Weaver

Chaper 1

Mom and Dad broke the news to me over eggs and bacon. 'The date is set with the movers," Dad announced while pouring his juice. 'We leave at the end of next month."

I put down my fork, no longer hungry. My dad looked at me. Really slowly. He does that, as if he's seeing through me, into my head. I don't like it; it feels like I'm one of the skeletons in the Anthropology Department where he works. But I guess it's nice to have parents who pay attention.

Not sure why he spent so much time staring; I'm not terribly exciting to look at. Rain-straight brown hair brushes my shoulders, and I chew on the ends when I'm nervous. Brown eyes my mom calls hazel. I'm too tall.

I don't like being taller than all the other kids in my class. The boys don't like it either. I'm not fat, but I'm not skinny. I'm never going to be one of those golden-haired cheerleaders everyone loves.

"Maggie, you've known for months about the move, why are you acting surprised?"

Yeah. I knew. But it didn't seem real until then. I wished they'd yell out "April Fool's!" and the move would turn out to be some sort of crazy joke. I didn't want to move to New Mexico, to the desert, land of the coyote and roadrunner cartoons; empty, barren and ugly.

Why would we want to move there? I wouldn't, but Mom and Dad couldn't wait. Mom found a dream job working with rockets at a lab. For Dad, getting close to different tribes of Native Americans couldn't be beat.

After school I went to the beach. Biting cold water kept me from swimming, so I just sat on the sand and watched the waves, throwing sticks for Jack until someone yelled at me about not having him on a leash. He's a border collie mixed up with something else pretty big, and sometimes that makes people nervous. The ocean is beautiful, big and open, and always helps me get my head in order.

I thought about the move, leaving all of my friends and starting over. The timing couldn't be worse: the summer between grades six and seven. By now everyone's groups of friends and enemies would be set. I knew already I wouldn't fit in, and wondered if they even had a swim team in the desert.

"So, have you met anyone in the neighborhood yet?" Mom's head was buried in a box, her voice muffled and funny. She straightened up and handed yet another stack of dishes to Dad.

I stopped texting Jenna, my best friend from home. My real home. "The old lady next door says there's a brother and sister, twins, that live down the street." I pointed out the window, through the little courtyard that we had instead of a patio. "They're at their father's right now. She doesn't know when they'll be back."

I slid off of the chair and scratched Jack's ears. Jack's a good dog, and always stays nearby when I need him. I loved him, but didn't much care for the idea of a summer with just him for company.

After lunch my folks sent Jack and me out. "You're driving me crazy," Mom said. "Just stay out of traffic, and be nice to our new neighbors."

I stood on the sidewalk and looked around; no one riding bikes in the street, nothing. But then I saw something that looked interesting

Mom and Dad had already started to tackle another pile of boxes when I ran back inside. "Can I go hiking on the trail?"

"What?"

"At the end of our street there's a little hill, and then a path on either side of a ditch. Can I go on that?"

My father figured it out first. "The acequia? Sure. It may not look like it now, but a hundred years ago when people farmed all of this area, that ditch brought water to the fields from the river, the Rio Grande. It's a common walking path now." He glanced at Mom, made sure they agreed. "Go north, to your right, and the furthest you can go is the river. All right, Miss Maggie? And try to keep Jack out of the water; I don't know how clean it is." With that final piece of advice they returned to battle with the boxes.

Great. Jack loves playing in water, but I don't want him to drag me in behind him. Duly warned, I went searching through the boxes in my room for our hiking stuff. All of the boxes were labeled, so it didn't take too long. I had my purple-and-black backpack and Jack wore his hiking harness with the little saddlebags. Mom thinks I'm a packrat, but I like to be prepared for anything.

In my backpack I always carry an extra bottle of water, sunscreen, a long-sleeved shirt with pockets in the front, a couple granola bars, my journal, a flashlight, a magnifying glass, a compass, and five pens, because you never know when you'll run out of ink, and odd stuff I hadn't cleaned out from last semester. Jack's saddlebags are always packed with a neat collapsible dish, and flat water bags.

I know it's a lot of stuff, but we've needed funny bits and pieces of things even out walking the beach at home. And I don't like going anywhere without Jack having water that's safe to drink.

I read an awful article online last year about how sick animals can get when they don't have access to clean water. I bought the collapsible bowl and water bags with my next allowance. I've been looking at a set of hiking boots for Jack too, to protect his paws from sharp rocks and the broken glass left by stupid people, but I'm not sure if he'd put up with them. He's pretty good about his harness, so you never know.

We scrambled up a little hill to get to the trail, and headed north. The trees looked old, with gnarled limbs as big as my waist stretched over the water and gray and craggy trunks. Sometimes I'd see one that looked like it had been split by lighting when young and had since grown up in two or three parts.

Tall grasses and purple wildflowers overgrew the steep banks of the ditch. I tried to pick one, but sharp spines on the stem pricked my thumb and changed my mind.

Cattails rose from the water, and after a while we saw ducks swimming along. A path ran on each side of the ditch, but I couldn't see how to get to the other bank without crossing through the water.

The trees spread over us to form a green tunnel with flashes of bright blue, so much more vivid than the hazy sky over San Diego, peeking between the branches.

Occasionally we saw someone on the other side of the ditch, but they passed on by with a little wave, jogging or walking, sometimes pushing one of those off-road strollers.

From the raised path I could look down into people's backyards. You think of your backyard as private, but we could look right in. Building projects left abandoned, patio furniture still covered up, gardens that hadn't been replanted, a little bit of everything.

And all the dogs. If Jack hadn't been convinced before that this walk was only for his benefit, the sheer numbers of his four-legged brothers would have done it. I think everyone in Albuquerque must have dogs. Not just one dog, either, but entire packs. As we walked behind houses, they would race up to their back fence, mad as all get-out because they couldn't reach us, barking as hard as they could. Jack strained at the leash, but I'm not sure how many of those dogs felt friendly.

A few of the yards didn't have dogs. They were huge, and

had horses or hens; one place had a little orchard.

One house had peacocks, another had sheep. It's hard to believe we're in the largest city in this state when people are keeping sheep and chickens in their backyards.

I ran my hand down the trunk of one of the cottonwoods. The bark split in little up-and-down slits over and over again, almost like a woven pattern. I put my arms out as if hugging the tree, but couldn't reach all the way around it. Standing there with my face tilted up toward the leaves, Jack pulling on my wrist, I wondered how long this tree had been here. Dad had said the ditch had been used for a hundred years. Was the tree that old? Older even?

After about an hour of walking we stopped for a break. Jack waited for me to pour his water and drank it in big noisy slurps. He curled up next to a tree stump, and I spread the long-sleeved shirt over the bark so it wouldn't be scratchy against my legs. Jack gazed at the world with half-closed eyes, the way dogs do, while I wrote a little in my journal, and thought a little, and then stood up and repacked everything.

"Another hour, boy. If we don't find that river by then, we'll try again tomorrow."

It took closer to half an hour to get there. The narrow path opened out onto a broad grassy area, with small trees dotting the ground. Nothing lush, nothing that looked like photos I've seen of rivers. Muted greens and grays painted this landscape. We followed the ditch as it led to the river, and I looked behind me every few steps to make sure I could find the way back.

Trees thickly lined the river, and small twisted bushes sprang up around them, trailing off the farther they grew away from the water.

We walked to the water. It flowed sluggishly, muddy, low. You could see across the river to the other side; in places the water looked shallow enough to wade across. I stooped to rest my hand on the bank, then looked closer.

The black mud sparkled in the light. I put my fingers in it and drew them across the back of my hand. It shone deep and rich. Jack came over to see what I had, and I put a streak of mud down his muzzle. Jack looked very handsome, gleaming in the sun, and I laughed watching him cross his eyes to see what I had done to him. I got my other hand muddy, then drew a mask around his eyes.

"There. You're now the Masked Dog of the River, mysterious and dashing."

Jack is the most patient dog in the world. I think if I had younger brothers or sisters, I wouldn't torment him like this. But I don't and, for the most part, he puts up with it.

Something nearby tickled my nose, triggering my allergies, and I had a sneezing fit. Reflexively, I went to cover my mouth like a good girl, and felt the mud from my hands smear on my face.

"Happy? Now we'll match."

Jack looked up at me with his tongue spilling out of his open mouth and eyes rolling, and I decided not to worry about my mud mask either.

With jumps and wags, Jack let me know he thought it would be much more fun to walk for a while right next to the river, and I decided to let him have his way. No one was around, so I let him off the leash, free to snuffle and explore as he wanted.

The time to return home came sooner than we wanted. About where I figured we needed to cut through the trees and get back to our path, I saw a boy, crouched on the bank, almost in the water. He wore loose pants, and no shirt, and I couldn't help but think about him getting sunburned; it happens to me so easily. Maybe his dark-gold skin and jet-black hair meant he didn't need to worry about it so much. He looked thin and wiry, and the way he knelt I couldn't tell his height. I saw him scoop up a great handful of black mud and put it into a little woven basket by his side.

I stood still for a minute. What do you do in a situation like that? Say something stupid like, "Hi, I'm Maggie, what on earth are you doing?" I'm never sure how to talk to new people, but I couldn't let the opportunity to talk to the first person I had seen close to my own age slip away. I needed a few moments to figure out how to approach him.

Jack had no such worries. He bounded toward the boy, stuck his broad head into the boy's side and knocked him off balance back into the dirt.

The boy yelled at Jack and I called him back. I ran forward to apologize and felt my face heat. The boy's wrist had gotten caught in something when he fell over. He tugged at it with his free hand, but it didn't look like he could untangle himself with only one.

"Here, let me." I knelt down and reached for his hand, but he snatched it away. "Please, it's the least I can do after my dog startled you." I held my hands out and waited.

He looked at me with wide golden eyes, and then slowly put his trapped hand back into mine. His eyes mirrored his skin; they made me think of hawks I'd seen caged at the zoo. I started working on the contraption. A frame of wood and bone held loops of string woven in complicated knots. I couldn't imagine its purpose, but it must have gotten knocked over when Jack struck the boy. The string had tangled and tightened over his wrist. It had to hurt a lot, but the boy never said anything.

I chattered while I struggled with the lines to fill up the silence. "Hi, I'm Maggie, and you've met Jack, and we just moved here. I'm sorry about this, I'll be careful to just untangle it and not break it." He still didn't say anything.

Maybe he didn't understand me. I knew a lot of people in New Mexico spoke Spanish, but I thought they would understand a little English.

I tried to think back to the phrase or two of Spanish I had picked up in California.

"Hola. Me llama Maggie?"

I didn't think that was quite right, but it should have been close enough. No reaction.

Jack curled next to me while I worked, as if to make up for his bad behavior. The knotted strings made an elaborate pattern, like cat's cradle but a million times worse. Untangling it, I saw that somehow all of the strings had pulled tight, snaring his wrist in a tangle of line.

"Almost, hold still for a little longer." The strings went back over the framework, one by one, pulling the frame together, relaxing the rest of the lines. "There." I slipped the contraption off his wrist. Throughout the whole ordeal he'd stayed silent, even though I could see the angry red marks where the lines had cut into his wrist. My own wrist hurt just to see them.

I stood up, brushed off my jeans and held out my hand.

"What's your name? Do you live around here?" Maybe this could be someone to spend the summer with. But once freed, he only stared at me for a few moments with his odd golden eyes, shoved the contraption into a bag at his side, grabbed the woven basket filled with mud, and ran for the trees.

Stupid boy. Not my fault he got stuck in that thing. He probably shouldn't have been carrying it. And he shouldn't have been so caught up in getting mud to not notice a big black-and-white dog galloping down on him. He could have said thank you. Even in another language.

As we turned for home I saw something under one of the bushes and spun back. For a moment I had seen something like a dog, but gray and tan, and somehow different, curled up, watching us with eyes way too smart to be in a dog's head. But I saw nothing now, only a light-dappled shadow.

The way home didn't take as long. Tired out, Jack didn't stop to investigate every smell. We paused for a while because I wanted to see the sheep a little closer. Sheep are not the white fluffy creatures you see in paintings. They looked dingy and yellow, and they smelled. Jack fought for a bit to stay when I tugged him to keep walking. Only the promise of cookies got him moving again.

Looking at the house as we scrambled back down the ditch was another reminder of how far we were from home. The new house sat low and long and didn't seem to have any straight angles. Plain, smooth walls confronted me instead of the detailed woodwork of our Victorian house back in San Diego.

A light-brown wall curved over the top of a wooden door, enclosing a courtyard, where bricks fit together in patterns to make the floor. A few trees stood in the back, huge, with rough trunks, and thick branches sprouting light green leaves curved into sharp points. The same thick, brown stuff formed the walls of the house, softly curved, like the half-melted battlements of a sandcastle. The bright-blue doorframe around the carved wooden double door provided the one bit of color on the entire house.

Our late arrival home surprised Mom and Dad, still unpacking.

"Good grief! How far did you go? And what is wrong with your face?"

"Just up to the river. Not any farther. Just like you said." Jack flopped down on the cool brick floor the instant I took his harness off.

I ran into the bathroom and burst out laughing. Smears of dried black mud covered my face. The pattern of my handprints wrapped up the side of my cheeks and up around my eyes. I scrubbed it off, and went back to the living room.

They looked at each other, with that parental glance that

never means well. I cut in again, before they could get started.

"I did just like you said. It's a perfectly safe path. And there were other people around, jogging and bicycling and stuff, so it's not like we explored the middle of nowhere. Besides, I had Jack with me."

We looked down at him, sprawled flat, tongue lolling out of his mouth.

"And I've got lots of questions." Questions are always the best way to deflect my folks, so I poured them out in a rush, in the hope that at least a couple would catch their attention.

"How old is the irrigation canal, anyway? Did you know people have sheep and chickens and horses around here? Isn't there some sort of rule about farm animals in a city? And what's the big wooded area by the river? Can we get Jack a sheep for Christmas? I think he'd really like one."

"The area by the river is called the Bosque, the Spanish word for woods, and most of it in Albuquerque and around the city is a nature reserve."

Mom cut Dad off before he got going. "A sheep? You want to get Jack a sheep for Christmas? Why?"

"Just a little one? I don't think he'd try to eat it or anything, just run in circles around it, and herd it and…whatever it is border collies do. I'll bet he's really good at herding."

Mom started shaking her head.

"Please? Wouldn't a sheep even keep the grass short? No more mowing." Dad hates mowing the lawn. I do it sometimes, and I hate mowing too.

Mom and Dad looked amused. I heaved a sigh of relief, amused meant I had distracted them from the worry.

"We'll talk about it closer to the holidays. By the end of the summer you can put together a report on what types of sheep would be suitable as a companion for Jack." Dad moved to the next room to get another box out. I leaned against the wall.

Typical of him to assign homework. I think he's been teaching for too long. Someday I'll learn.

Mom came over and put her arms around me. She used to be able to rest her chin on my head, but I've gotten too tall. I think it bothers her that I'm almost as tall as she is. Honestly, it bothers me too.

"Don't think you've completely distracted your father, dear." She dropped a quick kiss on my forehead. "Now come help me put away the dishes, will you? Your father started arranging his books, and I'll never dig him out."

The next morning, fright took the scream from my throat. I rolled over to look out the window to see what sort of day it would be, and nearly screamed. A face peered in at me, framed on either side with outstretched hands pressed against the glass. I jerked out of bed, but the face was gone by the time I reached the window, no smears left on the glass, nothing.

Made in the USA
San Bernardino, CA
19 December 2016